STAR WARS™

CLONE WARS GAMBIT:
STEALTH

CLONE WARS GAMBIT:
STEALTH

KAREN MILLER

arrow books

Published in the United Kingdom by Arrow Books in 2011

2 4 6 8 10 9 7 5 3 1

First published in the United Kingdom in 2010 by Century

Arrow Books
Random House, 20 Vauxhall Bridge Road,
London SW1V 2SA

Addresses for companies within The Random House Group Limited can be found at:
www.randomhouse.co.uk

The Random House Group Limited Reg. No. 954009

www.randomhouse.co.uk
www.starwars.com

A CIP catalogue record for this book is available from the British Library

ISBN 9780099533221

The Random House Group Limited supports The Forest Stewardship
Council (FSC), the leading international forest certification organisation.
All our titles that are printed on Greenpeace approved FSC certified paper
carry the FSC logo. Our paper procurement policy can be found at:
www.rbooks.co.uk/environment

Mixed Sources
Product group from well-managed
forests and other controlled sources
www.fsc.org Cert no. TT-COC-2139
© 1996 Forest Stewardship Council

FSC

Printed and bound in Great Britain by
CPI Bookmarque, Croydon, CR0 4TD

Book design by Susan Turner

To the fans of that galaxy far, far away,
who have made me so welcome

ACKNOWLEDGMENTS

Shelly Shapiro at Del Rey, for her unwavering support and guidance. Sue Rostoni at Lucasfilm Ltd., for being such a fabulous gatekeeper. The support teams of Del Rey and Lucasfilm Ltd., for helping to keep us writers on track. Karen Traviss, for lighting the way. Jason Fry, Mary Webber, and James Gilmer, for their insights.

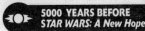

THE STAR WARS NOVELS TIMELINE

5000 YEARS BEFORE STAR WARS: A New Hope

The Lost Tribe of the Sith:
Precipice
Skyborn
Paragon

1020 YEARS BEFORE STAR WARS: A New Hope
Darth Bane: Path of Destruction
Darth Bane: Rule of Two
Darth Bane: Dynasty of Evil

33 YEARS BEFORE STAR WARS: A New Hope

Darth Maul: Saboteur*

32.5 YEARS BEFORE STAR WARS: A New Hope
Cloak of Deception
Darth Maul: Shadow Hunter

32 YEARS BEFORE STAR WARS: A New Hope

STAR WARS: EPISODE I THE PHANTOM MENACE

29 YEARS BEFORE STAR WARS: A New Hope
Rogue Planet

27 YEARS BEFORE STAR WARS: A New Hope
Outbound Flight

22.5 YEARS BEFORE STAR WARS: A New Hope
The Approaching Storm

22-19 YEARS BEFORE STAR WARS: A New Hope

STAR WARS: EPISODE II ATTACK OF THE CLONES

The Clone Wars
The Clone Wars: Wild Space
The Clone Wars: No Prisoners
Clone Wars Gambit: Stealth

Republic Commando
Hard Contact
Triple Zero
True Colors
Order 66

Imperial Commando
501st

Shatterpoint
The Cestus Deception
The Hive*
MedStar I: Battle Surgeons
MedStar II: Jedi Healer
Jedi Trial
Yoda: Dark Rendezvous
Labyrinth of Evil

STAR WARS: EPISODE III REVENGE OF THE SITH

Dark Lord: The Rise of Darth Vader

Coruscant Nights
Jedi Twilight
Street of Shadows
Patterns of Force

10-0 YEARS BEFORE STAR WARS: A New Hope
The Han Solo Trilogy:
The Paradise Snare
The Hutt Gambit
Rebel Dawn

5-1 YEARS BEFORE STAR WARS: A New Hope
The Adventures of Lando Calrissian
The Han Solo Adventures
The Force Unleashed
Death Troopers

STAR WARS: A New Hope YEAR 0

Death Star

STAR WARS: EPISODE IV A NEW HOPE

0-3 YEARS AFTER STAR WARS: A New Hope
Tales from the Mos Eisley Cantina
Allegiance
Galaxies: The Ruins of Dantooine
Splinter of the Mind's Eye

3 YEARS AFTER STAR WARS: A New Hope

STAR WARS: EPISODE V THE EMPIRE STRIKES BACK

Tales of the Bounty Hunters

3.5 YEARS AFTER STAR WARS: A New Hope
Shadows of the Empire

4 YEARS AFTER STAR WARS: A New Hope

STAR WARS: EPISODE VI RETURN OF THE JEDI

Tales from Jabba's Palace
Tales from the Empire
Tales from the New Republic

The Bounty Hunter Wars:
The Mandalorian Armor
Slave Ship
Hard Merchandise
The Truce at Bakura

5 YEARS AFTER STAR WARS: A New Hope
Luke Skywalker and the Shadows of Mindor

6.5-7.5 YEARS AFTER STAR WARS: A New Hope

X-Wing:
Rogue Squadron
Wedge's Gamble
The Krytos Trap
The Bacta War
Wraith Squadron
Iron Fist
Solo Command

DRAMATIS PERSONAE

Ahsoka Tano; Jedi Padawan (Togruta female)

Anakin Skywalker; Jedi Knight (human male)

Bail Organa; Senator from Alderaan (human male)

Bant'ena Fhernan; scientist first level (human female)

Lok Durd; Separatist general (Neimoidian male)

Obi-Wan Kenobi; Jedi Knight (human male)

Padmé Amidala; Senator from Naboo (human female)

Palpatine; Supreme Chancellor of the Republic (human male)

Taria Damsin; Jedi Master (human female)

Wullf Yularen; Admiral for the Republic (human male)

Yoda; Grand Master of the Jedi Order (nonhuman male)

STAR WARS™

CLONE WARS GAMBIT:
STEALTH

ONE

——◇——

As far as Ahsoka Tano was concerned, the only thing worse than being up to her armpits in battle droids was waiting to find out just how long it would be before she was up to her armpits in battle droids. She *hated* waiting. But it seemed that war was all about waiting—at least, when it wasn't about staring death in the face.

But I'm not scared. I'm not scared. I'm not scared. I'm not . . .

With *Resolute* out of rotation for a refit, she stood on the bridge of *Indomitable,* one of the next generation of cruisers to come out of the Allanteen VI shipyards. Cruisers that were faster and more responsive than ever before, thanks to her Master's—what had the chief shipwright called it? Oh yes. *Tinkering.* Thanks to Anakin's tinkering, the new vessels were a definite cut above the first Republic Cruisers that had rolled out of production for service in this war against Dooku and his Separatist Alliance.

The differences had been noted, and were talked about whenever and wherever military types crossed paths—in battle, in briefings, sharing some chitchat and a drink in this mess or that one, or even the occasional civilian bar. The Jedi who fought on the front lines were talking about them, too. Everyone who relied on the massive Republic warships knew that their odds of survival had increased because Jedi Knight Anakin Skywalker liked to muck about with machines—when he wasn't busy being the scourge of the Separatists.

Anakin.

That's how she thought of him now, after arduous months of fighting by his side, learning from him, saving him, and being saved by him. But she never called him that to his face. She *couldn't.* The idea of saying *Anakin* felt more disrespectful than a cheeky nickname. *Skyguy* was familiar but it wasn't . . . *intimate.*

First names were intimate. They implied equality. But she and her Master weren't equals. She suspected they never would be. She was pretty sure that no matter how hard she trained, how hard she tried, even after she'd passed the trials and been made a Jedi Knight, she would never come close to matching him as a Jedi.

How can I? He's the Chosen One. He can do things that aren't meant to be possible.

She snuck a sideways look at him, standing on the far side of *Indomitable*'s bridge in hushed conversation with Master Kenobi and Admiral Yularen. Letting down her habitual guard the tiniest bit, she prepared to stretch out her senses. To feel what he was feeling behind his carefully constructed mask. It wasn't prying. She didn't *pry.* As a Padawan it was her job—no, her *duty*—to make sure her Master was well. To be constantly attuned to his mood so she could anticipate his needs and more perfectly serve him. Since joining Anakin on Christophsis she'd lost count of the times that keeping a close eye on him had made the difference between success and failure. Life and death. Young she might be, and still in training, but she could do that. She was *good* at that.

Besides, once assigned to this man she'd made her own private and personal vow quite apart from the public oaths she'd sworn in the Jedi Temple.

I will not be the Padawan who gets the Chosen One killed.

Around her, the bridge crew conducted its military business with brisk efficiency. No chatter, since the admiral was present. When Yularen was elsewhere his officers sometimes indulged in a little gossip, a few jokes, a smattering of idle wartime speculation. Nothing detrimental to discipline, nothing untoward, just harmless camaraderie to help while away the tedium of days, like this one, when battle was yet to be joined and the void beyond the transparisteel viewports remained empty of enemy ships and impending slaughter.

She could hear, humming in the background, all the baffling hardware that made these warships possible. Sensor sweeps and multiphasic duo-diode relays and cognizant crystal interfaces and quasi-sentient droid links and—and *stuff*. So *much* stuff, and it made no sense to her. The slippery info-laneways of computers she could work with, but she didn't possess any kind of knack for nuts-and-bolts-and-circuits machinery—constructing her own lightsaber had nearly given her a nosebleed. Anakin, on the other hand . . .

Machinery was meat and drink to Anakin. He loved it.

But she was letting herself become distracted, so she pushed those thoughts aside. Her immediate task was to ascertain what Anakin was feeling. That way she'd have a better idea of what to expect from him when the news they were waiting for at last came through . . . and an idea of how best to deal with him, once it did. Dealing with her Master's sometimes overpowering emotions was becoming more and more a part of her duties—and as the war dragged on, and their losses piled up, that job wasn't getting any easier.

He feels too much, too keenly. Maybe that's what happens when you've got the highest midi-chlorian count in Jedi history. Maybe that's the trade-off. You feel everything, so you're brilliant. You feel everything, and it hurts.

Not that his emotions got in the way. At least, *he* didn't think they did. And to be honest, she didn't, either. At least not as often as some people thought. Like Master Kenobi, for example, who chided his former Padawan for taking crazy risks, for pushing himself too hard, for letting things matter too much and losing his carefully measured Jedi distance.

She didn't always disagree. And sometimes, when Anakin had given her a really bad fright or when his mood became difficult, she wished she could chide him, too. But as a Padawan she had to find another way to let her Master know he'd gone too far. So she sassed him, or invented nicknames that were guaranteed to get under his skin. Sometimes she even deliberately flouted his wishes. Anything to break him free of sorrow or frustration or some bleak memory he refused to share. Anything to let him know, *Hey, what you did then? That was stupid.*

But mostly she kept her fears for him to herself, because all his bright and burning passion for justice, his reckless courage, his hunger for victory and his refusal to accept defeat—they were what made him *Anakin.* He wouldn't *be* Anakin without his feelings. She knew that, she accepted that, no matter what Temple teachings said about the Jedi and their emotions.

And even though he scolds, I think Master Kenobi accepts it, too. He only scolds because he cares.

So . . . what was her brilliant, sometimes volatile Master feeling now?

Eyes drifted half closed, Ahsoka breathed out a soft sigh and let her growing Jedi awareness touch lightly upon him.

Impatience. Concern. Relief. Loneliness. Weariness. And grief, not yet healed.

Such a muddle of emotions. Such a weight on his shoulders. Months of brutal battle had left her drained and nearly numb, but it was worse for Anakin. He was a Jedi general with countless lives entrusted to his care, and every life damaged or lost he counted as a personal failure. For other people he found forgiveness; for himself there was none. For himself there was only anger at not meeting his own exacting standards.

Feeling helpless, she chewed at her lip. She didn't know what she could do to make anything *better* for him. She couldn't heal his grief for the clones who'd fallen under his command, or the civilians he'd been unable to save. She couldn't make him less tired, or order him home to Coruscant where his mood always lightened. She couldn't promise the war would end soon, with the Republic victorious.

At least he had Master Kenobi's company for a little while. She was sure that accounted for his relief. They cheered each other up, those two. No matter how dire the straits, Anakin and Master Kenobi always managed to find a joke, a laugh, some way to ease the tension and pressure of the moment. Between the two men lay absolute trust. Absolute faith. Now, *they* were equals. On the outside, looking in, she couldn't help feeling a little forlorn.

Will he ever feel that way about me? Will he ever believe in me the way he believes in Obi-Wan?

She opened her eyes to find Anakin looking at her. Though she'd tried so hard to be discreet, still he'd felt her sensing of him. She held her breath, expecting a reprimand. Anakin *hated* when she did this.

But no reprimand came. Instead her Master raised a tolerantly amused eyebrow at her . . . and in his eyes was a kind of tired appreciation. She felt herself shrug, a tiny twitch of one shoulder, and curved her lips into a small, rueful, *I can't help it* smile.

He took a breath, he was going to say something—but then his head lifted. So did Master Kenobi's. A few moments later she felt it, too: a sharp, almost painful tingle of awareness. Something was coming. And a few moments after *that*, the comm officer straightened in her chair and pressed a finger to the transceiver plugged into her ear.

"Sir—"

Admiral Yularen, lean and predatory as ever, and alerted already by the Jedi on either side of him, practically leapt for the comm station. "Lieutenant Avrey?"

The slight, blond officer danced her fingers over the ship's comm panel, frowning, then gave a pleased nod. "Sir, I have an incoming message from the Jedi Council, Priority Alpha."

"Recorded or real-time?"

The lieutenant checked. "Recorded, sir. Sent by triple-coded multiple-routed shortburst."

Priority Alpha. Skin prickling, senses jittering, Ahsoka held her breath. This was it. This was what they'd been waiting for as they dangled idly out here for hours in the middle of nowhere, an empty stretch of space on the border between the Expansion Region and the galactic Mid Rim, parsecs from anywhere remotely civilized.

This is it.

Yularen's nod was swift and grim. "Very good, Lieutenant. Master Kenobi?"

"I think we'll take this one in the Battle Operations Room, Admiral," Master Kenobi said. His voice was mild, completely unperturbed, as though an Alpha transmission from the Council came along once or twice a day . . . instead of only as a last-resort emergency.

Ahsoka eyed him with unbecoming envy. *One of these years I'm going to be as untwitchy as him.* "Masters—"

"Yes, Padawan, *we* means *you*," said Anakin. "So what are you waiting for?"

She nearly said, *An invitation.* The smart remark was awfully tempting. He'd practically asked for it. But she held her tongue, because she was no longer that uncertain, mouthy Padawan who'd met her new Master in the midst of battle on Christophsis. She'd changed. Grown. Smart remarks at a time like this weren't funny. They were disruptive and unhelpful and they made her mentor look bad.

She'd learned that lesson from Clone Captain Rex.

"Lieutenant," said Admiral Yularen, sounding almost as calm as Master Kenobi. "Comm the captains of *Pioneer* and *Coruscant Sky*. Stand by for orders, battle alert."

"Yes, Admiral," said the comm officer. Color washed into her space-white face. All around the bridge the crew snapped to stricter attention. The scrubbed air tightened with a palpable anticipation.

Yularen flicked a tight smile at Anakin and Master Kenobi. "Lead the way, gentlemen."

With an effort Ahsoka smoothed her expression into uncaring blandness, hating that Anakin and Master Kenobi could sense her true feelings. As her Jedi superiors and the admiral swept past her she fell into step behind them, lightsaber bouncing lightly against her hip. Her mouth was dry—how annoying. She'd seen plenty of action since the start of the war; surely she should be *bored* by this now. But no. Her body betrayed her with a dry mouth and a racing heart, and sweat slicking the skin between her shoulder blades.

Soon we'll be fighting. And if I make a mistake I'll get Anakin killed.

"Ahsoka," said Anakin, not even looking over his shoulder.

"How many times do I have to tell you? Our thoughts create our reality. Cut it out."

He always knew. "Sorry, Master."

It wasn't far from the bridge to the Battle Operations Room, just one short corridor and a single flight of stairs. As soon as they were ranged around the broad central holodisplay table, Admiral Yularen toggled his comm to the bridge.

"Patch it through, Lieutenant."

The holoimagers blinked on, bright blue-white light against the Battle Room's muted illumination. The air above the holodisplay shivered, mirage-like, and then an image flickered, partially disintegrated, flickered again, and finally coalesced into a recognizable form.

Master Yoda.

"*Confirmation we have, Master Kenobi, of the initial report,*" said the Jedi Order's most respected Master. "*Misled the Special Operations Brigade was not. A target have Dooku and Grievous made of Kothlis and its spynet facility. In Republic hands must they remain, for compromised the Mid Rim cannot be. Once the strength of the enemy you have determined, call for reinforcements you can if defeating Grievous without them is not possible. But contact the Council in real time do not until Kothlis you have reached. Stealth and secrecy are our most potent weapons. Use them wisely. May the Force be with you.*"

Master Yoda's image winked out.

"Well," said Master Kenobi, breaking the tense silence. "This is going to be interesting."

Anakin frowned. "What reinforcements? Our people are scattered from one side of the Republic to the other."

"*Coryx Moth* is on patrol near Falleen, is she not? That's the closest—"

"One ship?" Anakin shook his head. "Obi-Wan—"

"It's better than nothing, Anakin."

Anakin didn't think so, if the look on his face was anything to go by. He scowled at Master Kenobi and Master Kenobi stared back, his expression unreadable.

"I'm sorry, but Master Yoda's message is too cryptic for my tastes," said Admiral Yularen. One narrow finger stroked his mustache, a sure sign he was uneasy. "Bitter experience has taught us we can't attack Grievous with anything less than over-whelming force. Not if we wish to finish him once and for all—and avoid a catastrophic level of loss on our side."

"And in an ideal galaxy we would have that overwhelming force at our disposal," said Master Kenobi, arms decisively folded. "Alas, Admiral, this galaxy of ours is far from ideal. And cryptic or not, we have our orders. Yoda's right—we must keep Kothlis out of Separatist hands."

"I know that," said Yularen curtly. "But the notion we can't call for support until we're in the thick of the fight? We all know that'll likely be too late."

"True," said Anakin, stirring out of somber thought. "But we'll have to live with it. In fact—" He shot the admiral a dark look. "I think we'll have to think twice about calling for help at all. Because if someone does come to our aid, it means some-where else gets left undefended."

Yularen bristled. "What? You want me to risk this battle group—three cruisers—against—"

"I beat him with three cruisers last time," said Anakin, de-ceptively mild.

"I know!" Yularen retorted. "And that would be my point, General Skywalker. Grievous isn't stupid. He learns from his mistakes. He's going to make sure he has more than enough fire-power to easily take us down! I'm not prepared to risk—"

"I'm sorry, Admiral," said Master Kenobi, still calm. "But I'm afraid you might have to. Anakin's made a good point. What we'd prefer hardly factors in to this. We simply don't have spare battle groups idling about."

Abandoning his mustache, Yularen drummed his fingers on the edge of the holodisplay table, angrily resentful of the cold, hard facts. "I know. I know. I'm just—" He sighed. "I don't like it. That's all I'm saying."

"We should comm Grievous, then," said Anakin, his eyes glittering in the dull light. "Let him know his plans are inconvenient. Ask him to make sure he only sends in a couple of—"

"Anakin," said Master Kenobi quietly.

"Sorry," said Anakin, and made a visible effort to relax his gloved prosthetic hand. "I'm a bit . . . on edge."

Ahsoka looked at him from under lowered lashes, feeling his agitation as a hot breeze blowing over her skin. *No kidding.*

"So," her Master added. "I guess now we head for Kothlis."

"Without further delay," said Master Kenobi. "Admiral?"

Yularen nodded, his face grave. Resigned now to what had to be done, no matter how hard he found it. "Agreed. And with any luck we'll beat Grievous to the punch and be waiting for him. Even the smallest advantage might make the difference for us." He toggled the comm button again. "Lieutenant Avrey? We have a mission."

While Yularen relayed battle group orders with staccato speed, Master Kenobi drew Anakin aside with a glance. "I suggest we play to our strengths on this one, Anakin," he said, his voice low. "If we do reach Kothlis and find that Grievous has stolen a march on us, it's likely we'll be looking at both air and ground assaults. Should that prove to be the case, I suggest you lead the fighter squadrons and I'll take care of the ground assault with Captain Rex and our clone trooper companies."

Anakin almost had his edginess under control. Just a hint of disquiet churned in him now, like water on the brink of boiling. "And if we've stolen a march on him?"

"In that case," said Master Kenobi, his expression fastidious with distaste, "I shall join you in leading the fighters against Grievous's pilots."

Ahsoka watched them exchange quick smiles, then cleared her throat. "Um—Masters? What about me?"

They stared at her, startled, as though for a moment they'd forgotten she existed. In the silence she heard—felt—the shift in the warship's sublight drives as they broke their stationary position, getting ready for the hyperjump to Kothlis. Washing in its wake, the subliminal buzz through the Force as every sentient being on all three cruisers accepted the reality of imminent battle. Possible death. It was a song sung without words, in a minor key. Haunting. Sorrowful. Shot through with stark courage.

"You, Ahsoka?" said Anakin, blinking himself free of the same thing she was feeling. "If it comes to a ground assault, you'll fight with Obi-Wan and Rex. And if it doesn't, you'll stay here on *Indomitable*."

Stay behind? While he threw himself heedless into danger? "But—"

Anakin's eyes narrowed dangerously. "Don't argue."

Not fair, not fair, she raged in silence.

"Ahsoka . . ." Anakin gentled his tone. "This isn't about your competence. I know what you can do. But we have plenty of pilots. Your skills will be better utilized here."

"Master Skywalker's right," said Admiral Yularen. Finished giving his orders, he was unabashedly listening in. "If you do remain aboard ship, there'll be a tactical targeting array with your name on it." He unbent far enough to offer her a small, not unsympathetic smile. "I've yet to meet a Jedi who couldn't out-sense our best sensors."

"But it's more likely you'll be needed on the ground," added Master Kenobi. "With me. I do hope the prospect's not unbearable, Padawan."

He was being sarcastic. She felt her cheeks burn. Anakin was watching her closely. If she protested again, she'd disappoint him.

"Not unbearable at all, Master Kenobi," she said, staring at the deck. "Serving by your side is always an honor." She risked glancing up. "It's only—"

"I know," said Master Kenobi, more kindly. "You worry for Anakin's safety. But there's no need. And now the subject is closed." He turned to Yularen. "What's our estimated jump time to Kothlis?"

"Thirty-eight standard minutes," said the admiral. "I'm dropping us out of hyperspace just inside sensor range of their spynet. Close enough for us to contact them, and to sweep for Sep ships if we have beaten Grievous there."

"Our own intelligence agents will have alerted the Kothlis Bothans to the danger they're in," said Anakin, frowning again. "For all the good it'll do them. Without a standing army or space fleet of their own, they're ripe for plucking." His gloved prosthetic hand clenched. "I should've seen this coming. I should've known Grievous wouldn't forgive or forget the insult of losing to me at Bothawui. This is a rematch—and you know he's itching for the fight. If we lose Kothlis to him—if he manages to breach the Mid Rim . . ."

"Don't let your thoughts run ahead to disaster, Anakin," said Master Kenobi sharply. "As you say, you defeated Grievous once. There's no reason to think you—we—can't defeat him again."

Anakin's chin lifted at the reprimand. Ahsoka, watching him, felt her breath hitch, felt the flash of fury sizzle through him. And then he relaxed, pulling a wry face.

"Sorry," he said. "You're right. I should know better."

"Thirty-eight minutes," said Master Kenobi, his eyes warm now. "Give or take. Just enough time, I think, for a little pre-battle meditation. You're not the only one who's feeling a trifle on edge, my friend. I could do with some refocusing myself."

"You?" Anakin's eyebrows shot up. "I find that hard to believe."

Master Kenobi rested his hand briefly on Anakin's shoulder. "Believe it, Anakin. You know how much I hate to fly."

"I think you just say that," Anakin retorted, grinning. "You couldn't be such a good pilot if you hated flying as much as you claim."

Master Kenobi grimaced. "Trust me, if I'm a good pilot it's out of a well-developed sense of self-preservation. As far as I'm concerned, Anakin, anyone who actually *enjoys* flying is in serious need of therapeutic counseling."

Anakin was struggling not to laugh. "If you're not careful I'll tell Gold Squadron you said that. So—are we going to navel-gaze or aren't we?"

"Please excuse us, Admiral," said Master Kenobi, the amusement dying out of his face. "And look for us on the bridge ten minutes before the battle group drops out of hyperspace."

Admiral Yularen nodded. "Of course, General. In the meantime I'll have the fighters and gunships prepped for flight."

"Ahsoka," said Anakin, as Master Kenobi headed for the Battle Room's closed hatch. "Make yourself useful and give Rex the heads-up, will you? Run through the pre-battle routine with him and his men. Half of Torrent Company's still a bit green. They'll settle with you there."

Under his careless confidence, she sensed a hint of that un-healed grief. The loss of greenies Vere and Ince during the Jan-Fathal mission . . . the loss of other Torrent Company clones since then . . . his pain was like a kiplin-burr, burrowed deep in his flesh. Anakin had a bad habit of nursing those wounds, and no matter what she said, tactfully, no matter what Master Kenobi said without any tact at all, nothing made a difference. He hurt for them, and always would.

"Yes, Master," she said. She waited for him to leave so she could sprint to midships and let Rex know that like as not they'd soon be going into battle together. Again.

"So, WHAT'S THE SKINNY, little'un?" Rex asked, as Ahsoka skid-ded into the mess hall. "Since we're on the move at last, have we got that clanker Grievous in our sights?"

"Sort of," she said, dropping into a spare chair beside Checkers, one of Torrent Company's latest additions. "We've confirmed the preliminary intel—he's definitely after Kothlis. Now it's a race to see who gets there first."

Rex's perfect teeth bared in a feral smile. "Ah. Then it's game on."

The crowded barracks mess hall erupted into muttering and exclamation. Force-sensing from habit, Ahsoka tasted the clones' swirling emotions. A little caution. A lot of excitement. At first she'd thought the Republic's clone soldiers welcomed battle because they had no choice—because they'd been genet-ically programmed to fight and not question that duty. But while that was an uncomfortable truth, one she found herself wrestling with more and more as the war dragged on, it was also true that most of the clones she knew enjoyed combat— and not because some Kaminoan scientist had tweaked a test tube and made sure they would. No. They enjoyed winning. Outsmarting the enemy. Liberating citizens who were being used as pawns by Count Dooku, and Nute Gunray, and the other shadowy leaders of the Separatist Alliance.

Was it so hard to believe, really? Saving the innocent—that *did* feel good. Besting—or surviving—lethal foes like Asajj Ventress? Like Grievous? That felt good, too. She knew Anakin and Master Kenobi deplored this war, deplored the senseless loss of life, the suffering . . . but she wasn't blind. She'd seen in their faces the exhilaration that came with victory. It was no less real than their grief when lives were lost. She'd felt it, too. She'd celebrated when vicious, venal beings were defeated.

It's so complicated. If war is wrong, how come we can find moments of pleasure and triumph in it? Isn't there something . . . twisted . . . in that?

Disturbed by the thought, she heard herself whimper in her throat, just a little bit. And that alarmed her so much she crushed the notion, savagely. *Little fool.* It was exactly the wrong thing to be thinking when they were racing through hyperspace to confront that monster Grievous and save the helpless people of Kothlis from Separatist enslavement—or worse.

Ahsoka Tano, you know better.

Rex was deep in conversation with Sergeant Coric, so she turned to Checkers. He might be a newcomer to Torrent Company, but he wasn't a greenie clone. The deep scarring on his right cheek attested to previous combat experience . . . as did that certain glint in his eye. The same glint she sometimes saw in Rex, and Coric, and any number of Torrent Company's men. It set them apart as soldiers who'd been fought to a standstill, who'd stared down death—and survived.

Checkers felt her gaze on him and looked up. "Ma'am?"

She blinked. "Oh, I'm not a ma'am."

"What, then?" said Checkers, with a wry half smile. "Something tells me I won't get away with *little'un.*"

"You can call me Ahsoka," she said, charmed. "Everyone else does."

"Ahsoka it is, then," he replied. "Togruta, aren't you?"

"That's right. Checkers, can I ask how you got here? I mean, how did you get assigned to Torrent Company?"

Checkers flicked a glance at his fellow clones talking among themselves in the mess hall, pursed his lips for a moment, then seemed to reach a decision. His face relaxed, and his shoulders settled. "I requested the transfer. Used to be in Laser Company, under General Fisto."

Oh. "Is that when you were wounded?" she asked, her voice small. "In the Kessel encounter?"

His fingers came up, touching lightly to the bubbled scarring under his eye. "That's right."

"I knew there was only one clone survivor, but I didn't realize that was you."

He shrugged. "No reason you should. You weren't here when I joined Torrent, and there's no point talking about it. Can't undo what happened."

"But there's still a Laser Company, isn't there?" she said, frowning. "I thought Master Fisto—"

"There is," said Checkers, with another shrug. "But I wanted a clean break. After they got through patching me up at the clone medfacility, they offered me a posting of my choice."

"And you chose Torrent Company?" Charmed all over again, she couldn't help smiling, even though his terse story covered a chasm of pain and loss. "Don't get me wrong, I'm glad, but—why?"

"Not because I blamed General Fisto," Checkers said quickly. "Don't think that, Ahsoka." His dark-eyed gaze shifted and came to rest on Rex, still talking logistics with Sergeant Coric. "The truth is I want to survive this war. That means serving under the best officer I can find."

Checkers was keeping his voice down, but Rex still heard that last comment. Startled, he broke off whatever he was saying to Coric and shifted in his chair. Seeing *and* feeling his barely muffled astonishment, Ahsoka grinned. It wasn't easy to rattle Rex . . . and she did find it comforting to know he *could* be rattled. At least when they weren't on the front lines, facing death.

"Stow the chatter," he snapped. "We're on the chrono."

Silence claimed the mess hall, abrupt as a cut comlink. Ahsoka winced at the suddenly ratcheted tension buzzing through the Force like a vibroblade. It made her teeth ache and her vision blur.

"Ahsoka," Rex added, skewering her with his most direct, no-nonsense stare. "What's our ETA at Kothlis?"

She checked her almost infallible Jedi time-sense. "Twenty-three minutes, Captain."

"Ground assault's confirmed?"

"Not confirmed, but highly possible. If the Seps have beaten us there and started an invasion of Kothlis, General Kenobi will handle the counteroffensive while my Master and Shadow Company clear the skies."

Rex nodded. "That means you're with us? Good." His gaze swept the hall. "Then we need to gear up. Torrent Company—get to work!"

Within a heartbeat the mood changed again. Lingering anxiety and uncertainty disappeared in a wave of purposeful action as Rex's men began the familiar countdown to combat.

Because she couldn't help with that, because she couldn't do anything now but wait, Ahsoka got out of the way. She perched herself in a corner and tried, like Anakin, to calm herself with meditation. Which was fine, mostly—except one thought kept intruding, over and over.

May the Force be with us. And please, please, don't let my actions get any of these clones killed.

TWO

———○———

"IT'S NO GOOD, ADMIRAL," SAID LIEUTENANT AVREY, FLUSHED
with dismay. "I'm sorry. I don't know how they're doing it but
the Seps have every comm channel jammed, even our internal
network. We're silent across the board."

Yularen glared at her. "That's unacceptable, Lieutenant.
Find the problem and fix it."

"Sir—" The comm officer's face lost its hectic color. "Yes,
sir. I'll do my best."

As Yularen swallowed an unprofessional response, Anakin
looked to Obi-Wan. His former Master raised an eyebrow, resigned. "This time the advantage goes to the enemy," he murmured. "It's going to get ugly, I fear."

Beyond the bridge's main viewport Grievous's new flagship
and its four satellite cruisers hung low and threatening above the
Bothan colony world of Kothlis. Two of the planet's three small
moons were completely obscured by Grievous's fleet, and the
void of space lit up at haphazard intervals as the Separatist general's invasion troops blasted a path through the thin belt of as-
teroids ringing their intended target, bullying their blundering,
unopposed way toward the planet's undefended surface.

Joining his Jedi colleagues, Yularen blew out a furious
breath. "We've never lost communications like this before.

They've upgraded their countermeasures. How in the Nine Hells are they getting their intel?"

"That's an excellent question, Admiral," said Obi-Wan. "And we need to find the answer—just as soon as we've dealt with General Grievous."

"Obviously—but how can we do that if we can't talk to one another?" Yularen demanded. "And if it turns out we're outgunned and we're not able to send for reinforcements, how can we *possibly*—"

"Sir!" said Lieutenant Avrey, crawling out from under her comm console, her light hair darkened with sweat and grime. "Sir, I think it's a virus."

Yularen swung around. "How serious?"

With a grunt and a swipe of her sleeve across her face, Avrey scrambled to her feet. "It's corrupted the comm software, Admiral. As far as I can tell we've got ship-to-ship tightbeam—and most likely the clone troops' helmet tightbeam will work, too. Aside from that—" She shrugged. "We've been gagged. And the systems diagnostic can't recognize the virus coding. I can tell you it's complex and multi-stranded—three quadruple helixes at least—self-replicating on a random cycle and specifically targeted to our systems."

For a moment Anakin thought Yularen was going to burst a blood vessel. *"And it's on my ship?"* He turned, every muscle rigid. "General Skywalker—"

"Admiral, each new cruiser tested clean before it left Allanteen Six," Anakin said. "And none of my modifications could've introduced a virus. In fact, I designed blind-alley redundancies to make sure something like this couldn't happen." He glanced at Obi-Wan. "And if they've failed, that means—"

"Sabotage," said Obi-Wan, his eyes bleak. "The Seps must have infiltrated our shipyards."

Silence followed as they digested that unpalatable fact.

"Avrey, can you fix this?" said Yularen. "I can't send men into harm's way without communication."

Seated again at her console, Avrey looked up from punching in a swift succession of commands. "Admiral, I'm initiating a systemwide purge but it'll take time—and I don't know how effective it'll be. I've never seen a virus like this. I'm almost positive it was remotely activated—probably from Grievous's command ship as soon as we jumped into range. Whoever designed it— they're a genius. For all I know—" Breaking off as her console beeped and flashed, she adjusted her earpiece, listened for a moment, then turned back to them. "Tightbeams from *Pioneer* and *Coruscant Sky*. They report the same problem, Admiral. Battle group comms are down."

"Is there nothing you can do, Lieutenant?" said Obi-Wan. "No other solution but trusting this purge?"

Avrey dragged her fingers through her hair. "I don't think so, General. I don't—"

"What?" said Yularen, stepping closer to his officer. For all his formidable self-discipline, a note of hope sounded in his voice. "I know that look, Lieutenant."

She flicked him a frowning glance. Anakin, focusing all his senses on her, felt trepidation and a faint buzz of cautious optimism. "Sir, I did my Academy dissertation on pre-praxis crystal bio-anode circuitry," the lieutenant said. "The technology's years out of date, it's practically ancient history, but the theory's still sound."

"If it's ancient history, how can it help us?" Yularen demanded. "I need solutions, Lieutenant, not—"

"This might be a solution, Admiral," she said, meeting his hot gaze unflinching. "For all the upgrades and improvements we've got around here, I'm pretty sure we've still got some of that circuitry on board—in the waste core's tertiary adjunct conduits. They're another kind of triple redundancy. Pre-praxis bio-anodes used to have comm applications. If I can strip them out and rig them into the comm console, I think I can punch a signal through subspace strong enough to reach Coruscant."

Yularen stared at her. "You *think*?"

"Sir," said Avrey, the remaining color draining from her cheeks. "I know."

"You're saying you can restore communication?"

A muscle leapt along Avrey's narrow jaw. "I'm saying we've got a better than even shot at it, yes, sir."

"How long, Lieutenant?"

"To rig *Indomitable*? An hour, give or take."

"Then another two hours for *Pioneer* and *Coruscant Sky*?" Yularen shook his head, frustrated. "That's three hours neither we nor Kothlis have to spare. Have you looked through the viewport? Grievous's forces are invading as we speak."

"Lieutenant," said Obi-Wan, mildly, as though they weren't facing an utter disaster. "Can you tightbeam detailed instructions for the comm officers on our other two ships? If all three of you work simultaneously, your plan might still succeed in time to do us some good."

Avrey snapped out of her almost imperceptible slump. "Yes, General Kenobi. I can do that."

"Then get on to it," said Yularen. "Every minute wasted means more lost lives."

"Wait," said Anakin, abruptly unsettled. *I have a bad feeling . . .* "What about our fighters? And the larties?"

"They should be unaffected, General," said the lieutenant. "They're not linked into our comm systems."

He looked at Obi-Wan. "No. But if Grievous can remotely activate a computer virus—"

"Then he might have the power to jam our ship comms,"

said Obi-Wan. There was unease in him now, too, the bad feeling shared. "Despite our anti-jamming precautions. I suggest we
find out before we launch an attack."

Leaving dourly silent Yularen and frantically working Lieutenant Avrey, Obi-Wan and Anakin made their way to *Indomitable*'s flight deck. The hangar's deckhands, on standby
now that they'd prepped the fighters, watched them with wide
eyes. Gold Squadron's pilots were in their barracks, mentally
preparing for action.

"Don't disturb them," said Obi-Wan as he swung himself
into his own fighter's cockpit. "If it is bad news, best they're
spared hearing it for as long as possible."

And it was bad news.

Sickened, Anakin stared at his Aethersprite's unresponsive
comm panel. Then he looked over at Obi-Wan, whose expressionless face said it all. "So, Grievous isn't taking any chances."

Obi-Wan nodded. "Apparently not."

Computer viruses and broadband jamming equipment? *The
barve's gone and got himself some serious upgrades. I wonder
how long we've got before he can take out our tightbeam as
well?* "If he's jamming the fighters, it's a good bet he's taken out
the gunships, too."

Another nod. "A very good bet."

Stang. "Artoo—can you unjam us?"

Already locked into his wing position, R2-D2 emitted a dis-
mal whistle.

Anakin slammed his fist against the open cockpit's frame.
"Great."

"Come on," said Obi-Wan, all emotion ruthlessly repressed.
"Yularen's waiting."

The admiral took one look at them as they returned to the
bridge and spat a soft curse. "Then that's it."

"Not at all," said Obi-Wan, eyebrows lifting. "We can't afford to wait until communications are restored. Kothlis needs us now. We go in."

"You mean fight *blind*?" said Anakin, disbelieving. "*And* deaf? Obi-Wan—"

"I grant you it's not an ideal way to conduct a war," said Obi-Wan, the merest glimmer of bleak humor in his eyes. "But I don't see another choice. Do you?"

Stang. He didn't. Grievous was delivering mayhem and slaughter while they stood here helpless, watching. He wasn't even bothering to divert any of his cruisers or droid starfighters their way, so arrogantly confident was he that he'd rendered them impotent.

So let that be his first and final mistake.

"How do you want to play it, then?" Anakin said, his belly jumping with nerves. He felt shock run through the officers close enough to overhear this crazy conversation, and Yularen's dismay, swiftly stifled for the sake of his crew. "It's not like we can communicate with hand signals or color-coded flags."

"Actually, Anakin, your task is relatively simple," said Obi-Wan. "Engage the enemy and keep on shooting his ships out of the sky until none is left."

Simple? *Yeah, right.* Although, being coldly dispassionate, Obi-Wan wasn't too far off the mark, come to think of it. "Fine. But what about you?"

"Using the fighters as cover, the clones and I will run Grievous's gauntlet in gunships, make atmospheric entry, and insert on the ground. Kothlis has only two points of interest—the capital, Tal'cara, and the spynet facility on the city's northwest outskirts. We'll target those two areas first and see what happens once they're secured." Obi-Wan looked at Yularen. "Unless you can think of a better plan, Admiral."

Yularen shook his head. "No. We'll go with yours. For one

thing it's uncomplicated—barring disaster, we won't need communications once all cruisers and squadrons are reading from the same flimsi. Besides, it's too risky asking the larties to tackle Grievous's droid starfighter defenses."

Anakin nodded. Spaceworthy the gunships might be, but top-of-the-line fighters they assuredly were not. "Agreed. So, Obi-Wan, that gets you boots on the ground. And then what?"

Again, that wry, dry glimmer of humor. "Oh, I'm bound to think of something. Imminent death tends to stimulate the imagination." He turned. "Lieutenant Avrey—"

The comm officer looked up from her console while she was pushing the systemwide purge as hard and fast as it could take. "General?"

"Have you some spare data crystals? I've a few instructions for the other clone companies—and the captains of *Pioneer* and *Coruscant Sky.*"

"Sir," she said, and nodded at a slot in the comm console. "Help yourself."

"Excellent," said Obi-Wan, accepting her invitation. "Anakin, it's time you briefed Gold Squadron. I'll need you ready to launch in fifteen minutes."

"Obi-Wan, if you're recording orders for our other pilots then maybe I should—"

Obi-Wan smiled tightly, his hand full of data crystals. "Just this once let me speak on your behalf."

Again, that ugly jump of nerves. *Blast it, I think we really are crazy.* "Fine. Tell them to use their best judgment. Tell them to keep their eyes peeled and—and think of themselves as one-man squadrons. Tell them to launch on my mark—once Gold Squadron's clear of *Indomitable*, Hammer Squadron launches from *Pioneer* and then Arrow Squadron from the *Sky.* After that they're on their own. Obi-Wan—"

His mentor—his friend—nodded. "Yes, Anakin. I'll take care of your Padawan."

"Make sure you take care of yourself while you're at it," Anakin replied.

Obi-Wan just smiled. He smiled back, not even trying to muffle his feelings, then turned to leave—but Yularen raised a hand. "I know you Jedi don't believe in it—but I wish you good luck, General Skywalker. And don't worry. Comm or no comm, we'll have your backs."

"Thank you, Admiral," Anakin said, nodding. He trusted the man, even though Yularen's reservations about the Jedi lived close to his surface. "Good hunting to you, too."

On the way down to his pilots Anakin took a swift detour via the clone troops' barracks where Rex and Ahsoka and Torrent Company were geared up and waiting.

"Master!" said Ahsoka, practically gasping, as she and Rex answered his beckon from the opened hatch. "What's going on? What's the—"

"Be quiet and listen," he said, quelling her with a frown. "Grievous beat us here. His invasion of Kothlis is well under way—and to make things interesting the comms are jammed, so we're going in blind. *Indomitable* and the other two cruisers will be escorted through the upper atmosphere by our fighters. On my signal you'll go in on gunships, then while you're taking care of Grievous's ground troops we'll mop up his warships and droid starfighters. The action's going to be hard, fast, and dirty, so stay on your toes."

Ahsoka blinked at him, for once in her short life lost for words. Clasping his hands in front of him, Rex frowned. "When you say all comms . . ."

"I mean all comms," he said quietly, meeting Rex's concerned gaze. "Except your troops' helmet tightbeams—we hope."

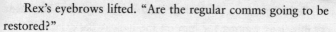

Rex's eyebrows lifted. "Are the regular comms going to be restored?"

"Maybe. And there's a chance we'll be able to call for help if we need it."

"Um . . . how good a chance, exactly?" said Ahsoka, her blue eyes wide.

Beneath her bold exterior Anakin could feel her anxiety. He resisted the urge to put a comforting hand on her shoulder. The last thing he needed was Torrent Company thinking either of them was worried.

"Good enough," he said, keeping his voice clipped and businesslike. "But that's not your concern. Follow Obi-Wan's lead and you'll all be fine."

"And what about you, sir?" said Rex. Nothing in his attitude indicated unease, but the Force told a different story. Like Ahsoka, the experienced clone captain was deeply unsettled.

And I don't blame him. I'm not exactly turning cartwheels myself.

"Forget about me," Anakin snapped. "I've got the easy job."

"So if we don't have communications," Ahsoka said slowly, "how will we know when it's time to launch the ground assault?"

"Don't worry. You'll know. Now hop to it, Rex. Get your men down to the gunship hangar—those larties are lonely. Obi-Wan will join you there shortly—and I'll see you both when the party's over."

"Yes, sir," said Rex, nodding smartly. "Good hunting, General."

"May the Force be with you, Master," Ahsoka whispered.

"The force will be with us all, Padawan," he replied. Then he left them, before his self-control slipped and he revealed the depth of his own doubts.

Gold Squadron, with their unerring instinct for imminent trouble, was waiting for him on the hangar deck, laconic and restively ready for action. Clone Captain Fireball, his clipped hair dyed an eye-searing scarlet, a single black-and-scarlet scalplock proclaiming his stubborn individuality, greeted him as he joined them.

"General."

"Game on, Fib," he said. "With a twist—we've got no communications."

His captain's only reaction was a raised eyebrow. "Fine. I'll take fighting over chitchat any day."

Oh, these men. He loved them. "It means we're going in hot and wild, no plan but this: blast those kriffing Sep ships out of my sky."

Fireball grinned with ear-to-ear ferocity. "It'll be our pleasure, General."

The rest of Gold Squadron was listening, their focused attention and absolute belief in him as warm and as reassuring as his mother's hand on his back.

"Grievous is out there, sitting on his clanky butt thinking he's got us whipped before we fire a single shot," he told his pilots, sharing with them his own unbridled ferocity. "I'm in the mood to contradict him, boys. How about you?"

They roared with one voice, clenched fists punching the air above their heads.

"Forget about the comm troubles," he added. "You don't need me telling you what to do. You were born knowing what to do. You've done it before, and after today you'll do it again."

Another roar, louder this time.

"Torrent, Cascade, and Waterfall companies are depending on us to sweep the streets for 'em," he finished. "And we are not going to let them down. Agreed?"

"*Agreed!*" his pilots shouted, so loud this time that the hangar's metal struts and deck plating thrummed with the sound.

He was so proud of them—and at the same time so afraid. The brutal reality of combat meant the odds were they wouldn't all come home. They knew it, too, but no one would read that in their faces—faces that were at first glance, to the uncaring observer, identical. But he knew them as individuals, and he loved them for themselves. He could list each man's scars, recite each man's quirks, describe each man's idiosyncratic hair. Close-helmeted, in full body armor, he knew every one of them by his walk.

Blindfold me and I'll tell you who laughed.

Letting his gaze touch each unique, committed pilot, he locked their faces tightly in his memory, in case this was the last time.

"Okay, let's go," he said. "On me in standard formation until we clear the ship. Once we hit free space take care of business in your own time. Last man home buys the drinks."

Laughing and eager, the clones broke ranks and headed for their fighters. R2-D2 hooted and whistled as Anakin climbed up to their ship's cockpit.

"Don't panic, Artoo," he told the agitated droid. "Someone's working on the problem."

More anxious whistling.

"No. Right now I need you more than Lieutenant Avrey does," he replied, starting his pre-flight check. "So while we're kicking tinnies into the gutter out there, Artoo, you do your thing and I'll do mine. And if you have to tell me something, write me a note."

This time the little astromech droid sounded dismayed.

"Don't worry, we'll be fine," he insisted, even as fear shivered down his spine. Padmé. *I will see her again. I'm not dying today.* "Grievous hasn't found the machine yet that can touch us. Got it?"

R2 beeped a mournfully hopeful reply.

"Good," he said, and took a quick look around the hangar to make sure Gold Squadron was locked and loaded. Yes. Every starfighter was tight and right, canopies engaged. He felt burning in the Force: his pilots' united determination to prevail, to defeat the enemy no matter what was thrown their way.

I'm so lucky to have them. Please, don't let me let them down.

His own cockpit canopy he left unsecured, for the moment. Waited for a messenger from the bridge to say they were go for launch.

Come on, come on. What are we waiting for? Time means lives, people. Let's not hang around.

OBI-WAN STOOD BY HIMSELF on the bridge, staring through *Indomitable*'s main viewport across the airless abyss between himself and the enemy battle group, at unseen Grievous, who stood on his own bridge orchestrating helpless Kothlis's subjugation. His skin was crawling with the need to act. The Separatist general's warship vomited another droid troop carrier. Sick with loathing, he watched its purposeful plummet toward the undefended planet.

Grievous.

Early in the war he'd tried to fathom what drove the creature. What fed its hate and violence, its mindless desire for death and destruction. An answer stubbornly eluded him, and finally he gave up. Understand Grievous or never understand him: it made no difference. There was not, could never be, a hope of peace between them. The sentient cyborg was committed to destroying the Republic. He was a creature of the dark side, and in joining Dooku, he'd sealed his fate.

Obi-Wan could feel, trembling on the edge of his awareness, a sense of what had transpired on Kothlis. If he opened himself, he'd feel it completely. The Force would show him in intimate, merciless detail; would plunge him deep inside the pain and the terror and the death that lay distant and waiting, that he and Anakin must stop.

He kept himself rigorously closed. At times like this, empathy was a curse.

Though most of his attention was focused beyond *Indomitable*'s bridge, some small part of his mind was aware of every being behind him, every conversation, every half-formed thought, every bead of sweat trickling down spines, tickling ribs, and sticking hair to foreheads. This was a fine crew, one of the Republic's best, but they were organic, not programmed droids. Beneath their disciplined veneers they were afraid.

I could be afraid, too, if I permitted it. But I can't. Fear is a luxury I cannot afford.

Yularen joined him. "Your tightbeamed orders are received and understood, General. Give the word and we'll get this mission under way."

Give the word . . . Such a small, innocuous phrase. *Give the word . . .* and sign who knew how many death warrants? How many clones would die today because he gave the word? How many more would be born in their sterile containers on Kamino, subjected to accelerated maturation and comprehensive conditioning, because he gave the word? He wouldn't know until the end of the engagement. If he perished during it he might never know. If he perished during it, defending Kothlis, protecting his men, would that make up for those artfully constructed lives drawing their first, stunted breaths, because he gave the word?

Hardly. One day there will be a reckoning for this. One day we will be asked to account for these duplicate lives. One day . . .

He felt a sudden stabbing ache behind his eyes, and sighed. So. It was back. The pain was an unkind legacy from his exploits on Zigoola. After all this time not even the Jedi healer Vokara Che had managed to banish it. Neither could he, despite deep meditations and the occasional, resentful surrender to chemical help. But then, perhaps he deserved it. Perhaps it was a reminder of mortality, a sharp lesson in consequences.

And perhaps I'm being morbidly maudlin. Enough. I've work to do.

Yularen, a patient man, was waiting for him to speak. With a sideways glance he nodded. "The word is given, Admiral."

"General," said Yularen, and raised a hand. It was the only sign his crew needed. As his officers prepared for battle, a junior officer sprinted for the bridge transport, heading for the starfighter flight deck. She carried with her a brief, portentous command.

Gold Squadron, you have a go.

And so it would start, the fighting and the dying.

Anakin, be careful.

He could feel Yularen's considering gaze. "Young Sky-walker's an extraordinary pilot, General. Don't forget that."

Sympathy, from Wullf Yularen? It wasn't what he'd expected. They had a cordial relationship and worked well together. But the admiral was a reserved, cautious man who didn't, at heart, appreciate Jedi on his bridge. He was too disciplined, too professional, to allow his doubts to interfere with his duties, but they did shape his attitude. And yet here he was, offering an awkward, odd kind of comfort.

Odder still, I do feel comforted.

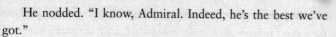

He nodded. "I know, Admiral. Indeed, he's the best we've got."

But if our best isn't good enough . . .

He wished he could see the outcome of this battle. He wished he could sense what would happen next. But even out here, so far from Coruscant and the Outer Rim Sieges, the dark side smothered his feeling for the future; torqued and twisted the light side, rendering it opaque. He was so much more sensitive to it now. Another legacy of Zigoola. Which he supposed was a good thing, even though it made him feel ill. He felt a constant hum of nausea, malignantly whispering.

In silence they waited. Two very different men, twinned by a single purpose, their differences set aside to serve the greater good.

And then—a sharpening of the Force. A leaping in his blood. The light side dazzled, beating back the dark. Beside him Yularen released a reverent sigh as he stared through the bridge's transparisteel window on the galaxy.

"They stop my heart, you know," the admiral said softly. Surprisingly. "Every time I see them they stop my heart."

Sleek and lethal, beautiful in their killing way, Gold Squadron's starfighters speared through the void beyond the viewport. Obi-Wan, reluctantly agreeing with Yularen's unexpected sentiment, felt his own heart thud as he kept his Force-enhanced gaze on the lead fighter, on Anakin, tearing toward Grievous at the head of his pack. He could feel his former Padawan's exhilaration in the flying, his fierce joy at the thought of crushing this impudent, implacable enemy.

That fierce joy chilled him. Somewhere, somehow, Anakin had discovered . . . not a taste for killing. No. Never that. But certainly a taste for vengeance. He'd learned to find pleasure in making an enemy pay for his crimes.

And did he learn it from me? In my thirst for justice, and the pleasure I take in perfecting my skills, have I led him astray?

The thought was a torment. Not all those who fought for the Separatists were droids. That he might, unwittingly, have failed his brilliant apprentice, be blind to something in him so crucial, so vital . . .

I don't care what Yoda says. He was Knighted too soon. And I fear we've yet to pay the price for our haste.

Movement to starboard caught his distracted attention. Hammer Squadron, fleeing the safety of *Pioneer*'s hangars, was following Gold Squadron to tangle with Grievous's droid starfighters. Moments later, to port, Arrow Squadron surged out of *Coruscant Sky*. Three full complements of fighters, the pilot of each metal canister a thin skin's distance from death.

Yularen gave his conn officer the nod, then turned. "General. We'll be in assault position shortly."

Indomitable was under way, ponderously heading for Kothlis, flanked by her sister cruisers and trusting to Anakin and his fearless pilots that they wouldn't come to grief before they could defend themselves. Some of Grievous's droid starfighters had broken off their prowling perimeter patrol of his battle group and were heading for the first wave of Republic starfighters, heading for Anakin, recklessly in the lead.

"Thank you, Admiral."

Streams of laserfire, blinking bright, crisscrossed the dark of space. Jinking and swooping, rolling and evading, Anakin and his clone pilots dodged destruction by a finger's-width. Four droid starfighters exploded in durasteel splinters and shards and slag.

"General—" Yularen was frowning. "When do you anticipate launching the gunships?"

Obi-Wan couldn't take his eyes off Gold Squadron—off Anakin. "I don't know yet. As soon as I do, I'll tell you."

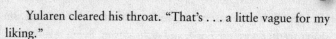

Yularen cleared his throat. "That's . . . a little vague for my liking."

"Really, Admiral?" Obi-Wan made himself look at Yularen and smile with quiet confidence. Through the Force he heard a clone pilot scream. "I don't find it vague at all."

"*STANG!*" ANAKIN CURSED, and scraped under the rolling belly of a shattered droid ship. "Careful, Gold Seven! Watch where you're shooting!"

It didn't matter that Flashpoint couldn't hear him. Yelling helped, so he yelled. Grievous's modified vulture starfighters were swarming them like enraged wasps. Best he could count, his people were outnumbered close on two-to-one.

But we've faced worse odds. We can do this. We can get the job done.

He'd made six kills in four minutes.

A Republic fighter streamed past his line of sight, hotly pursued by a pair of enemy ships.

"Look out, Arrow Nine, you've got two on your—"

The vultures fired, lethally accurate, and Arrow Nine's fighter disintegrated into fire and smoke. Punched through the Force he felt Stinger's fury, his brief, intense pain. *No. No.* The clone pilot's death echoed through him, blinding. And then there wasn't time to feel anything because three droid ships were on him—*where did* they *come from?*—and he was fighting to escape them, fighting his own whipping speed and trajectory, while they kept him pinned among them. Stang, they were good—*who programmed these barves? I want to meet him in a dark Coruscant alley*—and suddenly flying a fighter in combat wasn't so much fun anymore . . .

Fireball saved him.

Screaming out of a turn that should've been too tight for his fighter's structural tolerance, feeling like he was holding the ship together with the Force and desperation, flying through the vulture debris Fireball left in his wake, Anakin caught a glimpse of *Indomitable* from the corner of his eye. Laserfire streamed from the cruiser's gun turrets, welcome annihilation of Grievous's advantage. Flicking his gaze farther around, he saw that *Pioneer* and *Coruscant Sky* were pounding the Separatist warships as they headed for Kothlis's meager asteroid belt, diverting Grievous's resources from the desperately battling fighter squadrons.

And then Fireball dropped beside him so they were flying tandem, just for a moment. Turning his head, looking past smoke-scorched R2-D2, Anakin raised an acknowledging hand, thumb uptilted. Fireball's teeth flashed in a swift smile, and then he was peeling away to chase another droid starfighter.

Anakin shook himself. *Good idea. You're not a tourist, Skywalker.*

Hammer Two shot past his fighter's nose, a silent shout of panic blistering through the Force. Smoke belched from Wingnut's sublight drive and his cockpit canopy was bubbled in a wide streak, obscuring line of sight. Two droid starfighters pursued him, lethal projectiles spewing equally lethal plasma. Wingnut's fighter was struggling, pitching; its starboard stabilizer shot, his R4 unit a smoking ruin—and the droids were gaining—gaining—

No. No. Not Wingnut. He only joined us a month ago.

Grimly determined, he plunged his own fighter into the vultures' path, throwing the machine into a tight spin, hammering its laser controls so his weapons spewed death in a wildly expanding arc. The incendiary plasma sliced the droid starfighters to ragged, spinning pieces. One chunk grazed R2 on its way past, and the cockpit datapad lit up with a hysterical protest.

"*Sorry!*" he shouted through the spark-singed canopy. "*My mistake!*"

Wrenching the controls, he flipped his fighter right-side up again—or what counted as right-side up in this crazy fight—and tried to find Wingnut. There he was—limping back to *Pioneer*. Hammer Eight was covering him, keeping the tinnies off his smoking tail.

Stang, stang, speaking of tinnies . . .

His cockpit sensors screamed a warning, four of the enemy heading right for him. Where were they *coming* from? Every time he killed one, three more popped up in its place.

Grievous was throwing every last tinnie he could lay his metal hands on at the Jedi cruisers and the fighters protecting them. Space and time blurred and the void filled with explosions and shards and narrow misses and voices in the Force: his pilots, laughing and swearing and howling to their deaths. He laughed and swore and howled along with them, the silence unbearable.

Kill, kill, and kill again, slaughter the starfighters, slaughter the Tuskens, every loss is the same loss, every pain springs from one source. Save Kothlis, save Coruscant, save Padmé. Save them all.

THREE

SUNK DEEP WITHIN THE FORCE, SUBORDINATING WHAT HIS EYES could see to what his senses told him, Obi-Wan watched Anakin and his pilots savage Grievous's fleet—and watched the droid starfighters savage them in return. Someone on the Separatist's side had clearly tinkered with the vultures' operating systems; there was no Droid Control Ship in Grievous's battle group, yet the enemy fighters were functioning with fluid efficiency.

Wonderful. Just what we need—something else mechanical to distract Anakin from the larger picture.

Observing from outside himself, peculiarly detached within the Force's ebb and flow, he watched the three leviathan Republic warships add their might to the fray, weapons cleaving through enemy fighters and debris alike. And as he watched the furious battle, at once set apart from it and deeply involved, he felt clone pilots die. Felt Anakin's rage and grief for them. Felt his own grief, muted. Felt a faint echo of Ahsoka, still young and perfecting her mastery of the light side's strength, attempting to follow Anakin's progress from their gunship on *Indomitable*'s hangar deck.

Participant and witness, he stood before the bridge's viewport, waiting for the signal he knew would come. Not yet—not yet—not yet—

Yes. Now.

He saw Gold Squadron worry fleeing droid starfighters to pieces. Saw Hammer and Arrow Squadrons set their sights on Grievous himself. Felt Anakin's drenching relief. Heard his calm voice, clear as a shout.

Go, Obi-Wan. Tell Yularen it's now or never.

He turned. "That's a go, Admiral. Maximum sublight. Get us down to that planet."

"Done," said Yularen, his deep voice ripe with a violent satisfaction and his eyes just a little wide with the reminder of Jedi powers. "Captain!"

Behind them, needing no further prompting, the conn officer leapt to his duty. A heartbeat later *Indomitable* shuddered, her sublight engines powering them toward Kothlis and the beings trapped planetside who were desperate for their help.

Obi-Wan stepped back from the bridge viewport. It was time for him to join Ahsoka, Rex, and Torrent Company.

"Good hunting, General," said Yularen, his eyes fierce, his face grim. "You'll hear from me as soon as communications are restored."

If they were restored. Lieutenant Avrey was even now buried deep in *Indomitable*'s innards, attempting to graft into them those antiquated anodes.

May the Force be with her.

With a nod to Yularen he made his measured way to the gunship hangar. Even cocooned within the cruiser he could feel the dull thudding of her massive laser cannons as they pounded Grievous's new flagship and the smaller warships in his fleet. Through the Force he could feel the wrath of *Pioneer* and *Coruscant Sky,* the cruiser's sister ships lending their voices to the chorus of destruction raining down upon the enemy.

You should've stayed at home, Grievous. Coming here was a mistake.

The transport opened and there was Ahsoka, hanging out of

their open gunship, her eyes enormous with impatient eagerness. He jogged across the crowded hangar deck, threading through the other waiting, clone-laden gunships, and leapt up beside her. Sparing Anakin's apprentice a small, brief smile, he looked to Rex.

"Soup's on, Captain."

"Sir," said Rex, and reached into the cockpit to tap their helmeted pilot on the shoulder. The pilot smacked two console switches, and the interior lights came up to full. A second later the exterior shielding thumped into place. In the gunship's belly, crowded shoulder-to-shoulder, as many Torrent Company clones as would fit in the troop compartment slammed their buckets on their heads, becoming eerily alien.

"Master Kenobi?" said Ahsoka, quiveringly hopeful. "Is Skyguy—I mean—"

"He's fine, Padawan," he snapped. "*Focus*. Discipline your mind in preparation for battle."

"Yes, Master," she whispered. "I do know that. I'm sorry."

She was a good child. Anakin was training her well. *Better, perhaps, than I trained him. At least in some ways. He hasn't forgotten what it's like to be young and uncertain.* "Don't apologize. Making mistakes is a large part of being a Padawan. It's how we deal with making mistakes that determines our progress—and our ultimate success or failure."

Ahsoka's eyes were almost comically wide. "I can't imagine you making mistakes, Master Kenobi."

Despite his own simmering tension, he came close to laughing. "Padawan, in my time I have made more mistakes than there are sandfleas on a wild ban—"

A triple flash of red lights reflected on faces and flat surfaces as the hangar's launch beacon lit up in warning. Not needing to be told, the pilots fired up their engines. The throaty roar was echoed by the gunships on either side of them.

"Better hang on, General," said Rex. "That soup you mentioned has started to boil." With a nod to Ahsoka, he grabbed his own helmet and vanished inside it.

"Indeed," said Obi-Wan, snatching hold of a ceiling strap.

Rex's terse words tautened the gunship's atmosphere to the breaking point. The silence beneath all the normal operational noises was absolute, uncanny. Every clone stood with unnerving stillness, head tipped fractionally to one side. They were unified in a private conversation, attention trained on their captain. Last-minute instructions, a rallying pep talk, some kind of clone prayer? Obi-Wan didn't know. He'd never asked. The idea of asking felt—intrusive. Insensitive. Impolite.

"Weird, isn't it?" Ahsoka whispered confidingly. "I'm used to it now—but I'm kind of not, too."

He gave her a half smile. "I know what you mean."

The hangar doors were fully open, their exterior shields still engaged. Staring over the pilot's shoulder and out through the cockpit viewport, he could see they were close to their target, Kothlis. Just the asteroid belt left to negotiate, and then the steep plunge through the planet's thin upper atmosphere. *Indomitable* shouldered her way between the suspended chunks of rock, blasting some aside, taking the path of least resistance where she could by using the route carved out by Grievous's droid troop carriers.

At least the Separatist leader was proving useful for something.

Closing his eyes, Obi-Wan sought for Anakin in the Force. He was there, still in one piece, leading his surviving pilots in a ruthless chivvying of Grievous's warships and droid starfighters, drawing their fire away from the Jedi cruisers, giving them the best possible chance of reaching the planet unscathed.

Satisfied that Anakin was—and would be—all right, at least

for the time being, he turned his senses to Kothlis. What he felt, so close now, tightened his throat and his belly and flared the banked fires of pain behind his eyes to bright, angry life.

Terror. Agony. Bewilderment. Despair.

Breathing harshly, he turned aside—and saw that Ahsoka was struggling to contain her own undisciplined reaction to the overwhelming sensations and emotions boiling through the Force. As *Indomitable* plowed through the planet's upper atmosphere, the heat of reentry burning all around them, he took the child by one scrawny shoulder.

"You've opened yourself too wide, Ahsoka," he said, shaking her gently. "You've let yourself be overcome. You're not a river in flood, youngling, you're a faucet. Tighten your mind. Restrict the Force's flow. Control the amount and the speed of what you're seeing and feeling. You must *never* let it control you. That way lies madness, and a fall to the dark side."

The girl was trembling, her eyes squeezed tight shut. So distressed she didn't even bristle at his deliberate use of *youngling* instead of *Padawan*. In the gunship's dull illumination he thought he saw a tear escape between her extravagant lashes and trickle down her cheek.

"I can't—Master, I can't—"

"Yes, you can," he insisted. "You've great potential, Ahsoka. Master Yoda has high hopes for you, as does Anakin. *Control yourself.*"

"Yes—yes—" said Ahsoka, and opened her eyes. In her face a new and formidable determination. "You're right, Master Kenobi. I can!"

Obi-Wan felt a surge in the Force as she exerted control. Ahsoka exhaled one long breath as she regained her emotional balance. Impressed, Obi-Wan released her. "Well done, Padawan."

"General Kenobi!" their pilot said over his shoulder. "Hangar shields are disengaged."

"Then let's go, Lieutenant," Obi-Wan replied. "We've kept the people of Kothlis waiting long enough."

THE GUNSHIPS LAUNCHED in swift succession, bursting free of the Republic cruisers like akk dogs slipped from their leashes. Watching ship after ship dive toward the stricken planet's surface, Anakin allowed himself one brief, distracted thought— *May the Force be with you, Obi-Wan*—and then banished the ground assault troops from his mind entirely. Obi-Wan, Ahsoka, and Rex's men had their battle to win, and he had his. Worrying about them now would easily get him or his own people killed.

The cockpit console datapad lit up with a new message from R2-D2: *Still no comms. Comms not active.*

"I know, I know," he muttered. "Believe me, I've noticed." *Come on, Avrey. What's taking you so long?* "Hang in there, Artoo. We're doing all right without them." *So far.*

A partially damaged droid starfighter attempted to lock on to him. Braking hard, flipping end over end, he blew it to pieces then took a moment for a quick head count.

Twenty-three starships, excluding himself. With Wingnut back on board *Pioneer* that meant—

Twelve. I've lost twelve.

There was no time to feel it. New droid starfighters were pouring out of the Sep warships—*What, they've got an onboard foundry now?*—heading in a direct line for Kothlis, the cruisers and all those clone-laden gunships. Scarab fighters this time, configured to kill just as easily in atmosphere as airless space.

So you've run out of vultures, Grievous? Does that mean we killed them all? Hey, sorry about that.

Another glance showed him the last of the gunships, plunging out of sight. Showed him Grievous's scarabs swarming after it, bent on destruction. He turned his fighter sharply to port and executed a tight barrel roll to get Fireball's attention. The captain's gloved hand waved, acknowledging, so he flipped himself under a raggedly floating debris field and waggled his tail at a cluster of his people on its far side. Message received, his men formed up behind him. A hunting pack they were now, scenting fresh blood and eager for the kill. Soaked in the Force, his blood scalding with adrenaline, he set his sights on the scarabs, opened his fighter's throttle to maximum velocity—

—and attacked.

You're dead. You're dead. Every last one of you is dead.

The battle consumed him. The void of space fell away. Flesh became metal, thought burst into flame. The boundaries between space and time and self disappeared. Dissolved within the Force, he surrendered to the moment. Past, present, and future were one. He was Anakin. He was Obi-Wan. He was Shmi and Padmé and Ahsoka. He was Grievous in his greed. He was Rex and Fireball and Wingnut and all the clones he'd never met. Every friend, every enemy, left behind and yet to come. And he was his fighter, too, wings and thrusters and conduits and canopy. He was his fighter, tearing up the stars.

I am the Chosen One. Today I choose to win.

Indomitable, Pioneer, and *Coruscant Sky* joined him in battle. Like the warships of old, planetbound, on wide seas, they sailed the void's astral winds and pounded the Sep warships with proton torpedoes and laser blasts. Fire bloomed and died on both sides, its incandescence fleeting. The pilots of Gold Squadron, his Hammers and his Arrows, flung themselves at the enemy so the enemy would not prevail.

Sight—chase—kill. Sight—chase—kill. Over and over and over and—

Arrow Six gone. Hammer Leader gone. Gold Four gone. Arrow Three gone.

It's war. It's what happens. Don't think of them. Not now.

Scarab gone. Scarab gone. Scarab gone. Scarab gone.

The Force showed him Grievous, railing on his bridge. Showed him Padmé, sleeping. Showed him Palpatine, in thought. Showed him Obi-Wan and Ahsoka, fighting back-to-back. A sandstorm of images whirling past his mind's eye.

It shows me myself. It shows me victorious.

The battle raged on and he raged with it, man and machine in perfect killing harmony.

"LOOK OUT!" Ahsoka shouted. "Soldier, *look out*!"

The clone whose name she didn't know couldn't hear her. He was going to die. Locked in her own life-or-death struggle, deflecting a volley of blaster bolts from an oncoming droid on a STAP, nicked and singed and scorched in half a dozen places, Ahsoka reached through the chaos, reached for the Force, and *pushed* the clone sideways as a stream of plasma sizzled the air where he was standing.

I saw that! I saw it! Before it happened, I saw it!

A burst of elation gave her a fresh punch of strength. Her lightsaber a green blur in front of her, she leapt to meet the droid on its STAP and slashed both machines in half with a single swiping blow. Her Force-enhanced jump carried her up and over the spinning debris, up and over three charred clone troopers she couldn't save, a blood-soaked clot of civilians she couldn't save, and into the path of four shielded droidekas.

Four against one? That's just not fair!

She reached for the Force again—and suddenly that was harder: she was getting tired—and desperately pulled half a high stone wall down on the machines. Not even their enhanced shields could save them. Flattened, they sparked and spat and died.

Taking a moment to breathe and swipe the sweat from her

face, she took a wild look around Tal'cara's central plaza. Before the Seps it must've been a pretty place. Now it was smoke and ruins; pools of blood and rubble were strewn everywhere, surrounded by shorting power cables and burst water pipes pretending to be fountains. The air was thickly hazed with stinking smoke. It seemed the Sep droids had been given one order: *Kill everything that bleeds.* With brutal efficiency they were doing just that.

Master Kenobi wasn't here. He'd ordered her and Rex and others into the fray, then left her to cope while he and his own clone detachment headed for the strategically crucial spynet facility. She didn't mind, it meant he trusted her, but she couldn't help worrying—for him.

If he gets hurt again, Anakin'll blame me, I'll bet.

A sharp shock of foreknowledge spun her around, lightsaber raised and ready. Three pounding heartbeats later two more STAPs screamed up and over a partly demolished dress shop. The droids driving them caught sight of her and started firing, a blood-red volley of zipping laser bolts. Grimly she deflected their attack, angling the bolts back on the droids, exploding them into a shower of sparks and spare parts.

All around the plaza, clones from Torrent Company fought the entrenched Sep forces. As well as the STAPs, super battle droids thudded their emotionless, methodical way through the crumbling buildings and across the open spaces, smashing the statues, crushing the flowers in their scattered beds, splintering and torching the blossomed trees, firing blasters and launching grenades. Destruction and desolation—the Seps' stock in trade.

Right now they only had one gunship for air support, and Torrent Company's clones were taking a beating. With their comms still jammed—*stang*, she wanted to know how Grievous was doing it—there was no choice but for the other gunships to insert and then fly off to make individual sitrep assessments of the enemy's strength and troop disposition. It was a crazy way to run a war.

And not a very likely way to win it.

But she wasn't going to think about that.

Everywhere she looked beyond the plaza she could see columns of thick black smoke streaming into the hot summer sky. A light breeze swirled, bringing with it the stink of burning things, the faint screams of living—dying—beings, the *thud-thud* of concussive weapons, the higher-pitched *zap-zap-zap* of lasers.

Overhead, their lone shielding gunship opened fire. A Sep battery fired back and—*oh no, oh no*—the gunship was belching red and black smoke. She saw two clones plummet from its half-open belly, saw the gunship spin like a lassooed wild nerf. And then it plunged toward the ground, disappearing behind an obscuring belt of trees. A loud boom. A plume of flame. She felt the deaths jolt through her. Felt pain and tears and pushed both deep inside.

Off to her left a clone screamed, his voice muffled in his helmet. She turned, just in time to see someone else die in a weltering spray of bright scarlet blood. The super battle droid that had killed him trod on him afterward and kept walking. A sob rose in her throat but she choked it down. She had to stay focused, she had to—

Another STAP buzzed out of hiding toward her. Head spinning, heart racing, she flipped herself up and over its droid-rider's head, lightsaber extended, swinging, slicing around to dismember the machines.

And then in the final split second, acting on a half-thought impulse, she changed the angle of her blow. Her lightsaber de-

capitated the droid, sent its head spinning right and its gangly
body tumbling left. Guided by the Force she landed lightly on
the STAP, booted feet thudding onto the footrests, free hand
catching hold of the handle. The STAP dipped and whined,
protesting, but she wasn't much heavier than a droid and it held
her weight.

The super battle droids never saw her coming.

"Good job, little'un," said Rex, breathing harshly as he
looked up at her on her swaying, slip-sliding STAP. His white
armor was scorched in a score of places. Smears of blood
streaked the length of his right arm, leaking from the joint at his
shoulder plate. More blood trickled from beneath his chest plate
and down his left thigh. He was favoring that leg, a lot. A clone
soldier, Checkers, his helmet recklessly discarded, hovered beside him. He was bleeding, like Rex, but not as badly. His chin
and left hand were cut. His right arm was held out, ready to support his captain. Ahsoka flashed him a swift smile, liking him
enormously for it.

"Rex—you need to fall back," she said, scanning the plaza
for more signs of droid activity. Incredibly, for the moment, it
seemed they were alone. "In case you haven't noticed, you're
hurt."

"I'm not the only one," said Rex. The strain in his distorted
voice was the worst she'd ever heard it. "I've got men here who
need—"

The concussive boom of the nearby explosion made the
warm air shudder and sent the STAP bucking wildly. Ahsoka bit
off a startled cry and wrestled her aerial platform under control,
steadying it with a twist of Force push. All around the plaza broken windows broke free of their sashes and smashed to the
buckled ground. Loose bricks followed them. Dust rose in choking, billowing clouds.

"I know, Rex," she said, coughing and spluttering. "You've

got men who need medical assistance. Get the wounded under cover while you can. Better yet, barricade yourselves in somewhere. Who knows how soon before you get more company— and I think we're officially outnumbered. I'd help, but now that I've got this STAP I can go find a gunship to evac you out of here. Unless—" She snapped off her lightsaber, clipped it to her belt, then managed to activate the comlink in her gauntlet. "This is Ahsoka Tano calling *Indomitable*. Admiral Yularen, do you copy? Gunship One, do you copy? Does *anybody* copy? Can anybody hear me?"

"It's no use," said Rex, his voice tight with pain and ruthlessly controlled concern. "Whatever bright idea they cooked up to fix the comm problem doesn't seem to be working. At least not yet. We're on our own, Ahsoka."

She'd never heard him sound like this. She'd never seen him bleed so much. Not since Teth had they lost so many men in one engagement. Another look around the plaza showed her the surviving clones, only a handful unscathed, heading from all directions toward their captain. Many of them could only walk with assistance. Four were being carried, too wounded to make it alone.

Oh, this is bad. This is very, very bad.

"I'm going to find Master Kenobi," she said, willing her voice to sound bold and confident. "And another gunship. I'm getting you out of here, Rex. Do you hear me?"

"Yes, ma'am," said Rex, trying to sound like his unwounded self. He swayed, and Checkers grabbed him, keeping him on his feet.

She felt her throat close again. "You're not allowed to die. That's an order." She looked at the other clones. "Is that clear, everyone? No more dying. It's against regulations."

"Ma'am, yes, ma'am!" the surviving clones of Torrent Company chorused.

"Checkers—"

"Ma'am?" he said, his voice tight with pain.

"Keep an eye on Captain Rex."

He nodded. "Ma'am, let's make that two eyes."

"Okay then," she said, touched close to tears. "Stay here. Stay safe. I'll be right back. I promise."

And before the clones' courage broke her completely she wheeled the STAP away and gunned it out of the plaza in search of Obi-Wan, and help.

SLASHING HIS LIGHTSABER THROUGH yet another onrushing wall of droids, feeling the drain on his strength, the burn in his muscles, Obi-Wan blinked stinging sweat from his eyes.

I have a bad feeling about this.

"General Kenobi!" shouted Lieutenant Treve, darting out of the corridor behind him. "Sir, they're about to break through the second containment line. I don't know how much longer we can hold them."

As the last droid collapsed piecemeal at his feet Obi-Wan turned, breathing hard. The pain behind his eyes was vicious. "We'll hold them as long as we have to, Treve. There's no alternative."

Treve took one look at the scattered bodies of the Bothans killed before Republic help arrived, then pinged a finger to his helmet. "Yes, sir."

He didn't sound too confident. *And I don't feel too confident. I wish Anakin would get here.* "Number of casualties?"

"Sorry, General. I've been too busy to count." Treve shook his head. "Maybe a third."

A third? He took a moment to ease his aching shoulders. "What about gunship support? How is it holding up?"

Even with his expression obscured by the helmet, Treve's discomfort was palpable. "Ah—"

He closed his eyes, briefly. "How many?"

"At our location? Four shot down. Two destroyed, two disabled." Treve shrugged. "Could be worse, sir."

Really? How? "So we've *no* air support at all?"

"Not quite," said Treve, grim again. "We've got six gunships still up there but they're finding it hard to break through the Sep defenses."

Which would explain why he'd heard plenty of enemy fire but hardly any friendly. He could hear it now, booming and blatting beyond the barricaded front doors. Muffled, but still too close. Hammering beneath it was the familiar *dap-dap-dap* of Republic blasters shouting in reply.

"Very well. Get back to the line. Tell the men to hold on. Reinforcements will reach us soon."

"Sir." Treve started to withdraw, then hesitated. "General—are you sure you're all right here on your own?"

Obi-Wan wiped the sweat from his face. Scattered around him were the remains of all the droids who'd so far failed to kill him. The spynet facility's anonymous entrance hall was starting to resemble a spare parts warehouse.

"I'm not dead yet, Lieutenant," he replied. "Get back to your post."

"Yes, Gen—"

The entrance hall's transparisteel skylight shattered, spraying them with high-velocity lethal shards. A swarm of small and highly maneuverable remote droids, each armed with a miniaturized laser cannon and heat-seeking sensors, poured through the jagged hole.

"Stang!" Treve cursed. "*Mosquitoes!*" Raising his blaster he started to fire.

Obi-Wan felt his blood surge. Shockingly, his armor was pierced but there was no time for him to pull the slivers of transparisteel from his chest and arms and shoulder. No time to feel the white-hot pain, to worry about severed nerves or tendons. Fight or die. That was the choice.

He fought.

Fed a trickle of fresh purpose by the Force, Obi-Wan danced with the mindless, murderous droids. He slashed and sliced and annihilated as many machines as he could reach, and flung more aside with his diminishing strength. The blasted things were tough, resilient. They bounced off the walls and floor and came right back at him, silent and deadly.

A choked cry and a clatter sounded somewhere to his right: Treve was down. Dead or dying. It was hard to see. The rain of transparisteel shards had cut his face and his forehead. His laboring heart pumped blood into his eyes.

No time for this. No time.

Frustrated, he smeared his vision almost clear as more remote droids streamed through the obliterated skylight. Why had the Kothlis Bothans allowed a *skylight* in a place like this? Stupid, stupid. *I can't kill all those droids. Not alone.* But still—he had to try.

Cunning as Onderonian blood-beasts, the remote droids seemed to sense their advantage. So many swarmed him now he couldn't cleanly deflect every laser bolt. Fire seared his left thigh and he staggered sideways. His foot skidded on a piece of broken battle droid and he dropped hard to one knee.

A speeding STAP plunged through the smashed skylight, careering between Obi-Wan and the mass of remote droids. He brought up his lightsaber, ready to destroy it—then realized who was controlling the machine.

Ahsoka.

She rode the STAP like a circus performer, swooping and

sliding, her lightsaber a green blur. Such a little thing she was, scarcely more than a child. But a *lethal* child . . . droids were flying to pieces all around her.

Grinning, he regained his feet. Now, *this* was more like it. "Good timing, Padawan!" he called to her, rejoining the fray.

"I do my best, Master!" she said with a swift, cheeky smile. "Now what say we finish this? I've got better places to be!"

"Don't we all, Ahsoka?" he retorted and moved in for the kill.

Perfectly orchestrated, he and Anakin's apprentice took the fight to their enemy. The air filled with sparks and smoke, with the stink of burned metal and circuitry and the glorious hum of whirling lightsabers. Then a lucky droid blaster shot took out the STAP's antigrav projector. Ahsoka somersaulted gracefully off the falling machine and with a hard Force push smashed it through a flock of the remotes.

"Nicely inventive," Obi-Wan panted as Ahsoka leapt to him. "Anakin would approve."

"That's the idea," she said, whirling to press her back to his back, a classic defensive move. "Can you please remember to tell him?"

Oh, she was cheeky all right. It seemed Anakin was rubbing off on her. "You can tell him yourself. Now let's finish this, shall we?"

Panting, bleeding, they redoubled their efforts.

When it was over, the last droid sliced apart, Obi-Wan checked on Lieutenant Treve. He knew what he'd find, but he also knew that it was important to touch the man and feel it in the flesh.

"He's dead, isn't he?" Ahsoka asked. Sweat and smoke masked her face and turned her blue eyes sapphire-brilliant. Her voice wasn't quite steady.

He straightened, suddenly so weary. So sad. "Yes."

Seeing it—most likely feeling it—Ahsoka took a step toward him then stopped. Cheekiness vanished now, and grief rushed to take its place. "We've got a lot of troopers in trouble back in the central plaza, too, Master," she said, almost whispering. "And the communications still aren't working. If we don't get help—"

"I know. We're in a tight spot." Then he frowned at her. "And speaking of being in a tight spot, your arrival was most fortuitous, Padawan. How did you find me?"

Ahsoka blinked and regained a little self-possession. "Um . . . well, really, it wasn't hard. You kind of light up the Force like a bonfire, Master Kenobi. Almost as bright as Skyg—I mean, Master Skywalker."

Now it was his turn to blink, disconcerted. "Oh."

Beneath the dirt and blood of battle, Ahsoka blushed. "I'm sorry. I didn't mean to—" Her eyes widened on a gasp. "Hey! Can you feel that? It's—"

Anakin.

He didn't even bother trying to hide his relief or smother his smile. "Come on. This way."

She sprinted after him down the corridor and out of the spynet facility, bursting through an exterior door into the debris-littered loading dock where the second containment line had been established, at high cost.

It hadn't broken yet.

But the clones weren't fighting, they were staring and pointing into the smoky Kothlis sky, where the fighters from Gold, Hammer, and Arrow squadrons, along with five gunships, pounded the remainder of Grievous's invasion force to scrap metal.

Dizzy with relief, Obi-Wan watched Anakin finish what they'd started. And with this welcome respite from worry, he became aware of his exhaustion and the pains loudly clamoring for his attention. He heard an oddly distorted voice, calling his name.

"General! General Kenobi! Do you copy?"

Yularen.

Startled, he slapped the comlink on his arm. "Admiral! What's happening?"

"It's over up here, General. Grievous is on the run—thanks to a little help from Coryx Moth—and regular communications are restored, at least for the moment. What's your status?"

His status? *I've had better days.* "We're still standing. Anakin and his fighters are mopping up now. Admiral, I've got—"

"Medevacs are on their way, General."

And the relief of that made him weak at the knees. So many men lost and wounded. Now that he'd stopped fighting he could feel through the Force dreadful echoes of death, of searing pain. His belly churned a warning and sour saliva flooded his mouth. He spat it out, then raised his comlink again.

"Tell them to hurry, Admiral. What about the Kothlis Ruling Council? Have we heard—"

"Wiped out, I'm afraid. I've alerted the Senate—they're contacting Bothawui now. And they'll be sending a civilian disaster relief team ASAP. Hold on, General Kenobi. It's nearly over."

It was a moment before he could trust himself to speak. Beside him, Ahsoka was trying to pretend she wasn't flooded with hard-to-control emotion.

"Thank you, Admiral. I'll see you soon."

"I don't believe it," said Ahsoka. She sounded dazed. "I didn't really think we could—that we would—" Her voice broke. "Rex is really hurt. A lot of Torrent Company's really hurt. And—and dead. I tried to protect them, Master, I tried to—but there were so many droids."

Obi-Wan looked down at her, aware of a tired triumph as Anakin and his team pinpointed the last stubborn Sep fighters.

"I know, Padawan. Don't worry. The medevac transports will be—" He frowned. The child was holding her left side. He realized, too late, that she was hurt. He could hear her breath coming in suddenly difficult gasps and saw, beneath her pressing fingers, a vicious, spreading bruise.

Furious with himself, he reached for her. "Ahsoka!"

"Ah—Master Kenobi—" Abruptly a child again, she looked up at him, puzzled. "Oh. I don't feel so good," she whispered . . . and fainted, a dead weight, into his arms.

FOUR

ASIDE FROM THE EXPECTED BATTLE AFTERMATH CLATTER AND
bustle, and the distant wailing of civilian disaster sirens, the first
thing Anakin heard as he made his way onto the spynet facility's
loading dock was Ahsoka, indignantly protesting.

"No, no, I'm fine, I'm *fine*. Please don't worry about me.
You need to check on Captain Rex and the others, there's nothing *wrong* with me, it's just a *bruise*. And I *didn't* faint, I—I
tripped."

The second thing he heard was the clipped, impatient voice
of his former Master.

"Ahsoka, be quiet. Captain Rex and his men are in good
hands already. Besides, it's not a bruise, it's three fractured ribs,
which means—*ow!*"

Ow? *Oh, great. He's done it again.*

Threading a path between hurrying medics and clone troopers and scattered bits of Grievous's destroyed army, Anakin let
the Force guide him to where he needed to be.

Obi-Wan and Ahsoka sat side by side on crates in a hastily
setup triage area, just outside an entrance into the spynet building. One clone medic was encasing his singed and smoke-stained
Padawan's torso in an inflatable brace, and another was attempting to extract a wicked-looking shard of shattered trans-

paristeel from Obi-Wan's chest plate. Several more shards were deeply embedded in both arms and his right shoulder. He looked like an extremely cranky pincushion.

"General, please stay completely still," said the medic, sounding harried. "I don't want to hurt you any more than I—"

"Can I help?" Anakin said, joining them.

Ahsoka's pain-pinched face lit up. "Master! You're all right!"

"Of course I am, Padawan," he said. "Why wouldn't I be?"

His bored tone was designed to reassure her, but it wasn't working, as the answer to his flip question was lying all around them: triaged clone troopers, most stoically silent, waiting for the next medevac flight to arrive. Beyond them, decently shrouded, lay the bodies of those men who hadn't been so fortunate. And then, of course, there were the men who'd died going up against Grievous and his droid starfighters.

"Anakin," said Obi-Wan, self-contained as always. "There you are at last. Nice work."

He nodded. "You, too. Ah—should I ask what happened?"

"What happened is that your Padawan arrived in the nick of time and helped save the day."

"She did?" With his initial burst of relief fading, seeing them both more or less unscathed, Anakin felt a rush of pride. "Of course she did. She's my apprentice."

The clone medic treating Ahsoka sealed the brace. "Stay put and breathe shallowly. No fancy Jedi moves for the time being, or chances are you'll end up with a tension pneumothorax. A collapsed lung," he added, noting his patient's blank stare. "As of right now, Padawan Tano, you're officially out of commission."

Ahsoka frowned. "Wonderful."

She was awfully pallid beneath all the grime. And hurting a lot—Anakin could feel it. "No internal injuries?"

"There's a lot of bruising, sir," said the medic. "A few broken ribs, but no organ damage I can detect. Although, as I say, that could change if she tries anything clever."

Anakin scowled at his Padawan. "Trust me, she won't. How did it happen, anyway?"

"I don't really remember," Ahsoka said, shifting uncomfortably on the crate. "There was a lot going on. Except—there was this one super battle droid I tangled with on the way here from the plaza . . ."

He raised an eyebrow. "Just one?"

"Oh no, there were lots of SBDs," she said, as the medic pressed a spray injector to the inside crook of her elbow and hissed some drug or other into her bloodstream. "But only one of them was a problem."

He looked at Obi-Wan. *Please. Tell me I wasn't ever this cocky.* Obi-Wan, his face cut in several places and streaked with dried blood, rolled his eyes.

"You're sure my Padawan's going to be fine?" Anakin asked the medic.

"No reason to think otherwise, sir," said the medic, allowing a little unprofessional sympathy to show. "Provided she gets to a proper medfacility sooner rather than later."

"She will. Now, about General Kenobi . . ."

The medic treating Obi-Wan cleared his throat. "The general's life might not be in danger, sir, but I still really need to get this transparisteel out of him. It's not what you'd call hygienic." He looked down. "So, General, if you could please keep still and stop talking, that would be helpful."

"Yes, yes, all right," Obi-Wan muttered, hating the fuss. Refusing to admit any kind of physical weakness. "But do please hurry up. I can't sit here all day."

"Obi-Wan, you can sit there for as long as the medics need

you to," said Anakin, and turned to the harassed clone. "Have you scanned him? Is there any arterial involvement? Or nerve damage?"

"No nerve damage, no compromised arteries," said the medic. "There's a tendon that's not looking too cheerful, but we can take care of it once these transparisteel splinters are out of him."

"You're having some trouble with that?"

"A bit," the medic admitted. "They're stuck in him but good and if I use brute force to pull them out, I'll do more damage than they did going in."

"Please don't," said Obi-Wan. "I've wasted enough time as it is."

Ignoring him, Anakin frowned thoughtfully. "Right. I get the picture. Look, I don't mean to tread on your toes but do you mind if I try something?"

The medic stood back. "Be my guest, General Skywalker."

"Anakin, what are you doing?" Obi-Wan demanded. "We both know you're not a healer. Please, leave this to the exp—"

"Hush up," he said mildly. "You're distracting me."

As Obi-Wan opened his mouth in comical surprise, the medics exchanged amused glances. Ahsoka stifled a giggle.

"Fine," said Obi-Wan with poor grace, defeated. "But whatever you intend to do, get on with it. Captain Drayk and Sergeants Ven and Ando are coordinating what's left of our troops but I need to get back out there. It's going to take hours to clean up the mess Grievous has left behind here."

"Don't worry about that now," he said, and dropped to a crouch in front of his former Master. "Drayk's a good officer. Just relax, clear your mind, and don't fight me."

Resting his gloved human fingers on Obi-Wan's forearm, Anakin closed his eyes and breathed out long and slow. Allowing the Force to rise within him, warm and familiar, he let it show him the shape of the eight transparisteel splinters still lodged in Obi-Wan's body. Nasty. Painful. It was nothing short of a miracle they hadn't severed nerves or sliced major blood vessels, which meant Obi-Wan would heal as good as new once the shards were removed.

He lifted his hand and opened his eyes. Focusing the power of the Force, he summoned the first piercing splinter out of Obi-Wan's chest.

"Sorry," he murmured, as his former Master grunted. "This is going to sting a bit. Hold on . . . hold on . . ."

Dimly, he was aware of his fascinated audience: Ahsoka, the two medics, the less seriously wounded clones. All of them stared as he eased the shard of transparisteel out of vulnerable flesh and the armor that had failed to protect it. Bloody, the splinter of transparisteel clattered to the oil-stained ground.

He smiled. *Excellent.* "Okay. One down, seven to go."

When the final shard was safely extracted, he rose from his crouch and got out of the way. Warm and comforting, the Force resonated through him. Pride, too, for a difficult task perfectly executed. The medic moved in, stripping off Obi-Wan's armor and tugging him out of his spoiled Jedi tunic. Then he slapped a succession of pressure pads on each seemingly insignificant puncture wound.

"General, wriggle your fingers for me," he ordered, tapping Obi-Wan's right hand. It was the tendon in his right forearm that was the cause for concern. "Then make a fist."

Grimacing, Obi-Wan obeyed. "That feels fine."

"Looks fine, too," said the medic, patently relieved. "I think you dodged a blaster bolt this time, General."

"Actually, I dodged quite a few," said Obi-Wan as he eased himself back into his scorched and bloodstained tunic. "Thank you, Sergeant. Now perhaps you could turn your attention to those among us who aren't merely scratched."

"Yes, sir," the medic replied. "But let's get one thing straight, General—those aren't just scratches and you need to take care of them properly."

Anakin grinned. "Don't worry. I'll make sure he's sorted out."

"*Thank* you, General Skywalker," said the medic, and moved aside with his partner to confer quietly about their other charges.

"Master," said Ahsoka, heavy-eyed and starting to droop from the crushing fatigue that followed injury and the crazed intensity of battle. "They've sent Rex and the others to Kaliida Shoals. Can I go after them? They've got regular med droids there, they can fix my ribs while I'm waiting. And—well—" She bit her lip. "I think it'd mean a lot to the men, if one of us was there. Of course, if you need me here . . ."

Rex. Briefly, in teasing Obi-Wan, helping him, he'd forgotten. "How bad is he, Ahsoka?"

"Bad, I think," she whispered. "Sergeant Coric, too. Lots of them are bad."

Obi-Wan was on his feet, favoring his blaster-burned leg. Had he let the medic take care of it? It didn't feel like it. Typical.

"I see no harm in her going, Anakin," he said softly. "She's got to be treated somewhere. And she's right about a Jedi presence helping clone morale. Besides, with so many of our healers deployed to the front lines it'll ease the workload on the Temple."

Anakin nodded. "True."

"Anyway, neither you nor I will be rushing back into action anytime soon," Obi-Wan added. "There'll be significant fallout from this affair, I suspect."

There surely would. With industrial espionage in at least one Republic shipyard, striking at the heart of the war effort . . .

Obi-Wan was tugging at his beard. "I imagine we'll be on Coruscant for a week, at least. The Council and Palpatine, possibly even the Senate, will want detailed reports on these unfortunate developments."

Coruscant. *Padmé.* Anakin nodded, hoping Obi-Wan's physical discomfort was enough of a distraction to hide the unbidden leap of pleasure.

It's been so long since I touched her.

"I expect you're right. You usually are." He looked at Ahsoka. "Fine. You can go. But I want to be kept informed of Torrent Company's status. Don't make me chase you for updates, is that clear?"

She managed to smile. "Yes, Master. Thank you."

"And Ahsoka . . ." He felt his heart thud. "Tell Rex—tell all of them—that anything less than a full recovery is unacceptable. Tell Rex I—" He had to stop. Obi-Wan was in earshot, and they were *not* supposed to care so much.

But Ahsoka cared too much, too. She didn't need to hear the words. "I will. Don't worry."

Another medevac ship was coming in, the sound beating against his eardrums, bouncing off the nearby walls and the litter-strewn ground. The wind whipped up by its careful descent tugged his hair and his tunic and rattled the body bags and drove dust into the eyes of the helpless wounded.

"Your ride's here." Hugging her was out of the question, and not just because she had broken ribs. Anakin rested his hand on her head. "Go. Get yourself healed. You did well today, Ahsoka. I'm proud of you."

"I just did what you taught me, Skyguy." Then she swallowed. "Was it bad—you know, up there?"

He looked away. The medevac was grounded now, spilling more medics to help with the casualties. "Bad enough. Some good people didn't make it."

"What about Grievous?"

Grievous. He felt his metal fingers clench. "No."

Bloodshot and red-rimmed, her eyes reflected his own angry disappointment. "We will get him, Master. One day, we'll get him."

"I know."

"So how soon before we go after the clanky barve?"

She was so eager. No matter what the war threw at her she caught it and threw it back, twice as hard. If her reckless enthusiasm didn't get her killed, she was going to make one fine Jedi.

"I'm not sure," he said, and looked to ask Obi-Wan his opinion, but the medic had noticed the wound in his mentor's leg and had pulled him aside to take care of it. "I guess we'll find out soon enough."

She nodded, resigned. "I guess."

"Anyway, you've already got a job to do," he said sternly. "You're no good to me with broken ribs, Ahsoka. Or a collapsed lung."

"They won't be broken for long," she said, wrinkling her nose. "And my lungs are fine. So don't you get used to being without me, Skyguy."

She was teasing him, but the jab struck a nerve. He *was* used to having her around now. Maybe even had started to rely on her, a little bit.

Stang. When did that happen? Last time I looked I didn't want an apprentice.

He nodded at the medevac, which was preparing to leave again, burdened with the living and the lost. "They're not going to wait for you. Go on, get out of here. We'll talk again soon."

"We'd better," Ahsoka retorted, and made her slow, painful way to the transport.

Escaped from the medic, Obi-Wan joined him. "She really did save me, you know," he said while they watched the mede-vac ship dwindle out of sight. "As did you."

Anakin grinned. "Again."

"Oh, so we're keeping score, are we?"

"Everyone should have a hobby, Obi-Wan." He looked the older man up and down. "Seems yours is getting yourself shot full of holes. Are you sure you're okay?"

"I'm fine," said Obi-Wan. A small smile thanked him, but it faded fast. "So—at least tell me Grievous *limped* away."

"Hobbled, more like it. Him and his friends. We dented him, Obi-Wan. We bloodied his nose."

"Yes, well, that's what we thought last time," Obi-Wan murmured. "Let's hope this time it's not an exaggeration."

That was a depressing thought. Shoving it aside, Anakin turned to consider the spynet building. "What's the story here? Is this place still secure, or are the Bothans going to have to tear it down and start again?"

"I don't know," said Obi-Wan. "There were droids inside when we got here. We managed to clear them out, but whether they'd had enough time to compromise the security protocols and transmit sensitive data to Grievous I'm afraid I can't say. That'll be for the experts to ascertain." Abruptly, Obi-Wan looked exhausted. "Where are you parked, Anakin?"

He jerked his thumb over his shoulder. "Out in the street. Hopefully nobody's given me a ticket."

"And your squadrons?"

"They're on recon, picking off any of Grievous's stragglers. They're fine, Obi-Wan. If there'd been trouble, I'd have felt it. There's not."

"Good," said Obi-Wan—but he was frowning. "Now for the bad news. How many pilots did we lose?"

Anakin didn't want to say. Didn't want to see—to feel—Obi-Wan's shock and pain. He was too busy trying not to feel his own.

But I can't run from it. I can't hide. It has to be faced.

"Fourteen."

"*Fourteen?* Anakin, that's—"

"More than a squadron's worth. I know." He shook his head. "They've found some way to upgrade the droid starfighters. These vultures and scarabs were faster, smarter—and it didn't help that we were fighting them gagged. If this was a test run for his computer virus and his jamming equipment, Grievous got the results he was after."

"And if he and Dooku equip all of their warships with the same jamming technology—if they've managed to infiltrate more than one shipyard, infect other ships with that virus—" Obi-Wan sounded shaken. "It doesn't bear thinking about."

"Except that's our job, isn't it?" Anakin said. "Thinking the unthinkable."

He looked around the loading dock at the scattered flotsam and jetsam of battle. At the splashes of dried blood on the ground, the discarded blaster clips, the violently dismembered battle droids. Remembered the slaughtered Kothlis citizens he'd seen from his fighter cockpit as he'd flown to the spynet facility, his senses yammering with alarm. There'd been scores of bodies lying in the streets, crumpled in the forecourts of their offices and apartment complexes, and the dead or injured clone soldiers, their armor white and red and shining in the sun.

He glanced at Obi-Wan. "You know . . . some days I don't much like our job."

"You'll get no argument from me," said Obi-Wan, rubbing

the wound on his chest. "Master Yoda and the Chancellor must be apprised of this development as soon as possible, but only via a secure shortburst. Grievous may have fled the scene of his crimes, but we don't know what other tricks he's got up his sleeve. We can't risk—"

"*General Kenobi. Do you copy?*"

It was Yularen, sounding relieved. Obi-Wan tapped his comlink. "Kenobi here."

"*The Senate disaster relief team has arrived.*"

"That was fast."

"*They were in the neighborhood. Major flooding on Rishi. They—hold on—*" There was some background chatter, then: "*The Bothan delegation's here, too, General. They're on their way to your location now.*"

"That's excellent news, Admiral. I'll be here waiting for them. Kenobi out."

Anakin shook his head. "Ah—no, you won't."

"I won't?" Obi-Wan's eyebrows shot up. "Anakin, I don't recall needing your permission to—"

"Save your breath," Anakin said flatly. "I'm not arguing this with you. Medic!"

The clone who'd patched up Obi-Wan looked around from packing his medkit. "General Skywalker?"

"When's the next medevac due?"

"In a couple of minutes, sir. But it's not coming here, it's—"

"It is now. Arrange that, would you? Then see General Kenobi safe on board—and if it's not heading back to *Indomitable*, tell them to make a detour."

The medic nodded. "Yes, sir."

"*Anakin—*"

Exasperated, Anakin glared at his mentor. "Obi-Wan, you don't need to brief the disaster team and the Bothans. I can do that. *And* get a proper sitrep and sort out our troops while I'm at it."

"Well, yes, that's true, but—"

"But nothing," he snapped, not the least bit interested in good manners. Sometimes Obi-Wan needed a short, sharp shock. *Not your Padawan anymore, remember?* "You said it yourself—Chancellor Palpatine has to know what's going on. That's our top priority. And in case you hadn't noticed? You're bleeding again. You belong in a medbay. Now, I've given this soldier a direct order. Don't make him disobey it by being difficult and *don't* upset the chain of command by countermanding me."

Silence. Obi-Wan stared at him.

"Okay." Anakin patted his mentor on his undamaged shoulder. "Now I'm going to move my fighter, because it's probably in the way. I will see you upstairs when I'm finished down here. And I promise—in the unlikely event I run into trouble I can't handle, I'll contact you."

With a cheerful nod at his mute former Master, carefully not looking at the medics, he sauntered out of the loading dock, heading for his fighter. As he walked, he toggled his comlink. "This is Gold Leader. Check in, people. Tell me what's going on."

One by one, his surviving pilots replied. Good news all around. No more casualties, lots more kills, the last of Grievous's garbage disposed of. Kothlis was free at last.

"Good job. Head on home," he told them. "I've got a couple of things to do here but I'll be right behind you. And the drinks are on me."

As he hoisted himself into his cockpit, R2-D2 beeped and whistled a relieved welcome and a question. Coming in low overhead, the diverted medevac transport stirred the street's dirt and debris. He hit the cockpit canopy switch, fast.

"Obi-Wan's fine, more or less," he told the anxious droid, firing their fighter's thrusters. "Ahsoka's pretty banged up, though. So are Rex and Coric. They're on their way to Kaliida Shoals."

R2's mournful whistle said everything Anakin couldn't . . . or didn't want to.

"Yeah. I know," he said. "But they're in excellent hands. They'll be fine. Good as new in no time."

And who exactly was he trying to convince? The droid or himself?

Yes.

"Okay, Artoo. Hang on!"

And he gunned the fighter in a vertical liftoff, pointed its nose toward a nearby deserted speeder parking lot, and did his best to outrun inconvenient reality . . . for a few moments, anyway.

To HIS SURPRISE, Obi-Wan found Admiral Wullf Yularen waiting for him when he disembarked from the medical transport in *Indomitable*'s busy main hangar.

"Welcome back, General," the admiral greeted him, as around them deckhands and medics got down to business. "Nice to see you still in one piece, more or less."

"Thank you," Obi-Wan said warily. Since when did admirals loiter about in hangar bays? "I'm fine." Unless . . . *Anakin.* "If you were led to believe otherwise, Admiral, my apologies."

Yularen's sober gaze followed an antigrav gurney laden with a bloodied, half-unconscious clone—hurt, but not hurt enough to ship all the way to Kaliida Shoals. Only the worst cases, the touch-and-go cases that needed Kaminoan specialists, were sent there. "I wasn't. Precisely."

No? Obi-Wan found that hard to believe. "But?"

Yularen hesitated, then nodded. "But after bringing me up to speed on the Kothlis ground situation, General Skywalker did mention in passing that you might get—ah—sidetracked, on your way to the medbay."

Oh, really? *I'll sidetrack him the next time I see him.* "I see."

"I must say," said Yularen, unbending a trifle, giving him a once-over glance, "you don't appear to be knocking on death's door."

"I'm *not*," he said tightly. "I'm afraid Anakin is—" With an effort he stopped himself. Whatever irritation he might be feeling with his high-handed former Padawan, it wasn't appropriate to vent it at the admiral.

Yularen was looking at him closely, an odd and unexpected sympathy in his deep-set eyes. "He's upset about his lost pilots," the admiral observed. Only a fool forgot he was a smart, perceptive man. "And about our ground troop casualties—as am I. This was an expensive outing, General Kenobi."

Weariness rolled over Obi-Wan in a great wave, flattening his vision and dulling his ears. Underneath it, the pain he'd managed so far to repress flared a warning. "I know." He looked around the hangar, vaguely taking in the bustling deck crew as it unloaded technical supplies from a small transport vessel bearing *Coryx Moth* insignia. "How badly were you hit by Grievous and his warships?"

Yularen shrugged. "We'll be in spacedock for a couple of weeks. Perhaps longer. In fact—"

He started walking toward the hangar deck transport. Falling into step beside him, Obi-Wan waited for him to finish, keenly aware of his colleague's strictly controlled dismay.

"I was wondering, General—how would you feel about transferring to *Pioneer* for your return trip to Coruscant?" Yularen asked. "I'd rather not stress this lady with more hyperspace jumps than I absolutely need."

The admission shocked Obi-Wan. "*Indomitable*'s damage is that bad?"

"It's that bad," Yularen agreed grimly. "You wouldn't have seen it on your approach—most of it's portside. We'll be keeping a lot of hands busy, I'm afraid."

And if they didn't already have the repair downtime to worry about, now they had to fear Separatist insurgents on the repair crews, sowing more havoc under the guise of care.

Not a day passes without this war growing more difficult. More treacherous.

If he wasn't careful, he'd become disheartened.

"Of course, Admiral. Whatever I can do to assist you. If I might ask . . . how many people did you lose in this engagement?"

They'd reached the transport. Its doors hissed open, and Yularen let himself be waved in first. "Nine. And three times as many wounded."

"I'm so sorry," Obi-Wan said, stepping in after him. "What about the other cruisers?"

"Eleven dead on *Coruscant Sky*. Their wounded are still being tallied. *Pioneer* got off the lightest this time. Four lost, a dozen wounded." As the transport doors hissed shut again, Yularen hit the control toggle. "Medbay, then bridge."

Obi-Wan crushed the rising grief. "Actually, I should code my report to the Council before I—"

"Medbay, then bridge," Yularen repeated, frowning. "I didn't just speak to General Skywalker. I double-checked with the medic who treated you. Have you stopped yet to consider how much explosive force it takes to shatter transparisteel and puncture clone armor? No? I didn't think so. Therefore do please humor me, General. Ten minutes here or there won't make a difference to the Council."

Nonplussed, Obi-Wan stared at him. "Admiral—your concern is appreciated, but frankly, I believe it's misplaced. I'm not quite sure why you and Anakin feel the need to—"

"Not quite sure?" said Yularen, incredulous, as they headed toward the warship's medbay. "Since I know you're not a fool, sir, are you by any chance concussed?"

Temper was starting to burn away Obi-Wan's leaden exhaustion. "No, I am *not* concussed. Admiral Yularen—"

"*General Kenobi.*" With a slap of his hand Yularen halted the transport. "While as a rule I find your modesty refreshing, in this instance I'm inclined to feel *peeved*. You, Master Jedi, are a valuable asset. Your skills are irreplaceable, your contributions to the Republic's war effort immeasurable. You do *not* have the right to treat your person lightly. What you *have*, sir, is an obligation to guard your health and well-being as though it were the health and well-being of our precious Republic's Supreme Chancellor. And if you so cavalierly refuse to do that, then you can hardly be astonished when those of us who *aren't* blind to your value make whatever arrangements we deem necessary to keep you in one piece." Yularen's salt-and-pepper eyebrows shot up. "Need I continue, or have I made my point?"

Obi-Wan dropped his shocked gaze to the floor. Not once in the months they'd been loosely working together had this highly respected officer raised his voice to him, or even come close to raking him over the coals as though he were an errant subordinate. *Nobody* spoke to him like that. Not since Qui-Gon. Well, except for Yoda. And Yoda—like Qui-Gon—had earned the right.

Except . . . perhaps Wullf Yularen has earned the right, too. Today—like so many days—he threw his ship, his life, and every life he's sworn to protect between me and death. I suppose it's only natural he feels something of a vested interest in my survival.

"Admiral . . ." He looked up. "My apologies. Your point is made."

Breathing out a harshly relieved sigh, Yularen restarted the transport. "You know, General, some say young Skywalker's the crazy one, the reckless one, the Jedi most likely to go down in a blaze of glory. *I* used to say it—but now I'm not so sure. In your own quiet way you can be just as terrifying."

"I'm sorry—I don't know what to say to that."

A faint smile curved Yularen's lips. "You don't see it, do you?"

"No, I'm afraid I don't," Obi-Wan replied. "You seem to be suggesting that I take unnecessary risks. I can't agree. I only ever do what I feel is right."

"And rarely stop to think of the personal consequences," said Yularen, still wryly amused. "You and Skywalker are cut from the same cloth. And that little Padawan of his—she's been fashioned out of the discarded material!"

Ahsoka. Though he was worried about her, Obi-Wan had to smile. "She's certainly feisty. Master Yoda knew exactly what he was doing when he paired those two."

The transport was slowing. As it bumped to a stop, its electronic voice chirping "*Medbay*," Yularen nodded. "Just as you knew what you were about, training him."

It was a compliment, and as unexpected as the man's earlier sympathy had been. *I think Yularen is more rattled by this recent engagement than he cares to admit, even to himself.* As the transport doors slid open, Obi-Wan smiled, acknowledging the comment.

"I'll join you on the bridge as soon as I can, Admiral," he said. "Perhaps in the meantime you could ask Lieutenant Avrey to set up for a Priority Alpha shortburst to the Jedi Temple. That is, if our current comm capacity permits."

"It does," said Yularen, professionally impersonal once more. "I'll get Avrey on it immediately."

In *Indomitable*'s impressive medbay anteroom, Obi-Wan breathed in the antiseptic air and felt—and banished—the pain of its occupants, hidden inside the facility's treatment cubicles. A 2-1B med droid stood behind the anteroom's desk. Registering his presence it looked up, its visual sensors electronically gleaming.

"General Kenobi. We've been expecting you," it said politely, moving to join him. "Please come this way. I understand you've suffered a number of penetrating wounds, facial lacerations, a blaster burn, and injury to one of your flexor tendons."

I am far too busy for this. "Yes, but I assure you my situation sounds worse than it is," he said, stepping back. "In fact—"

"Please, General, there's no need for concern," the med droid continued, herding him toward the treatment area. "I was recently upgraded courtesy of the Rhinnal State Medical Academy. I assure you, you're in excellent hands."

Clearly there was no escape. Ungraciously surrendering to his fate, Obi-Wan followed the droid into the serious part of the medbay.

Anakin, there will be a reckoning for this.

FIVE

—⊙—

LIKE SUPREME CHANCELLOR PALPATINE, BAIL ORGANA PRE-
ferred to work with living breathing sentient individuals, not
droids. The thought of being surrounded by a staff of protocol
droids was enough to induce a migraine. How Padmé tolerated
that prissy, overbearing collection of wiring and circuits was beyond him. He'd have trashed the fussy thing for spare parts the
second time it metaphorically opened its mouth to lecture him
on the correct pronunciation of the Adikarian *Greetings Between Equals,* or whatever.

His own very human, very efficient personal assistant
tapped on his open office door. "Senator—you wanted to know
when *Pioneer* was due in?"

He hit the pause button on his slowly scrolling datapad and
looked up. "She's home?"

"Not quite," Minala said. As usual, even though they were
at the tail end of a long day, she looked immaculate. No matter
what kind of crisis blew up, Minala Lodilyn managed to remain
cool, calm, and effortlessly composed. The word *flustered* didn't
seem to be in her dictionary. "The ship's on approach, heading
for the GAR docks."

"All right. Thanks. Can you—"

Minala grinned. "Already done. You'll find your speeder on
Level Two, Bay Four-forty-five-Cee."

"Lady, you are a treasure and *twice* a treasure," he said, standing. "I've tagged Fli'teri and Jinmin Tokati for the Kothlis inquiries. If either calls back, let them know I'll be in touch later tonight."

She nodded. "Certainly, sir."

"Also, I've sent through those last five Tarik's Law amendments to your console, plus the latest stats for the Appropriations Committee and the draft Executive Data-Dumping Bill. I'm sorry they're so last-minute but I only got them an hour ago. If you could—"

Minala raised a soothing hand. "Don't worry, Senator. I'll see they're proofed and disseminated as and where needed."

Her unquestioning dedication flooded him with sudden guilt. "It'll mean a late finish."

And that prompted her elusive, zany grin. "Surprise, surprise."

"Come in late tomorrow to make up for it," he said, reaching for his workcase. He dropped it onto the desk and snapped open the lid. "I mean it."

"Can't," she said, with a decisive shake of her head. "Now that your meeting with the Chancellor's been rescheduled for the crack of dawn, I'll need to keep an eye on things here."

Grimacing, he powered off the datapad. "All right. But you'll go home early. No arguments."

"We'll see," she said, so very prim and proper.

Sweeping the datapad, his pile of notes and a few other bits and pieces into the workcase, he gave her an amused look. "Have you forgotten we're coming up on performance review season? If memory serves there's something about 'suitably deferential demeanor' in the questionnaire."

She was still straight-faced, but her eyes were amused. "Yes, sir. Will that be all, Senator Organa?"

"If anything urgent comes in after I've gone, flick it to my home console," he said, and clicked his workcase shut. "Oh—and aside from the Executive Office I'd rather not take any official calls unless somebody's sky is falling down. And even then, see if they've got a sturdy umbrella."

"Will do, Senator." Minala stepped back so he could get through the doorway. "Have a good evening. And you should try for an early—earlyish—night, too."

"Hah," he said, heading for the discreet exit in her outer office. "Chance would be a fine thing."

As promised, his speeder was waiting for him at the Level 2 Senatorial parking station. Leaving the shields down to let in the balmy weather, Bail eased into the southwest traffic flow that would take him out to the sprawling GAR docks and barracks complex. It was an industrial sector of the city that had been reclaimed with an executive eminent domain decree a few weeks into the war. The move hadn't been welcomed, but Palpatine had managed to smooth the affected company directors' ruffled plumage by promising that the inconvenience would be temporary, a matter of months at most. They weren't to worry: the Jedi would soon have the Separatists suing for peace.

But months had passed since the property seizures, and the galaxy's violent divisions were growing wider, not narrower.

Still. The war can't go on forever. Dooku and his cohorts must know they'll fail in their efforts to bring down our democracy. It's a thousand years' strong. It can ride out this storm.

Although . . . this wasn't the first time he'd told himself that. And he was starting to worry it wouldn't be anywhere near the last. Palpatine needed to tone down the optimistic rhetoric. The Jedi were being pushed to their limits and far, far beyond, and the Kaminoan cloning facility was struggling, as well. New clones were being deployed without the same depth and intensity of training as those who'd made up the original companies, most of whose soldiers had fallen in battle. That meant higher casualty rates, which in turn increased demand for replacements. It was a vicious circle that spun and spun with no sign of ceasing.

If we don't turn the tide soon, we're going to get washed away.

A chilling thought. To distract himself Bail stared at the glorious Coruscant sunset, bleeding into twilight at the edge of the world. Bands of purple and gold, and bold, shameless crimson, a welcome reminder that even in the midst of despair there was beauty to be found, if you looked for it.

This far out from the densely populated city center and the admin districts the traffic was much lighter. Though he piloted a speeder with the most up-to-date sensors and crash nets, vigilance when commuting to and from the Senate Building was crucial. It was a relief to be able to relax a little, to sit back and let his gaze take in more than the rear bumper of the crammed-in speeder ahead of him, to let his thoughts wander. Sure, these days they had a tendency to wander down dark alleys, but at least out here, for a short while, he had the luxury of chivvying them in a slightly more cheerful direction.

Like admiring a pretty sunset. I just don't do that often enough.

And why not? Because every time he turned around, the galaxy gave him something else to worry about. Like right now.

He could not forget his workcase, tucked in the speeder's luggage compartment and holding, locked inside it, his datapad, loaded with memos and statistical spreadsheets and reports. Lots and lots and lots of reports. As head of the Republic's Security Committee, he felt he was in very real danger of choking to death on reports.

But there was one in particular, buried amid all the others. Slow to reach him, its import had been ignored by the others who'd glanced at it in passing. On the face of things it was insignificant, almost irrelevant in the grander scheme of this conflict . . . and yet, for the life of him, he could not get it out of his mind.

So much for admiring a pretty sunset.

Eventually he eased his speeder out of the main traffic slipstream and into the restricted outer zone of the GAR hangar complex. And as the first of many security checkpoints scanned his speeder and personal ID chips he watched *Pioneer,* thrusters roaring, lining up for docking in the complex's largest central hangar. The ship looked . . . wounded. Scorched and visibly damaged by Separatist weaponry, there was something subtly *off* in the thundering note of her engines. He could hear it. Feel it, tickling the nape of his neck. Of course he'd been kept apprised of the Kothlis engagement, and he knew the Republic's forces had taken some brutal body blows. But reading a report and seeing with his own eyes what Separatist technology and ill will could achieve—those were two entirely different things.

Blast it. They really got themselves hammered this time. Hope the final casualty numbers aren't too bad. On top of the comm disaster and everything else we're up against that's the last thing we need.

But that same prickly feeling on the nape of his neck told him this was one wish that wouldn't be granted.

By the time he'd threaded his way through seven more security checkpoints, surrendered his speeder to a junior warrant officer, and signed in to the hangar sector with palm print and retinal scan, *Pioneer* was down and settled and disgorging clone troops. Various officers and civilian-aid personnel nodded as he made his way onto Hangar 5's uncomfortably crowded deck.

The noise was cacophonous: health-and-safety warnings blaring, antigrav transports beeping, booted feet thudding, voices raised in greeting and warning and the acknowledgment of orders. The air was engine-hot, stinking of spent fuel and sizzled industrial lubricants. Announcements and orders blared over the echoing public address system, almost too garbled to understand. Or maybe it was because after the civilized gentility of the Senate his hearing wasn't properly tuned in. From what he could tell, nobody else was having trouble following them.

Laden with battle-weary clone troopers, the first convoy of ground transports headed toward one of the hangar's four major exits even as the next batch of soldiers piled themselves into the first available empty—now, what was the nickname? Oh yes. *Wheelbarrow.* In the hangar's harsh lighting their scorched, stained white armor glittered, and their fantastically dyed, clipped, and intermittently bald heads shone like beacons. They caught his attention and made him smile.

At least they've got a sense of humor, these men. At least the war hasn't taken that from them. Yet.

A touch on his arm turned him. "Yes?"

"Senator Organa!" It was the deck officer, a smudge of dirt on her cheek, her surprise almost amusing. "Senator—sir—I'm so sorry, I had no idea you were—there wasn't anything in—"

"Please, it's all right," he reassured her. "Lieutenant—"

"Yarrow, sir."

"Lieutenant Yarrow." He favored the tall, gangly officer with his best politician's smile. "I didn't call ahead. This is an impromptu private visit, nothing official about it. I just wanted to welcome home a friend."

"Sir," said Lieutenant Yarrow, almost hiding her puzzled lack of comprehension. "Of course, sir. If I might ask, which friend were you—"

He caught movement from the corner of his eye—a flash of the familiar. He looked around and saw a slight figure dressed in a scorched and grubby cream-colored tunic and trousers and brown boots, the attire at odds with the sea of white clone armor, flight suits, and naval uniforms surrounding it at the base of *Pioneer*'s main ramp. A silver lightsaber hilt dangled from its clip on a wide brown belt.

He grinned. "That one. Excuse me, Lieutenant."

Obi-Wan, being Obi-Wan, sensed Bail's approach and turned. A moment's startlement, then a wide, genuine smile. "Bail! What are you doing here?"

"Playing messenger boy," he replied, hand outstretched. "And one-man welcome party."

"You shouldn't have come all this way," said Obi-Wan, clasping the offered hand briefly then releasing it. Smile aside, he looked tired, tension simmering beneath the surface. "We'd have caught up after tonight's security briefing."

"No, we wouldn't. Palpatine's office bumped the meeting over to tomorrow morning." Bail frowned. "Early. There was some diplomatic bash he'd promised to attend that got re-arranged at the last minute."

"I see." Obi-Wan was frowning now, too. "Odd that I've not heard about the change in plans from Master Yoda."

"That's because I told him I'd tell you. It's not a problem; I was done for the day anyway."

"How very organized of you."

"I do my humble best," Bail said, with a small, mocking bow.

Obi-Wan smiled, slightly. "Yes, well, I'm not so sure I'd call it *humble*." Behind him someone called his name. "Sorry, Bail. Give me a moment."

"Sure," Bail said. He stepped back as a clone NCO approached, bulky helmet tucked under one arm, a datapad in his other hand.

"Sorry to interrupt, General," the clone said. "But you wanted these final stats before you left."

"No, no, that's quite all right, Sergeant," said Obi-Wan, all brisk efficiency. "Let's have them."

Whatever the news was, Obi-Wan didn't like it. His face stilled as he read the datapad, and beneath the schooled blankness there was anger and distress.

Because they were friends, and because he'd come to feel a proprietary interest in this particular Jedi's well-being, Bail took advantage of the moment to consider Obi-Wan more closely. Whatever action he'd seen on Kothlis, he hadn't escaped from it untouched. Faint pink lines on his forehead and cheek suggested injuries, recently healed. His whipcord physique showed a suggestion of strain and discomfort. Small, familiar hints of pain. So he was walking wounded. Again. Apparently some things didn't change.

"Right," Obi-Wan said at last, quietly, and tucked the datapad inside his tunic. "Thank you, Sergeant. I think that'll do for now. You're stood down, along with your men. Your efforts on Kothlis are appreciated."

The sergeant nodded. "Yes, sir. Thank you, sir. See you on the next rotation."

"Indeed."

Obi-Wan watched the sergeant join a batch of clones on a waiting transport. As it departed the hangar he let out a sigh. "Sergeant Fyn. A good man. Single-handedly saved half his platoon when they were pinned down under enemy crossfire."

Which likely meant the other half of the sergeant's platoon hadn't been so lucky. Bail felt suddenly awkward. Like a pretender. Moments like this were a painful reminder that he stayed safe at home on Coruscant taking meetings and reading reports while others bore the brunt of his detached decisions.

"I know losing men is tough, Obi-Wan," he said, hesitant, needing to say something but afraid that whatever he said, it would be the wrong thing. "At least we got a good outcome. You saved Kothlis."

"Yes," said Obi-Wan, pensive. "There is that." Then his expression darkened. "There would have to be that, Bail. We came close to emptying our pockets on this one."

"I can tell. You look beat."

Eyebrows lifting, Obi-Wan stared at him, frustrated exasperation flitting over his face. "Why do people keep *saying* that?"

He nearly laughed, even though this wasn't really funny. "Ah . . . because it's true?"

"I am *fine*," Obi-Wan snapped. "And I will go on being fine unless one more person tells me that I look—"

"*General Kenobi?*"

Obi-Wan pulled a comlink from inside his tunic. "Yes, Captain Tranter?"

"*I'm signing off the flight log. Did you need to add anything?*"

"No. Thank you. How soon before you head out to Corellia?"

"*We'll depart within the half hour, General.*"

"Well, here's hoping your stay there is short and sweet. And again, my thanks for your efforts over Kothlis."

"*It was a pleasure, sir. Happy hunting on your next mission.*"

"And you, Captain."

"I saw some of *Pioneer*'s damage when you came in," Bail said as Obi-Wan flicked off the comlink transmit switch. "What's the extent?"

Obi-Wan sighed. "Far less than *Indomitable*'s—and *Coruscant Sky*'s. As I told you, this was a costly outing."

"I take it you're avoiding Allanteen Six's shipyards?"

"Ah." Obi-Wan's eyes narrowed. "So you've heard."

"Oh, yes," Bail said. "Espionage *and* an upgrade in Sep jamming technology? Trust me, the comlink channels were burning within moments of Yularen's first report. There's a task force up and investigating already."

"Good," said Obi-Wan with a bitter satisfaction. "Do whatever you must to see they get results, Bail."

The hangar's noise and activity level were starting to abate. The last of the clones were leaving, the deck crew squaring away equipment and detritus. Not wanting to be overheard, Bail lowered his voice.

"So. How many men did you lose?"

"Too many," said Obi-Wan tightly, his eyes shadowed. "And dozens of wounded shipped off to Kaliida Shoals—including Anakin's Padawan."

And that went a long way to explain the source of Obi-Wan's distress. "I'm sorry to hear it. What about Anakin?"

Obi-Wan flashed a fleeting smile. "Oh, he's fine. Anakin has more lives than a Sullustan moonbat. And speaking of my former apprentice—excuse me for just one more moment." He lifted the comlink again and thumbed the transmit switch. "Anakin. Anakin, do you copy?"

"Skywalker here."

"What's your status?"

"Well, Obi-Wan, right now I'm upside down inside my fighter's engine housing. What's yours?"

"I'm in Hangar Five, ready to return to the Temple. Have you forgotten that Master Yoda's expecting us?"

There was some grunting and a muffled curse. *"Right.*

Look—can you cover for me? Only my fighter's not the only one needing emergency first aid and they're shorthanded here and—" Another muffled curse, followed by a bitten-off exclamation of pain. *"Stang! You crippled barve-loving lump of—"* Then a short silence, humming with tension. *"Sorry. Obi-Wan, I have to stay and fix this. Hangar Three's almost empty. We're practically the only fighters in the place. If something comes up overnight—"*

Bail watched Obi-Wan close his eyes and shake his head before exhaling a slow, resigned sigh. "Yes. All right. I'll make your excuses. But whatever else you do, *don't* turn off that comlink. You might well be asked to join us via holoconference."

"Yeah. Fine," said Anakin, sounding distracted. *"Um—I might not be finished in time for the meeting with Chancellor Palpatine."*

"That's been postponed."

"Great. Sorry, Obi-Wan, I've got to get back to this. My manifold coupling's about to fall apart. Just—make sure you get some rest, okay?"

Bail struggled to muffle his laughter. Sparing him a single burning glance, Obi-Wan shoved the comlink back inside his tunic. "That young man is getting entirely too far above himself."

That young man was fast garnering a reputation for courage and brilliance under fire that was close to making him a Republic-wide celebrity. *Anakin Skywalker.* It was a name on many, many lips.

Not the least of which are Palpatine's. He couldn't be prouder of Obi-Wan's former apprentice if he were the young man's father.

But he decided not to share the thought, given that Obi-Wan wasn't overly fond of their Supreme Chancellor. "You said Anakin's Padawan has been hurt. Will she recover?"

"Yes. I'm more concerned about Captain Rex and Sergeant Coric," said Obi-Wan, passing a hand over his face. "The next day or two should tell the tale."

And now he really did look tired. Worn down. Weighted with grief and worry.

"Come on, General," Bail said quietly. "I'll give you a ride back to the Temple."

Obi-Wan patted his shoulder. "That would be very nice. Thank you, Senator."

CRUISING WITHOUT HASTE through the darkened Coruscant sky, dribs and drabs of traffic leading the way toward the brightly lit admin districts, Bail looked sideways at silent, brooding Obi-Wan, then gave a mental shrug.

On the other hand, sometimes a little impertinence is required between friends. And desperate times call for desperate measures.

"Okay. I'm going to say this now, while I'm flying, so you're less likely to pitch me over the speeder's side."

Eyes half closed, Obi-Wan smiled. "You do realize I could pitch you over the side and keep control of this machine at the same time?"

"Ah. So that would be the flaw in my plan."

Obi-Wan snorted. "Whatever it is you want to say, Bail, just say it."

He blew out a breath. "Fine. Here goes. You really do look tired, Obi-Wan. And not just *I've had a few late nights* tired." He hesitated. "I'm talking almost dead tired."

"Bail—"

"Master Jedi, I am warning you," he said sharply. "Do not tell me again that you're fine, or *I'll* pitch *you* over the side."

Obi-Wan muttered something under his breath and folded his arms tight to his chest. "I've just come back from a major engagement, Bail. I think I'm entitled to be a little weary."

"No. It's more than battle fatigue. This war—the way you and the other Jedi are being asked to fight without decent respite. It can't go on."

"It can and it will, for as long as the war goes on," Obi-Wan retorted. "You're the last person who should be surprised by that, Bail. You know better than anyone the truth of how matters stand between us and the Separatists."

"You're right," Bail said, slowing the speeder as they ran into the first hint of heavy traffic. Closer now, he could see the relentless glare of the city's nightlife; a hint of music blew fitfully on the breeze. "And that's why I'm concerned. There's no quick fix waiting around the corner. We're in this fight against Dooku and Grievous for the long haul and that means we need to conserve our assets."

Obi-Wan shifted in the passenger seat, staring. "Have you been talking to Wullf Yularen?"

"What? No," he snapped. "Stop trying to change the subject, would you? What I'm trying to say is—"

"I know what you're trying to say," said Obi-Wan, sounding close to snappish himself. "And while your concern is appreciated, it's not required. You seem to have forgotten that I am a Jedi, Bail, which means—"

"That you've got juice the rest of us lack," he said, scowling. "Like I'm going to forget that anytime soon. Look, I know how potent the Force is. I know how much you rely on it *and* the kind of difference it makes. But underneath all the flash and dazzle you're still no more than flesh and blood. You're vulnerable, Obi-Wan. And you Jedi have a bad habit of pretending that's not the case. All I'm saying," he added, more gently, "is don't let having the Force in your arsenal lull you into a false sense of security. Don't get into the habit of taking more credits from your bank account than you put in."

"Jedi don't have bank accounts."

Bail laughed, half amused, half angry. "Fine. Treat this like a joke. Treat *me* like a joke. I don't care—so long as you think about what I'm saying. You don't even have to admit I'm right. Just . . . try to cultivate some restraint, Obi-Wan. This Republic can't afford to lose any more Jedi."

"On that," Obi-Wan said with quiet intensity, "you'll get absolutely no argument."

They continued in silence for a while. The tips of the Jedi Temple spires were distantly discernible now, their nav lights blinking. Coding a course change into the speeder's onboard nav computer, Bail slipped into a different traffic stream. Obi-Wan stirred.

"I thought we were going to the Temple."

"We are. I'm taking the scenic route."

"The scenic route," Obi-Wan said slowly. "I see. In other words . . ." His arms folded again. "There's something else you want to get off your chest."

He should've known he wouldn't fool this man. "Yeah. Okay. So. Here's the thing—and you have to believe me, I *know* how this sounds—there's a whisper of something—some obscure intel—that's come across my desk."

This time it was Obi-Wan who laughed. "You *cannot* be serious."

"Serious as a heart attack, actually," he replied. "There's nothing confirmed. No encrypted messages or shady operatives. No clandestine meetings. Just . . . I've got a bad feeling."

"Which is even more worrying than any number of encrypted messages, shady operatives, or clandestine meetings!"

Obi-Wan tugged at his beard. "Very well. I know I'm going to regret asking this, but—what's your bad feeling about?"

Bail looked sideways. "Have you ever heard of a planet called Lanteeb?"

Obi-Wan sat forward, elbows dug into his thighs, face hidden in his hands. "We are not having this conversation," he said, muffled. "At this very moment I am asleep in the Jedi Temple having a nightmare."

"Hey, it's not that bad," he protested. "I happen to know where Lanteeb is and it's nowhere near Wild Space. It's a backworld of the Outer Rim."

"And that, of course, makes things *so* much better," said Obi-Wan brightly, lifting his head. "We should take the entire Jedi Council there for a picnic."

Bail looked at his tired friend. "Did no one ever tell you that sarcasm is a very undignified trait in a Jedi?"

Flinging himself back in the passenger seat, Obi-Wan pressed thumb and fingertip against his eyes. "I think you just did."

"Look," he muttered. "Lanteeb's not a Sith planet, it's a ball of grass and dirt and not much else in the middle of nowhere. It has no strategic value or wealth of *any* kind."

"In which case, Bail, why do you care about it?"

He shook his head. "No. The question you should be asking, Obi-Wan, is why do the *Separatists* care about it?"

"They care about it?" said Obi-Wan. At last he sounded interested.

"They do. In fact, nearly five standard weeks ago they took control of it. And I can't for the life of me work out why."

The Jedi Temple was almost within spitting distance now. Obi-Wan, who usually stared at the place as though it were a long-lost lover, tapped fingers to his lips and ignored its existence. "You're right," he murmured. "That is indeed . . . curious."

"Yeah. It's curious," Bail agreed. "And these days the last thing I want to deal with is *curious*. Do you?"

"Not particularly," said Obi-Wan, very drily. "Who else have you mentioned this to?"

"Nobody. I only read the report day before yesterday, and I've been buried in meetings and more urgent reports ever since. But it's been nagging me, Obi-Wan. And I trust my instincts."

Obi-Wan spared him an absentminded smile. "As do I."

The speeder's ID chip blipped a warning. The Jedi Temple, like the Senate Building, was part of an upgraded security net, and they'd just been tagged. Obi-Wan shifted his gaze, looking upon the ancient building with a vast and unspoken affection. Longing, almost. Did he know it?

Bail checked that they had the all-clear then dropped into the dedicated Temple traffic stream. The automatic speed limiters overrode his onboard controls, dropping their rate of progress to little more than a crawl.

"So," said Obi-Wan. "What are you going to do?"

He tapped his fingers to the speeder's control yoke. "That depends. How long will you be on Coruscant this time?"

"I've no idea," said Obi-Wan. "There'll be emergency meetings over Kothlis and its implications. And not only must we clear our ships of this computer virus and help track down the miscreants responsible, we're going to have to come up with a countermeasure for this new Separatist jamming equipment— and fast. The danger they pose to our people is almost incalculable."

And that was depressingly true. "So you'd be free to come over for dinner tomorrow night? I'd like to talk some more about Lanteeb. Thrash out a few possible scenarios for why

Dooku and his Seps are interested in it, and what that might mean to the war."

"You're not raising the matter in the Security Committee?" said Obi-Wan, surprised.

He shrugged. "The committee's bogged down enough as it is. And like I said, I have no proof of trouble. All I've got are the hairs standing up on the back of my neck. And, well . . ."

"Don't tell me. Let me guess," said Obi-Wan, torn between amusement and disgust. "Political complications?"

The Temple docking complex swallowed them. Bypassing its public parking sectors, Bail swung his security-cleared speeder up and to the left, heading for the restricted zone. There wasn't time to talk about committee entanglements, though he'd have welcomed Obi-Wan's wry, sarcastic input.

"A few complications, yes," he admitted. "Let's just say that for the time being I'd rather this stayed off the official table."

Obi-Wan nodded. "Understood. And of course I'll come to dinner, provided I'm free. I'll help you however I can, Bail, for as long as I can—though you'll appreciate that's not something I'm able to control. I could be sent back to the front lines at any moment."

"I know." It wasn't something he cared to dwell on. It would be a lot easier to fight this war from his office if he didn't know some of the people fighting it on the ground. "And there is one thing you could do right away, if it's not a problem."

"What?"

There was never any lack of traffic in the Temple. Idling the speeder, waiting for the opaquely shielded transport in front of them to move along, Bail flicked his friend a look. "You could ransack the Jedi Archives for anything you can find on Lanteeb. Anything that wouldn't appear in the Senate database or any public records."

"You think we keep secret files?"

"Obi-Wan, I *know* you keep secret files."

Obi-Wan's tired amusement faded. "Bail . . ."

"Sorry, sorry," he said. The transport moved on and he followed in its wake, looking for an empty bay to pull into. "All I meant was that you have resources I don't. And you can poke around without raising eyebrows. I can't."

"Why not?"

An empty bay revealed itself. "Things around here are changing, Obi-Wan," he said, nosing the speeder into it. "The mood's darkening. This war was supposed to be over by now. The fact that it isn't is making people . . . well, I hate to use the word but I can't think of another one. *Paranoid.*"

"Are you telling me you're being watched?" said Obi-Wan, incredulous. "Bail—"

"I know," he said. "*I'm* sounding paranoid. But I'm not. I promise. So you need to keep this Lanteeb thing quiet."

"Of course," said Obi-Wan, nodding. "Although—I'd like to bring Anakin to our dinner meeting. He has excellent instincts and a unique perspective."

Anakin, the wonder boy. *I wouldn't mind a closer look at this paragon.* "Sure. But don't tell anyone else. Not yet. Not even Master Yoda. All right?"

"You really are worried, aren't you?" said Obi-Wan, staring.

"Or I really am paranoid," he replied. "I guess only time will tell which it is."

Obi-Wan clambered out of the speeder and onto the concourse. "Indeed. Thank you for the ride, Bail. I'll see you in the Chancellor's briefing."

"You certainly will," Bail said. He touched a finger to his forehead and backed the speeder out of the bay. It was time to go home, where brandy and a hot meal beckoned. And even though he was nervous, even though every honed instinct he possessed screamed there was trouble coming—he felt better. Because he'd told Obi-Wan.

Crazy, but true.

SIX

——◯——

FIXING BROKEN MACHINES WAS LIKE A MEDITATION. FIXING broken machines was an antidote to every pain, every loss, every fear, every defeat.

Fixing broken machines kept him from going mad.

Hangar 3 was eerily quiet. After talking to Obi-Wan he'd sent everyone away: his clone pilots, the other mechanics, even the deck officer. Told them to take a little time off, relax in the mess, throw some darts, play some sabacc. Have some fun while they could, because who knew when the next crisis would erupt. Go on. It was fine. If anyone senior objected, he'd take care of it. And because he was Jedi General Anakin Skywalker, hero of the Republic, they'd obeyed—without too much reluctance, he'd noticed.

The first thing he'd done once he was alone was call Padmé.

"Master Anakin!" By some strange alchemy C-3PO, answering their apartment comm, had managed to sound delighted. *"How wonderful to hear your voice!"*

"Hey, Threepio," Anakin said, trying to appear casual, as though his heart weren't pounding its way through his chest. "Is Padmé there?"

"No, sir. I am sorry. Mistress Padmé is attending a diplomatic function on Chandrila. She won't be back for another four days."

What? *Stang.* "Oh. All right. I guess I'll have to comm her there and—"

"Oh dear. I'm afraid that won't be possible, Master Anakin. Mistress Padmé's function—well—to be precise, it's more like a sacred women's retreat. No contact with men is permitted."

He'd stared at his comlink in rank disbelief, disappointment a clenched fist crushing his throat, his heart. "Threepio, is this some kind of joke?"

"Joke?" The droid sounded offended. *"Certainly not, sir. I can assure you Mistress Padmé takes her participation in this event very seriously indeed. It was a compliment for her to be invited. As I understand it, the Sisterhood of Ta'fan-jirah hardly ever permits an outsider to witness their—"*

"Yeah, great, fine, whatever." With an effort he loosened his grip on the comlink. "Just—if she checks in with you, tell her I called. Tell her I'm home but I don't know for how long. All right?"

"Certainly, sir," Threepio said stiffly. *"I shall be sure to pass the message along."*

"Good. You do that."

"Ah—sir? If I might ask—is Artoo-Detoo with you? Is he—"

"He's fine," he growled. "Barely even a scratch. Which is more than I'll be able to say about you, Threepio, if you forget to tell Padmé I called."

He cut off Threepio's protestations mid-sentence.

Padmé. She wasn't home. He couldn't see her. Touch her. Hear her laugh. He couldn't feel her lips on his skin, or her warm sweet breath caress the back of his neck. The reunion he'd dreamed of on the journey back from Kothlis—ruined. Stolen. Carelessly trampled for some stupid, pointless women's gabfest. So overwhelming was his disappointment that he clenched his own fist and pulverized a cracked and discarded D-D-33 laser turret.

*Sacred retreat? What is she thinking? There's a war on. She's
not supposed to be romping offworld with a bunch of vegetar-
ian navel-gazers. She's a Galactic Senator, she's got a job to do
here. And I'm here.*

And what was the *good* of him being here if she wasn't?

Women.

Deprived of his wife's company, not at all eager to return to
the Temple where he'd have to rehash the events on Kothlis and
hide from Yoda all trace of his grief for the dead, he'd instead
hidden himself in the simplicity of machines.

Hours passed. He wasn't disturbed. No call from Obi-Wan
or the Jedi Council. Slicked with oil and hydraulic fluids, nicked
and scraped and pinched bloody in places, once the gross mechanical faults in five fighters were repaired he decided to give
every ship in the hangar a tune-up. After all, there was nowhere
else he needed—or wanted—to be.

But not even the sweaty, exacting work of bringing Gold
Squadron's starfighters to pitch-perfect performance status managed to ease his heart or lighten his thoughts.

Rex. Coric. Ahsoka. And fourteen dead pilots. Scores more
dead and wounded ground troopers.

*Why can't we stop this? Why can't we catch Grievous?
Dooku's only one man. How can he defy the entire Jedi Order?
Who is his Sith Master? Why can't we find him?*

Day and night the questions ate at him. They ate at Obi-
Wan, too, but somehow his former Master seemed able to live
without knowing the answers. Or else he was just better at hiding his dismay. His fear.

*I want Padmé. She's the only one I can be weak with. Every-
one else expects me to be strong.*

Three times he interrupted his tinkering to comm the Kaliida Shoals Medcenter. Every time he was denied permission to

speak with Ahsoka. Every time he was given the same bland, impersonal reply.

"All our patients are doing as well as can be expected, General. Your concern is appreciated. We'll contact you with any news."

Fresh frustration welling, feeling the dangerous stir of rage within, after the third infuriating conversation he relieved his seared feelings by Force-flattening an empty oil drum. He stood adrift in the middle of the echoing hangar afterward, ashamed of his outburst, wrestling with that part of himself that frightened him and fueled him and woke him gasping in the dead of night.

I am a Jedi. I am in control. I use the Force, the Force does not use me.

A precarious calm restored, he got back to work.

He'd been tinkering with his seventh fighter for not quite half an hour when he realized he wasn't alone. Rolling out from underneath the ship's space-pitted belly, he blinked at the politely inquiring face looking down at him.

"Good morning, General Skywalker," the spit-and-polished officer said, so respectful.

"Morning?" Vaguely, he stared around the hushed hangar. "Sorry, I don't—"

An apologetic smile. "It's after midnight, General. Technically that qualifies as morning."

Anakin locked the mech-cart's wheels and sat up, his shoulders and back aching. "I suppose it does, Commander—Jefris, isn't it?"

The commander's smile widened, just a little. "That's right, General. You've got a good memory." Turning, he considered the other starfighters. "Looks like you've been busy."

Anakin reached for a wipe cloth and smeared the mix

of oil and blood from his hands. His skinned knuckles were stinging. "Well . . . it keeps me out of mischief. Hope you don't mind."

"Not at all, sir," said Jefris. Although he was still smiling, his eyes were wary. "You're always welcome here."

Anakin looked at him, feeling the man's tension, his irritation. "But?"

"But I can't help noticing my men aren't at their duty stations," said Jefris. "I take it you stood them down?"

"That's right. I prefer to work without distractions."

Jefris took a moment, then nodded. His smile faded now; his eyes were more than watchful. "General, you don't have the authority to stand down my men. What you do with your clones is your business, of course. But the hangar crew is mine."

His temper, so lightly sleeping, stirred. Pushing to his feet, he tossed the wipe cloth aside.

Really, Jefris? You really want to get into a power match with a Jedi? Okay. Fine. We can do that. You'll end up sorry, but we can do that.

Jefris stepped back. "Though given how helpful you've been I'm prepared to let it slide this time," he added, almost smoothly. "Just—ask first in the future, General. Please. Chain of command, you know? It's there for a reason."

Coward. He smiled. "Of course. I'll remember that." With a sharp cracking sound, he unkinked his neck. "And since it is late, I guess I should get going. Don't suppose you can lend me a speeder? The Temple's parking bays aren't quite up to accommodating my fighter."

"I'll have someone take you wherever—"

"Thanks, but I prefer to take myself. Any old speeder will do. I'll see it's returned to you first thing tomorrow."

Defeated again, Jefris nodded. "I'll let the transport pool know you're coming, General."

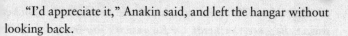

"I'd appreciate it," Anakin said, and left the hangar without looking back.

THE JEDI TEMPLE never slept.

After dumping his borrowed clunker with the droid transport chief, abruptly aware that his belly was achingly empty, Anakin made his way to the nearest dining hall and filled a plate with hot stew and thickly buttered fresh bread. The other three Jedi in residence, also eating late—Master Damsin and senior Padawans Biliril and Dorf—beckoned him to join them, but he refused with a suitably regretful smile. Chances were they'd want to talk about Kothlis and he still wasn't in the mood. Falling ravenous onto his meal, it wasn't until the plate was half empty that he let himself admit he hadn't handled Commander Jefris well.

He was doing his job. And he was right, I had no business standing his crew down. If anyone did that to me—I should know better. I should have better control.

A familiar *tap-tap-tap*ping on the dining hall's polished marble floor stirred him out of miserable self-recriminations.

"Master Yoda."

Yoda slapped his gimer stick on the table, hopped into the chair opposite, and tipped his head to one side. "Anakin. Welcome home."

This wasn't home. Padmé's apartment was home. This was—his halfway house. The place he'd fetched up in between the slave quarters on Tatooine and the bed he sometimes—not often enough—shared with his beautiful wife.

He nodded, cautious. Had Yoda sensed his dismay? "Thank you, Master."

"For the Kothlis engagement much praise have you earned," said Yoda. "Save Obi-Wan and your Padawan you did, as well as the spynet facility."

Praise from Yoda was rare. He should be thrilled . . . but he wasn't. *Because I'm tired? Or because it's too little, too late?* "So the facility is secure? Grievous didn't get the chance to steal what he was after?"

"This the Bothans have told us," said Yoda. "Their word on the matter must we accept."

"You *doubt* them?"

Yoda pursed his lips. "Say that I did not."

"You implied it."

"Late it is, young Skywalker," said Yoda, aggravating as ever. "Rest now you should. With Palpatine we meet in only a few hours. Ignore *that* conference you cannot. Asked for you especially the Chancellor has."

Palpatine. The only person in his life, aside from Padmé, who didn't scold him for his difficulties with the Jedi Council and its impossible expectations.

"Of course not, Master. I'll be there."

"Travel to the Senate with Obi-Wan and myself you shall."

"Master Windu's not attending the meeting?"

"To Kothlis has Master Windu gone," said Yoda. "His expertise have the Bothans requested."

Oh. Well, he wasn't about to lose sleep over that. Mace Windu made him profoundly uncomfortable. One minute critical, the next blithely reciting the old Chosen One prophecy, using it as justification to get his way in an argument.

Master Windu needs to make up his mind about me.

"Actually, ah, I have another question, Master Yoda."

"Recovering your Padawan is," said Yoda gravely. "Your Clone Captain Rex and his sergeant also. Serious their injuries were, but in sufficient time were they treated."

Relief warred with annoyance. "The Kaminoans gave you details? They wouldn't tell me a thing."

Yoda's ears lifted. "Surprised by that are you?"

No, he was—yes, admit it, angry—but there wasn't any point saying so. He'd only get another lecture about mastering his feelings. "What about the other casualties?"

Sighing, Yoda shook his head. "Troubling that news is. Four have died. Two may yet die. Recover the rest will."

They would recover—only to be thrown back into the meat grinder of this galactic civil war. A war the Jedi should have prevented. "Did you actually speak with Ahsoka or just—"

"Resting, she was. Speak with her tomorrow you may."

Hearing that, Anakin felt the tight knot of tension under his ribs dissolve. "Thank you, Master Yoda. Now, if you'll excuse me, I'll go to my quarters." Standing, he collected his emptied plate and used cutlery. "Good night."

Yoda nodded. "Good night, young Skywalker."

But after taking a couple of steps toward the refuse station he hesitated. *Go on. You might as well. You might not get another chance.* He turned back. "Okay. Obi-Wan'll kill me for saying this but I don't care. Master Yoda—"

Yoda's luminous eyes, which so often seemed disapproving, warmed. "Worry not for Obi-Wan, young Anakin. This night he spends in the Halls of Healing. Deep, untroubled sleep he requires and deep, untroubled sleep he shall have."

"No kidding," he said, impressed despite himself. "How did you manage that?"

"After nine hundred years a few tricks for dealing with wayward young Jedi have I learned," said Yoda, close to outright amusement. "Forget that you should not, hmmm?"

It wasn't often he and Yoda shared a joke. "No, Master. I won't," he said, grinning. But instead of leaving it there, he hesitated.

"Something else worries you, Anakin?" said Yoda, his head tilting again. "About Obi-Wan?"

"No. Yes. Maybe." He blew out a sharp breath. "I know

you can't betray confidences, Master. I know certain things must be kept privileged. Medical things. But—" And suddenly he wasn't sure what to say next.

Yoda's amusement faded. "Concerned you are that fully recovered from his encounter with the Sith on Zigoola, Obi-Wan is not."

Yoda's speech might be as twisty as a demented corkscrew but it never failed to hit the nail on the head. "And?"

"Zigoola," Yoda said thoughtfully. His eyes narrowed. "Your fault that misadventure was not, young Skywalker."

It wasn't an answer. Nor was it the first time someone tried to excuse him, but repetition didn't make it any easier to believe. If he hadn't lost R2 in the battle to save Bothawui—if he hadn't had to waste so much time looking for the little droid—

I never would've let Zigoola happen. I'd have sensed ancient Sith on that planet long before they could do any damage. I should've been there.

"Yes, Master. Thank you. But that doesn't tell me about Obi-Wan."

Yoda retrieved his gimer stick and hopped to the ground. "Observant you are, young Skywalker," he said, large eyes still half lidded in that inscrutable way of his. "Sleep well. Weary also are you. Mindful of that you must be."

Anakin watched the ancient Jedi *tap-tap-tap* his way out of the dining hall.

So, what . . . was that a yes? A no? Or a work it out for yourself?

Disgruntled, and suddenly so tired he was seeing double, he dumped his dirty plate and cutlery at the refuse station and staggered off to his quarters.

• • •

"*ANAKIN!*" WIDELY SMILING, Supreme Chancellor Palpatine came forward to meet him as though they were the only two men in his executive suite. "How gratifying to see you unharmed after your recent battle. Allow me to congratulate you on your fine showing against that monster, Grievous. You continue a credit to the Jedi Order."

Uncomfortably aware that they weren't alone, Anakin nodded. "Thank you, Supreme Chancellor. It's good to see you again, sir."

"Anakin, are you not well?" Palpatine peered anxiously into his face. "You're looking a trifle weary. This terrible war—it's taxing all of us, I know, but—" He turned. "I hope you're not asking too much of this young man, Master Yoda. The more I learn of his exploits on the front lines, defending our Republic, the more I come to believe we'll not win this fight without him."

Anakin stared at the carpeted floor. He didn't dare flick a look at Obi-Wan or Master Yoda, who by rights Chancellor Palpatine should have greeted first. His friendship with the Chancellor meant a great deal to him but sometimes—like right now—he wished Naboo's former Senator would remember that the Jedi liked to keep things calm and understated; that they were greatly attached to ceremony and the proper protocols.

But Yoda didn't appear perturbed. "Correct you are, Supreme Chancellor. Most valuable to our cause young Skywalker is."

"As, of course, is Master Kenobi," said Palpatine, offering Obi-Wan a gracious nod. "Please don't think I'm unaware of your contributions. Indeed, I had a long conversation with Kothlis's interim leader a short while ago and he specifically mentioned your heroic defense of the spynet facility. I'm told you were wounded in that engagement?"

Now it was Obi-Wan's turn to squirm. Nothing irked him

more than being singled out, especially by a politician. "A few scratches, Supreme Chancellor. The matter's hardly worth mentioning."

"And you'd much rather I'd not mentioned it?" said Palpatine, amused. "Master Kenobi, you are far too modest. I think—"

"Forgive me, Supreme Chancellor," said Bail Organa, as Mas Amedda ushered him into Palpatine's office. "I'm so sorry to delay you."

Anakin turned his head, just a little, to watch the Senator from Alderaan join them in front of Palpatine's desk. An interesting man. His presence in the Force was dynamic. Intense. Padmé trusted him implicitly, and more than once had urged him to do the same. And of course, after Zigoola, Obi-Wan had complete faith in him, too.

I've no reason not to trust him. The three people I trust most in my life trust him. I don't know. He just seems . . . awfully smooth.

Palpatine didn't appear put out by the politician's late arrival. "Nothing wrong, I hope, Senator?"

"No, no," said Organa. "I was held up at one of the checkpoints."

"How delightfully ironic," said Palpatine with a small, wicked smile. "My head of Republic security falling afoul of a security check."

"Yes," said Organa, charmingly rueful. "It serves me right for not following my own recommendations. Again, sir, my apologies."

"Accepted," said Palpatine. "And now that we're all here, my friends, let us get down to business."

Ordinarily, visitors to the Supreme Chancellor's office remained standing. This time, however, Palpatine led them to an offset alcove where chairs and a sofa had been arranged, conversation-style.

"Master Yoda," said Organa, following. "Good to see you again."

"And you, Senator," said Yoda.

"Senator," said Obi-Wan, with a noncommittal nod.

Organa nodded back. "Master Kenobi."

And that was very restrained. Very formal. But still watching closely, Anakin saw something warmer pass between Obi-Wan and his unlikely friend. And something else, too—the merest shiver through the Force. Uncertainty. A hint of danger.

Uh-oh. What are they up to now?

But there wasn't time to ponder that, because everyone else was seated. So he took his own place, folded his hands in his lap, and sat back, waiting to see what happened next.

"So," said Palpatine, congeniality set aside in the face of grim reality. "Kothlis. A desperately close-run affair, I'm afraid. Grievous's bold attack almost succeeded. And there is every reason to suspect he'll try again as soon as he has regrouped. My friends, we *cannot* afford to lose the Kothlis spynet to our enemy."

Bail Organa nodded. "I agree. It was sheer luck the Special Operations Brigade picked up that chatter about the impending attack. If not for random chance, Kothlis would now be in Separatist hands—and we need its capabilities, now more than ever with the war not going our way. We can't rely only on Bothawui, Special Ops, and our clone agents for intel. The conflict's spread too far."

"Exactly, Senator," said Palpatine, approving. "Which is why I have decided—after consultation with Kothlis's interim government—to establish a permanent GAR presence in their system and on their soil."

Anakin saw Yoda and Obi-Wan exchange discreetly alarmed looks. "A permanent presence, Chancellor?" said Yoda, ears lowered. "Using which troops?"

"Our best and brightest, of course," said Palpatine, eyebrows raised.

"From the front lines you would divert resources?"

"Master Yoda—" Palpatine throttled impatience. "Given Kothlis's importance I don't see I have any choice. Do you?"

"In theory your suggestion is sound, Chancellor," said Obi-Wan carefully. "But in practice I fear it might prove to be a miscalculation. Conditions on the front lines are extremely difficult. We've already lost too many of our most experienced clone soldiers and pilots. To take more out of rotation and station them permanently on—"

"Master Kenobi," said Palpatine, one hand raised. His voice was chilly now, his eyes hard. "Perhaps you should consider that while I have not seen action on the front lines, as Supreme Chancellor of our grand Galactic Republic I *do* have a firm grasp of this conflict's *big picture*. I would not have taken this step did I not consider it unavoidable."

Obi-Wan's face went still. "Of course, Supreme Chancellor."

"My friends . . ." Palpatine's intent gaze swept across their faces. "I regret the difficulties losing these troops will cause you. But unless I've been misinformed there are more clones due out of production within the next few months. Can we not hold fast until they reach us?"

Yoda sighed. "We can, Chancellor—if convinced you are that we must."

"I am convinced, Master Yoda," said Palpatine. "I know that, as a rule, I leave the strategic planning to you and your Jedi Council and the GAR war cabinet—but in this case I feel compelled to intervene. It was only thanks to young Master Skywalker that Kothlis—and before it Bothawui—did not fall into Separatist hands. But Anakin is only one man—and the Jedi cannot expect him to save the day *every* day."

Anakin closed his eyes. *Please, please, stop talking now, Chancellor. Really. Just stop.*

Bail Organa broke the excruciating silence. "I agree, Supreme Chancellor, that the spynet facility on Kothlis is an asset that must be protected. But with all due respect, Master Kenobi also has a valid point. So might I suggest a compromise?"

Palpatine leaned back in his chair, fingers delicately steepled. "Of course, Senator. Please, it's not my intention to dictate to any of you. I requested this meeting so we might have a free and frank exchange of views on our desperate situation. If you can think of another way to protect Kothlis, *believe* me—I'll seize it with both hands."

There was no mistaking the Chancellor's sincerity. Anakin flicked a look at Obi-Wan and Yoda, willing them to see Palpatine's point of view.

They can't make this personal. He's the Supreme Chancellor, it's his job to make difficult decisions. The Jedi serve the Republic, not the other way around. And if this is how we serve today—then so be it.

"I suggest," Organa said slowly, "that a mix of experienced front-line troops and newer soldiers be sent to secure Kothlis. And that once the newer troops have been trained by those experienced personnel, the latter be returned to the front lines without delay."

"That's an interesting suggestion, Senator," said Palpatine. "Master Yoda, your thoughts?"

Yoda smoothed one small hand over his seamed, roughly domed head. "An ideal arrangement it is not, but better than the alternative I think. Accept Senator Organa's compromise I do. On one condition."

Palpatine frowned. "Which is?"

"Of this arrangement a three-month review must be held,

Supreme Chancellor. To save Kothlis and lose the civilized galaxy is not an outcome to be desired."

"And if Kothlis isn't prepared to accept this compromise, or the imposition of a three-month trial period?"

"Supreme Chancellor you are," said Yoda, smiling grimly. "Explain to them you can that no choice do they have."

"I'll certainly do my best, Master Yoda," said Palpatine, very dry. "Now—if we might address our second pressing issue? How was Grievous able to infiltrate our shipyard and sabotage our warships' communications systems? How was he able to jam fighter and gunship transmissions? That argues he has access to our coded frequencies, which is alarming."

"I can offer no explanation at this time, Supreme Chancellor," Organa said flatly. "But a task force comprising military and civilian intel agents is working all hours to find one. My office is coordinating. As soon as I have answers, sir, you'll have them." He looked at Yoda. "And you, Master Yoda. I'm acutely aware of the danger the Jedi and the troops they command are in so long as this security breach remains unresolved."

"Greatly appreciated your efforts are, Senator," said Yoda. "Outwit Grievous we *must*. If help from the Jedi you require, ask for it. Every assistance shall we give you."

"I hesitate to suggest this," said Palpatine, "but should we consider standing our forces down until we can be sure GAR communications are safeguarded?"

"Stand down?" said Anakin, startled. "We can't. We'd lose too much ground to the Separatists. We'd be telling Grievous he won. Chancellor—"

"*Anakin,*" said Obi-Wan.

"It's all right, Master Kenobi," said Palpatine. "He's right, I fear, and I was mistaken to suggest it. No matter the dangers we cannot retreat. Instead, we must bear the consequences of courage. And we will." He favored them with a weary smile.

"Thank you all, for your time and your advice. Now we must trust to the Force to see us victorious."

The meeting broke up, amid promises and assurances of constant mutual updates. Then Palpatine cleared his throat.

"Master Yoda—I wonder if I might trespass upon your goodwill and ask that Anakin remain behind for a few moments?"

Yoda's nod was as close to a respectful bow as he would likely ever get. "Certainly. Young Skywalker—"

"Master," Anakin said, with his own version of a deferential nod.

"To the Temple you will return once finished is your business here. Your report on Kothlis I have yet to hear."

"Of course, Master."

Obi-Wan said nothing, only raised an eyebrow then followed Master Yoda out of Palpatine's office, Senator Organa by his side. As the doors closed behind them, the Supreme Chancellor turned.

"Anakin, Anakin." He shook his head, ruefully smiling. "I embarrassed you, didn't I?"

He felt heat rush into his face. "No, sir, I—"

"Yes, I did," said Palpatine. "You can say it. I won't bite." He gestured. "Let's sit down again, shall we? Have you eaten breakfast? It wouldn't surprise me if you hadn't—I was forced to convene this meeting at a most uncivilized hour."

"No, thank you, Chancellor," he said, dropping back into his chair. "I'm fine."

Palpatine frowned. "Are you sure? I don't like to think of you neglecting yourself, Anakin. You work so hard, risk your life for the rest of us on a daily basis. You mustn't be careless of your own well-being. As Supreme Chancellor I've quite enough worries to be going on with, young man. If you've any regard for me at all, you'll not make yourself another one."

Any regard? He couldn't speak for a moment. *This is the most important man in the galaxy . . . and he speaks to me as though I'm his own flesh and blood. He has cared about me since I was a boy.*

"Chancellor . . ." He had to wait a moment before he could trust his voice. "Please, don't ever doubt my regard for you. It's too deep for words."

Eyes moistening, Palpatine smoothed the nap of his rich blue velvet trousers. "I know it makes you uncomfortable when I praise you in public, Anakin. Particularly to Master Yoda or Master Kenobi." He looked up. "But I'm not about to apologize for that. Perhaps you're too close to things. Perhaps you've grown accustomed to being . . . treated in a certain way. But when I see how blithely they take you for granted, when I see how reluctant they are to acknowledge your extraordinary efforts in this awful war—well. It makes me see red."

Now it was Anakin's turn to look down. "Adulation is not the Jedi way," he murmured. "The knowledge that we've done our duty is sufficient for us."

"Yes, well, it's not sufficient for me," Palpatine retorted. "So I'm afraid you'll just have to get used to me telling you how splendid you are."

Anakin laughed. "Far be it from me to argue with the Republic's Supreme Chancellor."

"Anakin . . ." Smile fading, Palpatine regarded him intently. "How are you, really? The truth. Please."

"I'm . . . tired," he admitted, after a long pause. "I'm angry. I'm afraid."

"Afraid? Of what?"

"That we'll lose this war. That I'll lose more friends. That even if we *do* defeat Dooku and Grievous, what we're left with—our Republic—will be so damaged I won't recognize it."

He shivered. "I've seen so much suffering, Chancellor. Some-times it feels like I'm drowning in it. Like no matter what I do it's not enough."

Palpatine nodded. "I understand. I often feel the same way. And loneliness makes it even harder to bear, doesn't it?"

"Loneliness?" He stared at Palpatine, abruptly uneasy. "I'm sorry, sir, I don't—"

"Senator Amidala. Padmé." Palpatine's smile was gentle and full of affection. "You miss her, Anakin. I can see it in your eyes. I can feel it. Your pain."

Shocked icy cold, he struggled to remain calm. *How can he know? I've been so careful.* "I'm sorry, Chancellor, but I think you're—"

"Anakin, Anakin . . ." Palpatine rested a hand on his shoul-der. "You mustn't fret. I won't tell."

"There's nothing to tell, Supreme Chancellor." He felt sick. "Padmé—the Senator—I don't—"

"*Anakin.*" Now Palpatine's hooded eyes were fierce. "You can hide from the Jedi—but you can't hide from me. I know your heart. And *my* heart breaks that you must endure such sor-row. I wish there was something I could do, my boy. I wish I could snap my fingers and change their foolish rules. But I can't. All I can do is promise you—on my *life*—that I will never betray your confidence. I hope you know that. I hope you trust me."

"Yes," Anakin whispered. "Yes, of course I trust you."

Palpatine's relief hummed in the Force. "Thank you," he said. "That means a great deal. Anakin—my dear young friend—you're not alone. And if ever the need to unburden yourself be-comes too great to bear, if there's no one else you can turn to, turn to me. I am here for you, always. There is *nothing* you could tell me that would change my feelings for you."

Padmé had said that: on Tatooine, after he'd confessed to

her his slaughter of the Sand People who'd murdered his mother. A slaughter that still haunted his dreams. To hear Palpatine make the same promise . . .

"Thank you, Supreme Chancellor. I don't—I can't—" He breathed out hard. "Thank you." Then he stood. "But I should go now. I've duties in the Temple—and wounded to ask after."

"Of course," said Palpatine, rising. "We are both busy men. But if you can, come to see me again before you're flung back into the war. I enjoy your company."

"And I enjoy yours, Chancellor," Anakin said, with a bow. "If I can return, I will. I promise."

And feeling much better than he had upon waking, he made his way back to the Jedi Temple.

SEVEN

"He doesn't encourage it, you know," said Obi-Wan, threading the speeder through the slowly building morning traffic, taking the most direct route back to the Temple. "Friendly as he is with the Supreme Chancellor, Anakin doesn't ask to be singled out in that fashion."

In the passenger seat beside him, chin sunk to his chest, Yoda grunted. He was frowning.

"Besides. Palpatine wasn't wrong," he added. "The spynet facility most likely would have fallen if not for him."

"An accomplished Jedi has young Skywalker become, Obi-Wan," Yoda conceded. "But your own part in the saving of Kothlis did you play. Forget that I do not."

Warmed by the unexpected praise, he took advantage of their status, slipped their speeder into an adjacent lane, and kicked it along a bit faster.

"Still, I'm lucky Ahsoka was there," he said. "She's shaping up to be a fine Jedi, Master Yoda."

"Pleased I am with her progress," Yoda conceded.

"Although—" He had to smile. "I believe she's teaching Anakin at least as much as he's teaching her. You were right. Training her will be the making of him. Just as training him was the making of me."

"Hmm," said Yoda.

They weren't far from the Temple now. Changing lanes again so he could bypass the main transport complex and instead dock the speeder at Yoda's private landing platform, he glanced sideways at his mentor.

I've never asked. And if I don't ask now, there's a chance I never shall.

"Master . . . do you regret giving me permission to train Anakin? Even though our path wasn't always smooth, did we not manage to overcome your reservations?"

Yoda sighed. "Your best you did, Obi-Wan. Doubt that I do not."

Well. Talk about damning with faint praise. "That's not the same as saying I didn't fail."

"Obi-Wan . . ." Another sigh. "A difficult child he was. A difficult man he has become."

"Difficult? Master—"

"Brilliance is difficult, Obi-Wan," Yoda said sharply. "Know that better than anyone you should. Understand him better than anyone you do. A fine line always does your former apprentice walk. Taught him well, you have. But learned well, has he? Only time will tell."

It would be foolish—and arrogant—to argue. He was a Jedi Knight who'd trained a single Padawan. And in his long life Yoda had trained hundreds . . .

Still. I think he's wrong. Anakin may have his faults, we all have our faults, but he's surpassed every goal set for him. He's made mistakes but he's never let me down.

Swinging the speeder out of their public airlane and into the nearest Temple airlane, he decided to change the subject.

"Admiral Yularen feared *Indomitable* would be weeks in spacedock. Do you know if that's true?"

"True it is, Obi-Wan," Yoda said heavily. "Although—"

"So long as she's in spacedock she can't be diverted to Koth-lis," he murmured. "Which is reassuring. I understand the planet must be protected, but . . ." He glanced sideways. "Master Yoda, like Palpatine, you've got the best view of the big picture right now. I know I'm not on the Council but—can you tell me? Are things going as badly for us as I suspect?"

"What do your feelings tell you, Obi-Wan?"

The Temple was looming. Their journey was almost over, and with it this surprisingly forthright conversation. *Best make the most of it while I can.* "That we are a long, long way from victory, Master."

Yoda sighed. "Enslaved to the dark side the Separatists are. Strong this makes them. Very strong."

It was chilling to hear Yoda confirm his worst misgivings. "And the Force? What does it show you?"

"Not enough."

Obi-Wan felt a gibber of fear. Ruthlessly he quashed it. "We will win this war, Master. We have to. The alternative—"

"Must be faced, Obi-Wan," said Yoda. He sounded so grim. "Clouded is the Republic's future. Obscured by the dark side. Hope we must have, but not blind hope."

And what did that mean? Was Yoda coming to believe that defeat was possible? Probable? Even . . . inevitable?

I refuse to accept that. Too many have died defending the Republic for me to accept that.

With another sideways swoop he guided the speeder toward the Temple sector containing Yoda's apartment. "Master, perhaps Anakin and I should reconsider our furlough. Five days is a long time. Perhaps—"

Yoda's ears lowered. "No. Correct Palpatine was when he said rely on you too much we should not."

Though he was worried, he had to smile. "Actually, he said you weren't to rely on Anakin too much. Our Supreme Chancellor appears not to care for me particularly."

"And concern you, does that?"

"Not in the least, Master," he said. "Generally speaking, anyone a politician praises to the sky is someone I'd think twice about trusting."

That made Yoda laugh. "Young to be so cynical you are, Obi-Wan."

"Believe me, Master, the war is aging me fast."

"Aging us all it is." Yoda sighed. "Five days your furlough will remain. This short respite you have earned, Obi-Wan. Take it. No telling there is when rest again you will have."

"Well . . ." Obi-Wan frowned slightly, uncomfortably aware that everyone who'd nagged him about being tired was right. "I won't say it's not welcome."

Although who knows if I'll get to enjoy it? There's dinner with Bail tonight. That might change everything.

Yoda was staring. He could feel that bright, wickedly sharp intelligence assessing him. "Something else bothering you there is, Obi-Wan. Confide in me, can you?"

Blast. He should know better than to indulge in doubts around Yoda. Directly ahead lay the Jedi Master's private landing platform. Slowing the speeder he glided them in, the machine shuddering gently as the automatically triggered cushion-shield absorbed their momentum. He used the maneuver as a distraction, searching for the best response.

But really, telling the truth was his only option.

"There is a situation brewing, possibly," he admitted, "but I need to know more before I speak of it. When I do—if I need to—I will. You have my word."

"Your judgment I respect, Obi-Wan," said Yoda. "Come to me at any time you know you can."

Yes, he knew it. But it helped to hear Yoda say so, to know he had the ancient Jedi to lean on. There were days of late when he'd felt very alone.

"Thank you, Master."

He watched Yoda make his way into the Temple, then returned the speeder to the transport pool. After that, with Anakin occupied and nothing else to claim his attention, he headed for the Jedi Archives. With luck he'd find something of value there about Lanteeb. After all, it would be impolite to turn up at Bail's empty-handed.

But nearly two hours later it appeared he'd have no choice but to be bad-mannered. Beyond bare bones cartographic information, a passing mention of its colonization date and a brief note about mineral exports, with every last obscure primary, sub-, and super-sub-directory data file rigorously examined, it seemed the Jedi had no interest whatsoever in Lanteeb. Indeed, from what he could tell no Jedi had ever once set foot on Lanteeban soil. As he sat in the private cubicle he'd commandeered, pondering that inconvenient conclusion and feeling mildly peeved, Anakin found him.

"There you are. What are you doing hidden away in here?"

He glanced around. "Lanteeb."

Anakin blinked, then perched on the edge of the desk. "All right. I'll bite. Animal, vegetable, or mineral?"

"Planet."

"And it's important because . . . ?"

He sighed. *You and your blasted instincts, Bail* . . . "I have no idea."

"And yet we're discussing it."

"Apparently, yes."

"Obi-Wan." Anakin folded his arms, alight with baffled amusement. "Are you feeling all right? We have some time off. There has to be somewhere else you'd rather be."

"I could say the same thing to you."

Anakin's smile faded. "Yeah, well." He shrugged. "I'm still waiting to hear from Ahsoka. Or Rex. I'll even settle for a Kaminoan. I swear, if someone doesn't tell me what's going on in the medcenter, and soon . . ."

Obi-Wan sat back in his chair. "Stop worrying. Ahsoka and the injured clones are in the best possible hands. If something had gone wrong, you'd have heard by now. Bad news travels reliably fast."

"I suppose," Anakin muttered. "But—I don't know—maybe I'll—"

Obi-Wan slapped him lightly on the arm. "Don't even *think* it. The last thing they need is you under their feet, Anakin. Besides, how will it look to Ahsoka if you go running out to Kalida Shoals? She'll think you don't trust her."

"It's got nothing to do with trust," Anakin protested. "Those are my men, Obi-Wan."

"And your apprentice is there for them," he pointed out. "They need to know that, Anakin. They need to know that you trust her to lead them when you can't. This is a vital part of her journey from Padawan to Jedi Knight. Don't deprive her of it because you can't control your feelings."

Anakin opened his mouth to argue, then reconsidered. "Is that what I'm doing?"

"What do you think?"

"I think—" Anakin kicked his heel against the polished marble floor. "I think I hate it when I can't stop my men from getting hurt. From dying. I think—"

"What?" he prompted, when Anakin didn't continue.

"Never mind. It doesn't matter."

"It matters, Anakin," he said gently. "What you think matters."

Anakin flicked him a look. "You'll just lecture me about attachment. Again."

Careful, careful. *He's not your Padawan anymore.* "It's true," he said, after a moment, "that I sometimes wish you were more . . . moderate . . . in your feelings. But it's also true that your men follow you with such enthusiasm and loyalty because they know how deeply you care."

"So—that's it?" said Anakin. "That's all you've got to say?"

"Anakin . . ." He shook his head, recalling Yoda's somber words. *Taught him well, you have. But learned well, has he?* "Only you can decide what works best for you. How strongly you feel things—what you choose to care about—I can't make those decisions for you. I can tell you what *I* think. I can give you the benefit of my experience. But I can't live your life for you."

Anakin ducked his head. "I already know what you think, Obi-Wan. You think I'm hotheaded. I'm impulsive. That I let myself feel too much."

"Yes," he admitted. "Sometimes I do. And sometimes I can't imagine who I'd be today if not for you. Though you frequently drive me to distraction, Anakin, I cannot deny this: knowing you has made me a better Jedi."

Silence. In Anakin's wide eyes, astonishment. A shy, uncertain pleasure. He felt himself pricked with unexpected guilt.

I should have told him that long ago. I shouldn't have let him doubt himself. Lectures are all well and good, but there's a place for praise. I too easily forget that.

He cleared his throat and tried to lighten the mood. "By the way, do you have plans for this evening?"

A disgruntled look skimmed Anakin's face. "No."

"Good. Bail Organa has invited us to dinner. I'd like you to accept."

"Us?" said Anakin. "Why us? I mean, you I can understand, but he barely knows me. Unless—" He slid off the desk. "*No. He's stumbled into trouble? Again? Are you serious?*"

"As a heart attack."

Anakin stared at the datareader's screen, still showing the last unsuccessful query. "And it has something to do with Lanteeb? Don't tell me it's a secret Sith base, too."

The private cubicle's door was still open. He waved it closed. "Keep your voice down. And no. At least, Bail says not."

"Then what is this about?"

"I don't know. He doesn't know, precisely. Hence the dinner invitation, so we can talk about it without fear of interruptions."

"Talk about what?" said Anakin, bemused. "What's so special about Lanteeb? I've never even heard of the place."

Obi-Wan turned off the datareader. "I hadn't, either, until he mentioned it. But Bail's concerned about recent events there . . . and that's enough for me to at least hear him out."

"And if it's enough for you, then it should be enough for me?" Anakin perched on the desk again. "What do the Archives say?"

"About Lanteeb? Very little."

"And Dex?"

Vexed, he frowned. "Dex says nothing at all. He's offworld visiting family, and out of comm reach."

"Oh. Well, don't you have anyone else you can ask? What about that Arkanian smuggler we ran into last year, what was her name? Targio? Talin? Ta-something-or-other."

"*No,* Anakin. Bail's asked me to keep this confidential, and I am."

Anakin raised an amused, skeptical eyebrow. "Apart from trying to ask Dex, you mean."

"Dex doesn't count. Be patient. We'll find out more tonight—that is, if you're coming."

"I might as well," said Anakin, shrugging. "It's not like I've got anything better to do."

Excellent. "Chances are it's a false alarm, you know," he added. "But the food and wine will make up for that."

"And if it's not a false alarm?" said Anakin, no longer amused. "What then?"

Then we'll have one more problem to deal with, won't we? "I'd prefer not to speculate ahead of the facts."

Anakin frowned at him, his regard almost as intense as Yoda's. "You don't think it's a false alarm. Politician or not, you trust Organa."

"I have good reason to, Anakin."

"Never said you don't," said Anakin. "And Palpatine wouldn't rely on him so heavily if his judgment wasn't sound."

"There you are, then." Obi-Wan ran a hand down his face, washed through with sudden weariness. *I don't want any more problems. I want five days where I can sleep without bad dreams.* "So. Dinner. We should leave the Temple no later than—"

But Anakin wasn't listening. He was slumped a little on the edge of the desk, brooding.

"What's the matter?"

Anakin stirred. "Look. Obi-Wan. About this morning. Chancellor Palpatine." He sighed. "He means well. He's my friend, all right? He worries about me."

His instinct was to urge caution. Just because Palpatine meant well didn't mean his lavish praise was a good thing. On the contrary. Too often the Chancellor's uncritical support encouraged Anakin's regrettable tendency toward brash overconfidence.

But I daren't say it. He's so fiercely loyal to his friends. He'll just get angry and defensive if I criticize Palpatine—which won't do either of us any good.

He nodded. "I know."

"I don't agree with him," Anakin added. "About me being taken for granted. Or that I'm single-handedly defending the Republic. We all risk ourselves. We're all ready to die in this war. The Chancellor just—he gets carried away, Obi-Wan. That's all."

"It's fine, Anakin. My feelings aren't hurt. I understand."

"Do you?" said Anakin, cautiously hopeful. "Really?"

"Of course."

It was true. He understood completely. Palpatine always did have a soft spot for Anakin . . . and there was a part of Anakin that would always need emotional ties. Having lost his mother and Qui-Gon—and then being denied Padmé—of course he'd turned to Palpatine. A benign, uncritical father figure. A source of unconditional support. Anakin had come to the Temple years too late for anything or anyone to undo his need for love.

And what cannot be cured must be endured.

Shoving his chair back from the datastation, Obi-Wan stood. "I've been sitting for hours. I'm going to stretch my legs. Care to join me, or do you still have reports to file?"

Anakin shook his head. "No. They're done. But I was thinking I might take Artoo down to the droid workshop and give him a tune-up. He's seen some pretty heavy action over the last couple of months, and I've only had the time and equipment to make running repairs."

Tinkering, again. *Anakin and his blessed machines.* He should have known. "Fine. Just don't get any bright ideas for upgrading him. Or if you do, check before implementing them. Remember what happened the last time you got creative?"

They left the Archives' private cubicle, Anakin hotly protesting under his breath. "That *wasn't* my fault. Fleet Maintenance shouldn't have changed my onboard weapons protocols without telling me. If I'd *known* they'd recalibrated the targeting computer, I'd never have rewritten Artoo's rapid-response interface and—"

"—you wouldn't have accidentally shot me down. I know," he said, with weary forbearance. "Mistakes were made all around and hopefully we've learned from them. I'm just suggesting—"

"All right, all right," said Anakin, as they passed through the Archives' main doors and onto the Level 6 concourse beyond them. "Point taken. I won't upgrade anything without checking with Fleet first. You satisfied?"

"I'm ecstatic," he said drily. "Have fun. I'll comm you later."

They parted company.

Lacking any clear purpose for the first time in weeks, and finding the absence of urgency unnerving, Obi-Wan wandered the wide, stately concourse with its towering marble columns and artworks donated from countless worlds throughout the Republic. He smiled at the little flocks of younglings he encountered, so focused and serious as they were herded from one task to the next, and felt a wistful melancholy, remembering himself at that same tender age. He passed groups of older Padawans, a little less serious, a little more in tune with the Force. The awe in their eyes as they recognized him made him feel profoundly uncomfortable.

I am not a hero. I'm merely older than you.

He had several hours yet before he was due to meet with Bail. What to do, what to do? He supposed he could spend some time in the arboretum, meditating. Last night Vokara Che had strongly advised just that, once she'd finished what *Pioneer*'s med droid had started and repaired the lingering echoes of damage from those inconvenient transparisteel shards.

"*I know you've not forgotten our last talk, Master Kenobi,*" she'd said. "*And I know you resent what has happened to you. But resenting it changes nothing. Your body is different now. You must find a way to work with those differences, not against them.*"

Differences forced upon him by the Sith. By the dark side. Differences whose deleterious effects, Vokara Che believed, would accumulate over time. That he *would* find a way to conquer if it took him the rest of his life.

"Obi-Wan!"

His heart thudded, once, then settled back into rhythm, almost unchanged. Slowing, he turned. Stopped. Smiled. "Taria."

"I heard you were back," Taria Damsin said, joining him. Long blue-green hair tugged into a careless braid, athletic physique wrapped in dark green stretchskin, she looked fit and vital and burningly alive. Nobody would ever guess, looking at her, that she was dying. "*And* I heard you were injured. Again."

"You should know better than to listen to gossip."

She raised one strongly arched eyebrow. "I hope you bluff more convincingly than that when you're negotiating, Master Kenobi."

They'd been friends since childhood. More than friends for a short while, those memories cherished. The old friendship resumed, undiminished, when it was time.

He grinned. "As a matter of fact, I do."

"I'm pleased to hear it." She looked him up and down, a critical inspection worthy of a nerf breeder. "And even more pleased to see you're not prostrated this time."

Prostrated. She chose the most absurd words. She was a

most absurd woman. *She can't be dying. It's too cruel.* "Taria, I'm fine. How are you?"

"Me? I'm fighting fit," she said, the sudden glint in her eyes a warning. It was almost impossible to get her talking about the disease that was slowly consuming her. "But desperate. I've an advanced lightsaber class to teach and my assistant's managed to give himself food poisoning. I don't suppose . . ." She trailed off, invitingly.

Well, here was a conundrum. Tedious meditation in the arboretum or the always entertaining rough-and-tumble of a lightsaber session with Taria.

Hmm. Let me think . . .

"I'd be delighted to stand in for your unfortunate assistant, Master Damsin," he said. "Although—" He hesitated, wondering briefly if he should continue. But he decided to risk her displeasure, because they were never less than honest with each other. They had never shielded each other no matter the temptation or consequences. "Truth be told, Taria, I'm a little surprised you're still teaching advanced classes. Are you sure that's wise?"

Instead of snapping, she let her gaze slip sideways. No quicksilver temper, that warning glint fading. He'd rather she raged at him. The fear he could feel in her closed his throat.

"Taria," he said, wishing they were alone, his voice brimful of unspoken sorrow. A broken promise: he'd sworn he wouldn't burden her with his grief.

Her chin tilted, and suddenly he was reminded of Padmé. That same stubborn strength and pride and courage.

"I'm in remission, Obi-Wan," she said, carefully self-contained again, shutting him out. "For as long as it lasts I'll live my life on my terms. Now come on. I need to set up the dojo and we don't want to be late. How would that look? Our poster boy Jedi tardy to class."

He didn't protest her distancing of him. When she was ready, they'd talk. They always did. Falling into old, bad habits—how fortunate Anakin wasn't here—he used the Force to tug her long braid. "Call me a poster boy again and I'll tell your students about the time you tangled with that dragon-beast on—"

"You wouldn't *dare*!" she breathed, retreating. "You promised, you *swore*, you said you'd *never*—"

Wickedly grinning, he followed her. "Who's the Jedi poster boy?"

"Not you," she said, flinging up her hands in surrender. "It was never you. In fact, there isn't one. I made it all up. Happy now?"

"I could weep with joy. Do lead the way to class, Master Damsin."

And so, with the problem of what to do with himself solved for the moment, he walked with Taria from the concourse to the largest dojo on Level 9, where her eager students awaited . . . and where he could, for a little while at least, leave the war and his worries behind.

THE KALIIDA SHOALS MEDCENTER was a terrible place.

Ahsoka felt guilty for thinking that, but Master Yoda was very strict about Padawans not denying their thoughts. Good or bad they must flow through the mind, neither provoking nor denying action. Only when a Jedi was at peace with his or her thoughts could the right course of action be decided.

She didn't like Kaliida Shoals and she wasn't too fond of the Kaminoans, either. Nala Shan and her colleagues were brilliant scientists and miracle-working doctors, but it seemed to her that Anakin felt more connection to machines than the Kaminoans did to the clones they created. When they didn't think she was listening, they referred to Rex and Coric and the others as units. *Units.* They weren't *units,* they were men, living breathing laughing hurting brave and reckless men, who would lay down their lives for her and for one another without ever once stopping to think first and she loved them for that. So did Anakin. And Master Kenobi, well, he respected them.

But the Kaminoans? No love. Not even respect. Just pride. They were proud of their work. They were terribly impressed with how much damage a clone could sustain and how fast they could heal his torn flesh and broken bones. But care about them? Feel sympathy for their pain, or grief at their loss? No. She hadn't seen a hint of that. The Kaminoans were very detached. They were so detached they made Jedi like Master Yoda and Master Windu and Master Kenobi look like giddy, hysterical children.

With her fractured ribs swiftly and neatly healed and her other scrapes and burns and bruises consigned to memory—the Kaminoans even fixed the slight defect in her central montral, which was good of them, she grudgingly allowed—she was free to wander the unrestricted areas of the uncomfortably white and high-ceilinged medcenter, or keep up with her lightsaber drills along any handily empty circular corridor she could find.

What she *wasn't* allowed to do was contact Anakin with an update, or sit with Captain Rex and Sergeant Coric while they were in their bacta chambers, or visit with any other Torrent Company clones who'd been consigned here. And she hadn't been permitted to bid farewell to those who'd died in this sterile place despite the Kaminoans' best efforts to save them.

And that wasn't *fair.*

Being a refitted space station the medcenter had one observation platform, sited at the very top of its flat-topped spindle. It afforded a panoramic view of the Kaliida Nebula, and the beauty of that distracted her—at least for a little while—from darker thoughts.

Nala Shan's assistant, Topuc Ti, found her there a short time before lunch, local time.

"Padawan Ahsoka, it is permitted for you to receive a holo-transmission from your Jedi Master," the ethereal Kaminoan informed her. "Please follow me to the communications center."

Anakin. Leaping up from her cross-legged meditation, Ahsoka tried to calm her scudding heart. Did they have new orders? Had another battlefront opened up? Would she have to leave Rex and Coric and the others alone here to their uncertain fates? She didn't want to do that. The notion felt like a betrayal, like she'd be abandoning them. As though, like these Kaminoans, she didn't care.

"Come," said Topuc Ti, one elongated pale hand beckoning. "Your Jedi Master seemed most impatient."

"Sorry. Yes. I'm coming," she said, and scrambled after him.

"*Ahsoka!*" Anakin's hologram jittered and warped, the signal struggling to punch through the nebula's interference. "*What took you so long?*"

"Sorry," she said. "I was right up in the—"

"*Never mind. What's going on? You were supposed to give me regular updates!*"

Was it the poor transmission quality or was his face practically black with oil? "I tried, Master, only—" She looked around, but the two Kaminoans sharing the comm center were busy with their own conversations. Still, to be on the safe side she hunched over the holotransmitter and lowered her voice. "They wouldn't let me, Skyguy. They took my comlink and they won't give it back!"

"*It's probably procedure,*" said Anakin. "*How's Rex? How's Coric? Have you seen them? When will they be discharged?*"

"I don't know!" She was practically wailing, and she didn't care. "All I know is that Rex was hurt a lot worse than I realized. The last time I saw him he was talking, he didn't look like he was—" She couldn't say it. "But they won't let me see him, or the sergeant, and they won't tell me anything except they're not dead."

Anakin sighed. *"That's probably procedure, too. But if they're not dead—that's something. That's good, Ahsoka."*

He sounded so relieved. It made her feel better, knowing he was as sick with worry on Coruscant as she was here. It made him seem less far away.

"Skyguy, what's happening at home? Do we have another mission?"

"No. We're on furlough. Everyone's in a holding pattern until we eliminate all the computer viruses and figure out a way around Grievous's comm jammer. Word's just in the Seps have used it again. Twice."

Well, that wasn't good. Did that mean another influx of wounded clones?

"What happened?"

"Our forces disengaged."

She couldn't stifle her shocked gasp in time. "We *ran*?"

"No, Padawan, we executed a strategic retreat," Anakin retorted. Not even the poor-quality holotransmission could disguise his frustrated anger. *"You don't win wars with vainglorious last charges, Ahsoka. You fight smart or you waste lives. This was fighting smart."*

"Yes, Master," she said meekly. "Master, if you're on furlough, would it be all right if I stayed here until Rex and Coric wake up? They're still in bacta treatment. They could be swimming in gel for a few days yet."

"Are you sure you want to? It must be pretty boring there on your own."

"I don't mind. It's just—" She hesitated. "When they do wake up, they're going to be—I thought they might like—"

"*To see a friendly face?*" Mercurial as ever, Anakin smiled. "*Nice.*"

"I'm keeping up with my drills, Master. Lightsaber and general phsyical. I'm not being idle."

"*That must mean you're fighting fit again.*"

"Me? Oh, I'm fine. I just wish . . ."

Anakin smiled again. "*I know. Ahsoka, you—hold on.*" His head turned. "*What? Oh. Right. Thanks, Artoo. Tell him I'm coming.*" Looking at her again, he pulled a face. "*Sorry. I'm late for a dinner engagement. I'll call again tomorrow. But if anything happens in the meantime that I should know about, and you can't reach me, contact Master Yoda. If the Kaminoans have a problem with that, throw your weight around until you get what you need. Okay?*"

Her weight? She didn't have any weight. She was a *light*-weight. On the other hand, he was a heavyweight. As the Jedi who'd led the raid to save the medcenter, his name meant something around here. Up till now she hadn't used it, because that wasn't what a Jedi did.

But now he's given me permission. And I really, really want to sit with Rex and Coric.

She nodded. "Yes, Master."

Somewhere out of holotransmit range, Artoo whistled and beeped. He sounded almost frantic now.

"*I know, Artoo! I'll be right there,*" Anakin snapped. "*Ahsoka—*" He frowned. "*Can you get access to the Kaminoans' information database?*"

Their *database*? "I guess. Why?"

"*If you can, and if you can poke around in there without setting off any alarms—and if you can wipe your fingerprints off any searches you do—see what you can dig up about a planet called Lanteeb."*

"Lanteeb?" she said, baffled. Where was Lanteeb? She'd never heard of it. "All right. But—"

"Good. And keep it quiet. I don't want any alarm bells ringing on this, Ahsoka. You understand?"

Oh, stang. What is he getting mixed up in now? "Yes, Master. I understand."

"Good. I'll comm you tomorrow. Remember—low profile on this, Padawan. It stays strictly between us."

"Yes, Master. And Master—"

But he was gone.

Bemused, Ahsoka stared at the deactivated holotransmitter. *Lanteeb.* How very mystifying. And she'd look into it like Anakin asked. Soon. But first she was going to start throwing some of his weight around.

Hang on, Rex. Hang on, Sarge. I'll be right there.

EIGHT

OBI-WAN WAS A NEAT, UNFLAMBOYANT SPEEDER PILOT—WITH A long-standing habit of sticking to Coruscant's orthodox, tried-and-true traffic routes. Looking at him, recognizing the familiar signs of displeasure, Anakin cleared his throat.

Here goes nothing.

"Actually, if you wanted to make up a bit of time, I know this really good shortcut over to the—"

"No, thank you," said Obi-Wan, very clipped. "I've had enough of your shortcuts to last me a lifetime. And if you'd kept an eye on your chrono we wouldn't *need* a—"

"Hey, I said I was sorry!"

"Yes, yes, you're always apologetic afterward, Anakin, but—"

"Obi-Wan, I'm *sorry*." He grabbed hold of the speeder's passenger-side door as his former Master dropped them out of their crowded traffic lane into the cross-cutting corridor that would lead them away from the sprawling admin district and over to one of Coruscant's most expensive and exclusive residential enclaves. He knew the area intimately. Padmé's apartment block was hardly a stone's throw from Bail Organa's. They'd be there by now if he'd been flying the speeder. But Obi-Wan, tight-lipped at being kept waiting, had ignored his offer to take the controls.

Just like the good old days.

"I didn't mean to be late," he added, as the Temple dwindled into the distance behind them. "I got carried away."

That earned him a chilly glance. "Now, there's an excuse with a familiar ring to it."

Right. Time for some serious damage control before this turned into a miserable night. "Okay. Okay. You're annoyed. I get that. And you're entitled. No argument. I was careless."

Obi-Wan flicked him another glance then dropped them into the district's residents-and-visitors-only lane so they could follow the locals' leisurely, expensive speeders to their eventual destination. "Punctuality never was your strong suit, Anakin, but I was under the impression we'd sorted that out."

"Yeah, well, some habits are harder to break than others. I remember Mom used to—"

"What?" said Obi-Wan, his voice abruptly gentle.

Memories of his mother were always bittersweet. Lurking in his shadows was her last touch on his cheek. Echoes of her dying pain. But remembrances of his childhood eased that unhappiness. When he closed his eyes he could feel her arms warm and tight around him, keeping him safe.

But I didn't keep her safe. When she needed me most I—

With an effort he wrenched his thoughts from that unhelpful path. Like Padmé said, there was no point looking back. There was no way to undo past mistakes. His only choice was to find a way of living with them. But even with her help, that was proving a challenge.

Some things can't be forgiven. Some mistakes shouldn't be overlooked. I let myself get sidetracked. I—

"Anakin," said Obi-Wan. Not quite sympathy. Not quite a warning. Almost a question. Obi-Wan tried, but he'd never truly understand.

"Mom used to get just as mad at me for being late as you

ever did," he said, after a moment. "She never tanned me, but she was tempted once or twice. That's why I built Threepio. To say sorry. And to help her around our quarters when I wasn't there."

Irritation forgotten, Obi-Wan smiled. "And how often were you late to dinner, building that blasted droid?"

"Too often." Recalling his mother's exasperation with his chronic dawdling, how torn she'd get between aggravation and appreciation, he half laughed. "She used to say I'd be late for my own destiny."

"But you weren't," said Obi-Wan. "So I suppose there's that to be grateful for."

"Well, yeah. Except . . ."

Except the prophecy hasn't been fulfilled yet, has it? There's no balance in the Force. The dark side's winning. Planet by planet it's creeping across the galaxy. And there doesn't seem to be a thing I can do to stop it.

"Except?" prompted Obi-Wan.

He shrugged. "Nothing. Like I said, I'm really sorry."

"I know," said Obi-Wan, as he swung their speeder into an exit off the main residential traffic lane and threaded them along a narrower side lane. "Besides, I should be used to you by now."

At last they'd reached the residential sector's perimeter. Rising majestically on either side of them were the glossy apartment buildings that were home to some of the Republic's most wealthy and influential citizens. Business magnates. Celebrities. Politicians. Sports stars. Aristocrats and their heirs. Ambassadors from more than thirty prominent systems. It had made Padmé uncomfortable at first, moving into this exclusive community, but Naboo's Queen Jamillia and Supreme Chancellor Palpatine had insisted. Naboo's former Queen and current Senator was a high-risk Separatist target. She might not want to live

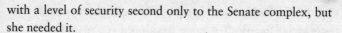

with a level of security second only to the Senate complex, but she needed it.

"Please, Padmé," he'd said, adding his voice to the chorus of common sense. Using her love for him against her without hesitation or compunction. "If you won't do it for yourself, then do it for me. Do you want me on the front lines worrying about you while I'm fighting to save the Republic?"

She'd given in, of course.

The security that meant so much to his peace of mind slowed their approach to Bail Organa's apartment block. As they traveled the designated visitors' lane they passed numerous discreet checkpoints designed to read and record the speeder's ID. Being Jedi they encountered no difficulties and eventually docked in the Senator's guest parking bay. The visitors' pedway was pass-coded. Armed with Organa's private key, Obi-Wan tapped in the sequence and they were whisked up to Level 300.

To Anakin's surprise, Organa answered his own front door. Dressed in casual trousers and an open-necked shirt, a glass of red wine in one hand and a kitchen towel tossed over his shoulder, he smiled when he saw them.

"There you are," he said, mildly reproving. "I was about to send out a search party. Come on in."

"Good evening, Bail," said Obi-Wan, entering the apartment's austerely elegant foyer. "My apologies for keeping you waiting."

Anakin followed him inside. "Please, Senator, don't blame Obi-Wan for our lateness. It's my fault. I'm not always the most reliable timekeeper."

Organa's smile widened as he closed the door. "So I've been told." He gestured. "This way. We're in the kitchen."

So he'd been *told*? Anakin let his accusing gaze slide sideways.

"Don't look at me," said Obi-Wan softly, as they made their way after Organa. "I've never mentioned you're incapable of—oh."

Oh was right.

They'd reached the kitchen. And standing behind a wide sweep of polished bench, knife in one hand, half-sliced tabba-root in the other, simply and beautifully clad in a sky-blue silk skirt and blouse . . . was Padmé.

ONE LOOK AT Anakin's face and Padmé knew he hadn't had the first inkling she was here. Shock, disbelief, pleasure, and alarm jolted through him in rapid succession, and that meant he hadn't sensed her presence—which wasn't like him at all. Considering her husband closely, she could see why. He was badly distracted and full of unease. His dearly familiar Jedi tunic looked just a little too loose on him, as though he'd recently lost some weight.

The war's wearing him down. He takes it so personally. He wants to fix everything that's broken. He thinks that's his job.

"Master Kenobi," she said, putting down the knife. She met his warily pleased gaze with every feeling masked. "It's good to see you again."

"And you, Senator," said Obi-Wan, at his most urbane. "I take it you're well?"

"Very well, thank you. You?"

"Oh, I'm fine. Thank you."

Ah, the commonplace banalities. Where would they be without them?

The urge to throw herself into Anakin's arms was almost overwhelming. But she wasn't a career politician for nothing. She offered her beloved an impersonally polite smile. "It's been awhile, Master Skywalker. How are you?"

Anakin swallowed. "Good. I'm good, milady."

"I asked Padmé to join us at the last minute," said Bail, wandering over to the impressive and immaculate kitchen's other bench. "She only got back a few hours ago—which is a stroke of luck for our team." He picked up the opened wine bottle, sloshed some more red into his glass, splashed a bit more into hers, then waggled the bottle at the Jedi. "I know you usually don't drink, but courtesy compels me to offer you a glass."

Obi-Wan sighed. "You really don't need to, Bail. We don't—"

"Thanks," said Anakin. "I'd love some."

Holding her breath, Padmé waited for Obi-Wan to object, to remonstrate, to tell Anakin no. Instead he raised an eyebrow. "I stand corrected. He'd love some."

Grinning, Bail took down another wineglass from the wall-mounted rack beside the small window above the sink. He half filled it with some of the finest vintage his family's vineyards had ever produced then handed it to Anakin.

"To your excellent health," he said, lifting his own glass in salute.

Anakin returned the gesture. "And yours, Senator."

"Why don't you make that *Bail*? This is my home, after all, not the Senate." Putting his glass down, Bail moved to the cooktop, where three saucepans were aromatically bubbling. He lifted the lid on the smallest one, grabbed a spoon and tasted. "Good. That's good." Then he glanced over his shoulder. "Well, gentlemen, pull up a chair. I'm pretty sure I can manage to cook and talk at the same time." He grinned again. "And you there, kitchen wench. Get chopping."

Padmé bobbed a sarcastic curtsy. "Sir, yes, sir."

"I've got chilled bolbi juice in the conservator, Obi-Wan, if you're determined to pass on the wine," Bail added, checking the contents of the next saucepan. "Second pressing."

Settling himself on one of the kitchen's tall breakfast bench stools, Obi-Wan nodded. "Perhaps later. Bail, are you sure there's nothing I can do to help?"

"*Ah!*" Bail said sharply, spoon raised. "Set one foot closer to this food, Obi-Wan, and I'll have you arrested."

"Bail," she said, surprised. Anakin was staring, too, wine-glass raised halfway to his lips.

"You don't understand," said Bail, replacing the lid on the third saucepan. "He may be a Jedi Master, but when it comes to cooking he's a dirty low-down spice smuggler. Trust me. I'm doing us all a *big* favor."

"Once," said Obi-Wan, over their laughter. "*Once* I had an unfortunate encounter with some minced maravia, two diced dipplis, and a pinch of Rodian spice."

"Once was enough," Bail retorted, emphatic. "You just—just sit there and be wise or something."

More laughter followed. The undercurrent of tension in the room eased. Padmé, quickly thin-slicing the rest of the tabba-root, risked a look at Obi-Wan. He smiled back, a shade wryly, sympathy in his eyes now. She lifted one shoulder in swift acknowledgment.

Not your fault. You weren't to know.

Anakin, declining a seat, wandered over to the kitchen's panoramic window. He sipped his wine and stared at the vista of bright lights and streaming traffic beyond the double-shielded transparisteel.

"So you've been away, Senator Ami—ah—Padmé?"

"On Chandrila, yes," she said, layering the tabba-root slices into a baking dish. "I wasn't due back for a few days yet, but there was an outbreak of Ralltiiri measles in the enclave where I was staying." Quickly she seasoned the vegetable with salt and pepper and chunks of the butter she'd cubed earlier. "Since there was nothing I could do to help, I came home."

"Well, Chandrila's loss is our gain," said Bail, ever the gallant. "Are you done with the tabba?"

"Obi-Wan, I heard about Kothlis," she said, handing Bail the dish so he could get it into the compression oven. "That was good work—and a lucky escape."

"In more ways than one," he said soberly. Like Anakin he looked fine-drawn. Weary. Not as awful as after Zigoola or even the battle on Geonosis, but . . .

The war's beating him down, too. It's so unfair.

"Didn't you tell me you don't believe in luck?" said Bail, teasing.

Obi-Wan gave him a half smile. "Yes, but too many more last-minute reprieves and I may be forced to change my stance." His wry amusement faded. "Speaking of Kothlis, Bail, what's the latest from the task force investigating Grievous's attack on Fleet communications?"

Bail closed the oven's door and hit the start button. "It's still investigating."

"They know we can't twiddle our thumbs indefinitely, right?" said Anakin, turning around. "They know we can't keep . . . *strategically retreating*?"

"Yes, Anakin, they know," said Bail. "And believe me, everyone on the team is working the problem as hard and as fast as they can. But if the Separatists weren't a formidable foe, well, this war would be done and dusted already, wouldn't it?"

"True," said Obi-Wan. "But Anakin's right. We can't afford to lose our offensive momentum. Dooku and Grievous are too skilled at taking advantage of our every stumble."

Padmé, watching Anakin while pretending to focus on cleaning up her section of the bench, saw his face tighten. She felt his tension reignite. *Oh, my love.*

"That may be the case," she said, "and I know we're here to talk serious business . . . but I suggest we leave that till after our meal, yes? Bail tells me you're both on furlough for a few days. So why don't we eat, drink, and be merry for a little while, before we tackle the Republic's latest crisis?"

A warm hand came to rest on her shoulder. *Bail.* Such a good, dear friend. "I second the motion," he said cheerfully. "Dinner's almost ready. Why don't you three go through to the dining room? I'll be with you in a few moments."

Walking with Obi-Wan, so aware of Anakin behind her, his burning gaze on the back of her neck, she glanced up. "Rumor has it you were hurt defending the spynet facility."

Obi-Wan sighed. "Is there no shred of idle gossip that escapes your attention?"

"None. Just tell me there weren't any lightsabers involved this time."

He smiled, faintly. "Anakin flew to the rescue before that became an issue."

Anakin. Oh, she wanted to turn and feast her eyes on him. She wanted to hold him and kiss away his cares. "Of course he did," she said, so terribly lighthearted. "I believe that's his job description, isn't it?"

"It is," said Anakin. "And I'm starting to think I should ask for a raise."

"By all means you can *ask*," said Obi-Wan, at his most droll.

Smiling, that undercurrent of tension eased again, they entered Bail's dining room. One entire wall was shielded transparisteel, offering breathtaking views across Coruscant's fantastically lit cityscape. Gleaming silver in the distance, stood the Senate Building, the symbol of everything they fought for and suffered to protect. As they crossed the lushly appointed room's threshold, soft music started playing from its hidden speakers.

She recognized it immediately: *The Spring Symphony* by celebrated Naboo composer Tofli Argala. She'd mentioned once, in passing, that Argala was her favorite of all Naboo's music makers. Trust Bail to remember. He knew she'd been homesick of late, having to miss little Pooja's birthday celebrations again. Of course she'd sent a gift and commed on the day, but a holographic aunt wasn't the same. Pooja deserved better.

"Milady . . . your seat . . ."

Anakin held out a dining chair for her. So old-fashioned. So sweet. So dangerously close to betraying himself. He'd recognized the music, too. There were questions in his eyes.

Oh my love. Don't be silly.

"Thank you," she said, sliding onto the chair. The dining table was already set, silverware and low, wide vases of fresh flowers on a filmy white cloth. Anakin's fingers brushed against her arms as he slid the chair into place. She shivered—and felt him shiver. She didn't dare look at Obi-Wan, already seated.

Does he feel it? He must. Oh Bail. What have you done?

As though summoned, Bail wheeled a cart into the dining room, laden with their meals and a fresh bottle of wine, clean glasses and a chilled pitcher of second-pressing bolbi juice. "Masters, milady, dinner is served," he said grandly. "Spiced tikrit, steamed yyla greens, herbed rice, and baked buttered tabba."

"What *are* you doing, Bail?" said Obi-Wan, staring. "What's happened to your server droids? Have they broken down? If they have, you should ask Anakin here to fix them for you. Provided, of course, you've nowhere urgent to be."

That had Anakin shaking his head. "You're not going to let that one go anytime soon, are you?"

"Certainly not," said Obi-Wan. "Only a fool discards a blaster with some charge left in it."

Warmed, Padmé watched her husband and his best friend

exchange wicked smiles. It helped her a great deal to know that the difficulties of the past were put behind them, that they'd found such solid ground upon which to stand as equals. She wasn't sure if Obi-Wan understood what he meant to Anakin. How much his regard mattered. How far Anakin would go to keep him safe.

And I can't tell him. But oh, he needs to know.

Feeling the weight of her troubled gaze Obi-Wan turned, quizzical. "Padmé?"

And now she could feel Anakin looking at her. She pretended distraction. "What? I'm sorry?"

"I thought—nothing," said Obi-Wan, with a swift smile. "Never mind."

Bail passed around the fragrantly steaming plates, poured the wine and juice, then took his own seat. He raised his glass, his eyes warm with affection. "To friends," he said quietly. "And an end to this blasted war."

"Friends," she and the Jedi echoed, and drank.

After that, while they ate, Bail regaled them with the latest gossip from the Senate. They laughed, they poked fun, they dredged up tales long-buried and worth retelling and for a couple of rare, precious hours the war receded. They were just four friends enjoying fine food and fine company . . . and pain was a dim memory from a long time ago.

"So," said BAIL AT LAST, nudging his dessert plate aside. "It's been fun, but all good things come to an end. I'm afraid the time has come for us to stop pretending we're not at war."

A moment's silence was followed by exchanged glances and soft sighs.

"Agreed," said Padmé, dropping her napkin on the table. "But let me clear the table first."

"That's all right, I'll take care of it after—"

She stood. "No, Bail. First rule of the kitchen: the cook never cleans."

"I'll help," said Obi-Wan, starting to rise.

"Actually—" Anakin leapt up. "Let me. My penance for making us late."

Another silence, awkward this time. Then Obi-Wan nodded. "All right."

"Come on into the study, Obi-Wan" said Bail easily, as though he hadn't noticed a thing. "I've got a little show-and-tell set up."

"We'll join you there shortly," she said, collecting their used silverware. "Don't start without us."

The moment Bail and Obi-Wan were gone, Anakin pulled her to him. He cradled her face in his hands and kissed her like a starving man. She felt her body turn liquid with heat, tasted wine and danger and sweet, sweet safety.

And then she pulled away.

"Anakin, *don't*," she whispered, heart pounding. "Are you mad? We can't—not with Obi-Wan here—he'll know, he'll sense—Anakin—"

"I don't care," he said roughly, his hands roaming her body now, setting her on fire wherever he touched. "I've missed you so much, Padmé. Every night I dream of you. It's been too long."

His scorching lips were a blessing and a torment. "I know, I know. But if you won't care I'll have to care for both of us," she said, and raised her hands to fend him off. "*Anakin*. Stop it. We'll be together again, just not here. Not tonight. Tomorrow. You're on furlough and I've got a couple of days to myself, too. We'll slip away somewhere. We'll make up for lost time. *Please*, Anakin. Be sensible."

She could feel what it cost him to pull back from the brink, and knew he felt the price she paid for not surrendering. Shuddering, she stood on tiptoe and touched her lips to his once, lightly.

"Come on. Let's clear the table, shall we? Like good little guests."

Stepping back, he ran an unsteady hand over his face. "I'll clear it," he muttered. "You go ahead. You're right. We can't give Obi-Wan reason to suspect anything."

Chilled by the thought of discovery, she left Anakin to play busboy and joined Bail and Obi-Wan in the plush apartment's study. A table had been pulled into the middle of the room, four chairs arranged around it. Bail and Obi-Wan were already seated, but not side by side, which meant she and Anakin wouldn't be sitting together. Was that deliberate, or simply coincidence? She couldn't read the answer in Obi-Wan's expression. On top of the desk a sleek holoprojector pulsed gently in readiness.

"Anakin's finishing up," she said, aware of Obi-Wan's discreet scrutiny. Fervently hoping the blush had faded from her cheeks, she fished in her skirt pocket and pulled out a data crystal. "Here's everything I could find on Lanteeb that I didn't already know."

Bail took the crystal. "Excellent."

"I'm surprised you know anything," said Obi-Wan. "I certainly don't. It seems Bail is making a career out of revealing the depths of my galactic ignorance."

"How can you say that, Obi-Wan?" said Bail, mock-wounded. "I know I'm a politician and therefore beyond hope, but—"

"I beg your pardon?" she said, taking refuge in their nonsense. Her lips were tingling, and where Anakin's desperate fingers had branded her, she burned. "Politics is an ancient and noble calling. Without politicians our societies would descend into anarchy and chaos."

"I thought they'd done that already," said Obi-Wan. "It certainly looked that way the last time I was in the Senate."

"I'm not claiming the system is perfect," she retorted. "Obviously there's room for improvement, when—"

"A great deal of room, yes. Enough room to house about a dozen Republic warships, I'd say," said Obi-Wan. "Possibly *two* dozen. Maybe three."

"Oh well, now you're just exaggerating," she said, annoyed. "For every one failed political initiative, I can name you *ten* that have succeeded beyond all expectations and—"

"What am I missing?" said Anakin, entering the study. "Anything exciting?"

Obi-Wan sat back, hands clasped loosely in his lap, his gaze sharpened again. "Not really. Senator Amidala was just berating me for my civic ignorance. Between her and Senator Organa I'm feeling positively wilted."

"But don't worry," said Bail drily. "He'll survive. And now that you're here we can get down to business." He patted the chair to his left. "Padmé?"

She sat beside him, and Anakin took the remaining chair next to Obi-Wan. He had himself perfectly under control. Bail dimmed the lights with a word, then activated the holoprojector. A three-dimensional galactic map bloomed above the imager. Bright red and oversized for emphasis, one planet in particular drew the eye.

"So that's Lanteeb," said Bail, in the brisk tone he used to brief the Senate and the Security Committee. "The only human-habitable planet in the Malor-Seventy-seven system. As you can see, it's located more or less equidistant between Rattatak and Bespin, right on the edge of the Outer Rim Territories and far off all the major hyperspace lanes."

"In other words," said Anakin, "smack bang in the middle of nowhere."

"Colloquial, but true," said Bail. "Topographically it's got three landmasses, only one of which is inhabited. There's a single spaceport facility in a small city that doubles as the planet's capital. Otherwise the Lanteebans live in widely scattered villages. They're farmers and miners. Nominally Lanteeb is part of the Republic but they have no Senate representation. Never asked for it. Until very recently, they were a self-governing independent settlement with no reason for anyone to give them a second look. Just another spinning rock in the unheeded wasteland of the Outer Rim."

Anakin leaned forward, elbows braced on his knees. "And now?"

Bail frowned. "Now they've been invaded, and are an unwilling member of the Confederacy of Independent Systems."

"Do we know why Dooku's taken over?"

"No, we do not. And *that's* what started my alarm bells ringing. There's no obvious reason why he would."

"Given its obscurity and distance from anything or anywhere of galactic importance," said Obi-Wan, stroking his beard, "how did we learn that the planet has fallen into Separatist hands?"

Bail looked pleased. "By happy accident. A gas freighter on the way to Ryoone had to drop out of hyperspace to make repairs. A faulty seal in one of the cargo holds. When they went to jump back they got a proximity warning and were forced to change hyperlane routes."

"They detected the Sep invasion fleet?"

"That's right."

"But how did that lead to the gas freighter's people working out Lanteeb was the fleet's target?" said Anakin. "And why would its captain care, anyway?"

"Don't tell me, let me guess," said Obi-Wan, smiling appreciatively. "It wasn't the captain. We had an agent on board."

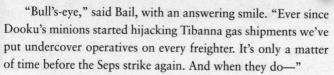

"Bull's-eye," said Bail, with an answering smile. "Ever since Dooku's minions started hijacking Tibanna gas shipments we've put undercover operatives on every freighter. It's only a matter of time before the Seps strike again. And when they do—"

"We'll have them." Obi-Wan nodded. "Good thinking."

Anakin was staring at Obi-Wan. "How come you know about this and I don't?"

Obi-Wan gave him the blandest of looks. "I expect you were late for the briefing, Anakin."

As Anakin made a face at Obi-Wan, and Obi-Wan indulged in a sly, teasing smile, Padmé cleared her throat loudly. "And this agent managed to ping a tracker after the Sep fleet?"

"She surely did," said Bail, briefly amused by the Jedi. And it picked up their comm chatter confirming the Lanteeb invasion."

"Which was when, exactly?" said Obi-Wan, sobering.

"During Dooku's last push through the Outer Rim. Which I'm guessing explains why no alarm bells rang any sooner. With four other systems falling at the same time, systems with actual strategic value, Lanteeb got lost in the excitement."

Anakin sat back, frowning. "It doesn't make sense. If the Council is right and Dooku's attempting to tighten a belt around the edge of the Republic to keep our forces hemmed in, then why take Lanteeb? The Seps having control of such an insignificant, out-of-the-way planet makes no difference to the galaxy's balance of power."

"Exactly," said Bail. "Which is why I asked you here. Between us we *have* to work out what his plan is—before he can implement it and make our already parlous situation worse."

"I concur," said Obi-Wan, staring at the holodisplay. "So. Lanteeb. Has it got *anything* worth stealing? What is its agricultural output?"

"Irrelevant. Any crops and stock they raise are for domestic consumption only."

"Then what do they mine?"

"Damotite. They've got the only known remaining, accessible supply."

"It's a mineral with a few limited applications," said Anakin, in answer to Obi-Wan's blank look. "A couple of manufacturing processes. Some industrial solvents. That's about it. It used to be a lot more widely used, but times change."

Obi-Wan gave him another look, one that plainly said: *Trust you to know.* "So it's this damotite that makes Lanteeb valuable?"

Padmé shook her head. "I don't see how. A few years ago, maybe, but not these days. The applications Anakin mentioned all have damotite-free alternatives and mostly they're preferred. Take Naboo, for instance. We still use damotite in our plasma-refining plants, but we're in the minority. When it comes to the plasma industry, damotite's been almost entirely superseded by trenomite. As soon as we finish upgrading our infrastructure we'll change over, too."

"Why?" said Obi-Wan. "Why reject damotite if it does the job?"

"Checks and balances," she explained. "While it's true damotite's a better product, trenomite's much easier to get hold of, which makes it cheaper. And it's more stable to work with. I'd say that within a year those of us who still aren't using trenomite will have made the transition. Damotite's about to become obsolete."

Obi-Wan stroked his beard again. "So there's no advantage to controlling its supply."

"None," said Bail.

"And when the demand for damotite finally dries up, Lanteeb will be even less relevant than it is now?"

"I'd say that's a safe bet."

"Great," said Anakin, disgruntled. "So we're back where we started, with no idea why Dooku would be interested in the place."

"The Jedi don't have any inside information?" said Bail, disappointed.

"None," said Obi-Wan.

"Hey—" Anakin turned to him. "You don't suppose—"

"No," said Obi-Wan. "It was the first thing I thought of. Alas, we've never found a potential Jedi on Lanteeb."

Anakin slumped. "Of course we've never. Because that would make this easy and why should anything ever be easy?"

"So the Jedi and Lanteeb have no history?" Padmé said, looking from him to Obi-Wan. "You've never been called in to sort out a local dispute? Or any kind of dispute where they were involved?"

"Not that I can find in the Archives," said Obi-Wan, shaking his head. "Our records are spectacularly silent on the subject."

"Ah . . ." Anakin was frowning again. "I don't suppose there's any chance that—"

"No," said Obi-Wan sharply. "Absolutely not. For one thing the Archives were thoroughly analyzed after what happened with Kamino, and for another I triple-checked. There's been *nothing* to do with Lanteeb deleted from our databases."

"I'm relieved to hear it," said Bail soberly. "One security breach of that magnitude is more than sufficient."

Lashes lowered, Padmé surreptitiously watched Anakin and Obi-Wan exchange discomfited looks. Aside from Dooku's defection, the tampering with their Archives was the greatest blow the Jedi had received in living memory. Anakin had fretted about it for weeks.

"Padmé . . ." Obi-Wan shifted in his chair. "What does

Naboo's business relationship with Lanteeb tell you about the planet?"

"And your extra research?" Bail added. "She researches everything. She's a one-woman galactic archive."

She could feel Anakin's sudden leaping tension, hearing that casual reminder of how well Bail knew her. *Be careful, Anakin. And don't be silly.* "Well, when I became Queen, it's true that I did make a point of learning what I could about Lanteeban society. Plasma refining is crucial to Naboo's economy—and it pays to know your friends as well as your enemies. But mainly what I turned up was a smattering of history, and I can't think of anything in Lanteeb's past that would prompt Dooku to invade it now."

Obi-Wan grimaced. "At this point I'll take whatever I can get."

"Okay." She hesitated, sifting through her memory. "Then sit back, children, and let me tell you a story."

NINE

"Lanteeb was colonized just over four hundred standard years ago, by humans from Rocantor," Padmé began. "Some kind of religious or political falling-out, I'm not sure exactly. You know what the Rocantori are like, they never tell you anything unless they're practically at blasterpoint. But I believe it's that cultural inheritance that explains Lanteeb's xenophobia."

Anakin looked at her. "Rocantor's xenophobic? Why?"

"About five hundred years ago the humans on Rocantor were infected by a plague that jumped the species barrier from the Rocanar—the planet's original sentient inhabitants. There was massive loss of life. When the last of the funeral pyres stopped burning, the surviving Rocantor humans took over. Banned all sentient nonhumans from the planet."

Anakin thought about that for a moment. "And what happened to the Rocanar who didn't die in the plague?"

She winced. *Oh dear. He's not going to like this.* "They were sold into slavery."

"Which is indeed tragic," said Obi-Wan, quickly, "but hardly germane to the topic at hand."

Though Anakin flicked him a dark glance, he didn't push the matter. "So you're saying that because they originally came from

Rocantor, the humans of Lanteeb won't have anything to do with nonhumans?"

"Oh, they'll take their credits," she said, not bothering to sweeten her cynicism. "But only from a distance. Nonhumans aren't permitted to set foot on Lanteeban soil or have any kind of financial or business interests there. Back when damotite was highly sought after and valuable, some offworld companies did have close industry ties to Lanteeb's government—if they met the species restrictions."

"That goes a long way in explaining why they weren't interested in seeking official Senate standing," said Bail. "All those pesky nonhumans to deal with."

"The Lanteebans' prejudices are culturally intriguing, if unfortunate," said Obi-Wan. "But they don't shed any light on why Dooku wanted to invade."

"True," Bail admitted. "But at least they tell us this much— if we want to solve the puzzle of his annexation of the planet, we'll need to rely on human investigators. Even if a nonhuman made it out of the spaceport they'd attract too much attention."

Obi-Wan drummed his fingers on the arm of his chair. "You're thinking of infiltration? An undercover mission?"

"Risky, I know," said Bail, his eyes grim. "But it's looking more and more likely that we won't have a choice." His gaze shifted. "Can you think of anything else useful, Padmé?"

No. She was too busy being horrified by wild speculation that maybe it would be *Anakin* who—"Well," she said, throttling fear, "with the reduced demand for damotite, Lanteeb's been suffering economically for a few years now. Despite their ingrained xenophobia some Lanteebans have grown desperate enough to go looking for work elsewhere in the Republic. From what I can tell, they mainly hire themselves out as unskilled labor, although we did have a Lanteeban engineer, briefly. His

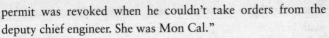

permit was revoked when he couldn't take orders from the deputy chief engineer. She was Mon Cal."

Bail was frowning. "So the planet's impoverished, and its population is panicking. I can't imagine why Dooku didn't snap it up sooner. Obi-Wan, are you *sure* you didn't miss anything in the Jedi Archives?"

"Quite sure."

Muttering under his breath, Bail switched off the holoprojector then ordered the study lights up again. "Okay. Let's get a little crazy, shall we? Let's just—start tossing ideas into the ring. Doesn't matter how ridiculous they sound. I don't care. There's something we're not seeing. Some connection we've missed. There *has* to be a reason Dooku would expend time, energy, and resources on taking over this pointless planet."

But they couldn't come up with a single reasonable explanation. Couldn't even cobble together an *un*reasonable hypothesis, despite more than half an hour's intensive brainstorming.

"This is ridiculous," said Bail, returning from the kitchen with four mugs of hot caf on a tray. "Among us we have more knowledge, more experience, more—"

"That's me," said Anakin, clapping his hand to his tunic pocket as the buzz of a comlink interrupted. "Sorry. It's probably Ahsoka with news about our wounded clones. Do you mind?"

"Not at all," said Bail, with perfect courtesy. "Answer it. I hope the news is good."

Hiding anxiety, not risking a glance at Obi-Wan, Padmé watched Anakin as he slid out of the chair and wandered toward the study window, thumbing the comlink to active. His face was tight again, as though he was bracing himself for the worst.

"Skywalker."

"*Master? It's me.*" Ahsoka's thin, distant voice was slightly distorted. *"I can hardly hear you. And how come I can't see you?"*

Finished handing around the steaming mugs, Bail put aside the emptied tray. "Anakin. If it's not a private conversation you can plug your comlink in to the holoprojector. It's got a secure comm panel with a boosted signal capacity."

"Thanks," said Anakin. "I'll do that."

After a bit of fiddling, Ahsoka's slight figure wavered on the holopad. *"Sorry, Master. Am I interrupting something?"*

"It doesn't matter," said Anakin, seated again and ignoring the mug Bail had left on the arm of his chair. "What's going on?"

"I've seen Rex and Sergeant Coric. They're not awake yet, but they look okay." The Padawan winced. *"Sort of. And I got to visit with some of the other troops, too. Nala Shan says everyone who's going to die has died, so—that's good news."*

Heedless of his audience, Anakin covered his face with his left hand—his organic hand—just for a moment. Then he let it drop. His eyes were bright. "That's *great* news, Ahsoka."

"And I managed to dig up something on Lanteeb," Ahsoka added, clearly very pleased with herself. *"Do you want to hear it now? I'm alone. It's safe to talk."*

Obi-Wan sat up, frowning. "Anakin?"

"Hold on, Padawan," said Anakin, raising a finger at hologram Ahsoka. "I'm sending you dark for a minute." And he flicked the holoprojector to standby.

Bail was looking equally displeased, all his warm geniality frozen. "Master Skywalker, I was under the impression you appreciated the sensitivity of this matter. Given that there are Separatist agents spread throughout the Republic, I didn't want—"

"Don't you think of questioning Ahsoka's loyalty, Senator," said Anakin. "I trust her with my life." He turned to Obi-Wan.

"And you can't talk, either. If Dex wasn't offworld we both know he'd be sniffing out whatever he could find on Lanteeb for you."

"That's true, Bail," Obi-Wan admitted. "I did try to enlist Dex's help."

Now Bail was staring daggers at Obi-Wan. "What? Obi-Wan, I thought—"

"Sorry," said Obi-Wan, his expression rueful. "But like Ahsoka, Dex's loyalty is beyond question. And he has ways of finding things out that make our Republic Intelligence look like amateur hour. Believe me, it's a great pity he's not here."

Bail wasn't much appeased. Leaning sideways, Padmé touched her fingertips to his arm. "Either you trust their judgment or you don't, Bail. And we know which one it is."

"Fine," said Bail tightly. "We'll take this Padawan's loyalty as a given. But what about her competence? She's practically a child."

"A child who saved my life on Kothlis," said Obi-Wan, gently stern. "And who's acquitted herself with a maturity far beyond her years on many other occasions. Besides, no Jedi is ever truly a child. Bail, it's all right."

And there it was. Beneath the teasing and the laughter and the spirited debates, beneath the flashes of hot temper when the debates got serious, was the bond that Zigoola had forged between Obi-Wan Kenobi and Bail Organa. Padmé, watching Anakin watch them, saw him stifle surprise and reassess, in a heartbeat, the parameters of this odd friendship.

Not quite relaxing, Bail nodded. "Fine."

With a glance at Anakin, his caf forgotten, Obi-Wan flipped the holoprojector off standby. "Padawan, this is Master Kenobi. What is it you've discovered about Lanteeb? And where did you find the information?"

"*Master Kenobi!*" Ahsoka's wavering image snapped to attention. "*Ah—well—*" She looked over her shoulder. "*I found it in the medcenter's billing records,*" she said, her voice lowered.

"The billing records?" Anakin echoed. "What made you look in there?"

"*Well, Master, I looked everywhere else that I could get into. And then, I don't know, it occurred to me to look in the financial files. I was just trying to be thorough, like you taught me.*"

Anakin was smiling. "Nice to know you pay attention now and then, Ahsoka. What did you find?"

"*A single reference to Lanteeb. From just over three standard months ago,*" said Ahsoka, still nearly whispering. "*Two genetically coded antidotes to damotite poisoning, whatever that is. I looked it up in the medical database but I couldn't find anything. The Kaminoans didn't make a huge amount of the stuff but it still cost a fortune.*"

"Damotite *poisoning?*" said Obi-Wan. "Padmé—" He looked over at her. "To your knowledge is damotite toxic? Do your people have to take special precautions when handling it?"

She shook her head. "No. But the damotite we work with is refined. I suppose it could be toxic in its unrefined state." She felt her pulse rate pick up. Felt a crawling sensation on the back of her neck. *Something nasty's brewing.* "Here's what I do know, though. If you were looking for protection on a cellular level, your smart first choice would be the Kaminoans. They're at the forefront of genetic engineering and experimental medicine."

"I wonder . . . ?" Bail said thoughtfully. "Is there any way of using those genetic codes to backtrack? If we can identify the antidotes' recipients, we might be able to find them—or at least use their identities to get some idea of what's going on."

"Possibly," said Obi-Wan. "It's a good idea. Ahsoka—"

"*I'm sorry, Master,*" said Anakin's apprentice. "*The actual genetic information wasn't listed on the invoice. I did try to find it but I couldn't get past the Kaminoan's security blocks.*"

"Not your fault, Padawan," said Obi-Wan. "It's good you thought to try. Who ordered the antidote?"

"*Sorry again, Master. No names were used. Only reference numbers.*"

"What about the delivery address?" said Anakin.

"*No,*" Ahsoka said, apologetic. "*That part of the invoice was left blank.*"

"Blast," said Obi-Wan, and tugged at his beard. "I'm beginning to find these dead ends tedious."

"Someone's being very careful," said Bail, fingers drumming again. "And organized, given that these antidotes were ordered three months ago. I suppose there's a chance this is all merely co-incidence, but—"

"There's no such thing as coincidence," said Anakin. "Just connections we haven't made yet."

Bail considered him for a moment. "That was very . . . Jedi . . . of you. But if I could bring us back to a more practical consideration? Has damotite ever been used in any weapons ap-plications?"

"Not that I know."

"Padmé?"

"Sorry. I don't know, either. And even with its plasma-refining usage it was never listed as an active combustible or cat-alyst."

Bail groaned. "So what does this mean? We need to do a crash course in damotite?"

Anakin leaned into the compact holoprojector's transmis-sion field. "Ahsoka—did you learn anything else?"

"*I'm afraid not, Master. But I could keep looking. Do you want me to ask Nala Shan about this damotite poi—*"

"No!" said Anakin, Obi-Wan, and Bail in an alarmed chorus.

Ahsoka jumped. "*All right. Sorry. I was only wondering,*" she said, aggrieved.

"Not a word to anyone about this, Padawan," Anakin ordered. "Not even Rex, when he wakes up. Secrecy is paramount. Are you sure nobody can trace where you were poking around the medcenter's databases?"

"*I'm positive.*"

"Be careful, Padawan," said Obi-Wan. "This isn't the time for overconfidence."

Hand pressed to her heart, Ahsoka stared earnestly into her own holoprojector. "*I promise, Master Kenobi. I've always been good with computers.*"

"Well done, Ahsoka," said Anakin. "Now, how do you feel about staying at the Shoals a few days more?"

"*Of course I'll stay, Master,*" Ahsoka said promptly. "*You won't get me out of here with a proton torpedo. Not without Rex and Coric and as many Torrent Company men as the Kaminoans will let go.*"

He'd been so reluctant to accept the little Togruta as his charge, convinced that he didn't need, didn't want, a Padawan. But looking at Anakin's face, Padmé saw his pride in the child. Saw genuine affection, and relief that he had someone to trust with his men.

He's grown. He's changing—and it's happening without me. Every time I see him he's more and more the man I always knew he could be. Would be. And I'm not a part of it.

That hurt.

"I'll be in touch, Ahsoka," said Anakin, and ended the transmission.

Obi-Wan stirred. "What made you think to ask Ahsoka to check the Kaminoans' database?"

"I don't know," said Anakin, his comlink tucked back inside his tunic. "A hunch."

That made Bail smile, despite the worry in his eyes. "So you don't believe in coincidence but you'll place your faith in a hunch?"

"I've learned to trust my instincts, yes," said Anakin, meeting his gaze steadily. "So far they've never let me down."

"And what are your instincts telling you about your Padawan's discovery?"

Anakin grimaced. "That we're in deep poodoo."

A glum silence descended as they sat around the deactivated holoprojector with their gazes lowered, contemplating the baffling situation.

At last, Padmé looked up. "The only reason someone would need an antidote to a substance that under normal circumstances can be handled safely is if something's been done to it to make it *un*safe." She frowned. "Damotite poisoning. A possibly deadly medical condition caused by a reaction to a rare mineral found nowhere else but on Lanteeb, which has just been taken over by Separatist forces. A condition that can only be treated by specifically targeted genetic manipulation, that isn't listed in the database of the most scientifically and medically sophisticated culture we know." She tapped a finger to her lips. Looked at her companions, these three extraordinary men. "*Stang*. Are you thinking what I'm thinking?"

"A bioweapon," said Obi-Wan, not even trying to hide his revulsion. "Dooku wants to turn Lanteeb's damotite into some kind of bioweapon."

• • •

WITH BAIL ORGANA'S BLESSING they took their concerns to Yoda, in private.

After listening without comment the ancient Jedi lapsed into silence, cross-legged on the meditation pad in his chamber. Small hands fisted on his knees, chin pressed into his chest, his eyes closed, he was sunk so deep within the Force he'd almost vanished.

With an effort Anakin controlled his impatience. They had to be here. Of course they did. He *wanted* to be here. Whatever Dooku was up to on Lanteeb, he wanted to finish it. To finish *him*.

I just want to be with Padmé more. At least I do tonight.

A few brief, paltry kisses after so long apart, it wasn't enough. It was a single sip of water offered to a man dying of thirst. He hungered for her, brutally.

Kneeling beside him, Obi-Wan stirred.

Stop it. Stop thinking about her before you ruin everything, you idiot.

Yoda opened his eyes. "A darkness there is surrounding this planet Lanteeb. Fear, I sense. Great fear and pain. Now and to come. Right you were to bring this to my attention."

"Have you any idea what's going on there, Master?" asked Obi-Wan. "Do you know anything about this mineral damotite and how it might be corrupted into a weapon?"

"Familiar with damotite I am not," said Yoda. "Heard of it I have, but in passing only. Certain are you, Master Kenobi, that a weapon is the danger we face?"

"Not certain, no," said Obi-Wan. "But we couldn't come up with a more plausible explanation for why Dooku would have taken control of such a negligible planet. Or why the Kaminoans would manufacture a genetically coded antidote to this mineral."

"Hmm." Yoda stroked his chin. "Given these facts not unreasonable is your conclusion. Already have we seen the Separatists' eagerness to develop bigger and more deadly tools of destruction. Expect their hunger for slaughter to diminish we should not."

"Whatever Dooku's planning, it's obviously got the potential to be devastating," said Anakin. "We have to shut him down fast."

"Agreed," said Yoda, eyes narrowing. "But send a battle group to Lanteeb we cannot. Already precious resources are diverted to Kothlis. Impossible it is to divert more. Not until revealed the truth of Lanteeb is."

"Then let us reveal it, Master Yoda," said Obi-Wan quietly. "Send Anakin and me to investigate. If we're right and Dooku's developing some kind of catastrophic weapon, then either we can destroy it in place or, if that's not possible, you can authorize a full military strike to take back the planet."

Yoda hopped off his meditation mat, summoned his gimer stick to his hand, and began pacing, head lowered again.

"A dangerous mission you propose, Obi-Wan," he said at last. "And intelligence agents you and young Skywalker are not." A sharp glance. "Suggest this course of action does Senator Organa?"

"Not specifically," said Obi-Wan, with care. "But I doubt he'd have mentioned this to me in the first place if he wasn't hoping for Jedi assistance."

Yoda snorted. "Devious, that is. A politician's move."

As Obi-Wan opened his mouth to argue, Anakin caught his eye. Shook his head, just a little. *Let me. He might call you biased.* "I don't think the Senator was being devious, Master. Given his relationship with Obi-Wan, and the potential seriousness of this situation, it's not surprising he'd reach out to him. Especially since he has no hard proof. Only . . . a hunch."

"Hmmm," said Yoda, eyes narrowed almost to closing.

"Head of Republic Security he is. Access to many agents he has. Use Jedi for this investigation he need not."

"Master, I understand your reservations," said Obi-Wan. "But the Senator can't use regular agents for this mission. Too much is unknown and uncertain. Our Jedi abilities might be all that can make the difference between success and failure."

Yoda stopped his pacing and stared at them, his gaze fiercely intent. "But as Jedi to Lanteeb you could not travel. False identities you would need. Behind enemy lines you would be, Obi-Wan. *Spies.* More dangerous than facing a droid army that is."

Exchanging glances with Obi-Wan, Anakin nodded. "We're aware of that, Master. And we're also painfully aware that we're neither of us trained in subterfuge the way regular Republic Intel agents are. But when it's something this important? We can play our parts convincingly."

Or I can, anyway. I've had a lot of practice at subterfuge since I got married.

"Sure of yourself you are, young Skywalker," said Yoda, and started pacing again. "But not so sure am I. Thanks to the HoloNet well-known your faces are."

"As far out as Lanteeb?" said Obi-Wan, skeptical. "Master Yoda, I doubt it."

Yoda rapped his gimer stick to the marble floor. "Separatist territory is Lanteeb now! Known to every Separatist you are. Eager to capture you and Anakin is Dooku. If care for your own safety you will not, care for it *I* must."

What? Anakin felt his temper flare. "Then set us to teaching younglings for the duration of this conflict, Master Yoda. Because that's the only way you'll keep us safe."

"Anakin . . ." Obi-Wan murmured, and touched a hand to his arm. "Master, if I thought this could be handled without our involvement, I wouldn't ask you to send us. But I don't. And Anakin is right. There is no safe place in a war."

Temper still simmering, Anakin glowered at Yoda. "I don't want special treatment because I'm supposed to be the Jedi's *Chosen One*. Anyway, if I do have this great destiny then I'm not going to be killed on Lanteeb, am I?"

Yoda's stare chilled. He met it defiantly, daring the old Jedi to deny such an obvious truth. Beside him, Obi-Wan held his disapproving breath.

"Pleased by this request I am not," Yoda said at last. "But grant it I will. Arrange your false identities Senator Organa and the Special Operations Brigade can, and a way onto this planet help you devise. If an unregistered ship you require, supply that the Jedi Council will. Secret will be your mission and where-abouts." He sighed. "Authorized you are to leave when finished are your preparations. Dooku's weapon, if there is a weapon, you must destroy."

Obi-Wan bowed. "We will, Master Yoda."

As THEY HEADED FOR the transport that would take them back to the Temple's public areas, Anakin looked sideways. "So, Master Kenobi, what now?"

Obi-Wan stifled a yawn. "It's late. I'll contact Bail and let him know what we need, then I think I'll turn in. You should get some rest, too. There's every chance this mission will prove—hectic."

Padmé. "Fine," he said, working hard to sound casual. "First thing tomorrow we should pick out a suitable ship from the transport pool. Reserve it, just in case someone else needs one like it and we miss out on the perfect disguise."

"Yes. All right. Anakin—" Aside from themselves the corri-dor was empty. Obi-Wan swung around in front of him then stopped, his expression coolly serious. "Look. I know it unset-tled you, seeing Padmé tonight. But it's happened before and it'll happen again. Like it or not she gets herself *involved* in things. She's never going to be a stay-at-home Senator. So it's up to you to find some way of dealing with your feelings when the two of you cross paths."

With an effort Anakin kept himself relaxed. "I am dealing with them."

"Yes, well, by dealing with them I *don't* mean being rude to Master Yoda."

He didn't need Padmé as an excuse to snipe at Yoda. "I wasn't rude. I told him what I thought."

"Yes, you did," retorted Obi-Wan. "Rudely!"

"Obi-Wan—" Exasperated, he half turned away. "It doesn't bother you when he says we're not up for the job?"

"Anakin—" Now it was Obi-Wan reaching for his self-control. "That isn't what he said. He's concerned—and he has a point. We *aren't* trained spies. We spend our lives walking through the Republic's front door, not—not sneaking in around the back when nobody's looking."

"Are you having second thoughts?"

Obi-Wan folded his arms. "No. It's just—I have a very bad feeling about Lanteeb."

"Which is why it's going to take us to deal with the problem," Anakin said. And then he sighed. "Look—Obi-Wan—handling tricky situations is what we do. You know that, and so does Master Yoda. So why is he making a fuss about this? And why are you defending him?"

Instead of answering, Obi-Wan headed again for the transport.

Anakin stared after him. "Oh—come *on*. Not you, too?"

"I don't know what you're talking about," Obi-Wan muttered.

Catching up to his friend in the lobby, Anakin slapped a

transport call-button. "Yeah. Right. You think I need to be protected because of the prophecy. Don't you?"

Obi-Wan glared. "If I thought that, Anakin, would I want
you with me on this mission? Would I be happy to see you risking yourself day in and day out on the front lines?"

"So you don't believe in it?"

"I didn't say that." Shaking his head, Obi-Wan stared at the
floor. "Qui-Gon believed in it. And I believed in him. And there's
no escaping the fact you're the most gifted Jedi the Temple has
ever seen." He looked up. "So *if* Yoda's reluctant to risk you,
Anakin, it's not on a whim. He has good reason."

"And like I said. *If* the prophecy's true I won't die on
Lanteeb."

Obi-Wan raised an eyebrow. "Then I suppose we must hope
the prophecy's true."

Their transport arrived. Obi-Wan directed it to the comm
center, then on to the accommodation sector. Said nothing more
until they reached the Temple's sprawling communications hub.

"So. Sleep well," he said, as the transport doors swished
open. "And I'll see you at breakfast."

Anakin nodded. "Breakfast it is. But not too early. I want to
enjoy a comfortable bed for as long as I can." *And make up for
the time I lost with Padmé by being late.* "Say—nine?"

"If you insist," said Obi-Wan, with the hint of a smile.
"Lazybones."

As the doors closed again and the conveyor zipped away, he
breathed a sigh of relief. Of dry-mouthed anticipation.

Padmé.

"Belay destination," he ordered. "Transport pool."

There was guilt, somewhere. Buried deep. Not weeping too
hard. He'd be leaving Coruscant within the next two or three
days. This might be his only night with her, their only chance to

be together in this cruelly short visit home. After tonight the mission would come first. And at any moment she could get called away.

And me? I could die. As long as we're fighting Dooku and his Separatists, every sunrise could be my last. Sleep in this place? Alone? Sorry, Obi-Wan. No way.

"VERY WELL," SAID BAIL. "*I'll get on this immediately. You should have everything you need—identification chips, flight plan, falsified backgrounds—within two days. Sooner if we're lucky. Are you sure you're right for transportation?*"

Sealed into a private comm cubicle, Obi-Wan nodded. "Yes. And we'll take care of our clothing requirements, too. There'll need to be some unique modifications."

"*Fine.*"

They were talking via comm panel, not holodisplay. Bail's face on the bright, flat screen was grave. Almost . . . uncertain.

"Is everything all right?"

Bail shrugged. "*Sure. Why wouldn't it be? You're only flying into a gundark's nest on my say-so and not much else.*"

Though he wasn't altogether comfortable himself, Obi-Wan smiled. "Well. It wouldn't be the first time."

"*Which might explain my trepidation,*" Bail said, unsmiling. "*I suppose I should be flattered that a Jedi would ask 'how high' when I say 'jump,' but—*"

"Bail," he said sharply. "Senator or not, you don't have the power to make the Jedi do anything we don't wish to do. I told you. Yoda has said we should look into this. That should be enough for you."

"*You and Anakin coming back in one piece will be enough for me,*" Bail retorted. "*Anything less than that and—*" He blew out a hard breath. *"Seriously, Obi-Wan. I can stop this before it starts. If you have any doubts, any kind of second thoughts— say the word and this mission is scrubbed."*

He was a good man. A good friend. "Bail, if you're asking whether or not I trust your instincts, the answer is yes. I trust them. I trust *you*. Anakin and I will be fine. We shall discover what Dooku's up to on Lanteeb and we shall thwart him and then we shall come home again. You have my word."

"And I'll hold you fast to it, Master Jedi," said Bail, not quite smiling. *"All right. I think that's it. I'll comm you when it's time for your intel briefing. Good night. Sleep well."*

"You, too," he said, though he suspected that neither of them would.

Entering the guest accommodation wing, nodding an absentminded acknowledgment to someone's greeting, Obi-Wan hesitated. Probably he shouldn't. He needed to stay focused, and she was unwell. She didn't need his burdens, she had too many of her own.

But it had been so good to see her again.

Motionless in the airy, softly lit antechamber, he closed his eyes. Reached out through the Force, delicately questing.

Taria?

Yes. There she was. Not on this floor, but close by. One level down, where the Jedi who either lived permanently in the Temple or who were here for longer than a few days made their home.

Taria?

Nothing. And then, a ripple of surprise. Cautious pleasure . . . and a definite feeling of welcome.

The door to her room slid open as he approached. He entered, and it closed softly behind him. The small chamber's lights were dimmed, its air warm. Wrapped in a vibrant blue

robe, she sat cross-legged on the meditation pad she'd placed between the plain, narrow bed and the other wall. Her blue-green
hair, freed from its braid, spread shimmering over her shoulders
and down her back like a waterfall caught out of time. Her
tawny gold eyes were too bright.

"Taria," he said, feeling fear and anger heat his blood. "You
overdid it in class today. I told you to slow down. Why don't
you listen? Your remisssion is *precarious*."

She laughed. "Am I your Padawan now Obi-Wan?"

"It's not funny," he said, unmollified. "I wish you *were* my
Padawan. Then I could make you mind me."

"As Anakin minded you?" she mocked. "Tell me again how
that went?" Then she relented. Leaned over and patted the bed.
"Don't stand there cross at me. Sit down."

He perched on the edge of the thin mattress, shamefully
close to sulking. Swiveling to face him, she reached out and
pressed her cool hand to his forehead. "You're so sad," she murmured. "So weary. Deep down in your bones. This blasted
war . . ." She stroked his hair, fingers skimming. "And now
you're leaving again. Where are you going?"

Of course she'd sense it. He let his eyes drift closed. How
strange it felt, to be touched with tenderness. His life was so brutal now. Loud and bloody and full of pain.

"I can't say," he whispered. "I would if—"

"No," she said. "It's all right. Can you say when?"

Her hand moved without ceasing. Her touch woke memory;
stirred sorrow. "Soon."

"You and Anakin?"

"Yes."

"You're frightened."

Never ever did he pretend with Taria. "A little."

Her small chamber smelled sweet. So did she. Her palm

came to rest against his cheek. He felt himself lean into it, felt something inside him give . . . or break.

"Sleep," she said. "I'll watch over you. You'll be safe. No bad dreams."

He opened his eyes. "No. You're not well. I can't take your bed."

"Obi-Wan . . ." Her generous lips curved in a wry smile. "No matter where you are tonight, I won't be sleeping."

Because she never ever pretended with him, either, not when it counted, she let him feel her encroaching disease. Took his face between her hands and pressed her thumbtips to his closed eyes, making sure his tears could not fall.

"It's not your fault. You didn't do this. Sleep."

So he pulled off his boots and eased out of his clothing and crawled exhausted into her bed. She sat beside him on her meditation pad, breathing gently, then sang to him until he slept.

In the morning, when he woke, he was alone.

TEN

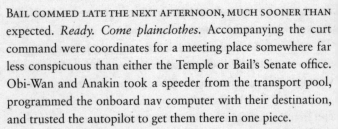

BAIL COMMED LATE THE NEXT AFTERNOON, MUCH SOONER THAN expected. *Ready. Come plainclothes.* Accompanying the curt command were coordinates for a meeting place somewhere far less conspicuous than either the Temple or Bail's Senate office. Obi-Wan and Anakin took a speeder from the transport pool, programmed the onboard nav computer with their destination, and trusted the autopilot to get them there in one piece.

It took almost an hour. In the end, *there* proved to be a dingy, tenantless office block on the outskirts of the run-down and poorly populated Bahrin industrial sector.

"Gentlemen," said the thin, nondescript woman in the building's open ground-floor doorway. She was dressed in the shabbiest gray tunic and trousers, and her gray hair was scraped back from her angular, unadorned face in an ugly rat's tail. "Follow me."

Obi-Wan exchanged a look with Anakin, who nodded. There was something unsettling about the woman's demeanor. But if Bail trusted her . . .

She led them to an equally dingy upstairs office, where Bail was waiting for them. Clad in a baggily ill-fitting brown suit and scuffed, badly worn shoes, with his hair greased down and his fingernails dirty, he looked like he'd be turned away from his own apartment complex. Beneath the carefully applied grunge he was hollow-eyed with weariness, as though he'd worked through the night and still hadn't stopped. Which had to be the case, surely, for him to have achieved such swift results.

"Nice outfits," he greeted them, turning away from the partially boarded window with the faintest shadow of a smile. "Very un-Jedi."

Obi-Wan looked down at his threadbare woolen overshirt and patched trousers. "So they're plain enough for you?"

"That was my stipulation," said the still-unidentified woman, closing the paint-peeled office door behind her. "This isn't an area known for its Jedi visitors."

"I sensed that," said Anakin, pulling his lightsaber from inside his own faded jacket and laying it on the room's battered conference table.

Bail glanced from Anakin to the nondescript woman. A perceptive man, he could feel the undercurrent of tension humming between them. "Master Kenobi, Master Skywalker, this is Agent Varrak from the Special Operations Brigade," he said, deliberately pleasant. "She's taking point on the Lanteeb mission. Agent Varrak, Masters Kenobi and Skywalker. Two of the best Jedi in the Republic."

"Yes, Senator," said Agent Varrak with a brisk nod. "I know who they are. And I'm aware of their reputations and their exploits."

The woman was almost overtly hostile, her distaste for the Jedi scraping his nerves—and Anakin's—unpleasantly. Puzzled, Obi-Wan looked at Bail. *Was it something we said?* But before Bail could diplomatically intercede, Anakin took a step sideways, away from the conference table. Opened space between himself and the agent. His face was calm, his eyes hotly focused.

"And when you say *aware* . . . ?"

Obi-Wan flicked a warning glance at Bail. Raised his hand, just a little. *I've got this.* "It's a pleasure to meet you, Agent Varrak. Your assistance with this mission is greatly appreciated, by us and the Jedi Council."

Pinch-lipped, the agent nodded again. "We all serve the Republic, Master Kenobi."

"And your service might well help to avert disaster. Thank you."

He held the woman's gaze, showing her nothing but sincerity, feeling Anakin's resigned annoyance. For all his efforts, his former Padawan never had developed a taste for pouring honey on a sour situation. Anakin tended to prefer a—blunter—approach.

Well, not this time, my young friend. Not when we need her more than she needs us.

Agent Varrak relaxed, fractionally. The smallest hint of retreat. "You're welcome."

He smiled. "Are we to understand you've prepared the documentation we'll require to infiltrate Lanteeb?"

"I have." She reached beneath the conference table and retrieved a plain, inconspicuous workcase. "Perhaps we might be seated and get this taken care of? I'm sure we're all busy, with other places to be." She glanced sideways. "Senator?"

"Yes, of course," said Bail, taking the nearest cracked-leather chair. "Master Kenobi, Master Skywalker, Agent Varrak is an identification specialist," he added as they sat. "You can be sure your new personas will withstand the most rigorous Separatist scrutiny."

"They'd better," Anakin muttered. "Seeing as how our lives are going to depend on them."

Agent Varrak looked at him, dispassionate. "Your lives are perfectly safe with me. This isn't my first nerf muster, Teel Markl."

Anakin came close to sneering. "Catchy name."

Uncomfortably aware of Bail's dismay, Obi-Wan tugged at his tunic. Snared Anakin's gaze with his own and held it hard. *Please. Let's not do this.* Anakin's jaw tightened, his eyes sharp with temper—and then he capitulated and looked away.

Oblivious, or uncaring, Agent Varrak opened the workcase and withdrew two sealed packets. "*Teeb*," she said, handing him and Anakin one each, her tone lecturing, "is the official designated honorific for any legally adult male Lanteeban. The equivalent female honorific is *Teeba*. Teeb Markl and Teeb Yavid—that would be you, Master Kenobi—are cousins. Farmers who lost the family holding after a prolonged drought put them into debt. They—you—are returning home to Lanteeb after working a three-season forestry laborer's contract on Alderaan. You hail from the village of Voteb, on the northernmost tip of the settled Lanteeban continent."

Obi-Wan frowned at her. "I don't understand. I thought our knowledge of Lanteeb was severely limited."

"It is," said Agent Varrak. "But there really are two Lanteeban cousins named Markl and Yavid, and they have helped us prepare for this mission."

"That's . . . impressive," said Anakin, with a grudging admiration. "How did you manage to find these men? And so fast?"

Bail shrugged. "Sheer luck, Master Skywalker. Senator Amidala's comment about the Lanteeban engineer got me thinking. Alderaan hires a lot of offplanet workers in the forests and the general agricultural regions. We're a popular destination for contract labor. The pay and conditions are good, and an Alderaanian reference opens many other doors. Fortunately our Ministry of Employment keeps meticulous records. It was a long shot, but I thought it was worth checking to see if we had any Lanteebans currently on the books." Another shrug. "Once I was apprised of the cousins' work status on Alderaan, I pulled the requisite strings and had them brought in."

"To help," said Obi-Wan carefully. He looked from Bail to Agent Varrak. "And when you say *help* . . ."

Bail sat a little straighter. "We—*I*—mean help," he said, and suddenly he was wearing his haughty politician's face, the princely face of a man who resented being questioned—or doubted. "No strings attached. And when they finished assisting us they were returned to their forestry camp."

"Which in my opinion was a grave tactical error," Agent Varrak murmured. "If they change their minds—"

"Pass up asylum and protected Alderaanian immigrant status?" said Bail. "That's not likely. Agent Varrak, you've already lost this argument. Drop it."

"Senator," said Agent Varrak, her eyes going blank.

Obi-Wan cleared his throat. "So you're saying these Lanteebans are free of further government interference?"

"That's right."

A glance at Agent Varrak showed him what she thought of that. "Surely it would have been less problematic simply to fabricate identities for us?" he asked.

"How?" said Agent Varrak sourly. "When, as you yourself pointed out, Master Kenobi, our knowledge of Lanteeb is as good as nonexistent."

Stang. He didn't have an answer for that.

"So," said Anakin, "these cover identities—you're sure they'll hold up for the duration of our mission?"

Agent Varrak nodded curtly. "We are. Voteb is one of Lanteeb's remotest villages. The chances of you stumbling across anyone in the city who knows the real cousins or is familiar enough with their home to ask awkward questions are negligible, at best."

"Looks that way," said Anakin, and turned. "I think Senator Organa's right, Obi-Wan. We got lucky. Without all this inside information, I doubt we could make it onto Lanteeb. And better yet—nobody we run across is going to be scared or suspicious of a couple of farmers."

Lucky or not, he didn't like it. Not at all. Not that he didn't trust Bail, or disbelieved his friend when he said the men were in no danger. That was the truth: They were in no danger from Bail Organa, one of the only two honorable politicians he knew. But that *didn't* mean they were totally safe. Agent Varrak's disapproval of their freedom was proof of that.

And while Bail is powerful, is he powerful enough to override the son of a Sith if they should push Palpatine for a change in the status of these Lanteeban cousins? I think he is—I hope he is—but can I be sure?

Bail was staring at him steadily, a challenge in his eyes. "It's done, Master Kenobi. Let's move on, shall we?"

Unhappy, Obi-Wan ran his fingers over the unopened info packet Agent Varrak had given him.

This wretched war. And to think I used to complain whenever Qui-Gon bent the rules even a little bit . . .

"Master Kenobi," said Bail, insistent. Wary. "Do we have a problem?"

He looked up. *Yes.* "No, Senator." He pushed the info packet aside. "We are indeed fortunate that these cousins were available to assist us."

"Your ship's new registry, your personal identichips, and your full bios are in those packets," said Agent Varrak, unmoved by the continuing tension in the dusty room. "Along with pertinent notes on Lanteeb and the spaceport's layout, rules, and regulations. Don't lose the chips, and destroy the bios and briefing notes once you've memorized them. If anyone on

Lanteeb questions your accents, make sure you stress you've been away from home for some time and you've picked up some alien inflections. Most importantly, *don't* talk about the great nonhuman friends you made on your travels. Do that and you'll attract all the wrong kind of attention. I'm told you're arranging your own transport?"

"Don't worry. We took care of that this morning," said Anakin. "Although—" He frowned. "If we're farmers turned forestry workers, how do you explain us having our own ship?"

"You won it in a game of chance," said Agent Varrak, and sniffed. "And learned to fly it in your free time. This vessel you've chosen—it's nothing too flashy, I hope."

Obi-Wan flicked another warning glance at Anakin. *Don't rise to her bait.* "On the contrary, Agent. It would, for example, attract no attention in this neighborhood."

"Make and model?"

"Hey," said Anakin, scowling. "This isn't my first nerf muster either, Agent. I grew up around tramp transports and shady operators, which means I know a thing or two about flying under the sensors."

"Of course," said Agent Varrak, her lips thinning into an ungenerous smile. "You grew up on Tatooine. The perfect preparation for a life of skulduggery."

Anakin smiled back, just as unamused. "Yeah. It was. Y'know, I'm surprised I never saw you there."

Instead of biting back, Agent Varrak nodded at Anakin's lightsaber, ostentatious in the office's shabby surrounds. "You know you can't take that thing with you."

"Excuse me?" Anakin flexed his fingers, and the lightsaber leapt to his loving hand. "That's not your decision."

Something close to contempt flitted over the woman's harsh face. "Don't be a fool. If you get caught with a Jedi weapon, you'll be shot dead on the spot. You'll have blown any chance of your mission succeeding or of anyone else following you to finish what you started."

This time Anakin's smile was dangerous. "Then I guess it's a good thing I won't get caught, isn't it?"

"So I think that's all we need from you, Agent Varrak," said Bail, standing. "The Supreme Chancellor appreciates your assistance, as do I. And please remember this is a coded operation. Compartmentalize as per protocols and discuss it with me, and me alone."

"Of course, Senator," said Agent Varrak, her expression smoothing to a cool, dispassionate competence. "Happy to be of service, as always."

After she was gone Bail dropped back into his chair. Ran a hand over his face then leaned his elbows on the conference table, letting his polished politician's mask slip to reveal the man who lived behind it.

"Don't say it, Obi-Wan. Just—*don't*."

"I wasn't going to," he retorted. "As you so rightly pointed out, it's done. And given our distressing lack of options there's no way to undo it."

"Exactly."

"Although I seem to recall you saying, only a few hours ago, that if I had any second thoughts—"

"I know what I said!" said Bail, glowering. "But it's not the mission you doubt, is it? Only my ability to protect those Lanteebans from Varrak's overenthusiasm."

"Is *that* what you call it?"

Anakin cleared his throat. "Ah—hey—"

"Are you saying that you trust her to take no for an answer?" Obi-Wan retorted. "Bail, I've only just met the woman and I can tell that she—"

"Will not be a problem!" Bail insisted, his voice rising. "Because I will not *permit* her to be a problem. Even though all she wanted to do was take the Lanteebans into protective custody for the duration of this mission."

"Protective custody?" he scoffed. "Bail—"

"*Yes,*" said Bail, shoving his chair back in frustration. "Obi-Wan, our government isn't the enemy. *I'm* not the enemy. And neither is Agent Varrak. We haven't turned into the Separatists while you weren't looking! Agent Varrak's security concerns are legitimate. I happen to share them. But I also happen to think she's erring too far on the side of caution, so I overruled her. End of story. But if you want to sit there and accuse me of—"

"*Hey!*" said Anakin, and slapped the table between them. "Is this helping? I don't think it is."

Shocked, they stared at him.

"Don't worry, Senator," he said. "We know you're not the bad guy here. We know the Lanteebans who've helped us will be safe—not only from overzealous operatives like Agent Varrak, but from any Sep spies who might be lurking around."

Nodding, Bail tugged his chair close again and leaned forward, intensely earnest. "They will be, Obi-Wan. I've tasked my own people with keeping them under surveillance. From now on they're protected by House Organa. Nobody will approach them again without my express permission. *Nobody.*"

"We had to use them, Obi-Wan," Anakin added. "You know we did. When it comes to defeating Dooku, we can't afford to be squeamish. War doesn't allow for a tender conscience. I mean, look at the choices we've made already. Some of them have been brutal. If we turn back now, all of that was for nothing. Our only hope is to keep going, believing that every hard choice we make is for the ultimate good of the Republic."

Obi-Wan frowned at the table. *He's right. I know he's right.*

And yet . . . "We've placed those men at risk," he said quietly. "We gave them no choice in this. And if something goes wrong—"

"I know," said Bail. He sounded abruptly exhausted. And beneath the exhaustion there was a kind of despairing anger. "You're right. There should be another way. But I can't see one. Not under the circumstances. Can you?"

"No," he said, slumping. "It's only—this shouldn't be *easy*. If we're going to do things like this it should be *difficult*. It should *hurt*."

Bail looked at him, not even trying to hide his wounded astonishment. "You think this is easy for me? Turning two simple, innocent men's lives upside down? Scaring the wits out of them in the middle of the night? You think I can do that and not *hurt*?"

"This isn't on you, Senator," said Anakin quickly. "Or you, Obi-Wan. Or me. This is on Dooku, and whoever he serves. Let's not lose sight of that."

In other words, don't waste time fighting each other. It was sound advice.

"Agreed." Searching for a safer subject Obi-Wan added, "You called this a coded operation, Bail. What does that mean, exactly?"

"That means it's eyes-only," said Bail, his mask back in place, bruised feelings thrust safely out of sight. "Specifically mine and Senator Amidala's. No data trail. No agent other than Varrak involved, on my side. I know you've told Yoda—but I'd prefer that what we're doing goes no farther than him."

Obi-Wan hadn't been expecting that. "You want Master Yoda to keep this from the rest of the Jedi Council? Surely you're not suggesting there's a question of—"

"Of course I'm not, Obi-Wan," Bail said. "Restricted mission access is standard for any coded operation. The fewer people who know its details, the better."

Anakin's uneasiness was stirring again. "That's understandable. But you've told the Chancellor, haven't you? He knows?"

Bail hesitated, then shook his head. "No."

"Senator Organa—" Anakin leaned across the table. He took any slight to the Chancellor so deeply to heart. "Supreme Chancellor Palpatine is the ultimate authority in the Republic. You can't set up a mission like this without informing him!"

"I can't?" Bail sat back, his casual tone masking a keen wariness. "So does that mean you Jedi tell him everything you're doing?"

"That's different," Anakin snapped. "There's precedent. The Jedi and the civilian government are separate entities. But you're *part* of the government. You owe Palpatine your allegiance."

"My allegiance is owed to the Republic," said Bail. "Chancellors come and Chancellors go, Master Skywalker, but the Republic endures."

Obi-Wan touched Anakin's wrist in warning, before something else unfortunate was said. "Why, Bail? Why keep Palpatine out of the loop?"

Bail's small smile was derisive. "You know why."

He did. He was one of the few who knew the truth. So was Anakin. Yoda had trusted them with it several months before. He'd been touched by the show of confidence—and sickened by the implications of what Yoda had shared.

"There's no proof the leaks are coming from his office or its adjuncts."

"There's no proof they're not," Bail retorted. "But what we *are* sure of is that the Seps have their own intelligence agency and they've got spies in our ranks just as we've got spies in

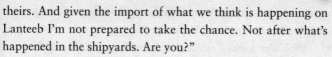

theirs. And given the import of what we think is happening on Lanteeb I'm not prepared to take the chance. Not after what's happened in the shipyards. Are you?"

Sighing, he shook his head. "No. You're right. The risk's not worth it." He glanced at Anakin. "You know it's not."

Anakin scowled, unconvinced.

"It's simple," Bail added, ignoring that. "The fewer people who know about this mission the safer you'll both be. I'll tell Palpatine what's going on when I'm sure nothing can get in the way of your success."

"Your blind confidence is comforting, Senator."

This time Bail's smile was warm. "It's not misplaced, either."

"Bail—speaking of the shipyards—"

His friend raised a hand, fending off the question. "No developments yet. I'm sorry."

In other words the Republic's war fleet remained vulnerable. Every Jedi on the front lines continued to face greater risk.

And there are too few of us as it is.

But that wasn't Bail's fault. He nodded. "I know you are."

"Obi-Wan . . ." Bail shifted in his chair, uncomfortable. "I've been thinking. It seems to me we've run into a lot of—well, since you don't believe in coincidence, let's call it convenient happenstance, shall we? Anakin's Padawan coming across that Kaminoan invoice—these useful Lanteeban cousins—even Agent Varrak's availability. Everything seems so *neat*. Should I be worried? I think I'm worried. Things are falling into place too easily."

Poor Bail. For him the ways of the Force must forever remain a mystery. "Don't worry. The fact that pieces of this puzzle have fallen into place to our advantage is a positive thing, Bail. It suggests we're on the right path."

"Yes?" Bail frowned, unconvinced. "Well. I'll have to take

your word on that, Master Jedi. Now—when do you think you'll leave for Lanteeb?"

Obi-Wan looked at Anakin, who shrugged. "First thing tomorrow unless something untoward happens between now and then."

"Tomorrow?" Bail nodded at the information packets. "That doesn't leave you much time for homework."

"It leaves enough," he said. "Trust me, we'll be letter-perfect on the fictions your Agent Varrak has invented for us."

"Ha," said Bail, pushing his chair back. "She's not my Agent Varrak. She's just the best at what she does." He stood. "I need to go. I've got meetings until midnight and I don't want to get people spreading rumors about why I'm not where I'm supposed to be."

"Yes, well," he said, and got to his feet. "You will be a politician, Bail."

"Every day," Bail retorted. "Because you've got your arena, Obi-Wan, and I've got mine."

Which was true. And a better warrior for peace and justice than Bail Organa the Senate would never see. The last traces of his disappointment and frustration fading, Obi-Wan nodded.

"Indeed."

"Do me a favor," said Bail. "Give me a decent head start before you two leave. I've no reason to think any of us was followed, or that we're being watched, but . . ." He shook his head. "Spend enough time with Republic intelligence agents and the next thing you know every shadow looks sinister."

He smiled. "Of course. But if it's any consolation, Bail, I don't sense danger."

"That's a lot better than consolation," said Bail, and held out his hand. His eyes were warm with rueful affection. "May the Force be with you, Teeb Yavid."

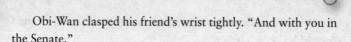

Obi-Wan clasped his friend's wrist tightly. "And with you in the Senate."

"Thanks," said Bail drily. "When it comes to the Senate, I need all the help I can get." He nodded at Anakin. "Happy hunting, Teeb Markl. And please—come home safe. Both of you."

"That's the plan," said Anakin, belligerent. "And I stick to my plans."

Bail considered him. "Yes," he murmured. "I'll bet you do."

Once they were alone Anakin leapt to his feet and with a swipe of his hand sent one of the office's chairs flying across the room.

Obi-Wan stared. *"Anakin!"*

"Oh, don't look at me like that," said Anakin, scowling. "I could do a lot worse, believe me."

And this was the story of Anakin Skywalker. Three steps forward and one step back, over and over and over again. "What I *believe,* Anakin, or at least what I hope, is that you'll remember your training," he said tightly. "Displays like that are unbecoming. How can you possibly hope to guide Ahsoka to Jedi Knighthood when you are yet so undisciplined yourself?"

Prowling, Anakin whipped around. "I'm not *undisciplined,* I'm *angry.*"

"Yes, I can see that! It's your anger, Anakin, that is the problem!" *It always has been. And no matter how hard I try, I can't seem to convince you to set it aside.* "Anger is one of the swiftest paths to the dark side."

"Maybe," said Anakin, the office's dusty air alive with his turbulent emotions. "Sometimes. But sometimes anger is justified, Obi-Wan. Like now. Because your friend the Senator is asking us—*me*—to lie to Chancellor Palpatine!"

"He's doing no such thing. He's following security procedures to safeguard the integrity of our mission."

"He practically accused the Supreme Chancellor of being a *traitor*!"

"Oh, Anakin." He sighed. "This is why Jedi teachings forbid attachment. It clouds your judgment. Nobody, least of all Bail Organa, is calling Palpatine a traitor."

"You're only defending him because he's your friend," Anakin retorted. "So whose judgment is clouded now, Master Kenobi?"

He watched Anakin pace the musty office. Felt the roiling of the Force within his former Padawan. It was tempting to answer fire with fire but that would only leave both of them burned.

"I understand your loyalty to Palpatine," he said, deliberately calm. "I understand why you don't want to feel as though you're mistrusting him. But Anakin, like it or not Bail is right about one thing. The leaks are coming from somewhere. And given how sensitive some of that information has been—given the price our forces have paid, lately—it's not unreasonable to look askance at the highest levels of government. Traitors come in many guises."

"That may be so," said Anakin sullenly. "But asking me to believe Palpatine is even the smallest bit responsible for top-secret intel being fed to the Separatists is the same as asking me to believe *you* could be a traitor."

Despite his own unsettled feelings he had to smile. "Yes, well, let's not get carried away."

"And that *woman*?" Anakin added, spinning around. Incredulous. "Agent Varrak? I don't care *how* kriffing good she is. She *despises* us. You know she does, Obi-Wan. You could feel it like I did."

"And if she does?" he said, suddenly tired. "How is that important, Anakin? We've got a job to do and she's helping us do it. *That's* important. The rest is nothing. You care too much for what others think of you. Let it go. Our lives are bigger than that."

Anakin stopped, breathing hard. Fisted his hands on his hips and let his head drop. The effort it cost him to release his anger, to regain his emotional poise, was palpable. At length he looked up.

"You're right," he said ruefully. "I'm sorry. You're right."

"I am?" Relieved, Obi-Wan tossed Anakin his information packet. "Then let me be right all the way back to the Temple. There's a lot to accomplish before we leave."

ANAKIN HATED TO ADMIT IT, but Obi-Wan was right again. They had so much to accomplish and so little time to do it in that there was no chance of getting away for a last night with Padmé. All he managed was a snatched comlink conversation with her, just before she headed into another late session of the Senate. She worked so hard. Too hard. He'd given up begging her to slow down, to resign from at least one of the six committees she was on. Every time he raised the subject she gave him the same answer.

"I can't, Anakin. I have to keep myself busy or I'll go mad worrying about you."

He couldn't really argue with that.

Safely alone in one of the Temple's guest chambers, having reinspected the ship he'd picked out, tuned up its hyperdrive and loaded its new ID specs, stocked it with provisions for the journey to Lanteeb, memorized his new identity, packed an old, battered travelcase with discreetly altered thirdhand non-Jedi clothes, contacted Ahsoka and let her know he'd be away and not contactable for a few days and no, he couldn't say where, eaten dinner then soaked in the rare, always delightful luxury of a proper bath, he sprawled on his narrow, unremarkable bed and listened to the music of his beloved wife's voice.

"You will be careful, won't you, Anakin?"

"You know me."

"Yes I do, which is why I'm saying be careful!"

He closed his eyes. Remembered her in his arms. How it felt to be lost in her. "You be careful, too. You're as much a target as I am."

"No, I'm not. You're the one with the great big SHOOT ME *sign stuck on his chest."*

The fear in her voice flayed him. She tried so hard to disguise it, struggled not to burden him with her nightmares. Just as he fought not to burden her with his.

"There's nothing to be afraid of, Padmé. I'm coming back to you. I will always come back to you."

"I know, my love," she whispered. *"And if you can manage to bring Obi-Wan back with you? I'd like that. Good friends are too hard to find these days."*

In the background noise surrounding her, a familiar, sonorous chime.

"The session's about to start. I have to go. Anakin—"

There was no one to see his anguish, but he covered his face anyway. "I know, *hatari*. I know."

The silence afterward mocked him . . . and the release of sleep was a long time coming.

"COME SIT WITH ME, Obi-Wan. Drink yarba tea we shall, and talk."

The invitation had stunned him. Not even Qui-Gon had been invited to take tea with Yoda. The honor was reserved for members of the Jedi Council, most often Mace Windu.

Cross-legged on the floor of Yoda's inner sanctum, tall candles flickering light and shadows on the richly tapestried walls, Obi-Wan watched the ancient Jedi Master fill a tiny porcelain cup with fragrant liquid then hold it out.

"Thank you," he murmured, accepting it. "Master—"

"Drink now," said Yoda, his fathomless eyes alight with warmth. "Talk later."

So he drank the tea, which was hot and tart. Yoda poured a cup for himself and sipped in reflective silence. When the cup was empty he placed it with care on the low, lacquered tanfawood table between them.

"Grieve you do, for Taria Damsin."

Taria. He put down his own emptied cup. "Does that displease you, Master?"

"No," said Yoda, gentle. "Lose your way in that friendship you have not, Obi-Wan. Let her go you will when her time is come."

The smallest spasm of pain. "When will that be? Do you know?"

Yoda closed his eyes, his lips pursing in thought. "Soon. But not too soon." His eyes opened. "But no more of Taria Damsin will we speak."

There was no question of dispute. "Yes, Master."

Yoda rested his small hands on his own cross-legged knees. "Watched you I have, Obi-Wan, from your first day in the Temple. Drawn to you I was. As an infant, a youngling, a Padawan, a Jedi Knight. Burn in the Force's light always you have."

Not knowing what to say to that, he said nothing.

"And now . . ." Yoda sighed heavily. "Touched by darkness are you. Not turned to the dark, but noticed by it. Dangerous this is, Obi-Wan. Very dangerous."

The chamber was warm, yet he felt chilled to the bone.

"To Lanteeb I send you for to Lanteeb must you go," Yoda added. "Needed there you are, that much the Force has shown me since first you told me of Senator Organa's concerns." He leaned forward, his eyes frightening. "But great care must you take. Death and darkness on Lanteeb await. Misery. Suffering. Lose yourself there you must not."

Profoundly unsettled, he stared at Yoda. "What have you seen, Master? I've tried to read the Force, tried to look ahead, but—"

"Never before so clouded has the future been," said Yoda grimly. "Never so oppressive the dark side. Struggle to see ahead *I* do. Your fault it is not."

But that wasn't exactly an answer. "Have you any other advice for me, Master? Any suggestion as to how Anakin and I should proceed with this mission? It would be greatly appreciated."

Yoda filled their cups again. Lifted his and sipped, inscrutable. "Trust your feelings, Obi-Wan. Guided you well they always have."

And if Yoda had watched him his whole life, surely he had watched Yoda . . . and knew enough of the Jedi Master to know their conversation was done.

"Master," he said, bowing. "I shall."

ANAKIN AND OBI-WAN left the Temple just before dawn, unremarked. Not even Yoda bade them farewell or good luck. Their leaving was unobtrusive. Subtle. Without needing to discuss it they blurred themselves within the Force. Faded from the world's attention and took a circuitous speeder route to the commercial facility where their dowdy ship had spent the night.

The spaceport's droid attendant checked them through without comment.

"Are we going to argue about who's flying this bucket?" Anakin asked as the hatch-and-ramp clanged shut behind them.

"Be my guest," said Obi-Wan. "I've nothing to prove."

"Ha ha."

He went forward to the cockpit, leaving his luggage for Obi-Wan to stow.

"Hey!" he called back. "You did remember to file the false flight plan, right?"

"What?" Obi-Wan called back from the passenger hold. "Oh dear. Let me think."

In other words, yes. He grinned, knowing exactly the look Obi-Wan had on his face. "Just checking."

Obi-Wan muttered something that was probably better not to hear or even acknowledge.

Anakin sent through the coded request for permission to depart Coruscant, then fired up the ship's marginally adequate sublight drive. Listened to the idiosyncratic *tink-tink-tink* underneath its deeper throaty roar. Shrugged. Thanks to his maintenance work the previous night they'd make it to Lanteeb in one piece, and that was all that mattered.

See, Obi-Wan? I am learning to let go of the little things.

The cramped cockpit's transparisteel viewport was intact, but badly scratched. He'd have to live with that, too. And with the sagging pilot's chair that threatened to separate his spine in three places.

A console light flashed green. Departure confirmed.

Even though this ship was a piece of poodoo, it was still a ship. He was flying. It was freedom. Lumbering into the pale sky, cleaving the atmosphere, Coruscant falling behind, he felt his spirits lift despite the gathering darkness.

Don't look now, Dooku. We're coming to get you and your friends.

ELEVEN

THE COMM OVERRIDE CAME IN LOUD AND BRASH, SHATTERING
the passenger compartment's comfortable silence.

"*Attention, unidentified vessel. You are entering restricted
Confederacy of Independent Systems space. You are ordered to
activate your ID beacon and stand by.*"

Seated at the small passenger compartment's table, Anakin
laid down his last sabacc card. "Well, it's about time. I was beginning to think this whole Lanteeb invasion story was the result of somebody's hangover. Oh." He grinned. "And you lose.
Again."

Obi-Wan tossed down his own cards. "Honestly, I don't
know why I bother."

"Honestly?" He stood, fighting the urge to laugh out loud at
Obi-Wan's disgusted expression. "Neither do I."

The Sep warning came in again as he entered the cockpit.
"Yeah, yeah, yeah," he muttered. "Keep your trousers on,
friend."

He turned on the falsified ID beacon then cut the sublight
drive. To be on the safe side he'd dropped them out of hyperspace well ahead of what would normally be the realspace reentry point for Lanteeb and they'd been crawling toward the
planet ever since, waiting for the Seps to challenge them.

The ship shuddered gently as it lost sublight momentum. Beyond the cockpit's scratched viewport the scattered stars shone beguilingly. Amazing. He was living his enslaved childhood dream, flying his own ship among the pinpoints of light that had been his only hope in those left-behind dark days. When he'd belonged body and soul first to venal, rapacious Gardulla the Hutt . . . and after her Watto, who hadn't been cruel, exactly, but was greedy and careless and willing to see him die racing a Pod.

I wonder what the little poodoo's doing now. I wonder if he's managed to claw his way back into another slimy Hutt's favor. If he's got some other little boy dicing with death in the Podraces, to make him rich.

When the war was over he'd go back to Tatooine and see. When the war was over he'd buy any child he found enslaved to Watto and find them a home where they might live and love in safety. Belonging to no one but themselves.

I should have done it before now. Wasn't that my other childhood dream? Become a Jedi and free the slaves. Instead I became a Jedi and let myself forget. Let them convince me that it's not our job to remake the Republic.

The Jedi were keepers of the peace, not legal enforcers. That was the Senate's job. How many times had he been told that? He'd lost count. But the Senate was falling down on the job, wasn't it? What was the use of having anti-slavery laws if the barves who broke them never paid for their crimes?

It was enough to shake his hard-won and harder-kept faith. If scum like Watto and Jabba and the other Hutts kept on making their fat profits on the backs of living property—and if the Senate continued to turn a blind eye—how could anyone believe in the Republic? How could he?

Padmé says she understands, but she hasn't pushed for a

Senate hearing. And Palpatine—he's promised he'll tackle the problem but nothing's been done. It's too political. Too corrupt. Too complicated. There are credits in slavery—and credits trump justice. Always have. Always will.

And the Jedi? They didn't want to get involved. Even Qui-Gon . . .

So I guess it's up to me. I failed my mother. I didn't go back for her and she died. But when the war is over I'll make good on my word. I'll fight slavery wherever I find it . . . and there'll be no mercy for those who steal lives.

Footsteps behind him. Wary of his former Master's ability to read him, he buried his stirred-up feelings deep.

"Any response yet?" said Obi-Wan, halting in the cockpit's doorway.

"No," he said, swiveling the pilot's seat. "Looks like they're being coy."

Obi-Wan folded his arms, considering. "Or careful. But if there's a problem, it won't be with the ship's ID."

"We hope. After all, we've only got Bail's word that Agent Varrak can be trusted."

"Anakin . . ."

He held up his hands. "I'm just saying. I know you trust him. I know you've got good reason to trust him. But people can be fooled, Obi-Wan. Even a smart man can trust the wrong person."

"Yes, well, while that might be true," said Obi-Wan, "did you by any chance sense the slightest deception in Agent Varrak?"

The ship was starting to drift. Turning back to the console, he adjusted the port stabilizers. "No. I was too busy drowning in the waves of hostility. But—"

"Civilian cruiser Registration Nine-seven-nine-seven-five-five-six-slash-Vee. You have passed the preliminary weapons

scan and are hereby granted provisional clearance. Disengage your nav computer protocols to receive coordinates and approach Lanteeb using sublight drives only. Any deviation from sublight speed or the designated trajectory will be deemed a hostile act and you will be eliminated."

"Huh," he said, and did as he was told. "They really are taking this seriously, aren't they?"

"Which only confirms what we suspect," said Obi-Wan. "Clearly there's something worth hiding on Lanteeb."

The nav comp chittered and flashed as their approach vector coordinates were remotely downloaded. Once the green ACCEPT light engaged, Anakin transferred helm control to autopilot and swiveled his chair around again.

"Well, Master Kenobi? Any last words of advice before we plunge into the enemy's maw?"

Obi-Wan frowned. "You could try not being quite so flippant."

Anakin grinned. "Nervous?"

"I have a healthy respect for the challenges that lie ahead of us, yes," said Obi-Wan carefully, "but I'd not go so far as to characterize that as *nervous.*"

"Don't worry," he said, still grinning. "I won't let anything happen to you."

"All right," said Obi-Wan, exasperated. "That is *it.* That is the *last* time I let you talk me into playing sabacc before a mission. Winning makes you altogether too cocky."

Teasing Obi-Wan was one of his favorite pastimes. His former Master always rose so satisfyingly to the lure.

"You should try harder to beat me, then. Because honestly, Obi-Wan, you were playing like a lame bantha. I know younglings who could've won that last hand. Wherever your head was, it wasn't in the game."

He waited for Obi-Wan to bite—but instead there was an awkward silence. A sideways shifting gaze. A sudden thrum of unease.

"Obi-Wan?" He sat up, his own senses alerted. *I thought there was something bothering him . . . and then I thought I was imagining it.* "What's wrong?"

"Nothing," said Obi-Wan, his denial automatic.

"Nothing. Really? You expect me to believe that?"

A flash of heat in Obi-Wan's eyes. "I expect you to—" He bit back the rest of his angry retort. Made an obvious effort to release his temper. "I'm sorry," he said, much more quietly. "I have a friend. She's very ill."

She? They'd only been back on Coruscant a couple of days and been nowhere save the Temple, Bail's apartment, and the Bahrin district. Who had he seen except for—

"No, it's not Padmé," Obi-Wan said hastily. "Don't you think I'd have said something if—"

It was hard to hear over the frantic banging of his heart. "Of course you would've." *Or she would've. Wouldn't she?* "Then who—"

Obi-Wan hesitated, then sighed. "Master Damsin. Taria."

Anakin stared. *I've known you all these years and you still surprise me.* "You're friends? I didn't realize. You never talk about her."

"I've had no reason to."

He was the most annoyingly *self-contained* man . . . "I'm sorry. I didn't know she was sick."

"Few people do. It's a private matter." Obi-Wan hesitated again, frowning. "I shouldn't have said anything. Anakin—"

"Don't worry," he said gently. He'd never felt Obi-Wan so upset. It was unnerving. Made him wish he'd paid closer attention to Taria Damsin. "Besides, who would I tell?"

Before Obi-Wan could answer, the console's proximity alarm emitted a feeble beep. Turning, Anakin looked through the viewport. Ahead, just visible to the naked eye, was Lanteeb, a tiny brown disk against the black backdrop of the insignficant Malor-77 system. The planet had a single orbiting moon, small and scurrying high above.

"Look at that," he said. "We're nearly there. Why don't you go aft and strap yourself in? If the sensors are reading right we've got the tail end of an ion storm to fly through between here and Lanteeb's spaceport."

"Fine," said Obi-Wan, subdued, and returned to the passenger compartment.

They did encounter the buffeting remnants of the ion storm. Their battered old ship tossed and shuddered, its pocked hull groaning, but it held together under the stress. With the turbulence safely negotiated the nav comp locked back on to their predetermined course, and minute by minute Lanteeb loomed larger. The Sep-designated approach was bringing them in on the planet's day side, which meant Anakin could see its single inhabited continent clearly. The landmass looked like a grubby greeny brown raft floating on the planet's enormous expanse of bluish gray water. Drab, uninspiring, not a single thing about Lanteeb struck him as romantic.

And new planets were *supposed* to be romantic, kriff it.

"Civilian cruiser Registration Nine-seven-nine-seven-five-five-six-slash-Vee. Disengage your autopilot and prepare for final approach and landing coordinates. Once received, return helm control to the autopilot and when you are docked stand by for inspection. Under no circumstances leave your ship until you are authorized to do so by a spaceport authority officer. Any deviation from these instructions will be deemed a hostile act and you will be eliminated."

Mindful of itchy Sep trigger fingers, he did as he was told without delay. As soon as the nav comp flashed green again he reengaged the autopilot. Then, with nothing more to do, he wandered back to the passenger compartment where Obi-Wan was calmly tidying away the scattered sabacc cards, no hint of his previous distress. Master Kenobi had himself in hand once more.

Sometimes I wonder what it would take to really make him let go.

"You know," he said, propping himself against a convenient stretch of wall, "whatever override technology they're using to control this ship, it's the best I've ever come across."

Obi-Wan shoved the dice and cards into a storage compartment and closed it. "That's hardly surprising. We are dealing with the Techno Union, after all."

Anakin grimaced. "True."

Which meant the only thing left for them to do now was wait until their ship made it safely to ground in Lanteeb's spaceport. He hated this part. Hated losing control, being at the mercy of someone else's whims. That was slavery's enduring legacy. He knew he'd go to his grave resentful of any being who tried to usurp his independence.

I will never be a slave again.

Obi-Wan patted his shoulder in passing. "Never mind, Anakin. It's not for long."

Trust Obi-Wan to know what he was feeling. "I'm fine," he said, pushing off the wall. The sharp movement bumped his concealed lightsaber against his ribs, and he frowned. It felt so wrong, not having the weapon hooked to his belt. Having to hide their lightsabers was another reminder that this wasn't an everyday, ordinary mission. That while being a Jedi would doubtless prove vital to their success, in this place it would also mean instant death if their true identities were revealed.

He'd grown used to being visible. To being welcomed *because* he was a Jedi. But thanks to the war everything was changing. Thanks to Dooku and his conniving cohorts, societies that had once welcomed the Jedi now viewed them with suspicion and hostility. He still found that hard to reconcile.

But then, perhaps he shouldn't be surprised. People tended to think what they were told to think by whoever got to them first—offered them the most—or scared them the worst.

The compartment intercom crackled.

"Civilian cruiser Registration Nine-seven-nine-seven-five-five-six-slash-Vee. You are now on spaceport final approach. All occupants must be seated in the passenger compartment when spaceport authority officers board. Any attempt to interfere with officers going about their lawful duties will be deemed a hostile act and you will be eliminated."

Obi-Wan's smile as he slid on the compartment's bench seat was particularly bland. "Oh dear. They do sound rather agitated, don't they? Come along, Anakin. Time to sit down. We don't want to distress the poor little Separatists, do we?" His smile sharpened. "At least, not yet."

THEY LANDED AND DOCKED without incident, remaining seated in the passenger compartment, as ordered. Turned out there was no need for them to let the Sep inspection team in. Whatever technology Dooku's misguided followers had used to control the ship made light work of the exterior hatch control. The ramp lowered and a gust of warm damp air blew into the ship's belly, carrying with it the raucous sounds of clanging metal, whining laser saws, raised voices, running feet, furious swearing, and an exotic tang of the familiar and the strange. They smelled ship exhausts. Spilled fuel. Burnt oil and hydraulic fluids. Overheated wiring. Sweaty, unwashed flesh. Something rancid and long overcooked. A sizzle of wet salt. Something else—fresh tree sap? Odd, in a spaceport.

Then the sound of heavy booted footfalls coming up the metal ramp, ringing hollow with purpose and authority.

"No," Obi-Wan murmured. "We're to stay seated, remember?"

Anakin sank back on the bench. "So how do you want to play this?"

A flash of amusement. Despite the danger—or because of it—Obi-Wan was enjoying himself. "Since I'm the older cousin I'd say it's only proper for you to follow my lead. Sir!" he said, managing an ingratiating bow at the short, stocky man striding into the passenger compartment. "I am Teeb Yavid. This is my cousin, Teeb—"

"Identichips," said the spaceport officer in Corellian-accented Basic, holding out his hand. He wore a dark blue uniform, military cut, military-issue boots, and a heavy-duty blaster in an ammo-laden holster on his right hip, the button unclipped. "Slowly."

Obi-Wan bobbed his head. "Do as the good man says, Markl." His voice was pitched higher than normal, and trembled. No threat here, no sir. Just a couple of inoffensive farmers. "We don't want any trouble."

With an anxious, vacant smile, Anakin fished his identichip out of his patched overshirt's pocket. "Here you are, sir."

"And here's mine," added Obi-Wan, pathetically eager. "Sir, as you will see we've been a long time away from home. You—you are not a Lanteeban, are you? And you're not from Alderaan. We've been on Alderaan, my cousin and me. Three seasons in a forestry camp. We—"

"Shut up," said the officer. He'd shoved one ID chip into a

reader unclipped from his belt and was staring at the information scrolling across the small data screen. Grunting, he glanced up. "Show me your hands."

"Me? Yes, sir." Anakin raised his left hand, palm-outward. Blessed the hours of rough quarter-staff training he'd undertaken with Ahsoka, preparing her to meet anyone wielding a double-bladed lightsaber.

The officer frowned. "I said *hands*."

"Oh—ah—I only have one."

"He lost the other one in an accident," Obi-Wan chimed in. "It was dreadful—there was so much *blood*—I thought—"

"I said shut up," the officer growled, switching identichips. "Last warning."

"I'm sorry," Obi-Wan whispered. He sounded close to tears.

"And show me your hands. You need telling twice? That can get a man shot around here."

"Shot?" Somehow, Obi-Wan managed to turn pale. "Oh sir. No, sir, please—"

"*Shut up*," said the officer. He stared at Teeb Yavid's smooth palms then back at the data screen. His gaze lifted, suspicious. "You've worked three years in a forestry camp? With those smooth hands?"

"Yes, sir. I'm sure it says so right there, sir," said Obi-Wan, pointing at the datareader. "One year and a half with a vibro-ax, sir. Then I hurt my shoulder and they put me in the office." His chest expanded with pride. "I have very good written Basic. Much better than my cousin's. He writes like fowl scratches."

What? Anakin bit the inside of his cheek. *Any minute he's going to break into a song-and-dance routine. What is this, stand-up night at the Coruscant Firebird?*

Grudgingly, the officer handed back their identichips. "Things have changed since you left home, boys. Lanteeb's joined the Separatist Alliance. You've got a new government. You're protected now."

"Protected from who, sir?" asked Obi-Wan, wide-eyed. "Lanteeb doesn't have any enemies."

The officer sneered. "The Republic is every planet's enemy. But you don't need to worry about that anymore. Count Dooku's taken care of that."

"And this would be why you're here inspecting our ship? Why we weren't allowed to fly it home on our own?"

"New security measures," said the officer. "Get used to them." He clipped the datareader back onto his belt, then wriggled his fingers. "Okay. On your feet."

Cringingly obedient, they stood.

"Right. Now strip."

Obi-Wan's mouth fell open. "*Strip?* Sir? You mean—take off our clothes?"

"Every last stitch," said the officer, with a bully's gloating satisfaction. "Standard procedure. Personal weapons search."

"Actually?" Obi-Wan straightened out of his self-effacing slump. Smiled, like a Jedi. "No. I don't think so. You don't need to search us for weapons."

A dreamy look crept over the Sep officer's broad, badly shaven face. "I don't need to search you for weapons."

"My cousin and I are *completely* harmless."

The officer nodded vaguely. "Yes. You and your cousin are completely harmless. Hold out your wrists, please."

"Why?" said Obi-Wan.

"All security-cleared citizens must be microchipped. Standard procedure. Only hurts for a minute."

Anakin glanced at Obi-Wan. But his former Master nodded, so he held out his wrist. The officer unclipped a different scanner from his belt and injected him. The man was right. It did sting.

"Thank you," said Obi-Wan, once his own chip was implanted. "Now run along. And after you've logged us into your security system as cleared, and granted us a full month's docking permit, be so kind as to forget everything about us."

"I certainly will," said the officer, his eyes glazed. "You gentlemen have a good stay. Pay close attention to all posted regulations and don't ignore the curfew. Anyone found on the streets after sunset is shot on sight."

Anakin watched as the Sep walked out without the slightest protest. Then he shook his head, and looked at Obi-Wan.

"Master Kenobi, you are *disturbingly* good at that."

Obi-Wan grinned. "Why, thank you. I do try. Although, to be fair, bullies make the easiest targets. Beneath their bluster they tend to be pathetically weak-minded. Now, what say we leave our little home away from home and find out what exactly these Separatist scum are up to?"

THE SPACEPORT WAS larger than Obi-Wan had expected, given Lanteeb's galactic isolation. A reflection of its more prosperous past, perhaps, when the planet's exported damotite had guaranteed a steady flow of credits. Standing at the top of their ship's lowered ramp, idly rubbing the still-burning point on his wrist where the Sep tracking chip had been inserted, he took a moment to breathe in the noisy, smelly atmosphere. Get a feel for the place. His innate time-sense told him it was still early morning. The milky-blue sky was patchy with clouds, the air thick and muggy. It had been raining. Pools and puddles spread across their docking bay's roofless central sector, the water sheened with iridescent oil-slick rainbows.

Wherever he looked there was construction work under way: upgrades to other docking bays, new lockdown grids, an extensive spiderweb of catwalks and rigging platforms. Across the other side of this sector was what looked like some kind of security cage arrangement complete with laser grid and targeting blaster turrets.

There were humans everywhere. Uniformed security types dominated, overseeing the construction work, each man armed with a high-powered blaster and a shock-stick. Clearly the Seps meant serious business here, and they weren't taking any chances. There were even some battle droids patrolling what he could see of the spaceport's inner perimeter. Instant death for anyone foolish enough to challenge them.

As for the native Lanteebans, they were easy to pick out. Hunched and nervous, skittishly aware of their armed supervisors, they were the ones lasering and sweeping and riveting and hammering and sweating to upgrade the spaceport to their new masters' specifications. They wore nothing but overalls and sandals. No protective eye goggles. No steel-capped boots. No sensor-harnesses to protect them from a fall. The indifference to their safety was breathtaking . . . and at the same time, unsurprising. Their fearful misery muddied the atmosphere.

Beside him, Anakin muttered something. Not in Basic. His outrage was palpable, a red shimmer in the Force.

Oh no. Not now. "Anakin . . ."

"Look at them!" Anakin retorted, low-voiced. "They've been turned into slaves!"

"I know. It's irrelevant. Focus on why we're here."

The Force shimmered again, reflecting Anakin's struggle. "Sometimes you sound just like Yoda."

A comment not intended as a compliment. "We're attracting attention. Let's go."

Still quietly seething, Anakin slapped the hatch control on the ship's hull then leapt off the rising ramp and headed for their docking bay's signposted exit. His imperfectly controlled agitation caught the attention of a strolling Separatist overseer. The man stared, suspicious, hand resting on the butt of his blaster. Not close enough to interfere but still too close for comfort. And this was far too public a venue for further mind-influencing.

Stang. Trying to look meek, Obi-Wan hurried after Anakin and plucked at his shapeless cotton sleeve. "*Stay in character.* We're humble laborers, remember, just like the unfortunates working in here. So less stiff-necked pride and more staring at the ground, please. I'm not interested in getting locked up in a cell—or shot."

Abruptly, Anakin's anger collapsed. "You're right. I'm sorry. Relax—Teeb. I'm fine."

The staring Separatist officer kept on staring until they were safely through the docking bay's exit. Wall sensors blipped as they passed through the autodoors.

"We should deactivate these chips," said Anakin. "Last thing we need is an electronic trail of our movements."

He shook his head. "Not yet. Perhaps later, if we really need to. I know the wretched things are a nuisance, but being found without an authorized identichip would surely cramp our style."

"Huh," said Anakin. "Tell me, do you ever get tired of being right?"

"Never," he said, with a small, swift smile. "Come on."

They reached the end of the narrow, winding corridor leading out of the docking bay. More sensors registered their progress beyond it, through a second set of doors and onto a narrow sidewalk facing a run-down public promenade. Immediately they found the source of the cooking smells and salt sizzle: a small open-air market situated twenty meters or so along from their spaceport exit. A scattering of food stalls jostled for attention with electronics exchanges and domestic droid repairers. Though it was still early, quite a few people wandered from stall to stall. Somewhere amid the jumble of Lanteeban humanity there was music, a thin reedy piping that tried to sound joyful, but failed. Competing with the pipes and the stall holders' raised voices was the cackling of live domestic fowl trussed up in wooden crates.

Mingling with the downtrodden Lanteebans were more armed battle droids. On patrol, it looked like. Doubtless the new Separatist government called it *keeping the peace*. Tyrants and dictators had a limited vocabulary.

As it had in the spaceport, the Lanteebans' fear made the Force feel heavy. Sluggish. Obi-Wan grimaced. "I wonder if this Separatist oppression is as prevalent in the outlying villages as it is here. Controlling the capital I can well understand—but extending that control over the entire planet might yet be beyond them. They've only been here a few weeks."

Anakin shrugged. "Does it matter? I thought you said social justice was irrelevant."

"It matters if what we're looking for has been hidden beyond the city limits."

Sticking his hand in his trouser pocket, Anakin jingled a few credits. "Speculation's not going to get us anywhere, Obi-Wan. Since we've got to start somewhere, I suggest we chat with the locals."

The roadway ringing the spaceport's perimeter was paved with Republic-standard ferrocrete, but its surface was pitted and potholed and buckled in scores of places. A steady stream of groundcars, most diseased with rust, many of them so antiquated they were fitted with wheels, not antigrav units, lurched and wove and bumped grindingly around the hazards, splashing through the remains of the recent rain. Droid-operated trundle carts fared slightly better, slipping between the groundcars, serenaded by curses and blaring horns.

There was no designated pedestrian walkway to get from the spaceport over to the markets. Crossing the road was going to be . . . interesting.

Obi-Wan felt a familiar Force ripple and poked Anakin with his elbow. "Don't. No using the Force unless it's an emergency."

Anakin stared. "You used it on that security officer."

"Yes. Delicately. But disrupting traffic isn't delicate, it's the equivalent of standing on a pedestal shouting *Yoo-hoo, we're here* to any Force-sensitive Separatist in the city."

"You don't know I was about to—"

Staring back at him, Obi-Wan raised an eyebrow.

"Fine," Anakin grumbled. "Just don't blame me if you get run over."

But as they tried to judge their dash across the road they were distracted by a distant booming sound and a painful pressure against their eardrums. Backing away from the road's dangerous edge, they turned and looked up.

"Techno Union starship," said Anakin, one hand shading his eyes. "*Excelsior*-class. Even more impressive than the Hardcell. Pricey—and very plush. Only Sep VIPs get to ride in one of those things."

Trust Anakin to know.

Another boom as the powerful vessel, its bulbous hull gleaming, reengaged the reverse thrusters to further slow its majestic descent. The strongly stirred air whipped up mini tornadoes, flapping the market stalls' awnings and the Lanteebans' baggy clothes. Sent a couple of caged fowl squawking into the middle of the road, where a groundcar flattened them in a welter of blood and feathers. The stall holder's wail of dismay was lost in the thundering roar of the Techno Union vessel's engines.

A wash of heat, sharper and brighter than the ambient humidity, spilled over the high curving walls of the spaceport, crisping hair and lungs and the stunted trees that dotted the marketplace.

Obi-Wan, immune to the landing ship's mechanical attractions, felt a faint shiver of anticipation in the Force. Felt the familiar sense of balance deep within that told him, *Yes. This is important. You're on the right path.*

"Well," he said. "It would seem our timing is fortuitous. If you're right, we have a Sep VIP to investigate."

Anakin lowered his shading hand. "*If* I'm right?"

"Come on, Cousin Markl," he said, smothering a smile. "We can hobnob with the locals later. Let's see if there's any way we can finagle ourselves into that ship's docking bay and discover the identity of our visiting Separatist bigwig."

But instead of following him, Anakin remained standing by the side of road, his face taut, something uncertain in his eyes.

Obi-Wan turned back. "What?"

"I don't—I'm not sure," said Anakin. "A sense. A feeling."

"Do you know that ship? Do you know who's on it?"

"No. At least—" Frustrated, Anakin pinched the bridge of his nose between thumb and forefinger, eyes squeezed tight shut. "It's on the tip of my tongue. There's something familiar there. I just—I can't pin it down. I can't *see* what's—" With a sharp head shake, he tried to refocus. "Give me a minute. I'll get it."

Anakin in this mood was little short of ferocious. He drove himself so hard. Too hard. Impatient of failure, wanting only what he wanted, when he wanted it . . .

In this mood he's likely to do something rash.

"Never mind. Don't push and the answer will come to you. Especially if we can get closer to that ship."

"Then what are we waiting for?" said Anakin. "Come on."

But the spaceport exit that had spat them onto the sidewalk wouldn't let them back in.

"*Great*," said Anakin, and punched the wall. "*Now* can I use the Force?"

With an effort, Obi-Wan controlled his irritation. "No. Let's keep wandering along this way, shall we? Perhaps we'll come across a legitimate entrance."

"You know," said Anakin, falling into step beside him, "for a man who once dived headfirst through a bedroom window three and a half kilometers above street level, you're being awfully cautious."

He sighed. "The word is *clandestine*, Anakin. I do wish you'd remember it."

"I know, I know," Anakin muttered. "Sorry. Guess I didn't realize how much I'd hate all this sneaking around. I prefer the direct approach. Overwhelming firepower. It cuts down on the fiddly details. Saves a lot of time, too."

"Don't worry," he said, letting some of his own tamped-down grimness show. "Once we've thwarted Dooku's latest plot we'll see every Separatist occupier on this planet wiped from its surface."

"That's not like you," said Anakin, after a moment. "You aren't the bloodthirsty type."

He wasn't keen to answer Anakin's unspoken question. Squinting against the soggy grit thrown up by passing traffic, oily fumes stinging his eyes and souring his mouth, he hunched his shoulders, ready to deflect his former Padawan's curiosity—

And changed his mind.

"No," he said, lifting his voice just enough to be heard over the erratic stream of groundcars and trundle carts, and the crashing reverberations of the just-landed Separatist ship some-where inside the spaceport. "I'm not. But you feel it, Anakin.

The dark side is poised to consume this planet and every innocent man, woman, and child living here. They were at peace, they were harming no one. And then the Separatists came—and they brought the dark side with them."

"Huh," said Anakin. "So. You're angry. I get that. But how come when *I'm* angry you jump on me and tell me my feelings are irrelevant? What is this, Obi-Wan? Do as I say, not as I do?"

"You want to know the difference, Anakin?" he retorted. "Fine. *I* have no intention of acting against this occupation until we've accomplished our mission. I *look* before leaping. And we both know the same can't always be said of you."

"Maybe not," said Anakin, truculent. "But it's funny how nobody ever complains when me not considering consequences like, say, I could get killed, ends up saving the day."

Taking hold of Anakin's arm, Obi-Wan tugged him to a halt. "Don't. This isn't about what I owe you, Anakin. I know what I owe you. It's about us setting aside our personal feelings, our disgust at the cruelties of this place, so we can do our job. Because if we don't, if we let the misery here cloud our judgment, then the Separatists win."

Already there was grime and sweat smeared over Anakin's face. Jaw stubbornly set, his gaze directed elsewhere, in his eyes shone frustration and resentment and hurt.

And then, with a sharp nod, he let them all go.

Hugely relieved, Obi-Wan clapped a hand to his shoulder. "Come on. Whoever Lanteeb's newest visitor is, he or she must be disembarked by now. We don't want to miss seeing who it is. And there *has* to be an entrance along this wretched wall somewhere."

Side by side they moved on, picking up their pace—but not to a run, because running would attract the attention of a passing Separatist official or one of the battle droids patrolling across the road. After a couple of minutes they saw the signs they were looking for.

LANTIBBA SPACEPORT DOCKING BAYS 11–16.
RESTRICTED ACCESS. NO UNAUTHORIZED ENTRY.

"What do you think?" said Anakin. "Will our entrance be counted as Unauthorized?"

"Oh, most definitely, I'd say," he replied, and flashed a sly grin. "But I don't see why that should stop us, do you? Let's go."

TWELVE

EXCEPT THEY WERE STOPPED—BEFORE THEY COULD TAKE A SINgle step off the sidewalk. Four MagnaGuards patrolled the spaceport entrance, each droid armed with two fully charged and activated electrostaffs. So much for influencing security to let them pass.

"*Halt! Hands up!*" the lead guard commanded, menacingly looming, its photoreceptor eyes burning with an almost sentient zeal. "*Your presence is unauthorized. Do not move. You will be scanned.*"

Snapping immediately into his meek Lanteeban persona, Obi-Wan swallowed a curse and raised his hands. At least here was confirmation that Bail's instincts were right. MagnaGuards weren't Sep cannon fodder, tinnies, or clankers. They were Grievous's elite, the most intelligent, aggressive droids in the Separatist arsenal. A MagnaGuard's level of AI programming was so high, the things were but a microcircuit or two from being alive. They wouldn't be stationed here if the prize they protected wasn't vital. Unfortunately this also meant that their chances of escaping this confrontation with whole skins were less than encouraging.

He didn't dare look at Anakin.

Clandestine, remember? Humble. Downtrodden. I know you can do it.

The ID chip in his wrist burned as the spaceport's security sensors passed through it. And though he had complete confidence in Jedi technology, still he held his breath while the scanner hummed over the shielded pocket inside his shirt. But his lightsaber wasn't detected, and neither was Anakin's.

So far so good. Now if only the droids didn't insist on a body search . . .

"*What is your purpose here?*" demanded the lead Magna-Guard. "*This area is restricted. You are breaking the law.*"

Ranged wide behind it, blocking the spaceport entrance, the other three droids stood poised to attack. Eager for any excuse to strike, they twirled their crackling electrostaffs idly. Suggestively.

"We're sorry," said Anakin, trying to watch all four at once. "We're lost. We just landed and realized we left something important on our ship. We need to get back to it and—"

The MagnaGuard's move was so swift Anakin couldn't save himself. The electrostaff in its left hand stabbed him in the belly, discharging a vicious micro-ionized energy blast into his body.

He dropped, limbs flailing, eyes rolled to white crescents.

"No, sir, please, no!" cried Obi-Wan and plunged to his knees, arms cradling his head. "This is a mistake! We mean no harm! We've been away from home a long time and everything's changed. We're confused. We didn't mean to trespass. We didn't know we were breaking the law. Oh please, *please*, sir, don't hurt us! *Please* let us go!"

Beside him, Anakin twitched and groaned on the recently resurfaced ferrocrete. But that was good. Twitching and groaning were good. They meant he wasn't dead. Frustratingly, tantalizingly, the interior of the spaceport was only meters away. Continuing his pretense of devastated cringing, through half-closed eyes he took in the scene beyond the intermittent wall of MagnaDroids.

More droids. Battle units, this time. Lethally armed but easily dispatched—by a properly armed, unencumbered Jedi. What a shame that wasn't his job description today. He could see humans, too—not browbeaten Lanteebans but more Separatist forces, at least a score of them, each man uniformed and armed to the teeth with blasters and shock-sticks. So far their attention was trained on whoever had arrived on the VIP ship, but that might change at any moment—and there were too many for him to mind-control on his own.

A sudden stirring beyond the Sep officials and ranked battle droids. Raised voices. A steadily blarping klaxon. He couldn't catch a glimpse of the Techno Union vessel, but he could see a large vehicle with opaquely tinted windows slowly advancing. The sleek, expensive groundcar carved its way between the Sep security officers and battle droids, who fell back to each side of the spaceport's restricted-access entryway. Red and orange laser beams flared as the vehicle negotiated a coded defense grid barring access to the inner docking bays.

Obi-Wan felt his jaw tighten.

So much security here. So much new infrastructure. The Seps certainly haven't wasted these past several weeks.

It was going to make getting to the bottom of this mystery a challenge.

Anakin moaned and blinked at the sky, his disordered nervous system trying to reassert control. He muttered something. Struggled to roll over.

Obi-Wan reached out. "No, no, Markl," he whispered. "Don't move. Don't—"

The lead MagnaGuard stuck one durasteel foot under Anakin's rib cage then lifted and shoved, propelling him onto the road and into the path of an oncoming groundcar. No need to fake fear this time. Obi-Wan dived after him, and grabbed

one elbow and an ankle and hauled him desperately onto the
sidewalk using mundane strength only. It was too risky to use
the Force. The groundcar swept by, its driver wide-eyed with
horror, not daring to stop or even sound the horn. Thwarted of
prey, of grisly entertainment, the MagnaGuards spat curses
and advanced, raised electrostaffs flaring. It would mean instant
death if they struck the face or throat or heart. And at this close
range the droids couldn't fail to hit their mark.

"Please," Obi-Wan whimpered, hunched over a still-dazed
Anakin. "Please let us go. We won't come back. We promise."
Knowing what would most appeal to these cold, ruthless droids,
he squeezed out a tear. "Please. We can't hurt you."

The lead MagnaGuard tossed the electrostaff from its right
hand into its left. With perfect precision, its three companions
followed suit. And then there were four built-in laser cannons
trained on them, muzzles glowing and primed to fire.

"We know you can't hurt—"

"Hey, you stupid barves!" the nearest Sep officer shouted,
noticing at last the commotion behind him. "What are you
doing? Let the feebles go and get out of the way before I decom-
mission you!"

The MagnaGuards stood down.

Not waiting for a follow-up question from the man who'd
just saved their lives, Obi-Wan hooked his arm around Anakin's
shoulders, roughly hauled him to his unsteady feet, and dragged
him pell-mell across the road in the face of traffic coming at
them from both directions. Horns blared. Somehow they made
it to the far sidewalk without mishap. Breathing hard, he turned
right and didn't stop staggering until they'd reached the farthest end of a line of shops facing the spaceport's high-security
entrance.

Every one of the outlets was abandoned. Boarded up. From

the freshness of the hoardings, it hadn't happened long ago. And it hadn't happened peacefully, either; the sidewalk was stained with smears and blotches of dried blood.

Coughing, his assaulted muscles still twitching, Anakin fell against one barricaded door and swiped his shaking forearm down his sweaty, dirty face. "Well, I think it's official," he rasped. "This is now my least favorite mission *ever*."

"I don't know, Anakin," said Obi-Wan, watching the Magna-Guards march onto the road and stop the oncoming groundcars and trundle carts in their tracks. "You're so hard to please."

"Ha." With a last dry cough Anakin pushed off the door to stand unassisted, swaying a little, but able to keep his feet. "What are we looking at?"

"*That*," he said, nodding at the groundcar. "In there is our mysterious VIP Separatist. Someone the security guards were anxious not to delay."

With the traffic held up, the VIP vehicle proceeded to make a left-hand turn onto the ill-maintained road. Pushing aside the city's ambient misery, Obi-Wan stretched his senses toward the retreating vehicle. But instead of feeling a sentient intelligence, for good or ill, he felt himself sliding like water over glass.

"That's odd."

"What is?" said Anakin.

"I can't pick up whoever's in that groundcar. Can you?"

The electrostaff shock had left Anakin pale, his gaze not quite focused. "Ah—wait—I don't—" He shook his head, frustrated. "Sorry. I'm still scrambled. Give me a minute."

The groundcar was picking up speed as it headed off down the road. "Anakin, I'd love to, but they're getting away."

Anakin rubbed at his eyes. "Yeah. I can see that. If I jump on your back, I suppose Force-sprinting after them is out of the question?"

"Very funny." Still—if Anakin could make appalling jokes he mustn't be hurt too badly. A minor victory. "But perhaps, until you're less scrambled, we need to think not of speed but of persistence."

The traffic was flowing again, coming toward them, an empty open-topped trundle cart. "Got it," said Anakin, and stepped unsteadily to the edge of the sidewalk. He stuck his fingers in his mouth and blew a piercing whistle.

"Yes, that's the idea," Obi-Wan sighed, as the vehicle changed lanes and started to slow, "but remember *subtlety*, Anakin!"

It was Anakin's turn to smile. "I'm hard to please? Come on, quick. Before our quarry manages to lose us."

Trying to appear casual, not the least bit hurried or desperate, they piled into the trundle cart. The droid operator's availability light flashed over from blue to red.

"Where to, good sirs?"

Anakin leaned forward. "No specific destination. See that flash groundcar up ahead? Follow it. Not too closely."

"Cannot comply, good sirs," said the droid. *"Programming overrides do not permit interactions with government vehicles. Please state another destination."*

Obi-Wan felt a twinge of irritation. "All this Separatist interference is getting on my nerves."

"Hold on," said Anakin. "You give up too easily."

Bending down, wincing, he used a quick burst of Force-enhanced strength to remove the droid's control plating.

"Okay. Let's have a look-see," he said under his breath, talking to himself as he often did when fixing machines. "Right. If I pull this wire—and *this* wire—and switch out *these* two control crystals—and cross-clamp *this* node with *that* one—"

"Anakin . . ." Obi-Wan flicked an uneasy glance across the

street, toward the MagnaGuards. They hadn't noticed anything as yet, but that could change in an instant. "Are you quite sure you know what you're doing?"

"Me? No," said Anakin, fingers still busily rearranging the droid's innards. "I'm making this up as I go along."

Obi-Wan looked at him. "So when I said before that you'd do well not being *flippant,* I was using a word with which you're unfamiliar? Is that it?"

"Hush," said Anakin, scowling with concentration. "Don't distract me. Why do you always have to distract me when I'm trying to work?"

By this time the VIP groundcar was a blip in the distance. Obi-Wan looked around. Any moment now, any moment, they were going to be accosted. There were patrolling battle droids farther down the sidewalk, heading their way. A handful of Lanteebans scattered as they approached, a miasma of fear rising from them, feeding the dark side.

"*Anakin.*"

"Yeah, yeah, I know, hold on," Anakin muttered, not looking up. "Almost there . . . almost there . . ." He sat back. "Okay. That's it. Manual override." Picking up the semi-detached interior control panel, he pressed a series of switches in swift succession. The droid beeped and the trundle cart's engine shifted up a gear out of idle.

The VIP groundcar had completely disappeared.

Obi-Wan breathed out sharply. *Well, this mission's off to an encouraging start.* "Wonderful. We've lost them."

"Only temporarily," said Anakin. "I hope."

"Can you feel what you felt when that ship was landing? Or are you still scrambled?"

"A bit," Anakin muttered. "My head hurts."

He took Anakin's wrist; felt its pulse beneath his fingers, and the burning behind Anakin's eyes. Felt the pernicious echoes of the electrostaff shock's disruption. Reaching for the healing Force, he settled Anakin's disordered senses. Melted the pain. Cleared his vision.

Anakin sighed. "That's better. Thank you."

"You're welcome. Now, can you find that groundcar?"

"I'll give it my best shot . . ." Anakin murmured, then handed over the doctored control panel. "Here. You drive. I need to concentrate."

He nudged the trundle cart into the sputtering traffic flow, and they chugged their way back past the spaceport's restricted entrance and its brutal quartet of MagnaGuards, past their human superiors, the open markets, and many more patrolling battle droids. It seemed the droids outnumbered the Lanteebans here: a standard Separatist tactic. Next they passed another long row of boarded-up shopfronts. Dismayed he stared at them. As if Lanteeb weren't suffering already. How many livelihoods had Dooku's people destroyed? How many lives?

And still there are systems who join his Alliance willingly. How can they be so blind? How can they not see the monster behind the smiling, urbane mask?

The stream of traffic swept the trundle cart onward. Lanteeb's spaceport was steadily falling behind them. Now they were passing through an odd, in-between stretch of abandoned buildings. Somnolent warehouses and smokeless chimneys. In the Force, a strong sense of decay.

Anakin shifted in the trundle's cramped seat. "Obi-Wan, you'll have to speed up. I think I'm sensing whoever's in the groundcar, but the contact's faint and—and—it's *weird,* it's *slippery* and—"

That fleeting sensation of water on glass. "Like you can't quite grasp it?"

"Sort of. I can grasp it and then it slithers through my fingers. Which means they're getting a long way ahead of us, so let's *hurry*."

He flicked a look at the other vehicles sharing the double-laned road, cruising along at a steady pace. "I appreciate your concern, but we can't go any faster. Droid transports are speed-limited, they—oh. Of course. That was the first control you disabled, yes?"

Anakin grinned. "Surprise!"

"No." He sighed. "Not really. But even so, we can't shoot off, Anakin. We'd only make ourselves conspicuous."

"We'll have to risk it," Anakin insisted. "We can't afford to fall any farther behind. So get a move on or this fascinating local tour we're taking will end up being a colossal waste of time."

"D'you know what your problem is?" he said, cautiously nudging the trundle cart's accelerator circuit. With a grinding whine of protest, the vehicle increased speed. "Your problem is that every time you get into a vehicle—*any* vehicle—you immediately think you're Podracing again."

Eyes half closed in concentration, Anakin chuckled. "You say that like it's a bad thing."

Still whining, the trundle cart passed an open groundcar. Its elderly Lanteeban driver flashed them a startled, disapproving look. *Vape it.* He eased off the accelerator.

"No. Don't," Anakin protested. "What are you doing?"

"Trying to avoid trouble," he retorted. "Who knows what kind of traffic-control measures the Seps have put in place? For all we know there are autospeed sensors monitoring our progress, and if we trigger one of those things we'll—"

"Yeah, okay, but Obi-Wan—I can practically walk faster than this!"

"Do stop exaggerating and *focus*. We need to find that groundcar."

"No, do we?" said Anakin. "I thought we were taking the air for our health."

That made him stare. "Really, Anakin, there's no need to be sarcastic. I don't know where you get it from, but it's most unbecoming."

Anakin stared back. "Are you—" He shook his head. "Never mind. Sorry. I just want to get this done and go home."

Trust me, that makes two of us. "Then stop talking and start sensing."

By now the spaceport was kilometers behind them and they were entering a run-down industrial district. There were smokestacks on many of the long, high buildings surrounding them, most belching greasy gray and dark brown effluvium. The air smelled burnt. Soaked in noxious chemicals. Obi-Wan felt his eyes sting. Felt every shallow breath scorch his mouth and throat. Stay here too long and surely their lungs would corrode to bloody sludge.

Coughing, Anakin pointed. "We need to go that way. Change lanes, quick."

He fiddled with the control panel.

"No, look where I'm pointing, Obi-Wan! *Right,* not *left*!"

"Sorry—sorry—" Amid a blasting of horns he managed to career the trundle cart across the next traffic lane into a turnout. Wrestling the control panel, he jiggled them to an idling halt.

"No, no, don't stop, Obi-Wan, *go*!" urged Anakin. "Come on, hurry, I'm losing the vaping groundcar!"

With an unwise burst of speed he scooted the trundle cart in front of the oncoming traffic, off the main road, and into a quiet street running between two long lines of active factories. Within meters their vehicle's engine cut out, the droid beeping ominously as they lost momentum.

"*Vehicle has exceeded permitted transport distance. Engine override. Engine override.*"

"What?" said Obi-Wan, fighting the trundle's sluggish controls to guide it safely to the side of the street. "Anakin, I thought you'd taken control of this thing!"

"I did!" Anakin protested. "But how was I supposed to know it had a built-in booby trap?"

On a deep breath he regained his calm. "You weren't. It's all right. It just means we'll have to make it on foot the rest of the way." Closing his eyes, he reached out in the Force—and felt it again, that peculiar deflection. "Blast. I cannot place that groundcar. What about you?"

Anakin nodded. "It comes and goes but yes—I've got it."

So they abandoned the defunct trundle cart and continued their pursuit, Anakin leading the way. The rain that had fallen on the spaceport must have been a local cloudburst; the buckled, potholed ferrocrete here was dusty dry.

"I don't like this, Obi-Wan," said Anakin after a while, staring around at the deserted street. "I can feel people in these buildings. I can feel their fear. But the area's like a cemetery. And there's danger . . ."

He nodded. "I agree. We're too exposed like this. I think we're going to have to risk a little Force enhancement before someone notices us and raises the alarm. What about the groundcar? Do you still have it?"

Slowing, Anakin closed his eyes. "Faintly. I think I can just hold on to it."

"Then let's pick up the pace, shall we? The sooner we get out of the open, the happier I'll be."

Lightly blurred within the Force, smearing their presence in the world like a thumb dragged through wet watercolor paint, they broke into a slow jog. Eyes still closed, running purely on Force-informed instinct, Anakin guided them deeper into Lanteeb's stinking industrial district. Three groundcars hummed by them, but they remained undetected. They jogged past the narrow mouth of a laneway. Glancing sideways Obi-Wan saw four battle droids poking their blasters into a kicked-down door. The blurring held; the battle droids didn't see or hear them.

One kilometer. Two kilometers. Three. Five. The polluted air thickened, became hazy and even less comfortable to breathe. He began to feel a distinct uneasiness, a *wrongness* that grew more pronounced by the minute. He felt a rasping in his throat. Heard the same distress echoed in Anakin.

And then, without warning, the Separatist microchip in his wrist burst into violent, burning life. Gasping, he let go of the Force. Stumbled into real time and struck the sharp edge of a fer-rocrete wall with his shoulder.

Somewhere up ahead, a klaxon started wailing.

"Vape it!" said Anakin, in real time beside him. "I can't *be-lieve* this Sep security!"

They'd stumbled into a sensor-monitored restricted zone.

No need to confer. Grabbing their wrists, they reached for the Force and used it to fuse the microchips' circuitry. That hurt even worse than the original insertion, but it was better than being found by the Seps. And any trouble the fused sensors caused them later on would have to be dealt with later on. Right now disappearing from the sensor grid was the only thing that mattered.

The wailing klaxon fell silent.

Shaking his hand, Anakin stared down the empty street. "With any luck they'll put it down as a false alarm."

Obi-Wan gave him a look. "You know the Jedi place no faith in luck."

Anakin snorted. "Right now, I'll place my faith in whatever I can find. The groundcar's up ahead."

Behind them, the chilling sound of tramping metallic feet and staccato, electronic voices.

"Roger, roger. Sensor net triggered by unauthorized personnel approach. Will check it out. Roger, roger."

"Wonderful," said Anakin. "Who invited tinnies to the party?"

They turned and ran.

IT WAS THE DARKNESS that warned him. Ablaze with the Force, running effortlessly in the light, it felt to Anakin like he'd stumbled abruptly into an abyss, a chasm so deep that the hottest sunshine could not reach its cold heart.

He wrenched himself to a stop, to find Obi-Wan alarmed and halted beside him. They stared at each other.

"You feel it?" said Obi-Wan, his face pale, his breathing unsteady. "The dark side, like a poison?"

He nodded. He had the feeling he'd turned a little pale himself. In his belly, a wrenching nausea. "Yeah. And we're in the right place. The presence I felt on the Sep ship and in the groundcar?" He pointed. "He or she—or it—is in there."

There was a massively protected compound, some six hundred meters distant at the end of the street. Its perimeter was marked by a forbidding durasteel wall, ten meters high at least, which was topped with laser turrets at three-meter intervals. A faint crackling in the air told them a laser net burned in front of it. Even this far away the technology was unmistakable. Two wide main gates, locked and laser-protected and guarded by blaster turrets, seemed to be the only way in.

Terrific. And here's us dressed like Lanteeban lumberjacks.

"Anakin," said Obi-Wan, slapping his arm. "Time to make ourselves scarce."

Even as Obi-Wan pointed he felt another sickening ripple in the Force. Looking up, he saw a security cam buzzing their way, flying what appeared to be a random search-and-alert pattern. They had a few moments' grace, surely; if they'd been actually spotted, that klaxon would be shrieking again.

"*Anakin,*" said Obi-Wan. "You can admire the technology later. Let's go."

Well, yeah, except where? Every building at this end of the street had been razed. A few piles of twisted, melted rubble was all that remained.

But it'll have to do.

The security cam swooped left, following its programming. Stopped in hover mode, focusing on something at ground level. The flickering red lights around its base blazed brighter, then held steady. And then it started to hum.

"Now, Anakin," said Obi-Wan tightly. "While it's distracted."

As they hurried sideways, heading for the nearest jumble of slagged debris, a laser blast shot out of the security cam's upper housing. *Great. The thing's armed?* Something screamed in brief agony. A native rodent, most likely. Another laser blast. Another scream. And then the security cam was on the move again.

Deftly, Obi-Wan manipulated the Force to dislodge rubble farther down the wrecked street. The security cam halted, sensors buzzing, then plunged off in pursuit.

"We don't have long," he said. "Hurry."

Within heartbeats they were belly-down and scrabbling across broken brick and melted glass toward long, broad sheets of durasteel heat-warped into fantastically impossible shapes. The mound of scorched debris had formed a kind of cave, and that was what they aimed for. Reaching it, they scrambled inside. Found not quite pitch blackness; three thin fingers of clouded sunlight fractured the gloom. Lightsaber banging against his ribs, Anakin stopped scrambling. But before he could look around and get his bearings—

"Vanish," said Obi-Wan . . . and disappeared within the Force. Following his lead, Anakin disappeared after him.

Oh, I remember this.

Childhood in the Temple. Playing hide-and-seek with his fellow students because he was still too young to travel the Republic with Obi-Wan. Vanishing was one of a youngling's most important lessons—but the Temple Masters hadn't needed to teach him. He knew that Jedi trick already. Much later, he realized he'd been doing it for years. That slavery had given him this one, priceless gift: the ability to disappear at will.

He'd used it to hide from Gardulla—eventually, not soon enough—when she came ranting with her whip. From his mother when he didn't want to come in to bed. From Watto, when he was tired of chores in the workshop. From Sebulba and Aldar Beedo and Gasgano, when the Podraces' most vicious pilots were out for blood and fighting them wasn't an option. He'd even used it twice while racing. Had somehow managed to vanish not only himself but his Pod, startling his targets so badly they'd both crashed out as he zoomed by, laughing.

He hadn't told anyone in the Temple that. Knew they'd never believe him, because that depth of vanishing wasn't meant to be possible. Certainly not for a child of eight.

But it had been. He could do that. So now? A man grown, with the Force obedient to his will? Hiding from a stupid security cam was a piece of poodoo. No sweat.

Like a leaf on a still pond he floated in the light, sharply aware of Obi-Wan floating somewhere close by. A warm presence. A dark gold glow in the Force, steadfast and unfaltering. After a time, since he had nothing better to do and it might prove helpful, he let his mind ride the Force's rippling currents. Let the Force carry him away from from misery-soaked Lanteeb.

Visions drifted before his quiet inner eye. Snatches of the past. He saw his mother laughing, and smiled despite the pain. Saw Padmé on her balcony, unbound hair blowing in the breeze. Felt desire flame through him and doused it, with regret. He saw Ahsoka with her lightsaber in the circular halls of Kaliida Shoals, her small face set in fierce concentration. Saw Rex, wrapped in a blue medcenter shift, watching her train with unspoken admiration.

Then the scene shifted, abruptly, and he was looking at Obi-Wan bending over someone stretched out on the ground. It was nighttime, no lighting, and he couldn't see where or when this was. *"Hold on,"* Obi-Wan was saying. *"Hold on. I'm with you. Don't go."* Naked pain in his voice. An awful raw grief he'd never revealed before.

Shocked, Anakin felt himself plunge out of the vanishing, plunge back into his body and the immediacy of danger.

Beside him, Obi-Wan swallowed, eyes gleaming in the dim, dust-ridden light. "Anakin," he said, almost too softly to hear, his lips barely framing the word. "Be quiet. Don't move. And keep your body temperature down. It's right on top of us."

He froze, again feeling that ominous ripple in the Force. Just audible, the buzzing hum of the Seps' armed security cam as it flittered over their heads. He held his breath and willed his thumping heart to ease. Willed his body's core temperature to remain low. Like a swimmer he sank himself just beneath the surface of the Force.

The security cam moved on.

Relief, sharp and scouring. He closed his eyes. Dropped his head. Let himself silently laugh, feeling a fierce and feral triumph. Then he opened his eyes again—and froze a second time.

Obi-Wan's fingers wrapped tight around his wrist. "I know," he breathed. "I know. Anakin, you mustn't make a sound."

They were lying on the charred remains of human beings.

And suddenly he could smell the blackened death in this place. Still and silent now, with that first annihilating, obliterating rush of adrenaline drained away . . . he could smell it. And he could see it, too, those three fragile fingers of light just bright enough to show him.

There were people in here when the Seps razed this building.

Oh. Oh. He was going to be sick. Echoes of fear and agony and despair raged around him, released by his own senses, by sight and smell and touch. Somebody's ashes were sticking to his skin. He was breathing in the detritus of murdered Lanteebans.

Looking up, beyond anguish, he stared at anguished Obi-Wan.

"It's too dangerous to move around out there in daylight, Anakin," Obi-Wan murmured. "We'll have to wait until nightfall."

Wait in here? With the dead?

Obi-Wan's eyes were full of shadows. "I know."

Banishing the horror, pillowing his head in his folded arms, he vanished again.

HOURS PASSED. Vaguely mindful of not borrowing trouble, Anakin resisted the temptation to seek for more visions in the Force. Instead used the time to rest and replenish himself. Week after week of dire battles had taken their toll. So had the injuries he'd sustained above Quell. Though the Lurmen had treated him on Maridun, and med droids finished the task on *Resolute*, there remained a lingering . . . not weakness. Not exactly. More like a memory of damage and pain. This was as good a time as any to summon the Force and allow it to work its will on him.

And it kept him too preoccupied to dwell on the dead.

Inevitably, as the sun set, those three fracturing fingers of light faded. First came twilight. On its slow heels, full darkness. His mouth was dry. His belly rumbled. The sweat of nausea had dried sticky on his skin.

At some point he heard the clanking procession of battle droids as they passed by on patrol.

"Roger, roger, base. All clear. No disturbances. Repeat, we're all clear."

Stupid blasted tinnies. Long may they stay so dumb.

Unmoving beside him, close enough to touch in the gathering darkness, Obi-Wan. Drifting in and out of wakefulness. Vanishing, then coming back only to vanish again moments later. Like a Whaladon in the ocean depths, coming up for air. He'd seen Whaladons once, in the waters of Agomar. Just like Obi-Wan they'd seemed monolithic and wise.

It started to rain.

The air was still warm and muggy. They weren't in danger of freezing. But the chemical-tainted water stirred the dead's ashes to pungent life. The stench was revolting. He felt bile burn his throat and coat his tongue.

At last Obi-Wan stirred again. "Well, I don't know about you, but I've had quite enough of this," he said, his voice rough. "Let's get out of here, shall we?"

It was a great idea, but—"What about the curfew?" His own voice was just as harsh. He hawked and spat. "If anyone breaking it gets shot on sight, that argues there's got to be someone around to shoot them."

The sound of shifting cotton as Obi-Wan shrugged. "It's a

risk we have to take. We must find a way inside that compound, Anakin. And the cover of darkness gives us our best chance."

He grunted. "If you say so, Master."

"Master?" said Obi-Wan. "Does that mean if our plan fails, you're going to blame me?"

"Well . . ." He grinned in the pitch darkness. "That's the general idea, yes."

A gentle snort of amusement. "I'm touched. Now get a move on."

Crawling out of their hiding space, Anakin closed his mind to the feel of sharp things like sticks, that most likely *weren't* sticks, breaking and rolling under his hands and knees. If he let himself think he'd get lost in dangerous anger.

Free at last of that particular nightmare, they stood on the sidewalk and tipped their faces to the sky. Easing off now, the rain spackled their skin. Dribbled through their hair. There were no streetlights. Hardly any stars. Half a kilometer down the road, the searingly illuminated secured compound, shouting loudly in the night.

Anakin shivered. "I want the longest, hottest bath . . ."

"A cold tap will have to suffice, I'm afraid," said Obi-Wan briskly. "I just hope we can find one, because at some point we're going to have to get clean. Although—perhaps not quite yet. Filthy as we doubtless are, it will come in handy as camouflage."

"Yeah—that sounds great in theory," he said. "But it's more a case of what we're camouflaged *with*."

Silence. Then Obi-Wan eased out a slow breath. "I know."

A longer silence—which was broken by the faintest thrum of an approaching vehicle. Together they turned and caught the dancing nimbus of distant headlights bouncing off the wet ferrocrete road.

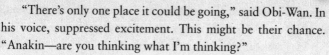

"There's only one place it could be going," said Obi-Wan. In his voice, suppressed excitement. This might be their chance. "Anakin—are you thinking what I'm thinking?"

"Depends," he said as the vehicle hummed closer. "Are you thinking that's our way in?"

"It's risky," said Obi-Wan. "If it doesn't work, we're almost certainly dead."

It was Anakin's turn to chuckle. "So—same old, same old? Then what are we waiting for?"

Running lightly, they headed back along the street. The vehicle was close now, headlights burning two holes through the dark. Some kind of delivery truck, looming tall. They reached the first untouched building. Pressed themselves into its wide, deeply recessed doorway, face-first, hands fisted against their chests so their skin wouldn't catch the light. The truck glided by on its antigrav cushion, the driver oblivious to their presence.

As soon as it was safely past they Force-jumped onto its roof, landing light as snowflakes. Cast themselves facedown, letting the Force pin them in place. Shared one brief, mutually encouraging look—

—and vanished.

THIRTEEN

ALONE IN HER LABORATORY, SCIENTIST FIRST LEVEL BANT'ENA Fhernan tossed down her electrostylus and pressed her cold, shaking hands to her face.

I can't do this. I can't do this anymore.

A chrono on the blank, pale gray wall opposite ticked away the dwindling dregs of her life. She'd been counting time for days. Weeks. No, it was months now, wasn't it. Two months, three weeks, and seventeen Corellian days had dragged by since she and her research team were swept up in the chaos and carnage that was the Separatist annexation of Taratos IV.

If my mother knew where I was, if she thought I was alive and could reach me on a comlink, she'd be saying I told you so. A lot. Very loudly.

But her mother didn't know where she was, or think she was alive. Nobody did. Well, nobody she cared about. It was a fair bet her family and friends and even her enemies believed she was dead and decomposing with the rest of her research team on the ruined sands of Niriktavi Bay.

Her mother, flamboyantly incoherent at the best of times, had begged her not to travel to the barely mapped lip of the Unknown Regions. But she'd long since stopped paying attention to her mother's tempestuous predictions of doom, and so she'd gone.

And why wouldn't she? The war was nowhere near that part of space and the chances of it reaching Taratos IV in the few weeks she'd be there, well. *"You're the gambler, Mother,"* she'd said, so scathing. So confident. *"The odds are minuscule and you know it. Stop inventing catastrophes. This is a once-in-a-lifetime opportunity. A career-making chance to impress the right people. Think of all the industrialists and philanthropists with credits to burn."*

Her working hypothesis about the antibacterial applications of radiologically treated and molecularly manipulated Niriktavi coral had attracted *enormous* attention. Several major biotech corporations had asked her to bring them her preliminary findings as soon as they were tabulated.

"Not go? Honestly, Mother, you can't be serious."

And then one beautiful morning, a month after beginning her life-changing, groundbreaking work on Taratos IV, as the planet's pale mauve sky exploded into riotous dawn color—explosions of a different kind had rent the warm and scented air. Without warning, out of nowhere, an enormous ship had appeared disgorging hordes of battle droids. On two feet, on no feet, rolling at lethal speed, armed with blasters and laser bombs, flying through the air on weapons-mounted mobile platforms. Without mercy or provocation, the Separatists attacked.

She and her research team weren't the only scientists at Niriktavi Bay. Oceanologists, marine biologists, archaeologists— so many *ologists* she'd given up trying to keep track. Just recently opened to exploration and academic investigation, the Taratos IV central government at long last cajoled into sharing its planet's wonders, the Bay was a treasure trove and had attracted the best, the brightest, the most astounding scientific minds in the Republic. Generations of knowledge and experience and painstaking study, gathered in this one place to celebrate learning and the mysteries of life. But the Separatists didn't care about that. They slaughtered indiscriminately, efficient as a plague.

Slaughtered nearly everyone. Slaughtered her friends and co-workers and people she didn't know, who might have become her friends if she hadn't been working so hard. But Bant'ena Fhernan, they took. A few other scientists, too, though she never saw which ones. And as the droids dragged her away, screaming, as afterward her human Separatist captors pumped her full of suffocating drugs, all she could think was *No, no, please, not for me. Not all this killing so you could take me.*

She still had no idea where the other captives were, or what had happened to them. What they were doing. She'd asked once, and been punished, and didn't dare ask again.

Grief rising like a tidal wave, Bant'ena pressed her hands harder against the jutting bones of her face. Two months, three weeks, and seventeen Corellian days ago she'd been plump. She wasn't plump anymore. Right here, right now, a cantina musician could use her rib cage for a xylophone.

If Raxl could see me he'd be horrified. Appalled. He hated skinny women. He loved the meat on my bones.

The thought of her research assistant and sometime lover scalded fresh tears to her eyes. Raxl was one of those decomposing bodies on the blasted remains of Niriktavi Bay. She hadn't seen him die but knew that one of the dreadful screams she'd heard had to have been his.

A convulsive intake of air as open weeping threatened to consume her. Savagely she struck her fists against her chest.

Stop it, you fool. Don't do this. Don't think of what happened. Don't think of him. It doesn't help. There's no going back, no undoing it. You're a ghost now—and so is he. So are they all.

Thanks to her captors, the laboratory she slaved in—her other prison—was state-of-the-art. When it came to equipment and resources there was nothing she could ask for that her Separatist masters wouldn't supply. As though a request for this electroscope or that particle divider meant she had joined them. That she didn't loathe them. That she was in fact one of them. But she did loathe them. And if she had joined them it was never an act of free will.

I just wish I believed that made any kind of difference. Who will care why I did this after it's done? When I'm finished— when I've succeeded—I'll be a murderer, just like them.

Unless she rebelled, of course. Unless she took a stand and refused point-blank to cooperate anymore. Let them punish her further, in large ways and small. Forced them to inflict upon her the ultimate retribution.

And if I do that—well, I'll still be a murderer. So it makes no difference, does it. Either way I lose.

Her chest hurt where she'd pounded it. She rubbed at the bruises. Looked again at the wall chrono. It wasn't that late. She should be working. Someone would be along to check on her soon. They checked her progress every day. And if she didn't have something positive to show them, if she wasn't able to demonstrate a gain, to justify her existence, to calm their easily woken suspicions, then they would indicate their displeasure.

They were very skilled at hurting her in ways that didn't interfere with her work.

Ranged down the long right-hand wall of her lab she had seven different experiments, each in a different stage of development. Three she had hopes for. Two were lost causes, but she'd decided to let them play out. The other two were winners. Not completed, not yet. Nearly. Just looking at them made her feel sick. She made herself feel sick.

Why was I born good at this? Why couldn't I be a talented ballerina?

The lab's back wall was taken up with cages, not quite half of them home to a soon-to-be-dead rodent. The ugly underbelly of science. Small, expendable lives. She'd long ago come to terms with their deaths. What difference was there between eating an animal in a restaurant and killing it in a lab, when diner and scientist shared the same goal?

There was no difference. In that case, at least, her conscience was clean.

Sublimely oblivious to their own dwindling time, the lab rodents chittered and snuffled as she began to clean out their cages. In her old life she'd had a droid to do such chores. But it pleased her captors to keep her humble.

And then behind her, the closed door swung open and her principal jailer swept into the lab.

"Doctor Fhernan! You're back! Welcome home, my dear."

No, you stinking barve. I'm not your dear. Never your dear.

Belly churning, ruthlessly she schooled her expression and turned to face him. "General Durd. I wasn't aware you'd returned to Lanteeb."

The slovenly, bloated Neimoidian smiled, unctuous and insincere. "Yes, yes. Several hours ago. I'd have been along to see you before now but I was engaged in other matters. But now I'm here and *you're* here. Isn't it delightful? Such a happy reunion, hmm?" A calculating look crept into his odd, alien eyes. "And how are you, my dear? Your little adventure went well, I take it?"

The coded secure-box she'd escorted back to the compound sat unbreached on its own bench against the lab's left-hand wall. Abandoning the doomed rodents, she crossed to it. Stood beside it, gaze subserviently lowered. Durd loved it when she abased herself before him.

"Yes, General."

"Yes, General—and?" Durd prompted.

She looked up. She had her pride, battered though it might be. "And I procured the substance we discussed."

"Oh, how *delightful*," said Durd, his eyes gleaming with unrestrained avarice. "And you're quite sure it's what you need to move the Project along to the next stage?"

The Project. That was what Durd insisted on calling this terrible weapon she was helping him create. As though an innocuous euphemism could somehow make it less evil. Not that he considered it evil, of course. In his sick and twisted mind, what they were doing was glorious.

On the far side of the lab, her experiments quietly bubbled.

"Yes, General," she said, her voice perfectly even. No hint, never a hint, of what she kept to herself. If ever once he suspected . . . *He thinks I'll come around to him. He thinks my passion for the science will seduce me to his side. But he's wrong, he's so wrong.* "The rondium you sourced for me is exactly what's required for the job."

"That's not a very big container," said Durd, frowning at the secure-box. "Will we have enough?"

His ignorance never failed to astound her. "Of course, General. I've brought us more than enough rondium to run extensive controlled laboratory tests and—" She cleared her throat and sent up a silent prayer for forgiveness. "And undergo multiple field applications."

"Hmm." Coming closer, Durd trailed one languid finger across a benchtop, in passing. "Curious, isn't it, that you had to travel to see our friends at Ralteb Minotech, instead of testing the rondium here? At home?"

This is not my home, you pustulent slimebag. This will never be my home.

She lowered her gaze again, terrified he'd read the revolted thought in her eyes. "I'm sorry, General. Did I not adequately explain the reasons for my trip? Colonel Argat seemed to think I did, which is why he gave me permission to go." She looked up. "With an armed security detail, of course."

Halted in front of her, Durd was smiling, unamused. "Colonel Argat miscalculated, Doctor, when in my absence he allowed you to leave Lanteeb. Even with an armed security detail. As a result, Colonel Argat is no longer in a position to authorize anything. Colonel Barev is your liaison now. You'll meet him when he arrives in the morning."

"Oh," she said faintly. Did that mean Argat was dead? Had she gotten the man killed? Did she care? He was one of them, a Separatist.

But he was never unkind. And there were times, when he didn't realize she was watching him, that he seemed sad. As though he didn't want to be here any more than she did.

"Tell me, my dear," said General Durd, one moist fingertip beneath her chin, tipping her face up so she had to look at him. "Were you thinking you might be able to evade your armed security detail? Or slip a note to someone at Minotech? Even find an unsecured comlink and send out a call to the Republic, for help?"

Of course I was. "No, General," she said, her mouth horribly dry. "As I explained to the colonel, rondium is highly idiosyncratic. Depending on where it was mined, it can contain impurities that would render it useless for our purposes. Minotech has rondium sourced from twenty-two different systems. It was less risky, less—less *conspicuous*—for me to go to them and test it on site than it was for them to transport twenty-two samples here to me."

Playfully, Durd tapped the end of her nose. "No wonder

Argat believed you, Doctor Fhernan. Such a *convincing* little thing you are. Tell me, why did you sit outside in your groundcar for so long? I was beginning to wonder if you'd *ever* come in."

So he'd been spying on her. Surprise, surprise.

I was talking myself into setting foot in here again, General. I was talking myself out of breaching the secure-box and committing suicide with the rondium.

She manufactured an earnest smile. "Oh. Yes. Actually, I was thinking. Just as we were on final approach to the spaceport I had an idea about the Project. About the problems we've been having with the conversion process."

Durd raised an eye ridge. "We?"

"I'm sorry. I mean me, of course, General," she said hastily. "I was thinking about the problem *I've* been having with the conversion process. I was still working my way through a possible new formula when the groundcar pulled through the compound gates and you—you know what it's like when inspiration strikes. You don't want to interrupt your train of thought. So I sat outside until I could get the whole formula clear in my mind."

Durd's pupils bloomed. "Is that so?"

"Yes, General." She crossed to her main workbench and snatched up the datapad she'd been scribbling on. "See?" she said, thrusting it toward him. "I've been double-checking my new calculations. I'm sure they're accurate."

"Hmm." Durd glanced at her notes as though he could actually understand them. "Well, my dear. It's a start in making up for your corruption of Colonel Argat. But I suggest you continue your reparations by giving us a breakthrough with that rondium. Tonight. Count Dooku was rather disappointed to lose the colonel's services, you know. Receiving an encouraging update on the status of our Project will surely put him in a forgiving mood."

Reparations? Forgiving? *Oh sweet mercy* . . . "I'm very sorry Count Dooku is disappointed, General."

"As you should be. And now—" Durd yawned. "I bid you good evening. I've been very busy and I want my bed. A general's duties are endless, you know." Hands clasped over his belly, he cast a pleased look around the lab, at her seven experiments and all the formulae and notes scrawled across the intelliboards and the benches of expensive equipment and the stacked cages of sacrificial rodents. "We're doing great work here, Doctor Fhernan. Great work. And when all is said and done, the galaxy will be deeply, *deeply* in our debt. We are on the brink of achieving freedom from the tyranny of the Republic and its raddled Senate. There'll be songs sung about us one day, my dear. *Songs.* I can hear them now."

Somehow she managed not to gag. "Yes, General."

Halfway to the lab door he clapped a hand to his clammy forehead and turned back. "My dear, my dear!" he exclaimed. "I was so excited to have you home again I completely forgot." He plunged a hand into his pocket. Pulled out a compact holo-unit and placed it gently on the nearest bench. "A gift for you. Enjoy."

She stood where she was for a long time after he left. Breathing, just breathing, until the urge to vomit passed. Until her tear-blurred vision cleared. The holo-unit sat on the bench like an unexploded bomb.

Don't look. Don't look. He wants you to look. Don't look.

But how could she not look?

The first recording was of her mother, shopping in the fresh produce market held every week in downtown Tiln. It meant an hour's uncomfortable traveling, but Mata Fhernan wouldn't buy her rubias and her chee-chee berries anywhere else. The shielded droidcam capturing the image had also recorded sound. Her mother was talking about Palpatine's latest address in the Senate with one of the stall holders. Durd's way of authenticating the recording. She'd watched the address herself, live, two days ago. It was the only news she'd been permitted to see.

Mother looked well.

So did her brother, Ilim, and his wife and the new baby, in their Corel City apartment. So did her sister Chai, and Chai's husband, Bem. Both their boys had colds, though, and runny red noses. Probably it wasn't a smart idea to take them on their annual camping trip to Alderaan, but Bem was so tenderhearted. He hated disappointing his young sons. The droidcam had caught them disembarking their transport at Alderaan's central spaceport, three days earlier.

Angry, despairing, Bant'ena smeared the tears from her cheeks.

I should've been born an only child. I should've been orphaned years ago.

And it was a pity she wasn't the kind of person who couldn't make friends, because if she *was* that kind of prickly person then Didjoa and Samsam and Lakhti and Nevhra wouldn't now be living with unseen, loaded blasters pointed at their heads.

A dreadful cramp of fear, revulsion, and grief doubled her over. Hanging on to the bench to stop herself from falling, she felt the tearing sobs rise in her throat. Heard them burst and break the lab's cool silence.

I have to do this. I have to. If I don't, they're all dead.

"HMM," SAID OBI-WAN thoughtfully. "I wonder if this was such a good idea after all."

Anakin looked at him. "I bow to your wisdom in all things, Master."

"Since when?" Obi-Wan retorted, half smiling. "Now hush a moment."

They were crouched deep in a concealing pool of shadows, at the rear of the Separatist compound's delivery station. After passing through four security checkpoints undetected they'd stayed on the truck's roof as it made achingly slow progress along a narrow ring road that took them past the compound's roofed parking area where the fancy groundcar had been left to keep company with two others, and around to the back of the searingly lit sprawling two-story complex. Eventually the truck pulled into an enclosed loading dock and a droid crew came out to unload its contents: three large antigrav pallets' worth of unmarked crates.

As soon as the driver was preoccupied with getting his documentation cleared, and the droids were busy juggling boxes, Obi-Wan had nodded and they'd leapt down from the truck's roof. Letting the Force blur their presence, they melted into the darkness around the edges of the delivery station.

By Anakin's estimation that had been nearly an hour ago. Since then another six crate-filled trucks had arrived, been unloaded, then departed. And still they were stuck in here because they had to be *clandestine*. They couldn't just take out the droids and march right into the complex's main building to find out what was being cooked up there. Because that would be acting like Jedi, and on this mission they weren't allowed to act like Jedi. Not proper Jedi, anyway.

He was starting to *hate* clandestine.

"Look," Obi-Wan murmured. "This might be our chance."

The delivery station was now crowded with loaded antigrav pallets. The next truck, if there was a next truck, would never fit inside. And it seemed the droids had finally noticed that because their designated leader, a boxy unit with a faulty vocoder that turned its voice into a ludicrous squeak, was issuing orders for the pallets to be convoyed up to the main building.

"*According to instructions, General Durd wants what's in these crates,*" it announced. "*And what General Durd wants, General Durd gets. So stir your servomotors, you bunch of rusty spare parts!*"

Anakin sucked in a sharp breath. General Durd? *Lok Durd,* Dooku's pet weapons inventor? But Durd was in Republic custody—wasn't he?

Obi-Wan leaned close. "I don't suppose there are two General Durds?"

"I doubt it." He watched the line of droid-propelled antigrav pallets snake out of the delivery station. "But that means the stinking barve's escaped Republic custody. How is that possible? And why haven't we heard anything?"

"Well . . ." Obi-Wan ran a hand over his beard. "We've been a bit busy lately. Perhaps we missed the memo."

"Or perhaps there's a cover-up," he retorted. "Because it doesn't look good, does it? Another captured Separatist slipping through our fingers?"

"Now, now," said Obi-Wan, soothing. "Let's not jump to conclusions."

"Maybe it was Durd in the groundcar. That would explain why I felt something familiar."

"Then I suppose we should be grateful for what happened on Maridun," said Obi-Wan. "Since it gave you the connection."

Grateful? Not really. "I suppose. Funny that I couldn't tell it was him, though. Or that you couldn't sense him at all."

"Yes. Very strange," said Obi-Wan. "But let's worry about that later."

The last of the droid-guided pallets floated out of the delivery station. And that just left the droid supervisor, checking off delivery stats on its datapad.

"Right," Obi-Wan added, rising out of his crouch. "I'll distract it, you incapacitate it, fast. But *carefully*—make it look like a circuit malfunction."

Incapacitate it, just like that. Without leaving a trace of tampering. A droid model he'd never seen before. Sometimes Obi-Wan's faith in his abilities was a bit daunting. Good thing there were no lasting aftereffects from that electrostaff shock.

As Obi-Wan approached the supervisor droid with his trademark swagger, Anakin had to grin. Filthy and dressed in cheap, dowdy clothing, no lightsaber in sight, still Obi-Wan looked like a Jedi.

"Excuse me," he called out. "I'm sorry to bother you, but I appear to be lost."

The warning light on the droid's head flashed. "*Who are you?*" it squeaked, turning. "*What are you doing in here? You're not authorized to be in here.*"

"I know, I know," said Obi-Wan apologetically. No trace of Jedi in him now—he was back in cringing native Lanteeban mode. His movements were casually and deliberately erratic, so the droid had no choice but to swing itself around to keep him in line with its photoreceptors. "There's been some dreadful mistake. Can you help me? Where am I? I think I fell down and hit my head."

Still grinning, Anakin eased himself out of the shadows. The droid had its back to him now. He could see the access plate between its two primary arms. That was his way in . . . but what would he find? Soft-footed, feeling his edges blur again, he drew on the Force in preparation for his task.

Obi-Wan was doing a perfect job of keeping this droid distracted. Yes, definitely Coruscant's Firebird Club was missing out on a crowd-pleasing act.

If he ever has to give up being a Jedi, at least he's got a ready-made job to walk into.

He was five soft steps from the droid. Four. Three. Two. One.

He reached for the machine's access plate. Why wasn't the droid designed like C-3PO, with an external deactivate switch? Why wasn't anything *simple* these days? His fingertips touched the scarred, dark brown metal—and a blinding shock of pain shot up his arm.

Vape it! Vape it! The blasted thing's shielded!

Time blurred. As the droid started to turn, screeching a protest, he used the Force to immobilize it, short out the access plate's shielding, and let him into its innards. Every insulted nerve in his body was shrieking. He was seeing double. Practically triple. It was the electrostaff shock all over again. Obi-Wan's lips were moving but he couldn't hear a single word.

Letting go of rational thought, he surrendered himself to instinct, to the odd quirk within that made him one with machines. The same quirk that had melded him almost effortlessly with his prosthetic limb and perhaps was the reason he'd lost none of his connection with the Force, even though his arm and hand were made of metal.

His vision cleared. His hearing returned. The pain receded. And he knew how to gain control of the droid. Metal and flesh fingers worked swiftly, confidently.

"Done?" said Obi-Wan.

He nodded. "Done. Are you in the mood for a little interrogation? I've managed to circumvent its limiter."

"Good job," said Obi-Wan with a swift grin. Then he focused on the droid. "What is this place?"

"A facility of the Confederacy of Independent Systems," replied the droid, its squeaky vocoded voice oddly slurred. *"Under the command of General Lok Durd."*

"What was in the crates those droids took up to the main complex?"

Something inside the droid's metal body hummed. Clunked. "*Supplies.*"

"What kind?" Obi-Wan persisted. "Some of those crates had breathing holes. What was in them?"

Another whirring clunk. "*Checking manifests—hold please—checking mani—laboratory rodents.*"

Anakin frowned. "Lab rodents?"

"For experimentation," said Obi-Wan grimly. "Which would suggest—"

"We were right," he breathed. "It's a bioweapon. Great."

Obi-Wan snapped his fingers in the droid's face. "What was in the other crates?"

"*Checking manifests,*" said the droid, its vocoded voice still slurring. "*Hold please—checking manifests—hold pl—*"

As the droid recited a long list of items, which included rodent food, nonperishable human food, a wide variety of Neimoidian delicacies, electronic supplies, industrial lubricants, holo-equipment, and many boxes of data crystals, Anakin checked to see if there was any sign of the other droids returning.

"Still in the clear," he told Obi-Wan, rejoining him. "But I don't know for how long. Better wrap this up."

"Agreed," said Obi-Wan. "Droid, what is the security complement of this facility?"

"*That information is outside my programming parameters.*"

"What's going on in the main building?"

"*That information is outside my programming parameters.*"

Obi-Wan's lips thinned, betraying his irritation. "What can

you tell me about any other CIS personnel currently stationed in this facility?"

"*That information is outside my programming parameters.*"

"So much for learning anything else useful," said Obi-Wan, giving up. "All right." He waved a vague hand. "Put this thing back together again, Anakin. Quickly."

He rolled his eyes. "Yes, Master."

While he took care of that, Obi-Wan headed for the delivery station's office, sited at the top of some battered metal stairs. But, being Obi-Wan, he didn't bother climbing them. He Force-leapt to the landing outside the office and disappeared inside.

It was the work of moments to rejig the droid's circuits—but he wasn't able to reestablish its shielding. If he'd had his microcircuitry kit with him, he could've done it in his sleep. But he didn't, and he couldn't see one conveniently lying around, so he covered their tracks by inducing a partial meltdown of the shielding unit. The next time anyone bothered to check the droid—and with luck that wouldn't be till long after they'd left this place in the dust—the damage would look like an energy surge and whoever noticed wouldn't think twice about it.

Last of all, he used a tiny tendril of the Force's power to subvert the droid's short-term memory chip. It was a common problem with older machines, and this model was a few years off the production line. The ruse should hold.

And then he was done, but there was still no Obi-Wan. With a frustrated glance up at the office, he left the droid on standby and returned to the front of the loading dock. Heard the measured tread of metal feet and geared wheels.

Oh, wonderful. The other droids were returning.

He Force-sprinted back inside. "Obi-Wan! Get a move on, we've got company!"

Obi-Wan appeared in the open office doorway. "Almost done."

"No, no, not almost done! You're done *now*! The other droids are—"

Obi-Wan held up a finger then ducked back into the office.

Stang.

He leapt back to the boss droid. Cradled its still-disconnected access plate in one hand and rested a finger on the machine's reset button.

Come on, come on, come on, come on . . .

Obi-Wan landed lightly beside him on the loading dock's ferrocrete floor. He was grinning anarchically. "Well, don't just stand there, Anakin. We haven't got all night!"

Oh, ha ha. Very funny. Obi-Wan, you're a riot.

"What were you *doing* up there?" he demanded, resetting the droid and slamming its access plate into place. "Taking a nap?"

"Playing fast and loose with their security recording," said Obi-Wan, still grinning. "We were officially never here. Oh— and because every good boy deserves a treat—catch!"

It was a comlink. He snatched it out of the air. "Great. Thanks. *Now come on!*"

As they bolted for the loading dock's entrance, the boss droid buzzed awake. A quick exchange of glances and they slipped into Force sprint, whipping around the rear of the delivery station just as the first returning droids came into view.

Once they were clear they slowed to a stop. Their sprint had carried them dangerously close to a security laser grid, laid out between the loading dock and the perimeter fence. Although the beams were invisible to the naked eye, still they could feel them humming in the Force. They retreated a prudent distance and dropped to the closely cut grass. The edge of a security light bled over the delivery station's roof, casting their immediate surroundings into stark black and white.

Obi-Wan rummaged inside his shirt then pulled out a flimsi. "I found this, too. A schematic of the main complex. As far as I can tell, electronic security inside the building is practically nonexistent. No laser grids or motion sensors. Just some rudimentary fixed-cam surveillance."

"That's not very smart."

"It's overconfidence," said Obi-Wan, pleased. "They're convinced the compound's external security is so comprehensive that there's no need for further inconvenience inside."

"Which makes life a little easier for us. For a change," said Anakin. "Hey—while you were busy pinching schematics and comlinks I don't suppose you came across any food?"

"I'm afraid not. And that's going to be a problem. We need sustenance and water."

"Well, you heard what that droid said. Lots of Neimoidian delicacies in those crates."

Obi-Wan shuddered. "I think I'd rather eat the rodents' food. Or the rodents." He grimaced. "Better yet, let's just not let ourselves get quite that hungry."

"Sounds like a plan to me." He let himself relax, just a little bit. "Okay. What now?"

"Now we need to investigate that main building. At this late hour it's unlikely anyone is working." Obi-Wan squinted at the schematic, holding it up to the faint light. "There appears to be a series of ventilation ducts networked throughout the roof and walls. If we can get inside without setting off any alarms, we should be able to move about with relative ease. Perhaps even access the main laboratory."

"Then let's go."

"Wait," said Obi-Wan, touching his forearm. "First, let's see if we can find out who we're up against in there. Since you're familiar with Durd you look for him, and I'll indentify how many other sentients we've got to deal with."

Look for Durd? *Wonderful.* He'd hoped never to cross paths with the Neimoidian again. Durd had a filthy mind, slimed with cruelty and avarice. The kind of petty spirit made monstrous by the slightest acquisition of power. But he couldn't afford to be squeamish. The mission came first. Like it or not he had to seek the barve out.

"Anakin?"

"Yeah. I've got it."

He closed his eyes and breathed in and then out, slowly and deeply, letting go of his hunger and thirst and uncertainty. Letting go of everything. He became one with the Force. Dimly he was aware of Obi-Wan on the grass beside him, treading the same familiar path.

The world vanished, then reappeared in different shades of red. Scattered imprints of distant, sentient life touched his awareness. On another exhaled breath he closed his mind to every living creature but the one he was seeking. He allowed his memories of Maridun to drift to the surface, carrying with them the psychic stench of Separatist general Lok Durd.

Where are you? Where are you? Show yourself, you vaping scum.

His belly twisted. He'd caught Durd's scent.

Overcoming reluctance, he quested closer. Followed the greasy trail Durd left in the Force until he ran the filthy creature to ground. The Neimoidian was asleep in a separate building in the compound.

Durd was alone in his room. There was no sense of sentience anywhere nearby, either. Withdrawing, Anakin cast his seeking mind farther afield. Surely Durd couldn't be the only living being in the whole place.

No. There were the lab rodents in the main complex, tiny pinpricks of life. And there was another imprint near them, much larger. Its shape in the Force was human. Female. Without warning he was swamped by a terrible fear. Misery. A cold and crushing guilt.

Startled, he opened his eyes. Obi-Wan was staring at him. "You felt that?"

He nodded, and for a moment couldn't speak. The woman's overwhelming pain shuddered through him, smashing flat his defenses. Touching buried, scarred-over places inside him.

Don't show Obi-Wan. Don't let him see that.

"Whoever she is she's in trouble. We've got to help her."

"And we will if we can," said Obi-Wan sharply. "But first things first, Anakin. We've got to get inside that building without raising the alarm. We're here to destroy a weapon. *That's* our primary mission."

Obi-Wan was right, but even knowing that, he felt a stab of resentment. They were Jedi. They could do two things at once. And what was the use of saving the galaxy if you let its wounded inhabitants fall by the wayside? When the big picture grew too big to see, what was left to focus on but the details?

"*Anakin.*"

"I know, I know," he muttered. "Don't worry. I'm with you."

Obi-Wan shoved the schematic inside his shirt. "Glad to hear it. Now come on."

Side by side and silent, on foot this time, they made their stealthy way back to the compound's main building.

FOURTEEN

THE COMPLEX'S AIR VENTS PROVED TO BE A BLASTED TIGHT FIT

Obi-Wan, facedown, the weight of his body supported on forearms and toes, face a mere finger's-width from the filthy vent flooring, closed his mind to the burning in his back, belly, and legs.

Behind him, Anakin muffled a curse.

The fit was even tighter for him, of course, being broader across the shoulders and more heavily muscled in general. But the discomfort couldn't be helped. Nor was it relevant. Their pain was temporary. The destruction caused by a Separatist bioweapon would likely be permanent.

Though he didn't believe in luck, he was forced to admit that the compound's lack of comprehensive internal security was . . . convenient. An enemy's overconfidence could indeed prove a powerful ally. Although—how far that overconfidence extended had yet to be seen. He and Anakin might yet face insurmountable obstacles once they ventured out of the venting system and inside the actual building. But he was feeling guardedly optimistic. So far they'd encountered only droids and a single sensor net, neither of which had registered their presence. He was even hopeful of outwitting any further security cams they might encounter.

And if at some point they did encounter sentient opposition, well, the Force was an even more powerful ally. Except if they didn't find food and water soon their ability to manipulate it would be significantly compromised. Every fire required fuel . . . and their reserves were running low. Trouble was, he hadn't anticipated such a swift start to this mission. He'd assumed they'd have a day, at least, to get their bearings and settle in. Find lodgings. Acquire supplies. Instead—

Now, now. Enough of that. Better a swift start than no start at all. Remember Qui-Gon's favorite saying: A solution to the problem is bound to present itself.

Glancing up, he saw they were about to reach the end of their current stretch of air vent. And that begged the question of which way to turn next: left or right? With a stifled grunt of relief he stopped crawling. Let his forehead drop against his filthy arm. So far they'd negotiated four long sections of vent set into the ceiling of the main building's first floor. Peering through every room's wall or ceiling grille, they'd accounted for two empty offices, a supply room, male and female refreshers, an unstaffed security monitoring station, and a droid maintenance bay. No laboratories yet, and no sign of personnel quarters. Still only two sentient presences in the compound—the repellent Neimoidian whom Anakin had apprehended on Maridun and that deeply troubled, unidentified woman. She was quite close now, farther ahead and higher up. The Neimoidian remained distant. Safely out of the way, for the moment.

So, Master Kenobi. Which direction will get us to her faster—left or right?

Or should they split up? They had comlinks now, and it would save time. He didn't want to be here a minute longer than they had to.

Anakin tapped his ankle, impatient, and he held up a hand.

Wait. Closing his eyes he sought for clarity in the Force. Encouraged instinct to inform him, and that sense of future events that had so often come to his rescue.

Instinct told him: *Stay together. Turn right.*

On a deep, measured breath he started crawling again. Anakin followed. When he reached the vent's intersection he paused, then began the spine-twisting process of negotiating its tight right-hand turn. He felt his vertebrae protesting, felt his tendons stretch and burn. Closing his mind to all sensation he thought of sinuous water, of a long braid of blue-green hair, silken and flexible.

Once he was well into the next straight stretch of vent he stopped and waited as behind him, Anakin bullied his long frame around the corner. He was doing his best to move silently, stealthily, but even so his knees and heels and elbows knocked against the vent's sides. In this confined space the muffled bumps and thuds sounded horrendously loud. If anyone was listening, if anyone noticed—a patrolling droid, say, or some Sep arriving at the complex unexpected, or Durd deciding to prowl his domain . . .

Obi-Wan held his breath. Not even their Jedi skills would save them if they were discovered now. But there was no sudden alarm sounded, no warning klaxon or blaster shots or any kind of indication that their presence was detected. He exhaled in relief. Like Anakin, he really wasn't fond of clandestine operations. Geonosis came uncomfortably to mind. He wanted this over with. He wanted to be himself again, unrestricted, with his lightsaber back on his belt, not digging painfully into his ribs.

Another tap, this time against the sole of his leather-shod foot. Anakin was ready.

He started crawling again, once more ignoring the hot, quivering protests of strained muscle and sinew. Refusing to acknowledge his dry mouth and throat, the headache behind his eyes, the voracious rumbling in his gut. The Force would sustain him a little while yet.

They reached another supply room, this one full of blasters and sonic grenades. A veritable arms cache. Wonderful. He started moving past it, but stopped when Anakin grabbed his ankle. He felt a tremor in the Force, a buildup of energy. Abruptly realized what Anakin was about to do and awkwardly snatched his ankle free.

Turning his head as far as he could, not quite able to catch sight of Anakin's face, he hissed a warning between his teeth. "No. Don't."

Anakin's frustration was palpable. "Why not?" he hissed back. "If we—"

Oh, Anakin. Still so reckless, so unwilling to look before the leap. "Shh!" He wriggled until his neck was jammed almost to the breaking point. Until he could see Anakin's furious glare. *"No."*

"But—"

Somehow he managed to shake his head. If Anakin fused every weapon in that supply room and the sabotage was discovered before they'd achieved their objectives, they'd likely never escape the compound—let alone the planet. The missing comlinks and schematic could be put down to carelessness. Their tampering with the droid could be attributed to sloppy maintenance. But an entire cache of ruined blasters and grenades? They might as well leave a calling card.

He didn't dare risk further argument. Instead poured his will into the look he gave his former student. Shamelessly played upon their earlier relationship, on the inviolate authority he'd once held over a small boy.

The old Master–Padawan bond held. Just. But the look in

Anakin's eyes said this conversation wasn't over yet. And that was fine. That he could live with. But neither of them could live with inconvenient discovery.

He smiled and nodded, wanting Anakin to know he wasn't being taken for granted. Anakin didn't smile back, but his taut expression eased.

Crisis averted, they kept on crawling.

Beside the weapons cache was a laboratory. Lots of unused equipment, but no people. Next door to it another unoccupied lab. They passed over a corridor, also empty. Passed some kind of office containing a desk and chairs and a wall of storage cabinets. Next came another corridor—but this one wasn't empty. This one was being patrolled by battle droids.

"*Roger, roger,*" the lead droid said into a comlink. "*Northeast sector secure.*" A faint buzzing as someone or something on the other end of the link spoke. "*Laboratory secure. Doctor Fhernan is still working. Second level secure.*" More buzzing. "*Patrol perimeter. Roger, roger.*"

The battle droids moved on.

"Obi-Wan," hissed Anakin. "The bioweapon."

Yes. Time to climb to the second floor and find the lab where it was being created, apparently by this Dr. Fhernan—who must be the woman sending those tremors of distress through the Force. But if she was resident in this Separatist compound working with Lok Durd, why would she be distressed?

Something's not right here.

They kept on crawling until they ran out of vent again. Ending at a wall, it instead became a chute leading to the sprawling building's top floor. Unfortunately its manufacturer had neglected to include a ladder, or any hand- or footholds. So inconsiderate. Rolled awkwardly onto his side, Obi-Wan squinted upward. They didn't dare risk a Force jump. There wasn' enough light to see what they'd be jumping into, or enough room to execute such a maneuver cleanly. If they tried, it was likely they'd make enough racket to end their mission on the spot.

This is going to be interesting. Time for a little inventive teamwork, I think.

Trusting that Anakin would follow his intentions, he kneed and elbowed and struggled his way upright in the chute, striving not to make even the tiniest untoward sound. It was excruciating. His joints burned in protest. His taxed muscles shrieked. Shift and stop. Shuffle around and stop. So slow, so *slow*, he was taking too long.

Again, he felt Anakin's fingers tap his ankle. Not a warning or a complaint this time, but a gesture of encouragement.

Heartened, he completed his arduous contortions. Took a moment to mop his sweaty forehead on his sleeve, then looked down. Anakin was wriggling his way to the bottom of the open chute. Once he was in place he looked up and nodded. Nothing but determined endurance in his face. With a swift, quirky smile he finagled his hands over his head, laying them flat, palms-up, on the vent's floor.

Obi-Wan indulged in his own swift smile. Yes. They were indeed working in sync. And he realized then how much he'd missed this. Had missed Anakin and the way they could read each other without the need for clumsy words. They were a better team than even he and Qui-Gon had been. And while he understood completely the need for them to unravel their partnership—not only because of the war, but also because Anakin was a Jedi Knight now, with his own responsibilities, still . . . he felt sharp regret.

Working without Anakin was like working half blind.

Anakin snapped his fingers. *Hey, are you ready?* Nodding,

he stepped onto his friend's hands. Centered himself within the Force, even as he felt Anakin gather its purpose for his own use. He tipped back his head. Focused his will and intent on the unseen lip of the chute, high above. Extended his arms, fingers lightly linked, like a diver—and leapt. And as he drove himself upward, drawing on the Force to propel him, he felt Anakin's answering explosion of will adding power to his power. Strength to his strength.

The walls of the chute flew past in a blur.

He reached the top easily, his fingers catching its lip, and used the Force as a brake to halt his momentum. His head swam dizzily and he nearly slammed into the chute's side—but managed to stop himself just in time. For a moment he hung there, like a carcass in a meat locker, then—once more drawing on the Force, and feeling the strain of that—heaved himself up and over the edge of the chute and into the next long stretch of vent.

Am I getting too old for this? I think I am.

More judicious wriggling saw him lying prone along the vent's floor, his chin level with the edge of the chute. Staring down to its base, squinting in the dim light, he was just able to see Anakin. Could sense him, of course, full of fire and resolution. He closed his eyes. Sometimes, especially when he was tired, like now, it was easier to focus without visual distractions. Reaching deep within, dredging himself for the last of his resources, he extended his arms into the chute, fingers spread and waiting. Felt Anakin gather himself, his arms upstretched. And then a surge of *push*, a surge of *pull*, as together they harnessed the power of the Force.

Anakin leapt.

They caught each other wrist-to-wrist, acrobats in a crazy secret circus. A bleeding edge of light from a nearby ventilation grille showed him a hint of Anakin's fierce grin as he braced his back and shoulders against one side of the chute and his leather-shod feet against the other so he was held fast, like a cork in a bottle.

Nodding his approval and appreciation, Obi-Wan wriggled backward, clearing the top of the chute, and waited for Anakin to negotiate the rest of the way. He did it easily. Folded himself into the next stretch of vent, breathing only a little bit harder than usual.

Ah, youth. *I remember it well.*

Anakin looked past him along the vent. "She's down that way," he whispered. "Can you feel her?"

Darkness and sorrow and revulsion and fear. "I can," he whispered back. "If I might make a suggestion, Master Sky-walker?"

"By all means, Master Kenobi."

"I suggest we eavesdrop awhile before we crash this Doctor Fhernan's party."

"Sure," Anakin agreed, sweat trickling down his face. He blotted himself dry on his sleeve. "That makes sense. We need to know what we're getting into." And then he pulled a face, the edge of his temper not quite dulled. "And since there's a better than even chance we're getting into trouble—I hope we don't end up regretting not wrecking those weapons."

It would be too easy to start an argument, and this was hardly the time or the place. So he shrugged and met Anakin's steady look calmly. "As do I. Now let's go."

They started crawling again.

This close to her location, the woman's—Dr. Fhernan's—emotional turmoil was much stronger. Obi-Wan felt it clouding the Force, muddying his own emotions. It was the last thing he wanted, or needed. But in order to find their quarry he had to embrace her pain, not resist or reject it. Behind him he heard

Anakin's breathing harshen as he, too, suffered along with the suffering woman they were trying to find.

In contrast with the ground floor, the rooms on this upper floor of the building were unlit. The darkness slowed their already slow progress but they had no choice; a headfirst tumble down an unexpected chute would be a disaster.

Cautiously they crawled to the end of the vent and negotiated its U-turn with panting difficulty. Crawled and crawled and turned another corner, following the woman's siren song of fear and pain and disgust.

Eventually they came to more light at last, farther along their current stretch of vent. Two rectangles of it, which meant they'd found the largest room yet. The lab? It felt likely. He could feel those pinpoint lives, the laboratory rodents in their cages—trapped, awaiting death. Washing over their life signs were waves of human distress billowing through the Force. Resisting the urge to speed up, Obi-Wan continued his painstaking way on forearms, elbows, knees, and toes. He couldn't feel another sentient keeping company with the woman, but there still could be battle droids or a roving security cam.

He reached the first grille and stopped. Anakin stopped behind him as he peered down into the laboratory. His field of vision wasn't perfect, but at least he could see—*her*. Yes, there she was, the source of the emotional pain churning through him. Tall and big-boned, with light brown hair cut raggedly close, she was dressed in a white lab coat over dark blue trousers. Her clothes didn't sit right, as though she'd recently lost weight. She had her back to him, and was hunched over a wide central lab bench strewn with a mini holoprojector and datapads and sheets of flimsi and electrostyluses and a plethora of scientific paraphernalia he couldn't begin to identify—or comprehend.

A mélange of odors tainted the cool, recycled air. Face

pressed against the vent's grille, Obi-Wan had no choice but to inhale the unsavory cocktail of chemical and rodent and hope it would have no lingering, deleterious effects.

Two clear, sealed containers on the lab bench caught his attention. One held a fist-sized chunk of a dark gray substance. He couldn't be certain from his awkward vantage point but he thought it was some kind of unrefined metal. The other container, larger, held an even bigger chunk of raw damotite, easily recognizable from the image included in Agent Varrak's briefing notes.

Even as he identified it, he felt a sickening twist in the Force, every instinct he possessed sizzling with alarm. It confirmed all their suspicions: damotite was definitely at the heart of this darkness. Anakin tapped his ankle—*Feel that?*—and he nodded, managing a confirming glance over his shoulder.

Scant meters below them, Dr. Fhernan stepped back from the lab bench, turning, and the long room's harsh lighting revealed her face. It was broad and angular, her eyes sunken and shadowed, her cheekbones razor-sharp against scarred, sallow skin. She looked deeply unwell. It was precisely the kind of face Obi-Wan had expected to see, given the depths of this woman's emotional pain. She was staring at something off to the left; he couldn't see what. The angles were wrong. But as she stared, a fresh wave of misery rose within her. She pressed two fingers to her trembling lips and held her breath until it passed.

Anakin tapped his ankle again. *Let me see, would you?* Fair enough. The woman started pacing, and he used the cover of her movement to ease himself along to the next grille so Anakin could see what was going on. Fortunately the unhappy scientist was too preoccupied to notice the soft shuffling sounds coming from overhead.

Settled once more, staring down at her, Obi-Wan waited.

Loud in the lab's silence, an electronic beeping. The woman—Dr. Fhernan—stopped her pacing. Crossed far left, out of his restricted field of vision. He heard the snapping of latex as it stretched over skin. Heard more beeping. Switches clicking on—or off. The doctor muttered something under her breath. Next, a chinking of tempered glass. Equipment being handled. Picked up. Put down. Then a slow, indrawn breath. A violent shudder through the Force. A moment later Dr. Fhernan walked back into view, holding up a slender, sealed test tube before her eyes. What looked like a spoonful of grayish green liquid sloshed inside it.

"Stang," she said softly. Mingled with her misery, an unmistakable pride. "Stang, I am *good*."

Obi-Wan felt some of his sympathy die.

Still holding the test tube she crossed back to the central bench and shoved aside a pile of flimsies, revealing a comlink. Raising it to her lips, she flicked the signal switch. A moment later she was answered. The indistinct voice on the other side of the transmission sounded displeased.

"Yes, sir. I know. But you need to see this."

Call completed, she dropped the comlink into her lab coat pocket then carefully placed the sealed test tube into a secure clamp-and-hold contraption. Swept projector, the datapads, and other materials to the far end of the bench, leaving herself a clear space in which to work.

Keenly aware of Anakin's intense concentration, his heightened emotions—for some unexplained reason his composure was rattled—Obi-Wan frowned at the scientist below them. Pride and misery. What did that mean? Was she or was she not a willing participant in this undertaking? He couldn't tell. And the uncertainty was making his bad feeling worse.

She's an enigma, blast it. A rogue factor. As if we needed another challenge tonight.

As he watched, Dr. Fhernan moved to the lab's rear wall where the caged rodents were kept. They chittered and scuttled nervously as she approached—and who could blame them? If any of the creatures had been here longer than tonight then they must surely know nothing good could happen to them in this place.

Poor things.

The scientist took a small, clear carrier from a shelf above the bank of rodent cages and extracted one of the animals from its prison. With practiced ease she thrust the squeaking, struggling creature inside, latched the cage shut, then returned with it to her bench.

Obi-Wan risked a look at Anakin, who looked back with his mouth twisted in disgust, pointed at the caged rodent then drew his finger across his throat in an economically eloquent gesture.

Indeed.

And then they both tensed. Someone was coming. *Lok Durd.* No more strange slipperiness about him. Like a slug in a garden, now the Neimoidian left an unambiguous trail.

Abruptly the cramped vent was full of Anakin's rage.

Pinned in place, Obi-Wan tapped softly urgent fingers to its floor. *Anakin, no. Don't do this. Not now.* His former apprentice appeared suddenly older. Ruthless and menacing. Not a man any sane being would willingly cross.

Anakin stared at him, sensing his desperate, unspoken plea. Nodded once, tightly, self-control reasserted, that obliterating flood of anger contained.

The laboratory door opened and a grossly overweight Neimoidian swaggered in. Dr. Fhernan stopped her pacing and stood to attention.

"General."

"My dear," said Durd. His voice was oily, his regard intent. "I hope there's a good reason you've disturbed my slumber. For if there isn't I'm afraid I'll have to—" And then his gaze fell upon the caged rodent. Shifted to the securely clamped, sealed test tube on the lab bench beside it. His breath caught. "Doctor?"

She didn't step back, but it was clear that she wanted to. Every line of her body showed her struggle with being in the same room as Separatist general Lok Durd.

As for Durd, his oddly-pupiled eyes were gleaming. He knew precisely how much this woman feared him and he reveled in it. Delighted cruelty rolled off him in cloying waves and his wide mouth glistened wetly as he breathed in her scent.

Obi-Wan frowned. First misery. Then pride. Now abject fear curdled through with hope. Defining this scientist was getting harder, not easier.

"*Doctor!*" said Durd, his voice a whipcrack. He pointed to the test tube. "Is that what I think it is?"

Dr. Fhernan cleared her throat. "Yes. After you left me earlier, I combined raw damotite with a distillation of the Minotech rondium. The new mix is stable and ready for testing."

"And will it work?"

"Yes," she said, and glanced at the mini holoprojector. "I believe so."

Durd shrugged. "You've believed that before."

"And it has worked before," she said steadily. Hot fear churned beneath her frozen exterior. "Just—not reliably."

The Neimoidian began to pace, close to waddling, plump hands clutched across his vast, robed gut. "But it's reliability we need, my dear. For your sake I do hope you've found it this time."

"As I said, General—"

"Yes, but I think you'll agree actions speak far louder than words," Durd said briskly. "I suggest you test your new formula, Doctor. I'll stay and watch. No need to worry. Thanks to the Kaminoans I've been inoculated, too, remember?" He smiled.

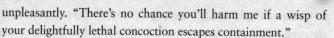

unpleasantly. "There's no chance you'll harm me if a wisp of your delightfully lethal concoction escapes containment."

What? Alarmed, Obi-Wan looked at Anakin. Their rebreathers were in the Jedi Temple, left behind with the rest of their standard equipment. If by some accident Dr. Fhernan bungled her experiment—

Oh, this is not good. This is not good at all.

Anakin shrugged, a gesture of almost amused resignation. *Cross your fingers, Obi-Wan,* his wry expression said.

How terribly helpful.

Having unclamped the sealed test tube, Dr. Fhernan unlatched the rodent's small cage and dropped it inside. The animal squeaked, startled, and cowered in a corner. The scientist closed the cage's lid, sealed its air vents, then searched the scattered equipment on the bench until she found a small silver implement, similar to an electrostylus.

"Wait, wait," said Durd, eager as a child at a naming day celebration. "I want to see *everything*. Wait till I find the perfect position."

Dr. Fhernan did as she was told, her face expressionless, as Durd fussed around and around the bench. At last he stopped, satisfied. Fortunately—or perhaps *un*fortunately—where he'd chosen to stand didn't impede the view from the air vent.

Obi-Wan wiped his damp palms on his shirt. *Bad* didn't come close to the feeling he had about this. A warm hand on his ankle. He looked back at Anakin, whose shadowed eyes reflected the same roiling unease.

"Are you ready, General?" Dr. Fhernan asked. Her voice sounded dead. She'd managed to tamp down her feelings. Achieve a level of scientific detachment. Warned by the Force, Obi-Wan felt his belly churn and fingers clench.

This is going to be unspeakable.

"Oh yes, quite ready," said the Neimoidian. He was almost wriggling with glee. "Hurry up, hurry up! I declare the suspense is almost killing me. My very first demonstration." He pouted. "Until now you've always managed to time your experiments whenever I'm called away to Count Dooku."

"And again, General, you have my sincere apologies for that," said Dr. Fhernan, toneless. "It was never intentional. The work dictates its own timetable. As a—as a fellow scientist, I'm sure you understand."

"Yes, well," said Durd, still pouting. "I think for your sake—and not only yours—it's a good thing that this time our timetables are compatible."

Dr. Fhernan nearly dropped the silver implement.

"Oh do come *along*, Doctor," Durd implored. "You've kept me waiting long enough!"

She bowed her head, as though in prayer or some other kind of profound thought. Then she looked up, her expression bleak, pointed the implement at the rodent's cage, and activated it. There was a hum, barely audible at first, then rising in pitch. Higher. Higher. The nervous rodent jumped, banging against the small cage's clear wall. It jumped again and again. Started leaping in a frenzy. The sealed test tube began to vibrate, rolling back and forth on the cage's floor. Lok Durd leaned forward, basted in pleasure, as though he could not get enough of the helpless animal's terror. And Dr. Fhernan, his accomplice, stared, too. But whatever she felt, still she kept it in chains.

With a loud splintering crack the test tube exploded. Its agitated contents, now a greenish black mist, curled and spread through the entire sealed cage. The rodent let out one shrill, agonized shriek then dropped to the cage floor and began convulsing. Hair and skin frothed and bubbled pinkly, obscenely, as the toxic vapor melted living flesh. Bone dissolved. The small animal was reduced to a soggy pile of slush.

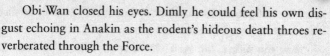

Obi-Wan closed his eyes. Dimly he could feel his own disgust echoing in Anakin as the rodent's hideous death throes reverberated through the Force.

General Lok Durd was clapping his hands in delight. "Oh, how wonderful. How *wonderful*. My dear Doctor Fhernan, it's true! You *are* a genius!"

The scientist fell to her hands and knees and vomited bile onto the laboratory floor.

"I *knew* it," said Durd, ignoring her. Pacing again as though his excitement were too great to be contained. "I *knew* that rondium would do the trick." He whirled. "Naughty, *naughty* Doctor Fhernan. You tried to dissuade me. You tried to tell me rondium would have *no* effect on the damotite. I think you were playing a game with me, my dear."

Still on her hands and knees, Dr. Fhernan smeared a sleeve across her mouth. She didn't look up.

"Is that so, Doctor Fhernan?" Durd demanded. "*Is that so?*" Suddenly angry, pouncing on the woman, he hauled her roughly to her feet. Fisted his pudgy fingers in the lapels of her lab coat and violently twisted. "Were you playing a game with me? Were you *lying* to me? Were you by any chance trying to ruin my plans? See me disgraced again before Count Dooku?"

Dr. Fhernan stood handspans shorter than the looming Neimoidian. Her breath strangled, she made no attempt to prise herself free of his clutching fingers.

"No, General," she croaked. "I would never do that. Why would I lie to you when I know what will happen?"

Durd thrust his moist, flat face into hers. "Perhaps you lied when you said you care! Perhaps their lives mean *nothing* to you!"

"No! I care!" The woman's words were a broken whisper. "I didn't lie, General. I have never lied to you. But I was wrong, I was mistaken and I'm so very, very sorry. I should've known you were right about the rondium. I thought it wouldn't be stable enough. I thought I knew better than you."

"But you *didn't*, did you!" Durd spat. "The great Doctor Bant'ena Fhernan, with degrees from the three most distinguished universities in the Republic. You *didn't* know better than General Lok Durd!"

Worked into a passion now, the Neimoidian was dangerously close to losing control. Dr. Fhernan's sallow face was dusky crimson, the air whistling in her throat.

"Obi-Wan!" hissed Anakin. "He's going to *kill* her! Come on—we can't sit here and watch!"

He shook his head, vehement. Yes, they could stop Durd's brutal assault—but only at the risk of betraying their presence and placing the entire mission in jeopardy. It was the scientist's life—or the lives of millions.

"No, Anakin," he hissed back. "Wait. *Wait.*"

"Do I need you?" Durd was ranting. "Do I need you, my dear Doctor? Do I? *Do I?*"

"Yes!" the woman croaked, desperate. "The refined formula's encrypted and I'm the only one with the key!"

Panting, Durd threw her to the floor. "Is that so? And were you by any chance thinking to keep that key to yourself, my dear? To alter our arrangement? Were you by any chance thinking to hold *me* hostage for a while?"

Dr. Fhernan groped her unsteady way back onto her feet, fear stark in her blanched face. "No."

"*No?*" Lurching to the cluttered lab bench, Durd snatched up the mini holoprojector. He turned and brandished it in front of her. "Are you sure? Are you *quite* sure? Because if you're lying now, Doctor—if you're lying to me—"

She dropped to her knees. "I'm not lying, General. I swear it. I'll give you the formula. I'll show you how to make it. I'll show anyone you like. Or I'll make it myself. As much as you want. I'll do anything you ask of me. Just don't hurt them. *Please.*"

Durd hurled the projector. It struck the doctor on the forehead, opening up a deep cut, then clattered to the floor. Blood sprang free of her body, pumped by her frantic heart. It slicked her open eyes, her hollowed cheeks, her parted lips.

"Please," she whispered, tears muddling with the blood. "I am begging you. Please, General Durd. Have mercy."

The Neimoidian's desire to hurt her shuddered him head-to-toe. His lips peeled back and his fists came up, desperate to strike.

"Do not test me again!" he snarled, reddish orange eyes glowing. "Do not be so foolish, my dear! Decrypt the formula, now. Make me a data crystal copy. I wish to inform Count Dooku of my success."

Shaking, the scientist did as she was told. Gave the data crystal to her tormentor and stepped back, out of his reach.

Durd tucked the formula into a pocket. "Very wise, my dear," he said softly, his voice ripe with menace. "I'll spare your loved ones—this time. But defy me again and there *will* be a consequence."

In a swirl of lush robes, he stalked out of the lab.

Dr. Bant'ena Fhernan stared after him, then covered her face with her hands and wept.

Every feeling conquered, Obi-Wan looked at Anakin. "Now," he said quietly.

They kicked the grilles off the vent and launched themselves into the room below.

FIFTEEN

STUNNED BREATHLESS, BANT'ENA STARED AT THE TWO RAGGED men standing in front of her. Who'd appeared, it seemed, out of nowhere. Like magic. Which was entirely impossible. So was this all a dream, then? Had she *dreamed* that moment when theory became fact and her reworked formula proved itself stable? Dreamed poisoning the Lanteeban rat? Was the pain in her throat where Durd had almost throttled her, was that—was all of it—a figment of her tormented imagination? Perhaps it was. Because this couldn't be happening.

"Doctor Fhernan, I know this is a shock, but you *must* pull yourself together and listen to me," said the older of the two men. His short hair and well-trimmed beard were clotted with dirt. Soot or charcoal smeared his face, his hands, and plastered the fabric of his plain, working clothes. He looked like a laborer on the run—and sounded like one of her biology professors. "Doctor, *please*. We might not have much time. Is this facility monitored? Are there security recording devices in your laboratory?"

She nodded, mute. Glanced at the man's younger, taller companion. He looked just as disreputable—but his eyes were unexpectedly kind.

"Are the recordings themselves monitored?" the older man

demanded. His eyes weren't *un*kind. Just terribly intense. "We passed a comm center on our way here—is that the only monitoring station for this facility?"

Another mute nod. She wondered when she was going to wake up.

"Good. And the recordings, Doctor? Are they assessed in real time? Or are they checked later, on some kind of roster?"

With an effort, she moistened her lips. *I might as well say something. It's a dream, after all. And Durd can't punish me for what I say in my sleep.* "I don't know." Her voice came out scratchy. Uncertain. "I don't think it's in real time."

The bearded man's brows pinched in a frown. "You don't *think* so? Doctor, I'm sorry, but I need more assurance than that."

Shaking, she pressed her hands to her face. "I don't—I'm not—" She let her hands fall. "Am I asleep or aren't I?"

"You're awake," said the younger man. "Don't be frightened. We're here to help you."

"Help me?" She tried to laugh, but it sounded like a sob. Turning away, she looked at the wall where the air vent's grilles had been kicked out. "If you were up there, watching, then you saw what I did." On a deep, painful breath she made herself face the specimen cage, and the appalling thing in it. "What I am. You know as well as I do—there's no helping me."

The younger man took a step toward her. "Durd is a monster." His voice was low and shaky. "None of this is your fault."

The older man started to say something, but his young companion raised a sharp hand.

Hope was a dangerous shudder inside her. "You can help me?"

"Not if we're discovered," said the older man. "Doctor, are you and Durd the only residents here?"

"At the moment," she said, dazed. "If you don't count the droids. A new military liaison officer arrives in the morning. I'm sorry—but who *are* you?"

"Friends," said the younger man.

"Who need your help if we're going to get out of here in one piece," his companion added, his voice snapping with authority. "So pay attention."

She jumped. This was no ordinary, downtrodden Lanteeban. Her fuddled mind cleared a little, and she looked at him more closely. Beneath all that dirt—was there something *familiar* about him? She didn't know him, had never met him . . . and yet she had the strangest feeling she'd seen him before. Had seen both of them, and not so long ago.

Memory stirred, reality shifted, and she wasn't in this terrible place, she was at home, on Corellia, cooking dinner and catching up with the HoloNet news . . .

"Sweetness and light," she whispered. "Are you—you're *Kenobi*." She turned. "And you're Anakin Skywalker. You're *Jedi*."

Anakin Skywalker, hero of the Republic, pulled a face. "Okay, so now we *really* have to take care of the security recordings."

Kenobi nodded. "Agreed. Doctor Fhernan—"

She couldn't believe it. The Jedi had come to rescue her. They'd save her family, her friends. The nightmare was over and everything was going to be all right.

"*Doctor!*"

"I'm sorry—what—"

"Obi-Wan," said Anakin. "Take it easy. She's doing her best."

Obi-Wan Kenobi, the other hero of the Republic, flicked his friend a warning look. "We've no time for *easy*. Doctor, is there

somewhere safe we can retreat to for a short while? Somewhere
Durd or those patrolling droids aren't likely to find us?"

With an effort she gathered her scattered wits. Kenobi was
right—and she was carrying on like a silly teenager instead of a
trained scientist. "I have rooms here. No one ever disturbs me—
but they're monitored."

"That won't be a problem. Anakin, go with Doctor Fhernan. Lay low. I'll deal with the security recordings and find you
afterward."

"Okay," said Anakin. "Need a hand tidying up?"

Shockingly, she caught a flash of wry, dry humor in Kenobi's
intense blue eyes. "If it's not too much trouble."

Anakin's face lit in a cheeky smile. "Of course it is. But for
you I'll make an exception."

Bemused, Bant'ena watched Kenobi line himself up with the
nearest open wall vent, high under the ceiling. Gasped when he
leapt to it, easily, and maneuvered himself inside the cramped
space. After a few moments, his face appeared. "All right."

Anakin tossed Kenobi the kicked-out grille, and he tugged
it back into position. Soon after he appeared in the other open
vent. When that grille was replaced, too, the younger Jedi turned
to her.

"Let's go."

Her life was *ridiculous*. When had that happened? *How* had
that happened? Murder and kidnap and blackmail and now
Jedi?

"Doctor Fhernan," said Anakin impatiently, sounding uncannily like Kenobi. "We have to *go*."

"What? Oh—yes—only—wait—just—just wait—" She crossed
to the lab bench and started scrabbling through its scattered
mess. "A few things," she muttered. "I just need a few things."
Data crystals. Notes. She grabbed her satchel from the floor be-

neath the bench and shoved everything into it, then looked at the young Jedi. "All right, we—no. No, wait." The holoprojector, she couldn't leave without the—where was it—where *was* it—

"Looking for this?"

Turning, she saw that Anakin was holding the projector. "Where did you—*how* did you—"

"Um—" He was giving her the oddest look. "Doctor, that slime Durd threw it at you. Don't you remember?"

"What?" Her fingers strayed to her forehead and touched the wound there. Her drying blood drew her attention to the dull, throbbing pain. Of course. Of course she remembered. *Oh, he must think I'm deranged.* She held out her hand. "Yes. Thank you."

Anakin gave her the holoprojector. "Doctor, please, we really have to—"

"I know," she said, shoving it into her satchel. "I'm ready."

He nodded, so reassuring, then crossed to the closed lab door. Rested his palm against it, fingers splayed, and let his eyelids lower. "Durd," he murmured. "He doesn't live in this building, right?"

"That's right. He has a private suite elsewhere in the compound. He says he can't sleep with the stink of human in his nostrils."

"And the rest of us won't sleep while he's breathing free air." Anakin's face twisted. "Or at all."

There was something in the way he said it. The way he'd called the Neimoidian a monster. "You know General Durd."

"Yeah. We've met." He dropped his hand from the door. "Okay. I think the coast is clear."

Shaken, she stared at him. "You *think*? Don't you—"

"Sorry. We can't sense droids." He gave her that charming, cheeky smile again. "But I've got very good hearing. Let's go."

They slipped out of the lab and down the long empty hallway to her room—her prison cell—which had been two adjoining offices before the Separatists took over. A dividing wall had been ripped out and the resulting space turned into a cramped, basic apartment that held a curtained-off bed, a tiny refresher, some shelves, and a makeshift kitchen. The leftover space had been turned into a living room—someone's crude attempt at interior decorating.

"Please," she said, closing the door then gesturing at the scattering of furniture—a sofa, a chair, a rickety table. "Make yourself comfortable. Can I offer you something to eat or drink?" And then she felt foolish. This wasn't a social occasion. Their lives were in deadly peril. If Anakin's Jedi friend Kenobi somehow got himself caught . . .

Idiot. Don't even think it. He won't get caught. They don't call him a hero of the Republic for nothing.

Anakin was looking relieved. "Water would be greatly appreciated, thank you. Food, too, but I'll wait for Obi-Wan to come back before I eat."

She crossed to the small kitchen table, put down the precious holoprojector, then nodded at the commercial-sized conservator her keepers had so kindly given her.

"It's entirely up to you. The water's in there. Help yourself to as much as you like."

He drank three full bottles, hardly taking a breath. Noticing her surprise, he shrugged. "Sorry. My manners aren't usually that bad. It's just—it's been a long, hard day."

"I can tell," she said, disposing of the emptied bottles down her makeshift kitchen's waste chute. "You should sit down. If you don't mind me saying so, you look tired."

He considered his filthy clothes. "Are you sure? I don't want to dirty the furniture."

"Why should I care?" she said, shrugging. "It's not my furniture. By all means, feel free to ruin it. Who knows? I might even help."

He almost laughed. "Yeah. Okay. In a minute. But first, do you have a medkit?"

"Why? Are you hurt?" she said anxiously. "Where? How badly? Yes, I've got a medkit, I'll go and—"

"Doctor Fhernan, I'm fine." His expression was a mingling of caution and pity. "You're the one who's hurt."

For a moment she couldn't think what he meant. And then she remembered, again, being struck by the holoprojector. Durd in a temper tantrum. Now, there was a surprise.

"Oh. That's right." There was still dried blood on her fingers, and a dull, throbbing pain in her head. "I'm sorry. I'm not normally this stupid. I just—" And then she felt her face crumple and heard herself sob. Her knees buckled and she began to sink toward the floor. "I'm sorry, I'm sorry," she choked. "Don't mind me. I'm fine."

He caught her before she tumbled completely. Lifted her without effort and carried her to the sofa. Boneless and unprotesting, she let him. Let her face turn to his roughly shirted, dirty chest and howled her rage and shame against him. Dimly, she felt his hand warm and comforting on her back and heard his soft voice saying, over and over, "It's all right. It's all right. You're safe now. It's all right."

The crazy thing was that she *did* feel safe. For the first time since those Separatist blaster bolts seared the air and sand of Niriktavi Bay, since she saw her friends and colleagues slaughtered, she felt safe.

Then, abruptly, she felt mortified. What was she doing? Weeping like a child all over a man young enough to be her son? Where was her *pride*? She shifted away from him, unable to meet his eyes. "I'm sorry. I didn't mean to—I'm sorry."

"Don't apologize," he said gently. "You've got a right to be upset. Now, where's that medkit?"

"In the refresher." She pointed. "Through there. Top shelf above the sink. But please, don't bother. It's nothing. I can—"

Standing, he frowned down at her. "It's not nothing. Don't go anywhere. I'll be right back."

Even if she'd wanted to, she didn't think she could move. Hope had vanished, leaving despair in its wake. Leaving her empty of everything save pain. Her eyes felt scrubbed raw.

"Right," said Anakin, returning with the medkit. "Here we go. And I'll say sorry in advance, because I'm probably going to hurt you."

Again, that extraordinary sense of being small, a child, as he carefully wiped the blood and tears from her face, cleaned the bruised, throbbing cut on her forehead with antiseptic, and lightly pressed a steriseal over it.

"You're very good at this," she murmured.

His face shadowed. "I've had a lot of practice."

Of course. The war. "Do you mind—can I ask—is the Republic really losing to the Separatists? Durd says we are, but I don't want to believe him."

He glanced at her, something fierce flickering deep in his eyes. "No. Don't believe him."

"So—that means we're winning?"

He swept the steriseal wrapper and used antiseptic wipes into one hand. Didn't answer.

"You mean we're *not* winning?"

A sigh. "It's complicated, Doctor."

"Please—" Wanting to touch his arm, instead she folded her hands in her lap. "Call me Bant'ena."

"It's complicated, Bant'ena," he said. "But you can trust we're doing everything in our power to defeat Dooku and his Separatists."

She watched him dump the medical rubbish into the waste chute, wash his hands, then fetch a bottle of water from the conservator and remove its lid. Returning to her, he held out the water and a couple of pain-tabs from the medkit.

"Here. You'll feel better for these."

Taking them, she looked up at him and shook her head, even though it still ached. "It's odd. You're nothing like I expected."

"Why?" he said, perching on the edge of the nearby chair. "What did you expect?"

"I don't know," she said, floundering. "I can't say I've ever given the Jedi much thought. I mean, not as individuals. I never expected to meet one—let alone two. I don't tend to go places where your skills are needed. But—well—you're *gentle*."

That made him smile. "As opposed to what?"

She swallowed the pain-tabs, washing them down with a mouthful of water. "Oh. You know. The HoloNet news—it portrays as you as this—this—heroic warrior. Larger than life. Charging into battle, lightsaber flashing. Scourge of the Separatists. That kind of thing." She shrugged. "And yet here you are and—and you're so young and kind and—" She put down the water bottle. "And you—oh, this sounds stupid."

"No," he said. "Tell me."

Feeling her face heat, she stared at her knees. "I feel like you understand what it's like to be scared and helpless. At the mercy of someone else. Someone . . . wicked. Which is of course ridiculous, because—you're a Jedi."

Silence. And then Anakin sighed. "I do understand, Bant'ena. I wasn't always a Jedi."

She looked up, ready to ask him what and when and how— but something in his eyes killed the questions unspoken. Instead she glanced at her wrist chrono. Stared at the closed door.

"Is he taking a long time?" she said. "Master Kenobi, I mean. That is the correct honorific, yes?"

"Yes," said Anakin. Pushing to his feet, he started to pace—then stopped himself, folded his arms, and frowned at the boarded-up square that had been a window. "Don't worry. He'll be here. He's very good at what he does."

He sounded calm, confident—but she'd always been skilled in reading people, whether they wanted to be read or not. He was soothing his own nerves as well as hers. She pretended she hadn't noticed.

"And he'll find us all right? I didn't tell him where to come."

"You didn't need to," said Anakin, with a small smile. "He'll find us."

"So . . . we wait?"

"Yes. We wait."

"Then I think, if you don't mind me leaving you, I'm going to clean up a bit," she said, standing. "Shower. Change my clothes."

"What?" Anakin stared at her. "Of course. Bant'ena, you don't need my permission. This is your place. I'm the visitor here."

He was a Jedi. Surely he couldn't be so naïve. "And what if I'm lying to you, Master Skywalker? What if I'm intending to raise the alarm? For all you know I've got a direct comlink to General Durd hidden in my bedroom or the refresher and I'm about to call him and tell him you're here. Trade you and Master Kenobi to him in return for something I want. My freedom, perhaps?"

Anakin shook his head. "You won't do that."

"How do you know?" She felt her lips tremble, and breathed hard until they firmed again. "You saw what I did to that lab rodent. You know what I've created for Durd. And you have to suspect what he intends to do with it. Obviously if I'm capable of *that,* then I'm capable of anything. Even the betrayal of two Republic heroes."

Anakin's boyish face hardened, aging him. "We'll talk about Durd and what you've done for him when Obi-Wan gets here. And I know you won't betray us because I'm a Jedi."

Her eyes filled with tears. "And how do I know *you* won't betray *me*? I can explain why I've done what I've done—but you might not accept my reasons. You might tell me you'll get me to safety so I'll cooperate and then hand me over to the authorities as soon as we're back on Coruscant."

"No, Bant'ena," he said quietly. "I won't do that."

"Yes, yes, of course you *say* you won't, but how do I *know*?"

He stood a little straighter and met her desperate gaze without guile. "Because I'm a Jedi."

He made it sound so simple. Could anything in the universe be that simple? How she wanted it to be true. She wanted to trust him. Could she trust him?

As if I have a choice now. If I was going to scream, I should have screamed back in the lab. Even if I did call Durd from the 'fresher, he'd never believe the Jedi and I aren't in collusion.

"Thank you," she said, subdued. "And for what it's worth, you're right. I've no intention of contacting General Durd. Help yourself to more water, if you're still thirsty. Help yourself to anything. I won't be long."

And she didn't intend to be, only once she stepped into the real water-shower, her sole luxury in this hideous place, once its soothing heat was beating down on her, she didn't want to get out. Sore head resting against the poor-quality prefabbed shower stall, she wept again and tried to pretend the tears were plain water on her face.

Don't cry. Don't cry. There's a Jedi on the other side of the door. He's come to save you. This will end soon.

Eventually the water started to run cool, so she turned of

the taps. Drying herself with an inadequate towel, she dressed in clean underclothes and a new shirt and trousers and bundled the lab coat and clothes she'd been wearing for the disposal chute. Her blood was on them, and they smelled like death.

When she returned to the living area, she found Obi-Wan Kenobi pouring a bottle of water down his throat. An empty bottle stood on the table beside him. Seeing her, he stopped drinking, put down the half-consumed bottle, and considered her, his face grave.

"Doctor."

"Master Kenobi." She crossed to the disposal chute and got rid of her clothes. "Were you able to—how do you phrase it? 'Accomplish your mission'?"

He wasn't warm, like Anakin. There was a cool, guarded watchfulness to him, though he was impeccably polite. "Yes. The security records will no longer be a problem."

Which meant, for tonight at least, for a few precious hours, for the first time in such a long time, she'd finally have some privacy. Although after her initial distaste, realizing Durd could see and hear everything she did, she'd stopped caring. After all, what was there to see? Durd had made it plain he found humans repellent. It was unlikely he'd be obsessed with watching her undress or shower.

On the other hand, I bet he loves to watch me weep.

"Bant'ena?" said Anakin.

She shook her head. "I'm fine."

"Good," said Kenobi. *Master* Kenobi. "Doctor—"

"You should eat," she said. "You've time. I meant what I said before—they never disturb me in here."

Kenobi exchanged a look with Anakin, then nodded. "Very well. Thank you."

"It's no trouble. It's not like I'll be cooking for you. My

meals are delivered in bulk, in heat-paks." The table had only one chair, so she nodded at the sofa. "Please. Have a seat."

As the Jedi sat on her ugly, lopsided sofa, she took four heat-pak meals out of the conservator and handed them two each. "You look hungry," she said when they stared at her, surprised.

"What about you?" said Anakin, activating the first pack without bothering to read its label. "You should eat something."

The confines of her skull echoed with shrill rodent screaming. "Maybe later. I—I had a big lunch."

He wasn't fooled. "Bant'ena—"

"I said no!"

They needed cutlery. She fetched her one spoon and her one fork and handed them over.

"Thank you," Anakin said quietly. Kenobi just nodded.

Retreating, she dropped into the lone chair at the table and looked at the floor in silence while the two Jedi ate. She didn't want to make them feel uncomfortable. Her future did depend on them, after all—and she'd grown adept at appeasing whoever held her in their power.

It didn't take them long to finish both meals. They must have been ravenous. She stood. "More? I won't miss them, and the droids don't actually count how many I eat."

"No, thank you," said Kenobi. Taking Anakin's emptied paks, holding them with his own, he started to rise.

"I'll do that," she said. She took the cartons from him and shoved them down the disposal chute. Then, turning back, she rubbed her palms down the sides of her legs, feeling the trembling deep in her muscles. "So. Master Kenobi. How did you find me? I'd given up hope of word getting out of Taratos Four. Was it one of the others? Did someone manage to escape and raise the alarm?"

The Jedi exchanged cautious looks. "Others?" said Kenobi. "What others, Doctor?"

"The other scientists who were taken with me. From the research enclave at Niriktavi Bay. That's where my team and I were working, where the Separatists attacked us. Did one of them—"

They were staring at her blankly—interested, but uninformed. She felt something twist in her guts. A sharp pain. A shattered hope. She had to wait a moment before she could speak again.

"It wasn't the other scientists, was it? You're not here for me at all. You found me by mistake."

"Not mistake," Kenobi said quickly. "Accident."

And was that supposed to make a difference? "I see."

"I'm sorry," said Anakin. "That we couldn't save Taratos Four. Or the people you lost in the attack. Or you."

"Did you even try?"

There was another exchange of looks. More silence. "No," Kenobi said at last. "The taking of Taratos Four was part of a larger Separatist push. We weren't able to defend every threatened planet."

Oh, the broken places inside her. "In other words, there wasn't anything worth saving there." Just Niriktavi Bay, with its corals and its sea life and her team, her Raxl, and the laughing games of tag on the beach as the sun set.

"I told you, Bant'ena," said Anakin. There was pain in his voice. "It's complicated."

She sat down again. "I understand. This is war. You have to look at the big picture. You can't afford to see the little people." Scurrying like rodents. Sacrificed for the greater good.

"That's not true!" Anakin protested. "That's what the big picture *is*. Lots and lots and lots of little people. You matter,

Bant'ena. The friends you lost on Taratos Four, *they* matter. We're fighting this war so no more like them will die."

He was very sweet. Very young. Full of grand ideals and breathtaking, intuitive compassion. She looked at Master Kenobi. Now, *there* was a pragmatist, a man possessed of a scientist's soul.

"Tell me," she said, holding his gaze steadily. "If you didn't come here for me, then why did you come?"

"I'm not sure that's relevant," Kenobi said. "We're here. And you're here. Developing a bioweapon for General Lok Durd—and Count Dooku."

Yet another silence followed, chilly this time, as all three of them silently relived the lab rodent's monstrous death. She wanted to rage at them, to stamp her feet and shout.

Don't you judge me for that. Don't you dare. Do you even know how much you've profited from the taking of little rodent lives?

"Since you were watching," she said at last, "and listening, you know perfectly well that what I'm doing here I'm doing under duress."

Kenobi frowned. "And yet you took pride in what you've accomplished."

He'd seen that small, unpretty moment? She felt her cheeks heat. "A brief weakness," she said stiffly. "Regrettable scientific ego. Believe me, I'm *not* proud."

"And yet—"

"What's Durd's hold over you, Bant'ena?" Anakin said, unapologetically cutting his companion short. "How exactly is he controlling you?"

Turning, she pulled the holoprojector toward her, switched it on, and activated the holograph slide show.

"My mother," she said, staring at the flickering image. After a few moments, the image shifted. "And that's my brother and sister-in-law and niece." Shift. "My sister, my brother-in-law, and both of my nephews." Shift. "My dear friend Didjoa." Shift. "Samsam." Shift. "Lakhti and Nevhra." The end. She deactivated the rolling display. "And probably, if they hadn't been killed when I was taken, my entire research team would be added to that list."

Master Kenobi nodded. "I see. Are they all being held hostage, like you?"

"In a manner of speaking. They're free—but under constant surveillance. Durd promises they'll die if I refuse to cooperate. I have no reason to disbelieve him. So you see, Master Kenobi, I'm in something of a bind. My mother—" Her breath caught. "My *mother* has a blaster pointed at her head."

If the notion appalled or alarmed him, he gave no sign. "And so you made Durd that bioweapon."

Her chin lifted. "Yes. I did." And then she smiled, so very unamused. "You're thinking I should have refused to work for him. Or better yet, taken my own life to make sure the good general and his precious Count's nefarious plans were thwarted?"

Neither was Master Kenobi amused. His blue eyes were cold, and tension thrummed in every line of his wiry, athlete's body. "As a rule—as a Jedi—I would never advocate suicide."

"But in this case you'd make an exception?" She laughed out loud, mocking. *You silly, stupid, arrogant man.* "Do you think I never considered it? Do you think I haven't tried already? Within hours of waking in this stinking festering hole, *do you think I didn't try?* But I failed, Master Kenobi, and Durd beat me nearly unconscious. And then he swore that if I tried it again, my mother would die in screaming agony and he would strap me to a chair with my eyelids taped open and make me watch a holorecording of her death a hundred times over. And if I tried and *succeeded,* they would *all* die in screaming agony."

The memory of Durd's fury, of the pain he'd inflicted, shuddered through her. She started to shake.

"Perhaps you could do it, Master Kenobi," she whispered. "I know little of the Jedi. And I don't know you at all. Perhaps you could take your own life knowing that those whom you loved best would be slowly tortured to death because of you. Perhaps—" Her voice broke. "Perhaps that's a fair price to pay to save millions of lives. I don't know. All I know is I don't have the strength to pay it."

"Obi-Wan," said Anakin, as she and Kenobi stared at each other. "*Obi-Wan*. A word in private?"

She stood. "I'll leave you to chat. Don't worry—I won't eavesdrop. I have a headset and some music. I won't hear a thing. Just—let me know when you've decided what you're going to do."

As BANT'ENA DISAPPEARED into her curtained-off bedroom, Anakin turned on Obi-Wan. Disbelieving anger made it hard to keep his voice down. "Tell me you're not blaming *her* for this mess."

Obi-Wan sighed. "Anakin—"

"Durd's threatening her *family*. Her *friends*. After murdering a bunch of other people she knew and cared about, right in front of her."

"Anakin—"

He leapt up, paced a few steps from the sofa, then swung around. "How can you blame her for cooperating? After what he threatened, after what the Seps have done here—Obi-Wan, we just spent *hours* breathing in the ashes of the dead. So how can you—" He dragged a hand down his face. "You think it's all a bluff? You think Durd won't make good on his threats? Obi-Wan—" He returned to the sofa and dropped to one knee beside it, his metal hand clenched to a fist inside its glove. *Hear me.*

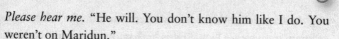

Please hear me. "He will. You don't know him like I do. You weren't on Maridun."

"I didn't need to be," said Obi-Wan. "I read your report."

"My *report*?" He shoved to his feet and stared down at his willfully obtuse mentor—his friend, whom right now he could cheerfully shake into tiny pieces. "That's just a bunch of words, Obi-Wan. *I was there. I felt him.* In my mind. In—in my *heart. I know* him. He's not bluffing. He'll do it. He'll kill everyone she loves."

Obi-Wan sat back against the sofa. Ran a hand over his beard. "You'd do well to calm yourself, Anakin. Getting emotional doesn't help."

"I'm sorry, but from where I'm standing it seems like one of us *needs* to get emotional!" he retorted. "Because *one* of us doesn't seem to care about what's happening!"

"Oh *Anakin* . . ." Obi-Wan pressed his fingertips to his eyes, the way he did when he had a headache. "Of course I care. And I know what Durd is. He's a cruel, rapacious creature entirely bereft of conscience. I *also* know that unlike him, Doctor Fhernan isn't evil. At least, she doesn't seek death and destruction on a galaxywide scale."

A little of his frustration subsided. "Well, then?"

"Well then, so what?" said Obi-Wan, implacable. "Talk is cheap, Anakin. She can protest Durd's villainy from sunup to sundown, but coerced or not, if she continues to assist him, *so what*? You heard her. To save twelve people she's prepared to sacrifice millions. If not billions. Yet every being she'd sacrifice has a mother and a sister and a brother and friends. Why do their losses matter less than hers?"

"I never said they did," he retorted. "*She* never said they did. But Obi-Wan—"

Obi-Wan stood. Rested a hand on his shoulder. "Listen to

me, Anakin. Forget whatever sympathy you might feel for this woman and *listen*. Doctor Fhernan has chosen to spare herself personal pain, knowing full well that her choice means genocide." His tired face tightened. "Imagine that bioweapon loosed upon Coruscant. Upon Alderaan, or Corellia. Upon every Republic world in the galaxy. *Any* world that refuses to submit to Dooku and his whims. Imagine hearing the death cries of millions, roaring through the Force like thunder."

Did Obi-Wan think he was stupid? That he didn't understand what was at stake here? Anakin shrugged away his friend's urgent hand. "It would be terrible, I know. It's what we came here to stop."

"And yet there you stand, Anakin, hesitant to stop it."

Oh. Right. "So you *are* saying she should let Durd kill everyone she loves."

"Certainly that would prevent an even greater tragedy," Obi-Wan said, very quietly.

"Well, that's easy for you to say, isn't it? You don't have a family to lose."

"Don't I?"

"That's different and you know it," he spat. "The Jedi are a lot of things, but family's not one of them."

Obi-Wan just looked at him. "I see."

Blast it. How had they ended up on angry, opposite sides of this? "No. Wait. That's not what I meant."

"I know what you meant."

As Obi-Wan turned away, Anakin grabbed his arm and pulled him back. "I'm sorry. I wasn't saying—" He let go. "Look, I hear you, Obi-Wan. War is anguish and there are terrible choices. But we can't expect Bant'ena to make *this* choice."

Obi-Wan's eyes were full of shadows again. "Someone has to make it, Anakin. If not her, then who?"

"That's a very good question," said Bant'ena, behind them. "I think I'd like to hear the answer."

As one, he and Obi-Wan rounded on her. He felt oddly betrayed. "You said you wouldn't eavesdrop!"

"I didn't mean to," she said, shrugging. "My music headset's faulty. The volume dropped and you were—heated."

Obi-Wan stepped forward. "Doctor Fhernan—"

"You know," she said, her chin tilted defiantly, "there is one option you haven't mentioned. You and Anakin could kill me and destroy my work. I'm not strong enough to stop you—and that would certainly stop Durd. Just know that if you do he'll assume I did it myself. My family and friends will die horrible deaths and their innocent blood will stain your hands *forever*."

SIXTEEN

"Don't worry, Bant'ena," said Anakin, so reckless. "That is *not* going to happen."

Obi-Wan flicked him a hard warning glance, but Anakin wouldn't look at him. His emotions were entirely engaged by this scientist. This woman who had permitted herself to be used by Durd and Dooku to create something almost inconceivably evil, with the potential to destroy the galaxy then see it remade in the Sith's image.

I can't allow that to happen. There is no price too high that we might pay.

"Anakin—"

"Wait," Anakin said, holding up both hands. "Just—*wait*. There has to be a way for us to destroy the bioweapon *and* keep Bant'ena's family and friends safe."

With an effort he kept his temper leashed. "Anakin, I know you believe that. But you of all people should know by now that *wanting* a thing does not mean *getting* a thing."

It was unkind of him to say it, but he had no time for kindness. He needed to break Anakin's inconvenient bond with Durd's captive scientist before it tightened any further. Before he completely lost sight of their goal. Their duty.

As Anakin stared at him, hurt, his anger stirring, Dr. Fhernan stepped forward. "Please. Don't fight because of me. I've done enough damage as it is."

Oh, this woman. *Bant'ena Fhernan*. Entirely unexpected. A hydrospanner in the works.

But she's right about one thing. I could end this here and now. I could kill her where she stands. Without laying a finger on her I could crush her throat or her skull or burst her heart in her chest. I could kill her ten times over without breaking a sweat. And then I could kill Durd. And if I do that, I bring Dooku to his knees.

Actions which would unleash a river of innocent blood.

"Obi-Wan," said Anakin. His voice was steady, but he was pleading. "We're not assassins. We're not murderers. There is a way out, we just haven't seen it yet. So let's find somewhere safe to hunker down and think this through. All right?"

"Anakin . . ." He shook his head. "There's no time. By now Durd has surely transmitted the bioweapon's formula to Count Dooku. For all we know Dooku's given Durd orders to eliminate Doctor Fhernan and the loved ones being used as leverage against her. The man is ruthless. He leaves nothing to chance. Forgive me, Doctor," he added, looking at her. "I realize such bluntness is painful but—"

"Forget it," she said. "What matters is that you're wrong. I know Durd. He's political to the core and he always takes care of himself first, last, and foremost. He might tell Dooku we're making progress, but he won't risk his valuable status by handing over my formula. He'll keep control of that for as long as he possibly can. And the only way harm can come to my family and friends is if he suspects my—" She sneered. "*Loyalty.* Which is why I won't even consider messing with that bioweapon."

She sounded cold, controlled, free of sorrow and regrets. But he'd long ago learned to see beneath people's masks—and what he saw in this flawed woman made him ache. Pride and passion. Loneliness. A single-minded dedication to the pursuit of knowledge, no matter where it led—or who got hurt in that pursuit. The desire to do good. A need for recognition. Her saving grace: a vast capacity to love.

"Doctor . . ." He gentled his voice. "I am so very sorry about this."

"*You're* sorry?" She half laughed. "Oh, Master Kenobi. You've no idea what sorry is."

He wasn't in the mood to contradict her. "Anakin is right. We're not assassins or murderers. But now that we know what Durd's planning—what will happen if that bioweapon is unleashed—our mission is more vital than ever. We *must* succeed in thwarting him."

She looked at him steadily, a mocking bitterness in her eyes. "You do realize that your best course of action is for you to get off this misbegotten rock and send in every warship the Republic can lay its hands on to batter Lanteeb into rubble?"

"No," said Anakin sharply. "Wholesale slaughter is Dooku's way. Not ours. Obi-Wan and I were sent in to deal with this quickly and quietly and that's the way it's going to get done."

Ah, the blind optimism of youth.

Dr. Fhernan was shaking her head. "Anakin, Anakin. That's a lovely speech. Truly. Very nearly reassuring. But what exactly does it mean? How do you propose to stop Durd without jeopardizing me and my family—or the innocent Lanteebans trapped on their own world, for that matter?"

"I don't know yet," said Anakin. "But we'll think of something. We always do."

She smiled at him then, so sweetly that her sallow, scarred face was transformed. Anakin smiled back, oddly shy all of a sudden. Obi-Wan stared at him, alarmed.

No, no. He's as bad as Qui-Gon. Picking up strays . . .

"Doctor Fhernan," he said, roughly breaking the moment. "I must be honest with you—I can't promise to keep you and your loved ones safe. All I can promise is that we'll try."

Slowly, she looked away from Anakin and nodded. "I suppose I can't ask for more than that."

"We could use your help," said Anakin. "I know you're afraid of making Durd suspicious—but we've got a better chance of winning if you're on the team. And like you say, you know the barve. And that means you know how to play him."

The fresh shirt and trousers she'd donned were as baggy on her as those she'd discarded. Hunched inside them, chin tucked to her chest as the implications of Anakin's request sank their teeth into her flesh, Dr. Fhernan looked fragile. Every day of her age.

She looked up. "I know you think I'm a coward," she murmured. "You're sweet, and polite, but you have to despise me." There were tears in her eyes. "Which is fine. I despise myself. What I've done here—it's abominable. I know that. It's a betrayal of every ethical code of conduct. And if I could undo it I would. But there is no going back, is there? I've done what I've done and I have to face it."

Fierce now, Anakin went to her and cupped her angular cheeks in his hands. "No. You can't go back—but you can go forward. There's always a way forward, no matter what you've done."

"And what about forgiveness?" Her voice was a bitter whisper.

He nodded. "Yes, Bant'ena. There's forgiveness, too."

"You promise?" she said, the brimming tears fallen. "Because I can't seem to find it."

He moved his hands to her shoulders and held her firmly. "Don't worry. I'll help you."

Obi-Wan had to look away. For if Bant'ena Fhernan had a vast capacity to love . . .

He humbles me, sometimes. He makes me feel small. He can't see a broken thing without wanting to fix it.

"Doctor Fhernan," he said, because they really couldn't afford any more time. "Can you give us a copy of the bioweapon's formula? And all the research and data you've accumulated during the process of its creation?"

Stepping aside from Anakin, she nodded. "Yes. Of course. But—"

"You'll attract no undue attention if a patrolling droid should find you in your lab so late?"

"No. The droids are used to me working odd hours."

"Excellent. Then could you do it now?"

"Yes. But after that—" She glanced at Anakin. "You should go. The longer you stay here, the greater the chance you'll be discovered."

And that was true.

"There's a lot of information to copy," she added. "It'll take a little time. You should eat again. Keep up your strength. Sounds to me like you're going to need it."

As the room's shabby door closed behind her, Anakin turned on him. "Obi-Wan, I don't care what you say, I'm not going to abandon Bant'ena to that Sithspit Durd."

"And I'm not going to have this argument again," he retorted. "Now, be quiet and—"

Anakin shook his head. "No. When are you going to accept it, Obi-Wan? I'm not your meek little Padawan anymore. Don't get me wrong, I'll *always* listen to you. But that doesn't mean I'll always agree."

"*Meek?*" he snapped, incredulous. "You've not been *meek* a single day in your life!"

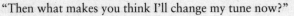

"Then what makes you think I'll change my tune now?"

"I don't know!" he turned away. "Someone must've hit me over the head when I wasn't looking."

"Obi-Wan—" With another of his mercurial mood shifts, Anakin sighed. "Bant'ena's right. We should eat some more while we can. Drink, too." He crossed to the conservator and started rummaging inside. "Any thoughts on where we should hole up?"

Stifling frustration, Obi-Wan returned to the sofa. "Nowhere in this compound, I know that much. I made the security system tampering look like a power surge, but I'd still rather not be here when it's discovered."

One by one Anakin tossed him a mealpack, a bottle of water, and his used spoon. "You want to go back to the ship?"

"I don't think we can," he said, activating the pack's heat seal. "Not until we're ready to make a fast getaway. We destroyed our identichips, remember? We might be able to talk our way out of that once, but not twice."

"Good point," said Anakin, and dropped onto the chair at the table. "Okay. We need somewhere quiet where nobody's going to stumble across us by accident. We need some kind of comm station, so we can use those 'links you took to contact the Temple. And we need access to a datareader, obviously, so we can sift through Bant'ena's research."

That made Obi-Wan stare. "Oh yes? Why not throw in a troupe of trained dancing tauntauns while we're at it?"

Anakin peeled off the lid of his mealpack. "What's a tauntaun?"

"Never mind," he muttered, and looked to his own heated meal. "I think our best bet is going to be—"

"Those abandoned shops near the spaceport?" said Anakin, with his mouth full. "Yeah. Among them they're bound to have what we need. If we're careful we can hole up in one for as long as it takes and the Seps won't be any the wiser."

He was grinning, temper abandoned. Elated because they had a plan, a solution, a way out of the dark. Obi-Wan swallowed a sigh. His former apprentice was so swift to anger. Swifter still to joy. So many years he'd spent trying to teach Anakin to keep himself balanced. All to no avail.

Perhaps the most I can ever hope for is that once his emotional pendulum stops swinging it will come to rest forever in the light.

"Hey—Obi-Wan—"

"What?"

Now Anakin was frowning, wheels and wheels of thought turning behind his eyes. "There's no way we can lift Durd out of here tonight, is there? Snatch him, the bioweapon, the research, the formula, Bant'ena, all of it—and get back to Coruscant before anyone's the wiser?"

Oh, it was a glorious thought. And for one brief, burning moment he let himself think it. Then sanity prevailed.

"No."

"No." Sighed Anakin. "I didn't think so."

Lapsing into silence, they finished their meals. They drank a second bottle of water each, took advantage of the refresher, then sat again to wait.

Dr. Fhernan returned at last, bearing four data crystals. "Here you are, Master Kenobi," she said, handing them over. "That's everything."

"Thank you," he said, tucking them into the shielded pocket holding his lightsaber and pilfered comlink. "But there is some more information I'd like." He nodded at the mini holoprojector. "Can you make me a copy of those holoimages, and a list of everywhere your family and friends might be found?"

As the doctor stared at him, silent, he felt Anakin's surprise, and his great leap of hope.

Don't get too excited, my young friend. It's a long shot at best.

"Yes," Dr. Fhernan whispered. "Yes, I can do that."

"Then hurry. Anakin and I have to go." As she rushed to burn the new data crystal, he added, "One last thing. We're aware two genetically coded antidotes to damotite poisoning were created by the Kaminoans—but they're specific to individuals. What I need to know is if you've created an antidote or a vaccine that would work on a general population."

Ejecting the loaded data crystal from the holoprojector, she winced. "I wish you wouldn't call it *mine*. And no. Durd made me design a cure-proof bioweapon."

Of course he did. "So you're saying that there's not even a hope of creating a generically applicable antidote or vaccine?"

"There might be," she said slowly. "I know of four scientists capable of breaking my bio-coding and extrapolating them from that research and formula I just gave you. Their names are appended."

She was a remarkably resourceful woman. "Thank you."

"Master Kenobi—"

Surprised, he looked down at her hand on his arm. "Doctor?"

Pale, her dark eyes filled with a quiet, desperate misery, she blinked back more tears. "I've been thinking. If I could trust my family and friends were safe from Durd, I would kill myself. I'd sabotage everything I've done, kill myself, and do my best to take Durd with me."

"Hey!" said Anakin, startled. "Don't you even think about it. We're getting you out of this, Bant'ena. You and everyone else. The only person not walking away from this is Durd."

She managed a tight smile. "I know that's the plan. And don't get me wrong, it's a good plan. I like it. A lot. But, Anakin, sometimes things don't turn out the way we want them to. So with that in mind . . ." She handed him the fifth data crystal. "If you can get my family and friends to safety—and if you can't come back for me or stop Durd any other way—find a way to let me know that and I'll do what I have to. No regrets. Agreed?"

"No, it's *not* agreed," Anakin retorted. "Bant'ena—"

"What? You can give your life for the Republic but I can't give mine? How very backward of you, Anakin."

"That's not what I meant."

She patted his arm. "I know what you meant. And I don't want to die. But if I have to do this, Anakin. You have to let me."

"You won't have to do it," said Anakin, holding the data crystal tight. "We'll save your loved ones *and* you, Bant'ena. My word as a Jedi. Do you believe me? Do you trust me?"

The fear and dread in her face eased, just a little. "You're a very sweet young man, Anakin Skywalker."

With an effort, Obi-Wan kept his face blank. *He's a very sweet young man who should know better than to make promises he knows full well we might not keep.* He pulled out his stolen comlink.

"Doctor Fhernan, can you carry this safely? And if we contact you, will you be able to answer?"

She looked at the 'link as though it might bite. "Yes. They only search me traveling to and from the compound, and I'm not due to go anywhere for the forseeable future. If I leave it on silent call I'll know you want me. And as soon as I can I'll answer you. Will that do?"

"Perfect," he said, with an encouraging smile. "I've no idea when or how often we'll try to contact you. Just sit tight, and keep it with you."

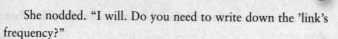

She nodded. "I will. Do you need to write down the 'link's frequency?"

"No. I've memorized it. But I do need that contact list."

"Of course." She found a blank flimsi and an electropen and scribbled for a few minutes. "There," she said, handing it over. "Every address and 'link contact I can think of."

He took the list and tucked it safely inside his shirt. "Doctor Fhernan—"

"Bant'ena."

"Bant'ena." He clasped her shoulder, briefly. "You must understand I can make you no promises. I will not put the lives of your family and friends above the safety of every living thing in the Republic. But I will do my utmost to protect them. And you."

She nodded. "I know you will. I know there are no guarantees. Now go. But take some water with you. Some mealpacks, too. Jedi or not, you need sustenance."

"Don't worry," said Anakin. "We're pretty good at finding what we need. We found you, didn't we?"

And that made her smile. "Yes. Yes you did. Please, *please,* both of you, *be careful.* There's a strict curfew after dark and—"

"We know," said Anakin. "Don't worry. We'll be fine."

"Remember," Obi-Wan added. "It might take awhile before we've any reason to comm you. Don't be concerned. You will hear from us again."

Always demonstrative, Anakin gave her a swift hug. "Be strong, Bant'ena. You're not alone."

They left her small apartment—her prison cell—via the venting ducts, just to be safe. Crawling through the cramped metal corridors, every ache and pain awakening with a roar, Obi-Wan found it hard to forget the look on Bant'ena's face as they left her behind.

But since they'd had no choice in the matter, he closed his

heart and his mind and focused on getting out of the building alive.

IF THEY HADN'T NEEDED to keep everything so *clandestine*, Anakin would have indulged in forty fast backflips to celebrate getting out of those stifling vents in one piece.

He and Obi-Wan crouched in the bushes growing along the building's side wall. Everything was quiet. Peaceful. The night sky was patched with low clouds, the ground freshly damp. It had been raining again. There was a nip in the air. He was going to start shivering any moment. He hated a cold, damp climate. Give him the desert any day over chilly rain—and that was something he never thought he'd think.

It was too dark to see anything, but he glanced at Obi-Wan anyway. Something wasn't quite . . . *right* . . . there. Obi-Wan seemed oddly subdued. And why was that? Because they'd argued? That wasn't new. They'd been bumping heads one way or another since the day they met. So what had changed?

Maybe the fact that now I don't back down? Get used to it, Obi-Wan. I'll say it as many times as you need to hear it. Until you believe it. Not your Padawan anymore.

"So how do you want to get out of here?" he whispered. "Wait for a while and see if we can hitch another ride?"

"That's a little too random for my tastes," Obi-Wan replied. "There's no guarantee of any more delivery trucks coming in tonight, and we can't risk waiting until morning. We have to get back to those boarded-up shops before sunrise. How energetic are you feeling?"

"I'm good. Why—you're thinking of going up and over?"

"I don't see we've got another choice. Do you?"

He wished he did. If it was a simple matter of Force-leaping the perimeter fence, no problem. But it wasn't just the fence they

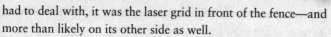

had to deal with, it was the laser grid in front of the fence—and more than likely on its other side as well.

"You'll be fine, Anakin," said Obi-Wan. "I doubt anyone will ever break your Temple leap record."

The one he'd set just over a year ago. The one that had smashed Mace Windu's leap by nearly fifteen meters. No, probably no one ever would break that. But it wasn't himself he was worried about.

How do I say this? I mean, there's cocky and then there's downright insulting.

There was a soft slithering sound in the dark beside him, and then Obi-Wan was pushing something at him. "Take these. If I can't follow you, if anything at all happens to me, you know what to do."

What? "No," he said softly, as Obi-Wan fumbled Bant'ena's data crystals and folded flimsi into his hands. "Obi-Wan, forget it. Nothing is going—"

Obi-Wan hissed, impatient. "It might. Anakin, *please.*"

His former Master was right. He was usually right.

Obi-Wan, this time you'd better be wrong.

He took the crystals and the flimsi and shoved them into his shirt's concealed pocket with the other crystal, his lightsaber, and their remaining comlink.

And then his head lifted. Someone—something—was coming.

Battle droids.

They folded themselves in half, arms wrapped around their shins, faces hidden against their knees, doing their best to stop breathing. Unlike the spycam droid, these clankers weren't equipped with heat sensors, but even so, accidents happened.

And for all we know they've been treated to an upgrade, just like the vulture droids we scrapped above Kothlis.

He could feel Obi-Wan vanishing beside him. He let himself

sink into the Force a little way—but not too far. He wanted to be ready if something went wrong.

I hate clandestine. I hate it. I hate it.

The battle droids were stupid clankers. Sneeze on them and they fell apart. The droids weren't going to find them . . . they were safe . . . they were safe . . .

"Patrol reporting in," the lead clanker wheezed. "All clear. Roger, roger."

The battle droids clanked away.

Slowly, cautiously, they swam back to the world's surface and unfolded themselves.

"Right," said Obi-Wan. "Let's get this—"

Anakin bumped his hand against him. "Wait. Just—wait." Embarrassed, he took a deep breath. "Look. Don't take this the wrong way. It's just—it's the mission, right? That's what matters. So—"

"Anakin." Obi-Wan's whisper sounded amused. "It's fine. I was about to suggest it myself when the droids turned up."

"You were?"

"Play to your strengths and minimize your weaknesses. That's how a battle is won. That's how we'll win the war."

Anakin had to smile. *I should've known he wouldn't take it personally.* "Yeah. So—once I'm up and over and nobody raises the alarm, give me a five-count then follow. I'll give you the best Force boost I can. Not that you'll need much. Your leap was only a meter and a half behind Master Windu's. Remember?"

Obi-Wan gave a breathy chuckle. "I remember I had nosebleeds for a week afterward. Don't ever feel bad for being extraordinary, Anakin. Now off you go. We don't have all night."

Nobody in his life could rile him like Obi-Wan. And nobody could make him feel so lucky to be called friend.

With a deep breath, he centered himself in the Force. Opening his mind to its limitless power, he surrendered his will to its overwhelming might, then looked toward the perimeter fence. He could feel the buzzing, lethal laser lines, the height of the barrier, and its formidable width. He rose lightly to his feet, adrift in that place without thought, without words, where he was one with the Force—where he could no longer tell where he ended and it began.

He leapt the laser-guarded security fence like he was jumping over a stream, or over one of the stone paths in the Temple's arboretum.

The night continued, silent and undisturbed. Standing in the empty road outside the compound, he felt Obi-Wan's admiring approval. Felt spattered rain against his face. Felt a stirring in the Force as Obi-Wan sprinted toward the barrier. He could see his former Master, a bright gold shape against his crimson inner world.

As Obi-Wan leapt, Anakin reached out and swaddled the Force around him gently, not interfering, not getting in the way— just enough of a push to ensure his safety. How could he be extraordinary and let Obi-Wan come to harm?

"Thank you," said Obi-Wan, landing safely and joining him.

Anakin grinned. "You're welcome. So—what now?"

"Now?" Despite the obstacles they yet faced, Obi-Wan's answering grin was wickedly cheerful. "Now I rather think I'd like to run away. How about you?"

"That sounds good," he said. "Running away sounds good."

So they ran.

BLURRED BY THE FORCE, they made it back to the abandoned shops near the brightly lit spaceport without discovery or incident. That was the good news. The bad news was that such a prolonged use of Force-sprinting left them both dangerously tired.

Panting, letting himself fall against a barricaded back door, Anakin mopped sweat from his face with one sleeve. "Ha. So maybe not extraordinary after all. My legs feel like they've turned to creamed Roa rice."

Obi-Wan, just as winded, braced his hands on his knees and bent over, gasping for air. They were safe for the moment. No droid patrols or mobile spycams in sight.

Thank the Force for small mercies.

"Well, that's all right. You like creamed Roa rice."

He laughed. "Not anymore I don't."

A gust of wind moaned down the street on the other side of the abandoned shops. Dull brownish lighting barely lifted the night out of gloom. There was dampness in the air, and above, more clouds were gathering like a frown. Any moment now it was going to rain. Again.

With a groan, Obi-Wan unbent his spine. "Come on," he said, and slapped Anakin's arm. "We need to get inside before we're soaked. Or discovered. Whether it's a blaster bolt or raging pneumonia, dead is dead. You start this end. I'll start the other. Remember what we're after: high-end electronics."

"Yes, Master," said Anakin. "Whatever you say, Master."

Such a pity he was being sarcastic.

Still light-headed, Obi-Wan made his cautious way to the farthest boarded-up shop. The lighting was so poor, it was impossible to read the partly obscured lettering above the barricaded front doors, so he pushed himself, hard, to read the premises through the Force. His body rebelled, resentful of the demands being placed upon it. Gritting his teeth, he ignored the vivid pain behind his eyes, in his bones, and sought for the faded echoes of this place.

A crying child. A weary mother. A customer, dissatisfied. With what? What had he bought here? What was it he brought back and tossed down on the counter, loudly shouting for the credits he'd spent or else?

Show me. Please show me. Please let me see.

Tappa weed. The customer claimed it was moldy, that it gave him bad dreams. This had been a smokery supplier. Nothing of use in here.

He moved to the next shop.

As he tried to focus, tried to sink himself into the past, he was tensely aware of the present, of the nearby sprawling spaceport. Though he couldn't sense its battle droids or MagnaGuards, he could feel the petty, quarrelsome peril of its humans. The occupying Separatist troops. So hushed was the curfewed darkness that the spaceport's noise seemed unnaturally enhanced. There was a rumbling roar as a light carrier's thrusters ignited. The echoes bounced within the port's encompassing ferrocrete walls. Then the engines were cut. Somebody shouted. A loud altercation was followed by the sound of two blaster shots. Someone was not having a good night.

Focus, Master Kenobi. You're no better than a Padawan, your mind's flittering all over the place.

Suitably reprimanded, he rested his forehead against the next shop's front door—and was immediately sorry. Images of terror and pain and panic exploded behind his closed eyes. He felt his blood leap, his heart pound. The screaming was awful.

Just go! Just go! This place isn't worth dying for! Take your lives and go! These are droids. They have no pity.

But the Lanteebans couldn't hear him. They had died here twelve days before. Died in their paint shop. They were rotting behind the door. Trapped in their death throes, he struggled to pull free.

A hand touched his shoulder and he nearly cried out.

"Obi-Wan? What is it?"

"Nothing, Anakin. It's nothing," he said, and stepped away from the paint shop, sweating. "What have you found?"

Anakin was grinning again. "An actual electronics shop. Come on. I've got the back door unboarded. There's power, but no alarm."

"Well done," Obi-Wan said, his voice still sour, his heart still pounding. "Let's get inside, quickly, before a droid patrol comes along."

There were no dead, rotting bodies in this shop. It was small and crowded floor-to-ceiling with shelves and cupboards spilling circuits and crystal components and infohubs and comically outdated holoprojectors. The carpet was threadbare. Anakin lifted his ignited lightsaber a little higher, dispelling the immediate darkness with its pale vivid light.

"I'm thinking if one of us works under the front counter and the other works under this desk here, we should be able to risk a lamp each," he said. "The front of the shop's pretty solidly boarded up."

"Yes," Obi-Wan said slowly. "Yes, I suppose that'll do."

Anakin stared at him. "What? This place isn't good enough?"

"Well, you must admit, Anakin," he said, "everything in here seems terribly antiquated."

"What d'you mean *seems*? It is." Anakin shrugged. "But you're overlooking something. I'm extraordinary, remember?"

Though he was tired and hurting, Obi-Wan smiled. "I'm going to regret that word, aren't I?"

"Probably," said Anakin, grinning again. "Right, let's get settled in. The faster we can get through to the Temple and co-ordinate a battle plan, the faster we get Bant'ena away from Durd. Here—" He held out his glowing lightsaber. "Hold this for me."

Troubled, Obi-Wan watched him as he unplugged a small desk lamp. "Anakin . . ."

"What?" said Anakin, dropping to his knees to set the lamp up again on the floor under the front counter. He looked over his shoulder—and his expression changed. He plugged the lamp in and switched it on, then sat back on his heels. His face was wary now, and his fists rested combatively on his thighs. "Obi-Wan, *what*?"

Obi-Wan wasn't going to let himself be sidetracked by the tone. Deactivating the lightsaber, he tossed it back. "Anakin, don't do this," he said, as his former student caught the weapon and put it aside. "Don't—" He took a moment to rein in his own temper. *Fixing broken things is all very well—but not when we're up to our armpits in a dangerous mission.* "Qui-Gon used to do this. He used to roam around the galaxy picking up strays."

"Like me, you mean?" said Anakin tightly. "Useless hangers-on like me?"

"You were never useless. Anakin, please, you must *listen*," he insisted. "On almost every mission he and I went on we came across someone in trouble. Sometimes they'd brought it on themselves. Sometimes they were like Doctor Fhernan, victims of another being's machinations. But there was always someone. And he would try to help them."

"So?" said Anakin. "What's wrong with that? He helped me. He *saved* me. And this is my way of paying him back for that. Every person I help or save is me saying thank you to Qui-Gon. Why do you have a problem with that?"

"I don't," Obi-Wan protested. And then, at Anakin's look, he grimaced. "Well—yes, all right. I do. But not because it isn't an admirable ambition. It is, Anakin. It's admirable, it's laudable, it shows you have a good heart. But—" He ran a hand over his beard, searching for the right words. "For one thing, we're

Jedi, not social workers. It's not our job to collect the galaxy's waifs and strays."

Anakin's chin came up, defiant. "Then it should be. What is the point of having all this power if we don't use it to make people's lives better?"

"But we *do* make people's lives better! You know we do!" he retorted. "Right now the Jedi are *dying* to make people's lives better. I can't believe I need to remind you of that!"

"You don't," said Anakin, glowering. "And I'm not saying we should drop everything and devote all our time and resources to picking up strays. I'm not saying we should go looking for them, either. What I'm *saying* is that if we happen to fall over one we shouldn't just—just pick ourselves up and keep on walking."

"Oh, Anakin." Sighing, he dropped cross-legged to the dusty carpet. "I know it's hard. I know it seems cruel. But—"

"That's because it *is* cruel, Obi-Wan," Anakin snapped. "Cruel and unfeeling and unworthy of the Jedi Order."

He was so like Qui-Gon. This was like arguing with a ghost. *Don't waste your breath, Obi-Wan. I will do what I must.* "It rarely ends well, you know," he said gently, willing Anakin to hear him, to believe him. "Entangling yourself in these transitory lives? And when it *doesn't* end well, when you *can't* save these people, when we can't save Doctor Fhernan or her family or her unfortunate friends—"

"You don't know we can't save them. You're giving up without even trying!"

"No, Anakin. I am *not* giving up. I am merely facing facts." He hesitated, because what he wanted to say next was dangerous. On the other hand—it needed to be said. "Don't misunderstand me. Your compassion is admirable. You are a truly good man. One of the very best I know. But you're also a Jedi, and we cannot allow ourselves to become emotionally involved." A deep breath. A sharp sigh. "Bant'ena Fhernan is not your mother."

Anakin leapt to his feet. *"You leave my mother out of this!"*

"Anakin!" he hissed. "For pity's sake, keep your voice down."

Hard-breathing silence as Anakin struggled for self-control. And then he shook his head. "You don't understand, Obi-Wan. You'll *never* understand. You've never been a slave. You have no idea what it's like to be completely helpless. To know your life could end at any moment on someone else's whim."

"That's true," he admitted. "But—"

"No. There is no *but*," Anakin said flatly. "You're wrong. Okay? You're wrong. So just sit there and be wrong. Or get the other lamp set up. Or start looking for a comm hub so I can hopefully punch a signal through to the Temple. Do something, Obi-Wan. Do anything. Anything except try to tell me that *I'm* wrong. Because I'm not."

Obi-Wan looked at Anakin, astonished. Ignoring him, Anakin turned away and began to rummage through an over-stocked cupboard. So he did as he was told, and started setting up the second lamp.

SEVENTEEN

It took some doing, but Anakin finally found a comm hub that he could rejig. Perhaps. He also found a reader that would accept the modern data crystals Dr. Fhernan had given them. It was slow and temperamental but it was better than nothing, so Obi-Wan hunkered down beneath the table, shielded the desk lamp's glow with his body—as much as he could—and started reading the background research notes on Lok Durd's precious, pernicious bioweapon.

"Do we really need to know that stuff?" said Anakin, looking askance.

Obi-Wan shrugged. "Possibly not. But you never know when an obscure piece of information could come in handy."

"Huh. Does that mean you want me to read it?"

"No," Obi-Wan said, glancing up. "I want you to be quiet and fix that comm hub."

Muttering under his breath Anakin took the old comm equipment apart, using a tool kit he'd found in a drawer.

Time passed, painfully slow. Once they stopped what they were doing, frozen, as a battle droid patrol clanked past the shopfront. But the machines didn't so much as break stride, so they started breathing again and got back to work. As best as they could guess they had six more hours of darkness before Lanteeb's sun rose, and they needed every minute.

Coming back from the shop's tiny refresher, Obi-Wan found Anakin trying to raise Dr. Fhernan on their sole remaining comlink.

"Any response?" he asked, folding himself back under the low desk.

Anakin shook his head and put the comlink aside. Tipping the gutted comm hub toward his own lamp, he examined its stripped-down basal connections. "No."

Oh. That wasn't encouraging, but worrying about it wouldn't help. "I'm sure she's all right, Anakin. She's a strong, intelligent woman. And I don't sense any trouble. Do you?"

"No," said Anakin, frowning. "No trouble. Only—that she's afraid."

She'd be a fool if she weren't. "Well, I'm sure she just fell asleep. It's very late."

"Yeah. Probably. I'll try again in an hour or so."

The little Obi-Wan could see of Anakin's face was drawn with weariness. "Could be she's got the right idea. Why don't you take a short nap? I'll keep watch."

"No, I'm fine," said Anakin, picking through the tool kit. "Why don't you?"

"No, no. I'm fine, too." He rubbed his tired, burning eyes and tried to ignore the leaden exhaustion in his muscles. "Besides, I've barely scratched the surface of this research. There are hours of reading on these data crystals."

Anakin selected a small-gauge wire stripper, then glanced over. He wasn't angry, not anymore. But he was definitely withdrawn. "Come across anything useful yet?"

"Unfortunately it's not easy to tell," he said, frustrated. "Chemistry was never my strong suit, I'm afraid."

"Then skip it," said Anakin. "And you can transmit all the science stuff through to the Temple. Let them figure it out."

"Good idea. And when will I be able to do that, do you think?"

Anakin snorted. "When I've got this blasted thing working. And provided I can bounce the signal around the HoloNet grid enough times so that if the Seps do manage to pick up our transmission, they won't be able to figure out where it originated."

"You can do that?" he said, impressed. He wasn't bad with electronics himself, but Anakin was—he hated to say it—extraordinary.

"In theory," said Anakin, shrugging. "Whether I can do it in practice has yet to be seen. It's complicated."

Obi-wan got the unspoken message: *In other words, shut up and let me work.*

Silence fell again. He gave up on the science behind the bioweapon and instead turned his fading attention to Dr. Fhernan's comprehensive data on damotite and its uses. But after a while his vision kept blurring, the words running together like melted wax. He found himself re-reading the same paragraph and failing to understand any words more challenging than *and* or *but*. Dropping the datareader into his lap, he let his weary mind wander . . .

. . . only to have it stumble right into the conundrum of Durd's kidnapped scientist. Attempting her rescue—not to mention the rescue of her threatened family and friends, scattered across five planets—could well jeopardize the mission. One false step, one small mistake, and Durd might be alerted to his danger. While he imagined himself safe here on distant, obscure Lanteeb, there was every chance of not only disrupting the creation of his bioweapon but also taking him back into Republic custody.

Now, that *would be* my *definition of mission success.*

On the other hand, *not* trying to save Durd's thirteen

hostages—abandoning them to his brutal revenge—while that might well be the pragmatic thing to do . . .

Could I live with myself if I did it? Could I forgive myself their slaughter?

Probably not. And neither would Anakin forgive him. He frowned at his former student, so diligent in his task. Anakin, feeling the scrutiny, looked up.

"What?"

"Nothing," he said. "Only—you were very good with Doctor Fhernan tonight."

Anakin's jaw tightened. "Obi-Wan—"

"No, no, I mean it," he said quickly. "I'm not trying to—my intention isn't to—it's a compliment, Anakin. What you said to her. About forgiveness. It was very powerful. That's all I meant."

"Oh," said Anakin, wary. He exchanged the wire stripper for a micro-pulse-reader, then tested a circuit and muttered, "Okay."

"So . . . who forgave you?"

Anakin stilled. His expression, in profile, was a muddle of surprise and resignation. As though he'd been expecting the question and yet couldn't quite believe it had been asked.

Obi-Wan was feeling a little surprised, himself. He hadn't meant to ask it. As a rule he avoided deeply personal conversations. Especially about the past, which couldn't be changed. And especially about Anakin's past, so gnarled and tangled and littered with traps.

I really am weary. I think I'll quit while I'm ahead.

"I'm sorry," he murmured. "It's none of my business. Forget I asked. I'll—"

"My mother," said Anakin, his voice low. "My mother forgave me."

Oh. Well. And how, exactly, could he answer that? Because the odds were good that whatever he said it would be the wrong thing. Shmi's death was a minefield of regrets and failures, for both of them.

"Just before she died," Anakin added. "She didn't—she was—" He took a deep, shaky breath, then let it out incrementally. "She didn't actually say *I forgive you, Anakin*. You know. For not saving her. For not going back to Tatooine and freeing her. But I could see the words in her eyes. I could feel them. She forgave me."

What that meant to Anakin, Obi-Wan could only imagine. But his mother's forgiveness was only half the equation. He rested his head against the solid side of the desk.

"And when are you going to forgive yourself?"

Anakin returned his attention to the comm hub. "Who says I haven't?"

"Anakin. Please," he said. "If you'd rather not talk about this, just say so. But don't treat me like an idiot."

"Fine," said Anakin, and pulled out another comm relay circuit. "I don't want to talk about this."

Except—that wasn't good enough. This thorny, unhealed issue needed some kind of resolution. Unless Anakin could find a way to reconcile himself with Shmi's murder, he would never find peace. Her cruel death would continue to haunt him, to feed his fear of failing those he cared for the most. Fear was Anakin's greatest weakness. It always had been.

Such a dichotomy. He is the most fearless man I have ever fought with . . . yet a part of him remains that small, frightened boy who left Tatooine eleven years ago.

The boy he knew, to his shame, he'd sometimes failed to reach.

"You shouldn't blame yourself, you know," he said. "If you want to blame someone, Anakin, blame me. We both know I encouraged you to leave Tatooine behind. What happened wasn't your fault. You really must stop punishing yourself for it. I'm sure your mother wouldn't want that. She wouldn't want—"

Anakin dropped circuit and mini pliers and stared. Such an intimidating, *adult* stare. The atmosphere crackled with a sudden, dangerous tension.

"Yeah. Okay. And which part of *I don't want to talk about this* just—slipped right on by you, there?"

All right. This was a mistake. *He's not a child anymore, Obi-Wan. You keep forgetting that.* "Sorry. I'm—tired. I don't know what I'm saying. I think I will take a nap after all. Wake me in half an hour, would you? If I don't wake of my own accord?"

For a moment he thought Anakin was going to change his mind, was going to break his self-imposed silence and tell him everything that had transpired on Tatooine, when Shmi died. Because there *was* more. He had always known there was more than the bald fact of Shmi being kidnapped and killed by Tusken Raiders. He just didn't know what. And he'd never let himself think about it. He had only let himself hope that one day Anakin would find his way to telling him the whole story.

Please. Let one day be this day. I have a feeling it's important.

Anakin nodded. "Yeah, you get some rest, Obi-Wan. You look beat."

So. Not this day after all.

Disappointed—fleetingly aware that somehow he'd managed to mishandle a rare, important moment—Obi-Wan closed his eyes and was instantly asleep.

IT TOOK HIM the best part of another three hours, but eventually he did it. He upgraded the clapped-out, antiquated Sigtech Industries comm hub until it was good enough—just—for them to make contact with the Jedi Temple, and Yoda.

Triumph washed away the acid weariness.

I'm good. I am. I don't care if I'm not supposed to say it. I'm good.

Sharply, achingly, he found himself wanting Padmé. Needing her so viciously that her lack was a physical pain. He almost never got to celebrate his victories with his wife. Mostly he had to imagine her joy on his behalf, and console himself with memories.

But he'd rummaged through them too often. They were starting to wear thin.

We need to make new ones. I need to be with her again. I need to hold her. To feel her. I need to know I'm not alone.

He was tired, he was so blasted tired, but unlike Obi-Wan he didn't dare fall asleep. Bant'ena Fhernan had stirred up the past. If he fell asleep he might dream of Tatooine, and in dreaming he might betray himself. And Obi-Wan could never know.

Padmé, Padmé, I need you. You're the only one who understands. You're the only one who can make the dreams stop.

His desire for her was like a dragon, sleeping. The slightest breath could awaken it, fan the flames until they threatened to consume him. He had to fight it. Innocent lives were depending on him. Obi-Wan was depending on him. Letting him down was unthinkable.

Breathing harshly, fist pressed to his lips, Anakin beat the roaring dragon into submission.

Curled on his side beneath the electronics shop's battered desk, Obi-Wan didn't stir. The stipulated half-hour deadline long behind him, he slept like the dead.

He's going to be furious when he does wake and realizes I disobeyed him. Ah well. It isn't the first time. And it won't be the last.

With his primary task completed he retrieved the comlink, crawled out from under the counter, retreated to the rear of the shop, and tried contacting Bant'ena again. This time she answered.

"*Anakin! Are you all right? Where are you?*"

"We're fine," he said, keeping his voice low. "But I'd better not say."

"*Oh. Of course.*"

"Are you all right? Has there been any trouble since we left?"

"*No. Everything's quiet. Anakin—*"

"What?" he prompted, when she didn't finish.

"*I don't understand. Why do you care so much?*"

There wasn't time to tell her. He wouldn't tell her if there was. "I just do."

Her sigh crackled over the 'link. "*Whoever you lost—you must have loved them very much.*"

His fingers tightened on the comlink. "Bant'ena, I have to go. Remember, keep this 'link open. When things happen, they'll happen fast."

"*I'll remember. You be careful.*"

Not even the conversation with Bant'ena had woken Obi-Wan. Concerned, Anakin held one hand just above his mentor's sleeping face and sought for a sense of him within the Force. Sought to feel if anything was seriously wrong. But no. Obi-Wan was just tired.

But is he too tired? Is he more tired than he should be? I know it's exhausting, fighting a war, but—there's still Zigoola. When is he going to tell me about what happened there, with him and Bail? He should tell me about that. Zigoola's something I need to know.

And as soon as they'd put this mission behind them, he'd

corner his former Master and get the truth out of him, one way or another.

It was still dark, the city still under curfew. In his estimation there was too much risk attached in trying to contact Yoda yet. Not enough ambient comm chatter and signal traffic for their illicit transmission to hide in. So he filched the datareader from sleeping Obi-Wan and plowed through reams and reams of fascinating facts about damotite.

Lanteeb's pale dawn came at last. And as the sense of the world around them changed, Obi-Wan woke. Knew instantly he'd been asleep much longer than half an hour.

"*Anakin!*"

"Don't start with me, Obi-Wan," he said, not looking up from the reader. "We both know you needed it."

"*I* will be the arbiter of what I need, not *you!*"

Now he did look up. "Not this time. Obi-Wan, what's the problem? It's not like we had somewhere else to be. And it's not like both of us were working on the comm hub."

"The hub." Obi-Wan uncurled himself and cautiously sat up as far as he could. Propped himself on one elbow. "Is it fixed?"

"Of course it's fixed."

"Then why didn't you *wake* me? We have to contact Yoda, we have to—"

"Piggyback our signal on one of the Sep signals, to hide it," he said, putting the datareader aside. "It's the only way I can guarantee—almost—that we won't be detected."

"What about coding our transmissions?" said Obi-Wan, still looking for fault. "I tell you, Anakin, I don't like the idea of sending data this sensitive without some kind of safeguard."

"Well, I've wired in the scrambler chip I brought with me but—" Anakin shrugged. "The whole thing's a bit wobbly, Obi-Wan. It's not like we're talking compatible technology here, you know."

Obi-Wan tugged at his beard. "But you are sure we can at least cover our tracks?"

"As sure as I can be," he said. "Once I've piggybacked onto a Sep signal and we hit the first holorelay, I can bounce our signal in a different direction and in theory nobody here will be any the wiser. But to do that, I have to wait for there to *be* a Sep signal."

"There was no comm traffic through the night?"

"Not the kind we need." Anakin raised an eyebrow. "A couple of local comms only. Seems the Separatists, unlike *some* people I know, believe in sleep."

"Ha," said Obi-Wan, and scrubbed a hand across his face. "What about you? Did you get any rest?"

"I'm fine." He tapped the datareader. "No chance of falling asleep with this riveting tale to read. Although—did you get up to the bit about how Lanteeb's other two continents are uninhabitable due to damotite contamination?"

"No. I didn't," said Obi-Wan, his interest piqued. "Hmm. I wonder if that's what gave Durd the idea for his filthy bioweapon?"

"Probably." He grinned. "When we catch him, we can ask him. Oh—and I talked to Bant'ena."

"She's all right? There's no trouble?"

"Well, not unless you consider her talking to me at blasterpoint trouble."

Obi-Wan straightened so fast he whacked his head on the underside of the desk. "*What?*"

"Sorry, sorry," he said hastily. "Bad joke. Sorry."

"*Very* bad joke," Obi-Wan muttered. "D'you know, there are times when you and Bail Organa are uncannily alike."

Anakin kept a straight face, just. "Thank you."

"That *wasn't* a compliment," growled Obi-Wan, then rolled out from under the desk and unfolded to his feet. "How soon before we can risk contacting the Temple?"

Anakin checked the comm hub signal monitor. "Not yet. Relax, Obi-Wan. As soon as the right kind of signal comes along I'll be all over it. This is what I do, remember? I fiddle with things and make them better."

"What you *do*," retorted Obi-Wan, "is drive me to distraction."

"Well, you know," he said, this time letting his amusement show, "everyone needs a hobby."

"I thought you already had a hobby."

"What—I can't have more than one?"

"*No*," said Obi-Wan.

Anakin grinned again, and got back to his reading.

YODA WAS TEACHING when he got word that Obi-Wan and Anakin were seeking to speak with him, urgently. Because these students were not younglings, but almost Padawans, he left Ruchikila to lead the blindfolded seeking exercises and hurried to the Temple comm center as requested.

"Master Yoda," said Master Ban-yaro, greeting him. "This way. The comm signal's very weak. Voice only, no holoimaging. I don't know how long we'll hold on to it. It's being pinged back and forth over half the Outer and Mid Rim relay network. And they've asked us to mirror their signal pattern when responding, which isn't helping matters. Also, their security scrambling's patchy. Sounds to me like they're calling home with a tin can and some string."

Yoda guided his float chair beside the Temple's energetic communications chief as they hurried through the center's main comm area to the pass-coded high-security section. "In immediate danger of discovery are they?"

Ban-yaro flipped his long red hair out of his face. "They

haven't said as much but—it seems likely." He was on the brink of breaking into a jog. "We've got them routed through the superconductor. That's the best signal boost and protection we can offer. We'll just have to hope it's enough."

Yoda looked at him sideways. "Worked out, have you, where their location is?"

"Yes," said Ban-yaro. "I'm assuming you need me to forget that little bit of information?"

They'd reached a security-coded door. As Ban-yaro supplied the requisite clearance data, Yoda nodded. "Assume correctly you do."

Ban-yaro flashed his rare, crooked smile. "Done. After you, Master Yoda."

The Temple's most secure, most powerful comm station was empty. As Ban-yaro excused himself to monitor the signal strength, Yoda maneuvered his float chair so he could easily access the comm panel.

"Obi-Wan. Hear me, can you?"

"*Master Yoda! Good. Please listen carefully—I don't know how long we can sustain this uplink. We've already transmitted some important data to you. Has it been received yet?*"

He looked at Ban-yaro, who checked his monitors then raised an acknowledging hand. "Received it is, Obi-Wan."

"*Excellent. Master, we were right. The Seps are manufacturing a bioweapon. The formula's included in the data we sent.*"

"Good work this is, Master Kenobi."

"*Lok Durd's behind this. Yoda, did you know he'd—*"

"Know that I did, Master Kenobi. Matter now it does not. More of this bioweapon tell me."

"*Durd's in charge of the project, answering to Dooku, but the scientist who actually invented the stuff says it's possible to*" *create an antidote and a vaccine. We've sent you the names of four scientists who could do it."*

"Helping you Durd's scientist is?" Surprised, he stared at the comm panel. Even for Obi-Wan, this was impressive. "Manage that how, did you?"

"Doctor Fhernan is not a willing participant in this business, Master. Durd's holding her family and friends hostage to ensure her compliance."

Fear and intimidation: a typical Sith tactic. As for Lok Durd . . . *Cross paths with him again, I knew we would.* "Obi-Wan, a way to stop production of this weapon have you found?"

"Master Yoda, this is Anakin. There's no easy answer to that. Damotite's the key here. It's the weapon's main component. Eliminate the mineral and we'll halt production in its tracks. Problem is, according to Bant'ena's research, Lanteeb's subject to random theta storms, and damotite's the main component in their storm shields. Sure, a Republic assault could take out the mines but—knock down those shields and we'd be condemning the people of Lanteeb to slow, excruciating extinction. At least, any of them who survived the bombardment and the toxic fallout that would follow it. And under the circumstances a planetary evacuation isn't an option."

Sighing, Yoda closed his eyes. "No alternative to damotite for these shields is there?"

"No, Master. Not in the short term."

"Good news this is not."

"Master, we could attempt to wrest Lanteeb back from the Separatists," said Obi-Wan. *"But given its value to them I can promise you they'll not give it up without a fight. I suspect we'd be looking at a prolonged military engagement with a high proportion of civilian casualties."*

No easy answer indeed. Another prolonged military engagement with high civilian casualties was the last thing the Republic needed right now.

"*Master, there is a third alternative,*" said Obi-Wan. "*Not ideal, by any means, but quite possibly our only viable course of action.*"

"Explain."

"*Master Yoda, we need to rescue the twelve hostages.*" And instead of Obi-Wan that was Anakin, sounding anxious. "*Once Bant'ena knows they're safe, she'll help us destroy everything connected with the bioweapon. And then we can get her off Lanteeb so Durd can't use her again. It'll be tricky, but I think we can do it.*"

Hmm. "Agree with Anakin do you, Master Kenobi?"

There was a significant pause before Obi-Wan answered him. "*As I said, Master, it's a risky plan. The hostages don't realize their endangered status. We would need to mount a number of separate rescue missions, any one of which could fail and alert Durd.*"

"Help us without their rescue this scientist will not?"

"*They're her family, Master,*" said Anakin. "*Her friends. She doesn't want to be responsible for their deaths. We can't ask her to be responsible for their deaths.*"

Yoda sighed. "Possible is it, Obi-Wan, for you and Anakin to destroy this scientist's facility and research?"

"*Yes, Master,*" Obi-Wan said, after another long pause. "*But that would guarantee her death, as well as the deaths of her family and friends. We'd be responsible for thirteen murders.*"

Ah. Yes. Everywhere they turned, it seemed, the blood of innocents waited to be spilled. "If young Skywalker's plan we follow, Obi-Wan, some time on Lanteeb you would be forced to remain. Dangerous, that is."

"Believe me, Master, I'm well aware of that."

"This scientist, Obi-Wan. Trust her, do you?"

"Yes, we do," said Anakin.

"Obi-Wan?"

"Master, given the circumstances I don't feel we have another choice," said Obi-Wan. He sounded worryingly reserved. *"Do you?"*

Closing his eyes he sought clarity from the Force, sought to find a path through the clouding dark side—but the future eluded him. Any sense of how this situation might play out shifted and taunted, dancing just out of reach. He felt a dangerous shiver of fear. Never, *never*, not in nine hundred years, had his abilities been so compromised. The dark side had rendered him virtually deaf, blind, and voiceless.

"No, Obi-Wan," he said at last. "I do not."

"And we have one thing in our favor, at least," Obi-Wan added. *"The successful formula has only just been finalized. The weapon is not yet in full-scale production."*

But it would be, and soon. There was no time to discuss this with anyone else on the Council—or with Palpatine. He would have to make the decision, and bear its consequences alone.

"Master Yoda, please, let us do this," said Anakin. *"We have to stop Durd—without hurting anyone else."*

Yes, they did. And while the thought of risking these particular Jedi filled him with dread, this was war. And in war one could not play favorites—no matter how overwhelming the temptation. "Very well," he said. "Identify these hostages for me, can you?"

"We can, Master," said Obi-Wan. *"Stand by for data transmission."*

Yoda turned to Ban-yaro and waited long moments for his acknowledgment. At last Ban-yaro nodded. "Received the data

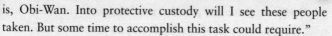

is, Obi-Wan. Into protective custody will I see these people taken. But some time to accomplish this task could require."

"We understand that, Master. Don't worry. We'll manage well enough where we are for a few days, I think. Now I don't dare keep this uplink active any longer. We'll contact you again as soon as possible. Kenobi out."

For a long time Yoda sat unmoving in his float chair. Given this new information, secrecy was now even more important, trust in ever-decreasing supply. He had Jedi available to send after the hostages—but what of the antidote and vaccine for the bioweapon? Production of both needed to get under way in case Obi-Wan and Anakin did not succeed.

"Master Yoda?" Ban-yaro said quietly, joining him. "Here's the downloaded information."

He took the two data crystals. "My thanks. Leave me now. Myself I can see out when finished I am."

Ban-yaro bowed. "Of course, Master Yoda. If you require me again, you know where I'll be."

As soon as he was alone, Yoda swiftly reviewed the data Obi-Wan and Anakin had sent. Found the names of the four scientists who could perhaps perform a miracle—and smiled.

Even in these dark times the Force could find a way.

He opened a new comm channel. But instead of reaching the person he wanted, the signal was diverted.

"Senator Organa's offices," said a warm, pleasant voice. Organa's personal assistant. What was her name? Ah, yes. Minala Lodilyn. Discreet and efficient, he sensed no duplicity in her. *"How may I help you?"*

"Master Yoda this is. With Senator Organa I need to speak."

The briefest hesitation. *"Yes, sir. Senator Organa is meeting with the Supreme Chancellor. I can reach him if you need me to, Master Yoda."*

But if she did that, Palpatine would know that he had business with Alderaan's busy, important representative. He preferred to be discreet. Doubtless he'd bring Palpatine into this mission at some point. But not yet. The Supreme Chancellor was a busy man. Best to keep his desk uncluttered.

"Necessary that is not," he said. "Speak with him, will you, when released from his meeting with the Supreme Chancellor he is?"

"Yes," said Organa's assistant. "*Shall I tell him you wish to see him?*"

"Thank you. Appreciate that I would."

"*Sooner rather than later? And discreetly?*"

"Indeed."

"*I understand, Master Yoda. I don't imagine he'll be much longer than a couple of hours.*"

Which would give him just enough time to deal with the less straightforward of Obi-Wan's requests. Tucking the data crystals into his float chair's pocket, he left the communications center and returned to his own domain.

JUST OVER A DAY returned to the Temple, kicked out of Kaliida Shoals for being underfoot, and already Ahsoka felt like climbing the walls. She wanted to be back out there, fighting, but with Skyguy mysteriously somewhere else, here she was stuck in a stupid dojo with only four remote training droids for company.

That was until Master Taria Damsin came to visit.

Ahsoka deactivated her lightsaber and stared at the older Jedi in surprise. "Me? Master Yoda wants to see me?"

"Us," said Master Damsin. "And no, Padawan, I don't know why."

"Oh," she said, and wrinkled her nose. "Does he want us

right now? Only I've been practicing for a while and—well—I think I need to clean up."

Master Damsin grinned. "I think you do, too, Padawan. But when Master Yoda says *At once come and see me,* I'm pretty sure he doesn't mean, *After your shower come and see me.*"

"No," Ahsoka said faintly. "No, I don't suppose he does."

Anakin. Had something happened to Anakin? She hadn't felt anything. There'd been no disturbance in the Force. And when she was by herself in the dojo, practicing, focusing on her lightsaber forms, that was when she usually tapped into it the best.

"I'm sure your Master and Obi-Wan are fine, Ahsoka," said Master Damsin. In many ways she was a disconcerting woman. "I've known Obi-Wan a long time. I can usually tell when he's landed himself in hot water and I'm not feeling that right now."

"You're not?" she said, relieved. *So it isn't me making stuff up because I want to feel it?* "You aren't just saying that?"

"I never just say anything, Padawan," said Master Damsin, loftily. "Now come on. No smart Jedi keeps Master Yoda waiting."

"Master Damsin, Padawan," said Yoda as they entered his private chamber. "A mission I have for you."

Ahsoka barely managed to keep her mouth from falling open. A mission? Well, that was wonderful. While Anakin and Master Kenobi were off doing whatever they were doing—*not* getting themselves into hot water—a mission was exactly what she needed.

She could feel the same kind of excitement in Master Damsin. And that was interesting. Since when did Jedi Masters get mission-giddy like a Padawan?

"Is this an offworld assignment?" said Master Damsin.

Yoda was looking at her with an unnerving intensity. And

Master Damsin was looking at him the same way, as though they were having a different, private conversation.

"It is," said Yoda, after a moment. "And very important. To a woman in danger am I sending you and this Padawan, Master Damsin. Under enemy surveillance she is. Know that she is in danger she does not. Alarm her you must not. Bring her back to the Temple you must, without alerting those who would harm her. Upon your success do many lives depend." He held out a data crystal. "Your instructions these are. Fail this mission you cannot."

As Master Damsin accepted the crystal from Yoda, Ahsoka took one very small step forward. "Master Yoda—does this have anything to do with Master Skywalker's mission?"

Yoda's eyelids lowered, and he stared at her in silence. She swallowed.

Oh no. I shouldn't have said that. I shouldn't have said anything. He's going to change his mind now. He's going to send me away. When will I ever learn to keep my mouth shut? Skyguy keeps telling me, but I don't seem to learn.

"An interesting question," Yoda said at last. "Why ask it, did you?"

Why? Why? She didn't know why. The thought popped into her head and out of her mouth before she could stop it. That was why. That was the story of her very short life.

"Um—"

"Fear not," said Yoda, gently encouraging. "Tell me."

Beside her, Master Damsin was considering the data crystal with mild interest, as though she could read its contents without needing a machine.

"I don't exactly know, Master Yoda," Ahsoka replied, almost whispering. "It's a feeling. As soon as you mentioned this woman we need to fetch, I had this feeling. And I could kind of sense Master Skywalker. Worried. About her."

"Misled you, Padawan, your instincts have not," said Yoda, opening his eyes wide again. "Tell you more than that I cannot." His inscrutable gaze shifted. "Leave soon you must, Master Damsin. Return soon. Tell *no one* of your task."

Master Damsin bowed. "We'll not fail you, Master Yoda."

"No, Master, we won't," Ahsoka added, because in this case failing Yoda would mean she'd failed Anakin—and right now she couldn't say which would be worse.

"Come on," said Master Damsin, as they left Yoda's chamber. "I've got a secured datareader in my quarters. We'll see what this is about, and then we'll get out of here. Sound like a plan?"

She didn't know Taria Damsin very well. She'd taken a few classes from her, but beyond that they hadn't interacted much in the Temple. Still, she found herself smiling. Liking her, a lot. There was energy and humor here, and a refreshing carelessness toward protocol.

"Yes, Master," she said happily. "That sounds like a very good plan."

Hurrying to keep up—Taria Damsin had a long stride, almost as long as Anakin's—she sent a thought winging through the Force to her absent Master.

Don't worry, Skyguy. Whoever this woman is, whatever she means to you, we'll look after her. We won't let you down.

EIGHTEEN

THERE WERE TWO WAYS MOST VISITORS ENTERED THE JEDI TEMple: on foot through the main public concourse, or by speeder into the enormous transport complex.

Bail Organa entered by a lesser-known, third route, one used almost exclusively by the Jedi. It required a special security pass allowing him to fly his speeder into the vigilantly patrolled restricted traffic zone around the Temple and dock at one of the private landing platforms attached to its publicly inaccessible sectors.

So far, since being gifted with that particular security pass, he'd only made use of it once. It wasn't the kind of privilege he was keen to abuse. Generally speaking, it didn't matter if people knew he'd visited the Temple. Usually he had nothing to hide.

But this time was different.

As his small, nondescript speeder nudged against the platform's docking field, holding fast, he disengaged the privacy shield, pocketed that special security pass, then climbed out. He took one quick look around at Coruscant's cityscape, gilded in the late-afternoon sun: lots of distant, streaming traffic, no one on his tail. Good.

Once upon a time he'd have laughed at the thought of taking such precautions. This was *Coruscant*, the proudly beating heart of the Republic. And this was the Jedi Temple, a galaxy-wide symbol of peace and safety and elegant civilization.

He wasn't laughing now. Times had changed, and he'd changed along with them. Every night he fell asleep with the thought they'd see the good old days again . . . but until then? A weaponized security scanner cleared him into the Temple.

"I'm here to see Master Yoda," he informed the first Jedi he saw crossing the airy twelfth-level concourse, with its soaring columns and pale polished marble and sweetly scented air of serenity. It was such a contrast to the galaxy's turmoil.

She nodded. "Of course, Senator. Please, follow me."

He still found it unnerving, so many people knowing him when he didn't know them.

Yoda was in his private chamber, comfortable on a meditation pad, engrossed in a datareader. He looked up, gravely smiling. "Senator Organa. Good of you it is to come. Very busy you are, I know."

"No busier than you, Master," he said, returning the smile. "I take it there's news from Lanteeb?"

"Yes," said Yoda, putting the datareader aside. "Come in. Come in. Sit. Refreshment, can I offer you?"

As he stepped farther into the light-filled chamber, its door closed behind him. "Thank you, no. The Supreme Chancellor was kind enough to offer me tea during our meeting."

"Hmm," said Yoda, his gaze intent, his small hands resting loosely on his knees. "And how is Chancellor Palpatine today?"

Bail hesitated, then awkwardly arranged himself cross-legged on the chamber's other meditation pad. His knees were going to punish him for this. "He's Chancellor Palpatine. Witty, urbane, and troubled by the war."

"Yet something troubles you about him, I think. Hmm?"

Bail frowned at his linked fingers. That privileged security pass he carried was only one reminder of how his life had altered since Zigoola. This new relationship with Yoda—it was still disconcerting. They weren't friends, not like he and Obi-Wan had become friends, but there was a mutual trust here, an understanding born of shared secrets and shared misgivings and an absolute determination that the Republic would survive. That no matter how bleak things got, or how tempted they were to despair, light would prevail over darkness and all that they loved would not slip away.

He looked up. "Rumor has it that Senator Yufwa of Malastere is about to propose a constitutional amendment."

"Another one?" Yoda's expressive ears lowered. "The sixth amendment this would be, Senator, since the start of the war."

"I know. And believe me, I don't like it. Our Constitution was never meant to be this malleable."

Yoda stroked his chin. "This new amendment. Grant more powers to the Supreme Chancellor's Office, would it?"

"That's right."

"Know of this, does Palpatine?"

"He's the one who told me," he said wryly. "He wondered what I thought, since the amendment involves security issues and that's my area of responsibility."

"And what think you, Senator?"

"I think it'll happen," he said, shrugging. He was aware of a creeping resignation—and anger beneath that. "Palpatine may be reluctant to shoulder more authority, but the Senate can't seem to push it on him fast enough."

"Reluctant, you say." Yoda pursed his lips. "Believe that do you, Senator?"

Sitting still and silent, Bail felt the dull thudding of his accelerated heart. This was the first time he and Yoda had ever directly discussed the Supreme Chancellor. They wouldn't be discussing him now, except that he'd . . . opened the door.

Yes, I opened it—but Yoda stepped through it. And what does that mean? That my misgivings aren't wild fancy? The result of too much work and not enough sleep? Does it mean that nasty tickle in the back of my mind is telling me the truth?

"Do you believe it, Master Yoda?"

Yoda's eyes gleamed. "Believe I do, Senator, that a free society must guard its freedom zealously, lest wake one morning it does to find all freedom disappeared."

Which both was and wasn't an answer. But he knew enough of Yoda, by now, to know it was the only answer he'd get. And that was fine. It was all the answer he could deal with at the moment. This was something he'd need to think about very carefully. One wrong word to the wrong person and—well. There'd be trouble—and on a scale he wasn't sure he could cope with.

If only I could talk it over with Padmé. But Palpatine and his powers are the one subject she and I can't discuss. She's known him so long. Her faith in him is absolute. I just wish mine still was . . .

With an effort he pushed his fresh worry aside and turned his thoughts to an old worry instead. "So. What's the news from Lanteeb, Master Yoda?"

Yoda raised his hand, and something floated through the air from a shelf mounted onto the chamber wall. A data crystal. The Jedi Master caught it in his fingers. Held it lightly, frowning.

"Know any biochemists do you, Senator?"

Biochemists? "Yes," he said, warily. "A couple, as it happens. Why?"

Yoda's gaze was boring into him. "Tryn Netzl?"

Tryn? "Yes. Yes, I know Doctor Netzl. He's one of Alderaan's most respected scientists. Master Yoda—"

"This Tryn Netzl," said Yoda, politely ruthless. "Trust him with your life, would you?"

"I don't—I've never given it any—" He stared at the data

crystal, cold rushing through his blood. "Are you telling me we were right? We're dealing with a bioweapon?"

Nodding, Yoda held up the data crystal. "Yes. The formula I have here. Found on Lanteeb by Obi-Wan and young Skywalker. Created it was by a scientist working for General Lok Durd."

Lok Durd. Bail felt his stomach clutch tight. The Neimoidian's escape from Republic custody was a closely guarded secret. And now Obi-Wan and Anakin knew?

Oh no. I'll bet they're . . . peeved.

His mouth was dry. His worst nightmare was coming true. "This weapon. It's bad?"

"Terrible," said Yoda. "Attempting to prevent its use are Obi-Wan and Anakin. Fail, they might. A defense against it we must have."

"Which would be where Tryn comes in," Bail said, nodding. "We need him to synthesize some kind of antidote?"

"Correct you are, Senator."

"What made you think of him?"

"Think of him I did not," said Yoda. "Suggested he was by the scientist whose formula this is."

Suggested by . . . Bail felt a tiny flicker of hope. "Obi-Wan's turned him against Durd?"

"Her," said Yoda. "Yes."

Bail let out a shaky breath. "Then I guess it's a good thing he and Anakin went to Lanteeb."

"A good thing?" Yoda's ears lowered again. "Remain to be seen that does, Senator."

Which meant the Order's two best Jedi weren't close to being out of danger yet.

Great. Obi-Wan, don't you make me chase after you. I'm a Senator, not a blasted soldier.

"Master Yoda . . ." Shifting on the meditation pad, ordering his disordered thoughts, he pulled one knee up to his chest, hands wrapped around his shin. "There's no question of Doctor Netzl's brilliance. If anyone can extrapolate an antidote from the bioweapon's formula, he can. But even if he succeeds—do we know how much of the weapon Durd and his scientist have created? If they've already got a huge inventory ready at hand—"

"They have not," said Yoda. "A little time do we have before in danger any planet will be."

But from the look on Yoda's face, not much. "There's no question of Tryn refusing to help. He's as committed to the Republic as we are. I'll contact him immediately and see he gets whatever resources he needs. If I have to, I'll provide him with the funds he'll need myself."

"Necessary that will not be, Senator," said Yoda, his eyes warm. "The Temple's discretionary spending I control. And more easily than you can I mask certain . . . purchases."

Oh. Of course. They lived so simply, it was easy to forget that over the generations the Jedi had amassed vast wealth. Which was understandable—the Temple and its widespread activities were enormously expensive to maintain, and the Order received no Republic funding.

Yoda held out the data crystal. "In person I suggest you deliver this, Senator. Out of your sight it should not be."

"Agreed," he said, taking it. "And of course I'll let you know as soon as Tryn's started work, and keep you regularly updated on his progress."

"Senator—" Yoda seemed almost uncomfortable. "This Doctor Netzl—meet with him I would before the antidote he begins to create."

He looked at the ancient Jedi. Meet with Tryn? Why would

Yoda need to—*Oh. He wants to read him. I forgot. The Jedi can do that.*

"You don't trust me to know if he can be trusted?"

"Trust you I do, Bail," Yoda said quietly. "But deceived even the best of us can be."

And of course he couldn't argue with that. Bitter experience had taught him that lesson, comprehensively. "I understand, Master Yoda. I'll bring him to see you as soon as possible."

"Thank you, Senator."

Bail clambered off the meditation pad and bowed. "No, Master. Thank you. I'll be in touch soon."

Sealed again inside his speeder, zipping along the priority Senate traffic lane, he requested a secure comm channel and contacted Padmé.

"It's me. Where are you?"

"On my way home. Why?"

"Need to talk. Can I swing by?"

She laughed. *"That sounds mysterious. Yes, of course. Do you want to stay for dinner?"*

"Love to, but I can't. I'm heading offworld."

"Offworld?" she said, surprised. *"Why are you—oh, don't bother. Tell me when you see me."*

He spent the rest of the ride to Padmé's apartment organizing his transport to Alderaan, tying up various loose ends that he couldn't leave untied, burdening poor Minala with more work than was remotely fair, dictating two memos and leaving Tryn a bland message that he'd be home on a quick visit in the next day or so and wouldn't it be wonderful if they could catch up?

It was funny how things worked out. When Tryn had told him, almost a year ago, that he was returning home to take up a teaching post at one of Alderaan's more modest universities, he'd tried to talk his old friend out of it.

And if he'd listened to me, I might not be able to take this problem to him now. Looks like Obi-Wan's right. Again. The Force has a habit of creating useful connections.

As he came into sight of Padmé's apartment block, he commed Breha. "Leave a light burning in the window this evening, my dove. Your shamefully neglectful husband is making a lightning visit home."

Her soft, sultry laughter lit a fire in his blood. *"I'll do that. How long exactly will the lightning last?"*

"Not long enough," he said, regretful. "As long as I can manage."

"Ah," she said. *"So—not a pleasure trip, then?"*

He grinned. "I'm pretty sure I can squeeze in a little pleasure here and there. But no. It's business."

"I see." The two small words told him she understood perfectly. She knew him so well; could read every nuance of tone in his voice. *"I'll be waiting."*

Padmé's droid answered her front door. "Oh. Senator Organa. Are you expected?"

"Stop being officious, Threepio, and let him in!" Padmé called from somewhere inside the apartment. "And get him a drink. Corellian brandy. Pour one for me, too."

The droid stepped aside. "Senator."

As he made his way to the living room, Padmé came out of her bedroom, careless in loose green silk tunic and pants, barefoot, fingers tugging her intricately bound hair free of restraint. She looked tired and frustrated.

"Have you heard what Yufwa's proposing?"

He grimaced. "Certainly have. What do you think?"

Dropping into the nearest chair, she wriggled until she could drape her legs over one armrest and let her head fall against the chair's high, comfortable back. "I think poor Palpatine's going to need a stiff drink and a lie-down. They can't keep doing this. He's one man. It's not fair."

Bail wandered to the living room's panoramic window and hid his unease from her by staring at the cityscape. Dusk was falling fast; all the bright lights were winking on. "He can always say no."

"I don't see how," Padmé objected. "People are frightened, Bail. They trust him to take care of things. It makes them feel safe, knowing Palpatine's in charge. And right now, we need people to feel safe." She sighed. "But I do wish it didn't involve more burdens for him. He's already got more than enough to contend with."

Oh, he could argue with her, so easily. Except he hadn't come here to argue. Hiding every misgiving, he turned. "You're right. But then, we all do."

Padmé sat up, dropping her feet to the carpet. "What is it? What's happened? Is it—" Her face paled. "Lanteeb? You've heard something?"

As though a switch had been thrown, she'd gone from sympathy to fear. He didn't need to be a Jedi to feel it. But who was she afraid for? He was beginning to wonder.

"I've just come back from meeting with Master Yoda," he said. "He's heard from—"

"Here we are, Mistress Padmé," said her fussy protocol droid as it entered the living room. Halting beside her, it offered a little bow then extended the drinks tray.

"Thank you, Threepio," she said. She was so funny. Treated the thing like it was a living, breathing person. Taking the quarter-filled glass the droid offered, she drank most of its contents in a single gulp. The droid did a small double take, but amazingly forbore comment.

"Sir," it said, tottering over and offering him the other glass.

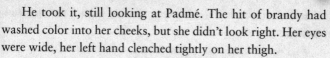

He took it, still looking at Padmé. The hit of brandy had washed color into her cheeks, but she didn't look right. Her eyes were wide, her left hand clenched tightly on her thigh.

Does she realize what she's betraying? Or is it just that she thinks it doesn't matter, in front of me?

He wasn't sure, and he had no intention of asking.

"Go on," she said, once the droid had left the room. "Yoda's had word from Anakin? And Obi-Wan?"

He nodded. "It's what we suspected."

"Great," she muttered, and swallowed the last of her brandy. "As if comm viruses and signal jammers and super ion cannons aren't enough, now we've got bioweapons. What's next? A planet killer?"

"Hey," he said. "Look on the bright side. At least we've got a working anti-signal-jammer prototype."

"But no answer to the comm computer virus," she retorted. "Sorry, Bail. Your eyes are playing tricks on you. The glass isn't half full, it's empty." She rubbed at her temple. "We're going to need an antidote. Better yet, a vaccine."

He loved the way her mind worked. She'd make a brilliant Supreme Chancellor one day. Not that she'd ever thought of it. But he had—and for the sake of the Republic he was going to get her thinking about it, too—and soon.

"We surely are. But that's some more good news." Though he was chock-full of worries, he had to smile. "I don't know how they did it but our Jedi friends have managed to get the rogue scientist who made the bioweapon to help them. We've got its formula. I'm going home now to speak with a good friend of mine. A biochemist."

An answering smile lit Padmé's face. "You're right. That *is* good news."

Stang. And now he had to bring her down. "The bad news,"

he added, reluctant, "is that Lok Durd's behind this Lanteeb business."

Her smile vanished. "That barve. D'you know, Bail, I did wonder."

"Yeah. So did I."

"You never said."

"Neither did you," he pointed out.

"Wishful thinking."

And that made two of them. Which was pretty stupid, really, given the times.

"So are they coming home?" she said, putting her emptied brandy glass on the armchair's side table. "Anakin and Obi-Wan. Did Yoda say if they were on their way back?"

"No," he said, cautiously. "I don't think the mission's quite over yet. But they contacted him from Lanteeb, so I'm assuming they're all right."

"I see," she murmured.

He drank the rest of his brandy. Felt it hit his empty stomach, hot and potent. "Look. I know it's dangerous, what they're doing, but those two eat danger for breakfast, remember? Try not to worry, Padmé. They really are the best."

"True," she said slowly. "But sometimes being the best isn't enough."

He put his glass down on a nearby occasional table and crossed to her. Dropped to a crouch, and rested his hand on her arm. "Hey. How many times have they spat death in the eye? So many times I'm thinking right now death's wearing an eye patch."

"Ha ha," she said, but she managed to smile. And then she patted the hand on her arm. "I know. I know. I'm borrowing trouble. I should have more faith. But it's not easy, being—being friends with people who risk their lives on a daily basis. There should be a how-to manual. Or a survival guide."

Yes, there really should. As Alderaan's elected Senate representative—and as its Prince—he'd been writing too many letters to bereaved families lately. Sending his sincere condolences for the loss of a loved one who'd perished in the battle to save the Republic.

It's not only the Jedi and the clones who are dying. My people are dying. And there's no manual for that, either.

"Hey," said Padmé. "You okay?"

He stood. "I'm fine. But I have to go. Breha's expecting me."

"Give her my love," said Padmé. "Tell her I'm still trying to juggle my schedule so we can catch up at the Crystal Bird Festival."

"I will. Don't get up—I'll see myself out."

"Bail," she said, as he reached the living room archway. "Master Yoda—did he say when they'd be back?"

Slowing, he turned aound. Behind the casual inquiry she was anything but casual. In her eyes he saw a terrible fear—and hope.

Oh, Padmé. My dear friend. What have you done?

"No," he said. "I don't think he knows."

She shrugged, pretending nonchalance. "Okay. That's fine. I was just wondering."

He could see in her face that she knew she'd betrayed . . . something. But he made sure she couldn't see that he'd seen it. She deserved a little privacy. He couldn't bring the Jedi home safe—but he could give her that much, at least.

"I should be back well in time for the briefing day after tomorrow, but I'll comm you if there's a problem."

She waved a hand. "Don't worry. I can cover for you. Focus on this, Bail. This is what's important."

"Yes, ma'am," he said, smiling, and reluctantly left her alone.

• • •

At first Ahsoka was surprised when Master Damsin said they were taking one of the public shuttle flights to Corellia. Then she thought about it, and of course Master Damsin was right. Given the nature of their mission they needed to be inconspicuous—which was also why they'd abandoned their regular Jedi clothing. It was actually a bit exciting, even if it did feel odd to be all covered up, long sleeves and trousers and a baggy overtunic down to midthigh so nobody would notice the lightsaber on her belt.

Hey, look at me. I'm a plainclothes undercover Jedi, like Skyguy.

The dowdy but serviceable shuttle they'd chosen was timed to arrive onplanet just as the working day began. That way they'd be swallowed up in the bustle of rush hour, just two insignificant bodies among many hundreds. Leaving so early from Coruscant meant the transport was barely half full, so she and Master Damsin—Taria—had a whole seat row each to themselves. And tucked away right up the back, too, so they could talk in low voices and not have to worry about being overheard.

She couldn't remember the last time she'd traveled on public transport. That felt odd, too, after months of gunships and starfighters and the soaring majesty of Republic Cruisers like *Indomitable* or *Leveler*. This shuttle, it was so *ordinary*. And it wasn't armed, not even with a single laser cannon. But then why would it be? Who was going to attack a public shuttle on the tedious back-and-forth hop between Coruscant and Corellia? And their fellow passengers? Not a single one of them was scared. They listened to music headsets, or watched vids on the HoloNet Entertainment feed, or read datapads, or snored. It was as if in here, the war didn't *exist*.

Leaning closer, Master Damsin—no, Taria, she had to remember that—tapped her on the arm. A small smile was lurking
and her eyes were amused. "It's called 'culture shock,' Ahsoka.
You'll get used to it."

"I don't know if I want to," she said, frowning at the oblivious passengers in front of her. "I think I want to smack their
heads together and shout *wake up*."

"But isn't this what you're fighting for?" Taria said softly.
"The chance for them to go about their lives without fear and violence?"

You're. Not *we're*. That was curious. But she wasn't going
to say anything. She was going to keep her mouth shut, for once.

See, Skyguy? I'm learning. I am.

She looked again at the scattering of drowsy passengers. "I
know. I just can't help wondering if they get that right now, *right
now*, there are people fighting and dying for them. Hurting.
Bleeding."

"Is that what you want?" Taria said, curious. "To be burdened with gratitude?"

Burdened with gratitude. She'd never looked at it like that.
"I don't—I guess—" She leaned her head against the seat.
"Maybe," she mumbled. "Maybe a thank-you once in a while
would be nice."

"And is that why you became a Jedi? To be thanked?"

"No!" she said, shocked and staring. "I became a Jedi because I couldn't be anything else."

Taria smiled properly. "Good answer."

Warmed by that, Ahsoka settled herself more comfortably
against her seat. "But still . . ."

Taria's sigh sounded sympathetic. "I know," she said. "Especially when you see them doing stupid things, yes? Selfish and
thoughtless and reckless things that put others in danger. That

prove they care about nothing and nobody save for themselves. And then when the inevitable happens, and they scream for the Jedi to come get them out of trouble—" Taria shrugged. "But what can we do? We're the galaxy's troubleshooters, Ahsoka. That's our job."

Well, it was more than a job. Really it was a sacred calling. But she'd feel stupid putting it that way, so she just nodded. "Yes."

"Yes," Taria echoed. "But even so—don't think you're alone in wanting to smack some sense into them sometimes."

Charmed, Ahsoka stifled a giggle. Taria Damsin was the most *un*-Master-like Master she'd ever met. She was finding it hard to remember that this female *was* a Jedi Master, with years of experience and seniority. *Oh please, what am I, ninety? Call me Taria.* And then there was the way she'd excitedly rummaged through the Temple's wardrobe warehouse as they'd looked for something suitable to wear for their mission. Taria's squeal of satisfaction as she pulled out a drab, dark brown two-piece traveling suit, as though they were headed on some kind of adventure, not a serious important mission for Yoda, had left her astonished. No other Master she'd ever met was so . . . so *informal*. Not even Skyguy.

Also, Taria had *amazing* hair. Long and thick and such an amazing color. Even carefully confined in its braid, it seemed to make her tawny eyes glow.

I've never ever been jealous of human hair before. Not until now.

Curiosity got the better of her. "Where are you from, Taria? I've never—"

Another smile, mischievous this time. "Seen anyone who looks quite like me?"

Oh, no. Was it rude, to ask? Probably it was. She was blush-

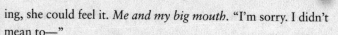

ing, she could feel it. *Me and my big mouth.* "I'm sorry. I didn't mean to—"

"*Relax*, Ahsoka," said Taria. "I'm not going to bite. I'm from Ghaina. Have you heard of it?"

"Sorry. No."

"I'd be stunned if you had," Taria said cheerfully. "It's one of the earliest settled colony worlds. Remotely situated and not at all interested in galactic affairs. I'm the first—the only—Ghainan Jedi. What you might call an aberration."

Oh. "Is that—does that make you—lonely? Being the only one?"

Taria gave her the strangest look. "D'you know, you're only the second person who's ever asked me that."

"Who was the first?"

"A friend," Taria said, after a moment. Her sharp face softened, and her gaze lost its focus. Then she blinked and pulled herself back from wherever she'd gone. "So. Tell me about Anakin."

She was going to have whiplash before this mission was over. "Master Skywalker? Oh. Um. I don't—I'm not sure—well, what did you want to know?"

Taria leaned close again, confidingly. "Basically—how good is he at not getting himself killed?"

Ahsoka stared. "You don't *know*?"

"Well, I know he's the Chosen One," said Taria, shrugging. "The Council didn't manage to keep *that* secret very long. Other than that . . . see, the thing is, I've led kind of an odd life for a Jedi. Maybe it's because I'm Ghainan or maybe it's because I'm me. Whatever the reason, I never trod the regular Jedi path, Ahsoka. I've had long-term postings in far-flung places. Been on quite a few extended retreats. Not so many visits back to the Temple. That makes it tricky to keep up with the news."

And it explained why their paths had rarely crossed. "It sounds—exciting."

"It had its moments," Taria said, and chuckled. "Now. About Anakin . . ."

"Anakin—Master Skywalker—is really, *really* good at not getting himself killed."

"Hmm." Taria flipped the end of her braid over her shoulder and fiddled with it. "What's his track record on not getting anyone else killed?"

Something the Jedi Master had said niggled. What was it? *I've known Obi-Wan a long time.* Risking censure, Ahsoka sank a little way into the Force and extended her senses . . .

"Hey," said Taria. "No peeking. It's rude."

And asking a Padawan to gossip about her Master was polite? "My Master would die before he'd let anything happen to Master Kenobi," she said quietly. "You don't have to worry about him."

"Have to?" Taria flipped her braid back. "Well, no, of course I don't *have* to. But every girl needs a hobby, Ahsoka. Yours is worrying about Anakin, remember?"

Ow. "I'm sure they're both fine, Master Damsin," she said firmly. "Master Yoda—"

"*Attention, passengers. We are on final approach to Corellia, for spaceport docking in Coronet. Prepare for sublight and have all relevant inbound documentation ready for Transit Authority inspection.*"

"Right then, Ahsoka," said Taria, suddenly briskly businesslike. A Jedi, through and through. "Let's run the plan one more time before we hit dirtside."

They both remembered it perfectly. Of course. Encountering no trouble with Coronet's Transit Authority, and with minutes to spare, they made their connecting shuttle to the satellite retirement suburb of Visk, where Bant'ena Fhernan's mother made her home. The nav computer on their hired groundcar—speeder access was restricted to local law enforcement personnel—guided them without incident to the address the captive scientist had provided.

Mata Fhernan wasn't there.

"Market day in Tiln," her chatty neighbor said helpfully as they stood stranded on her doorstep. "Always traipses down to Tiln for her shopping, does Mata." A disapproving sniff. "My Herold's tabba-root isn't good enough for her."

"I'm sorry to hear that," said Taria, self-contained and polite. "Thanks for your help."

They returned to their groundcar and looked up Tiln on the nav comp.

"That's a long way to go for tabba-root," Ahsoka said, frowning at the readout.

Taria punched the nav comp's ACCEPT DESTINATION button and grinned. "I don't know. I've gone farther for less."

Really, she was the most *disconcerting* woman.

Reaching the small rural township without incident, they soon found themselves bogged down in traffic. It seemed that Tiln Markets were a shopping destination in their own right. The crowds were going to make finding their oblivious quarry something of a challenge. Disengaging the autodrive as they reached the end of the queue for access to parking, Taria took over manual control of the groundcar, lowered its shield, and swept her narrowed gaze around the other vehicles and the roadside stalls and the meandering pedestrians loaded down with boxes and bags and little carts full of fruit.

"Well, Ahsoka? What do you feel?"

A cool breeze across her skin. Clouded sunshine on her face. The dampest hint of rain coming on. Soft like the ocean, a steady sussuration of human and nonhuman emotions. Contentment. Avarice. Anxiety.

Danger.

"Yes," Taria murmured. "Someone unsavory's here. Very dark side. They might as well shoot up a flare. Let's tread carefully, shall we?"

Stop start, stop start, they crawled their erratic way into the public parking station and then into a coded slot on the third level. After paying their credits, they took their ID chip for later, rode down to ground level in the turbolift, and joined the throng heading into sprawling, popular Tiln Markets. Partly covered, partly open-air, it was crammed full of sentients from at least sixty different systems, ripe with smells and sounds and a thousand ways to make and lose money, and, according to the welcome board at the entrance, they now swallowed almost a quarter of the town.

"I don't know," Ahsoka muttered, staring in dismay at the shifting sea of shoppers as it spilled and surged among the endless rows and cross-rows of stalls and displays. "Maybe we should've stayed in Visk and waited for Mata Fhernan to come home. We're never going to find her in here!"

"Patience," said Taria, patting her shoulder. "We'll find her. And unlikely as it sounds, it'll be much easier spiriting her away in this madhouse than it would've been in that neat and tidy retirement estate with its empty streets and nosy neighbors."

Maybe. And of course Taria was an experienced Jedi. But there was no denying it, all these people made her nervous.

"Don't think about our quarry," Taria added. "Focus on the creature hunting her, Ahsoka. Wherever she is, it won't be far away. And so long as we're careful and don't send up any flares of our own, it'll do most of our work for us."

Admiring, Ahsoka looked up at her. "That's really smart."

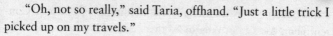

"Oh, not so really," said Taria, offhand. "Just a little trick I picked up on my travels."

The creature sent to shadow Mata Fhernan left a smear in the Force like something dead and dragged across ferrocrete. Rancid. Rotten. A corruption of the light. Gagging, Ahsoka tried to close most of her mind to it. Let only enough of its putrid essence past her defenses so she could track it through the echoing cacophony of every other sentient in this enormous place.

"Good girl," said Taria, as they made casual, careful, apparently random progress from stall to stall, closing in on their prey. "But I think that's close enough." She shuddered. "Time to start looking for Mata."

They'd both memorized the woman's holoimage. Medium height, straight brown hair muddied with gray and cropped short. A singular individual who, it seemed, had never chosen anti-aging or physical enhancement therapies, so she was wrinkled and hook-nosed and bigger-boned than civilian society deemed acceptable.

Her face was a map of a life lived brashly, on its own bold terms. Before her retirement she'd lectured in Galactic theater across half of the Republic.

Ahsoka, struggling to stay hidden from Mata Fhernan's shadowy observer, struggling to keep that shadow as close as she could bear, felt Taria Damsin stumble beside her.

"Stang," the Jedi Master muttered. "No. No. Don't mind me."

Beneath her light caf-colored skin she was pallid. Cutting through the shadow's darkness and the mayhem of the markets, Ahsoka felt pain. A corrosive quiver of fear.

Something's not right. She's—

"Ahsoka!" Taria snapped. "On the job."

"Sorry," she whispered. "I didn't mean to—"

The press of bodies around them eddied like a stream striking rock. She felt a tugging, off to the left. Feeling that peculiar rightness in the Force, she turned and looked.

"There," she said, pointing. "Taria, there."

NINETEEN

FEAR AND PAIN CRUSHED TO SILENCE, TARIA LOOKED. "YES, that's the woman we're after. Well spotted, Ahsoka."

A Jedi wasn't supposed to care about praise. And yet, she realized with a shock, Taria Damsin's approval mattered—which was almost as odd as Taria Damsin herself.

Never mind. I'll figure it out later.

Mata Fhernan was chatting animatedly to a man selling hand-carved, hand-painted wooden stirring spoons. Ahsoka couldn't believe it when their quarry handed over good credits for *two* of the spoons. Cooking with wooden utensils? *Urrggh.* That was so *unhygienic.*

She glanced at Taria. "What now?"

Taria's eyes were half closed, her lips tight with concentration. "Now, Ahsoka, we proceed with extreme caution. The sentient watching her—I still don't see him, but I think he's Anzati."

Oh. Well. *That* wasn't good. Anzati were born predators, even better hunters and trackers than the Togruta. Highly sought after as criminal assassins. He'd be difficult to shake off.

"The good news," Taria added, "is that he hasn't spotted us."

Ahsoka grimaced. "Yet."

"Now, now," said Taria, nudging her with an elbow. "Would Anakin let you get away with saying that?"

No, he wouldn't. He'd give her a look. "Sorry."

"Forget it. Come on. Let's make a new friend."

Threading their circumspect way through this covered section of the markets, toward Mata Fhernan who'd shoved her spoons in her shopping bag and was now inspecting handcrafted lace doilies, they gradually and unobtrusively began to drift apart, angling themselves so they'd end up flanking her. When they were almost close enough to reach out and touch the woman, Taria flicked a sideways, warning glance.

Let me do the talking.

Ahsoka nodded. Drifted her hand closer to the hilt of her hidden lightsaber. Strong in the Force, that sense of lurking danger.

"Mata Fhernan," said Taria, fingers closing gently on the old woman's arm. "Mata, I have a message for you. From Bant'ena."

Mata Fhernan's eyes were sharp with intelligence. Hearing her daughter's name, she gasped. "*Benti.* She's *not* dead? Oh, I knew it. I *knew* it. They said I was a crazy old woman to believe she'd survived the Separatists' attack but—" She pressed shaking fingers to her lips. "A mother knows. Where is she? *How* is she? How do *you* know her?"

Taria's free hand twitched away the folds of her overcloak, drawing discreet attention to the lightsaber on her belt. "She's— a friend of a friend. And she wants you to come with us."

Mata Fhernan's eyes narrowed, and her unpainted lips framed a single, silent word. *Jedi.* "She's in trouble?"

Taria nodded. "As are you. So please, let's go. Slowly, no rushing. No making a fuss. A nice casual stroll, Mata, toward the nearest exit."

"Why?" the old woman demanded. "Am I being watched?"

"Don't worry," said Taria. "We'll protect you."

"We?" Turning, Mata Fhernan looked down and blinked. "Oh. Aren't you a little small to be a Jedi?"

Ahsoka managed a polite smile. That sense of danger was uncomfortably flaring. "No. Please, we really do need to go."

"You're taking me to Benti?"

Ahsoka looked at Taria. *I'm Jedi. We aren't liars.* But sometimes the truth was more dangerous than a lie.

"Yes."

Mata Fhernan's amazing face tightened. "Then why are we standing around here gossiping?"

"Smile, Mata," said Taria, slipping her hand into the crook of the old woman's elbow. "Relax. We're three good friends who've spent a lovely morning at the markets, and now we're going home. Nice and slow. No sudden movements."

Casually, they made their way through the market throng. Like a shadow under bright water, the Anzati slipped after them. It didn't matter that he hadn't spotted them. He had Mata's scent and he wasn't letting go.

"Blast," Taria murmured. "This is exactly what I didn't want to do."

This was use the Force to blur their presence in the crowd. Ahsoka felt the ripples around them. Felt the sensitive sentients in the marketplace jostle as reality twisted, ever so slightly.

"Okay," said Taria. "Now. While he's distracted."

With the crowd seething and surging, a packed school of bimi fish startled by a thrown rock, they ducked out of the covered markets—and into pattering rain.

"It couldn't have held off ten more minutes?" said Taria.

The crowds outside had thinned dramatically, chased away by the cloudburst. Ahsoka risked a look behind them. There was no sign of the Anzati, but she could still feel him in the Force, angry and uncertain, raw violence simmering.

"What is it?" said Mata Fhernan. "What's gone wrong?"

"Nothing," said Taria, with a reassuring smile. "But it would be good if we hurried." She pointed to the not-too-far-away but still not-close-enough multilevel parking station. "We're in there."

One hand resting on the hilt of her lightsaber, the other under Mata's elbow to help her along, Ahsoka crushed every flicker of alarm as they made tracks for their groundcar.

I've smashed battle droids and SBDs, I've flown starfighters and STAPs. I've faced down evil Sith henchmen—and women—and I'm Anakin Skywalker's apprentice. One Anzati is no match for me.

Even so, her heart beat like a drum.

"I think we've lost him, don't you?" she asked Taria, trying to sound unworried.

Taria reached into the Force. "Not exactly," she murmured. "He's still there, though he's a long way behind us and definitely confused. But it's better than nothing. To be on the safe side, let's pick up the pace." She glanced at the old woman between them. "Sorry, Mata. It'll be over soon. I promise."

Breathless, the old woman nodded. She was fit, for an aging human, but their hurrying was taking its toll.

The crowd had grown again, fresh arrivals streaming out of the parking station and heading for the markets. Ahsoka let out a tiny sigh of relief. The more people the better. Camouflage, each and every one.

"Hey," said Taria, looking over Mata Fhernan's bowed head as at last they made their way into the station. "Don't suppose you remember where we parked?"

For one terrible moment, she thought Master Damsin was serious. And then came that swiftly flashing mischievous smile.

"Not funny, Taria!" Ahsoka choked out. "Really, really *not funny*!"

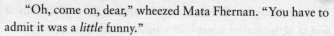

"Oh, come on, dear," wheezed Mata Fhernan. "You have to admit it was a *little* funny."

"Hey," said Taria, impressed. "I like you."

Almost hobbling now, still Mata Fhernan managed a smile. "You're taking me to my daughter, dear. I *love* you."

They made it safely to an empty turbolift and let it whoosh them up to the third level, where it spat them out again. They paused.

"Feel anything?" Taria asked.

Ahsoka shook her head. "You?"

"Not so far." Taria scanned the entire third level, frowning as she worked her way through all the other shoppers arriving and leaving. It was raining again, heavily, water blowing in through the station's open sides. "I think we're good. Let's go."

They made it to their groundcar, freed it with the ID chip, and piled inside.

"Backseat, Mata," said Taria, slinging the old woman's shopping bag on the floor. "And lie down."

"You're very bossy, dear," Mata complained, doing as she was told.

"I know. I'm sorry. And it's Taria, not dear. All set? Good. Off we go." As she backed the groundcar out of its slot Taria activated its shields. "Wish they were armored," she muttered. "Still, we should be all right."

Ahsoka nodded, her heart pounding, lightsaber unclipped and in her hand. "Yes. We should be."

And they were, until they hit the last section of exit ramp—where everything went wrong.

Their only warning was a red screaming in the Force, half a heartbeat before the Anzati attacked.

"Hold on!" Taria shouted, slamming the brakes as he leapt lightly from the level above onto the exit ramp directly in front of them. He carried two heavy concussion grenade launchers and fired them as he landed. One volley missed and exploded the small groundcar behind them. The death of its driver flared brief and bright in the Force. The other concussion charge clipped the side of their groundcar, bounced onto the close-by ferrocrete retaining wall, and erupted into gouts of crimson flame.

Its systems overwhelmed, their groundcar's shielding collapsed.

"*Ahsoka!*" said Taria, with one single, burning look. "Alive, remember? Stick to the plan! Mata, stay where you are. Don't you dare move. Ahsoka?"

In perfect harmony they Force-jumped out of the groundcar, lightsabers igniting as they speared through the air. Smoke and flames and screaming and klaxons, horns blasting, feet running. Chaos and madness.

Plunged into the harsh otherworld of combat, Ahsoka was dimly aware of Taria fighting beside her, a brilliant tawny gold flame in the Force.

Alive. Alive. If we end up confronting him, the plan is to take him alive.

The Anzati was Force-sensitive but he hadn't been trained. He was working on instinct and years of bloody practice. Ferociously swift and heavily armed he fired again and again until there was so much smoke and fire around them it was hard to breathe or see. But even so they were beating him back, deflecting his lethal concussion grenades, dousing his raging hunger for their deaths with the light side of the Force.

"*Ahsoka!*" Taria cried again. "Get ready!"

What? Get ready? What did she—

And then she *saw* it, the Force showed her, the way it showed Anakin things all the time and showed her not so often. She saw the split second where their desperate battle could turn.

Yes. Now. Leaping forward and across, she drew the Anzati's eager fire, her lightsaber a blurring whirl designed to frighten and defend. And in that tiny moment of his uncertainty, Taria lowered her own guard and leapt directly at him. Using the Force to pluck the concussion grenade launchers from his hands, she flipped him upside down to strike his back to the ferrocrete ramp with a brutal finality.

He shouted his pain once, then fell silent.

Giving him no chance to recover, Taria leapt again, planted her booted right foot on his heaving chest, and pointed the tip of her green lightsaber at the hollow of his throat. His grayish skin had paled with shock; his cheek proboscises were unfurled and lying limp across his shoulders. His eyes were open, his lips peeled back in a snarl.

Shaking, Ahsoka heaved great gasps of filthy, stinking air into her lungs and stared at Taria, who was gasping just as hard—even as she grinned.

"*Stang*, Padawan. You are *good*!"

Ahsoka grinned back. "You're not exactly a slouch yourself, Master," she replied. "I think—"

"What?" said Taria. Then she stopped and dragged the back of her hand across her face. The bright red blood leaking from her nose and eyes smeared her skin, mixing with the smoke and sweat from the fight.

She swallowed. "Taria?"

"It's nothing," Taria snapped. "Forget it. Not your concern."

Not her concern? But—

"Hey, Mata!" Taria was looking past her, back at their groundcar. "Mata, are you all right?"

"Yes, dear," came Mata Fhernan's quavering reply, barely audible over the shriek of approaching sirens and the hubbub of shocked spectators milling in disarray. She was still tucked in-side the groundcar. "I'm all right. How about you?"

"We're fine, Mata! Hold on. We'll be on our way soon."

"All right," said Mata Fhernan. "But hurry up. I want to see my daughter."

Taria's grin slipped. "I know you do, Mata. You'll see her soon, I promise."

"Taria—"

"Don't," said Taria, her eyes flashing a warning. "It's not a lie. Not exactly. At least it won't be, if we can help it."

On the ground, a captive, the Anzati started to laugh.

BANT'ENA STARTLED AWAKE on her lumpy sofa to feel five fat, clammy fingers clamped tight around her bruised throat. To see a moist, flat face and two lidless, oddly pupiled eyes looming over her.

Oh no. Oh no. Let this be another dream.

"Well, well, my dear," said the general, almost purring. "I think you have a little something to tell me. Don't you?"

She'd dimmed the lights after the Jedi left, but now they were kicked up to full illumination. With the window boarded over she couldn't tell if it was day or night. How long had she been asleep? Had she missed Anakin's next call? Stang, where had she left the comlink? Was it in full sight, where Durd would find it?

"Silence won't help you, Doctor!" said Durd, tightening his grip. "Silence is the last thing in life that will help you." Letting go of her, he straightened his vast bulk and stepped back. "If you value your whole skin—if you value the well-being of those you claim to love—you will not remain silent. Do I make myself clear?"

Warily she sat up, not taking her eyes off him. Touched fingertips to her burning throat. "General—" Her voice was raspy. Talking hurt. It was a wonder he hadn't crushed her larynx. "I don't know what—"

"Lies will get your family and friends killed faster than silence!" Durd snarled. And then he was holding up the comlink, brandishing it in her suddenly bloodless face. "Where did you get this?"

She felt her heart stop. Felt the air freeze in her lungs. Icy tears blurred her vision.

It's over.

"I am not a foolish creature," said Durd, his voice thick with rage. "I am a personage of *great* value. Wanted by the Republic and prized by Count Dooku. Did you think I wouldn't take *precautions*, my dear? At my insistence the comm equipment in this compound is tagged, and an automatic sweep is regularly performed to account for each comlink. The last sweep found that two 'links were missing from their designated location." He waggled the comlink again. "Here is one. Where is the other?"

"I don't know, General," she said, her lips stiff and cold. And that wasn't a lie. She had no idea where the Jedi were hiding. "I swear it. I don't know where it is. I don't understand any of this. I don't know how that comlink got in here. Perhaps one of the battle droids was inspecting my quarters and dropped it."

Durd threw the comlink at her and began to pace between the sofa and her curtained-off bedroom. "I have more to tell you, Doctor. You might think the news is cause to celebrate, but I promise you, you're wrong."

If she asked him to tell her, he would win. Ignoring the comlink, landed on the sofa beside her, she said nothing. Durd waited. Waited. And then he gave in.

"A short time ago," he said, hating her, "someone rescued your mother."

It nearly killed her but she kept her face blank. *Anakin. Oh, Anakin. You kept your word.* "I don't understand."

"Oh my dear, I think you do," said Durd, menace rolling off him like marsh stink. "And I expect you're dying to know how *I* know that your mother is rescued. Well, since I don't want you dying—at least not quite yet—I shall satisfy your lethal curiosity. The Anzati who was watching her told me. We had an arrangement. *Precautions,* you see? He sent me a signal to let me know he had failed."

Mata. Mata is safe. No matter what else happens, this barve can never hurt her.

"I'm afraid I don't know any more than that," Durd added. "But you would do yourself some small good if you were to enlighten me."

My mother was an actress. I am her daughter. I can bluff this fat fool.

"I won't lie to you, General," she said, meeting his furious stare. "I am overjoyed that my mother is safe. But I *do not know* who rescued her, or why. How could I possibly know that? I am your prisoner. And even if I did steal this comlink, which I didn't, it's not powerful enough to reach anyone offworld. I couldn't arrange my mother's rescue no matter how much I wanted to."

Durd didn't curse, or hit her. Instead he pulled a compact holotransmitter from his pocket and balanced it on his palm. Flicking it on with his thumb, he pressed a coded sequence of buttons on its base. A moment later, a small holoimage shivered into view. It was her childhood playmate Samsam. He was power-gliding along the shore of Corellia's Lake Radu. It was dawn there, his favorite time of the day. She knew it was the lake because that was the Radu Lighthouse behind him. She'd know it anywhere. And she knew it was Samsam because she'd know *him* anywhere. He always wore a bright yellow glide-suit.

Samsam. Oh, Samsam.

Still unspeaking, Durd pressed the transmitter's comm panel a second time. Nothing happened. Samsam kept on gliding.

"What did you do?" She couldn't take her eyes off that gliding yellow figure, carefree and laughing as it rode the wild wind. *"What did you do?"*

A high-pitched buzz. Instead of answering her question, Durd answered a comlink he took from his pocket. "Yes?" A metallic voice buzzed. She couldn't make out the words, but Durd's face flushed with more choking anger. "I see. Fix them."

Samsam was still gliding. Terrified of what the comlink call might mean, still she feasted her hungry gaze on her friend.

He's all right. He's all right. Durd's just trying to scare me. Samsam's all right, he's—

Between blinks, the bright yellow chest of Samsam's glide-suit turned red, and then he was tumbling out of the dawn sky. Lazily falling, like an autumn leaf from a tree. Down . . . down . . . falling so far down. In utter silence he fell into the lake and sank beneath its ruffled surface.

Dimly, through the ice storm roaring in her head, she heard Lok Durd laugh.

"That was a lie." She couldn't recognize her own voice. "That wasn't real. You're trying to trick me. You faked it. Samsam's not dead."

Durd laughed again, delighted. "You can think that if you want to, my dear. You're wrong, but you can think it. And you can keep on thinking it as I order the death of another person you love. Or better yet—" He smiled, widely. "Why don't I let *you* choose your next victim?"

She wished she could cry, she wanted to cry, but the roaring ice storm had frozen her tears.

"No."

"Doctor, there's no point playing this game anymore," said Durd, his murderous fury transmuted to something worse: to gloating glee. "Someone has erased several sections of security recordings. Footage from your lab. From this room. A few corridors. It was cleverly done. It could be a malfunction—it *looks* like a malfunction—but we both know that's not true. Tell me who did it. Tell me who's helping you."

"No one's helping me," she said dully. *Samsam.* "You've made a mistake."

"Oh, my dear," said the general. "One of us has."

He fetched her single kitchen chair and placed it in front of her. Then he punched a fresh code into the compact holotransmitter and put it on the chair. Nothing. Nothing. And then the air flickered, an image coalesced, and she was looking at her nephews playing tag in a park.

She stopped breathing.

"Who is helping you, Doctor?" the Neimoidian asked, so gently, as though he were concerned for the state of her health.

She shook her head. "No," she croaked. "No, you can't do this. Those are *children*. They're practically *babies*. You *can't*."

"They're not babies to me," said Durd, indifferent. "Little squirming pink bloodsacs. That's all they are."

Samsam gliding. *Samsam* falling through the air. Her nephews were laughing. Irek, the older, was sitting on Tam's head. And now those icy tears were falling. They were freezing her face. Her heart was a lump of ice, freezing her blood. One tap and she'd shatter.

I have to. I have to. I don't have a choice.

"The Jedi," she said, fingers fisted in her lap. "The Jedi are helping me."

Durd's moist face turned sickly. "*Jedi?*" he croaked. "There are *Jedi* here? How did they find me? I have protection from

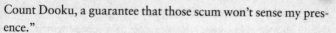

Count Dooku, a guarantee that those scum won't sense my presence."

She swallowed. *What is he talking about?* "Perhaps your protection's stopped working, General. If I could take a look at it—"

"I took it off," he snapped. "It hurts my skin." He pressed his palms to his fat cheeks. His hands were trembling. *"How did they find me?"*

"I don't know."

Durd exploded into rage. She didn't try to defend herself as he slapped and scratched and punched her. He dragged her onto the floor by the hair and kicked her back and her belly and spat in her face. She did nothing to stop him, just closed her eyes and let him hurt her, wishing he'd snap completely, and break her neck.

"*You* did this, didn't you?" he screamed. "When you were offworld. You contacted the Jedi Temple for help. How many have come to destroy me, Doctor? *How many?*"

Half blinded with pain, she curled on her side and stared up at him. She could feel blood dripping off her chin. "Two."

"Only two? You're sure of that?"

She nodded. "Yes. I swear it. Two."

He stamped around the room, arms flailing. "*Jedi*. They got their filthy hands on me once. They won't get me again. The Count will never forgive me if they get me again." He turned on her. Rushed at her. Loomed over her, fists waving. "You let the *Jedi* in here? I should kill them all! Your brother and your sister and their stinking offspring and your little friends. I want to hear you *screaming*, Doctor! I want to see you rend the flesh from your face as the grief drives you *mad*! The *Jedi*? Where are they now? Are those vermin still here? In the compound?"

"No," she whispered. "They left."

"I don't believe you!" he shouted, and turned to the holo-transmitter.

She lunged at him, frantic. "It's true! They left! They left! I swear it on my life!"

"No," said Durd, pointing at her beautiful nephews. "You swear it on *their* lives. But I think you're *lying*."

Again, his fingers fisted in her hair. Her head was dragged back so far and so hard she did think he'd snap her neck. And now she didn't want him to.

"*No no no!*" she gabbled, trying to pull his fingers free. "Please no, you're hurting me! Don't hurt me and I'll help you. Don't hurt them and I'll give you the Jedi, I swear!"

Leaning down, he breathed foul air into her face. "How?"

"They're going to call me. On that comlink you found. They took the other one with them."

"*You're lying!*" he shouted—but he wanted to believe her. She could see the need to believe her raging in his eyes. His hatred for her was outstripped only by his fear of Count Dooku.

"I'm not," she said, tears of pain streaming down her cheeks. "I will give them to you. I'll test the weapon on them. I'll do anything you want."

Hope and greed flared in his eyes. "Anything?"

"Yes. You show me my loved ones every day, General. You show me so I can see it's not a trick and they're alive and you've not harmed them. Show me that and I will get you your revenge on the Jedi and earn you Count Dooku's undying trust."

He stared at her greedily, mouth fallen open, his skin wet with avarice. Unfisting his fingers, he let go of her hair.

"If you are lying, my dear—if this is a trick—I'll bring those pink bloodsacs here and then I'll gorge you on their screams."

"No lies, General," she whispered, choking. "No tricks."

Still Durd stared at her. Desperately wanting to believe her promises. Desperately afraid this was a trap.

"Do we have a deal, General?"

Durd nodded, hating her. "We have a deal."

"Good," she said, and collapsed facedown on the floor.

The Jedi said they'd protect my family and my friends, but Samsam is dead. So either they lied or they failed. Either way I can't trust them. I am my loved ones' only hope. Let the galaxy save itself. I will save who I can.

"SORRY," said ANAKIN, as his empty belly rumbled again. "I can't help it."

Obi-Wan looked at him. "Try drinking some more water."

"No, thank you. Lanteeban tap water tastes like pond sludge," said Anakin, sounding grumpy. "We should've brought some of Bant'ena's mealpacks with us. I mean, she offered. It wouldn't have been stealing."

"And carried them how?" He shook his head, sighing. "We'll be fine, Anakin. You know perfectly well a Jedi can function without food for extended periods."

"Well, yes, I know we *can*," Anakin muttered. "I just don't want to." Grunting, he shuffled around a bit under the front counter. "Are you *sure* there aren't any biscuits in here? I'm *hungry*."

Temper stirred. "Anakin, what precisely are you hoping for? That somehow in the five minutes that have passed since you last asked if I was sure there weren't any biscuits, biscuits have miraculously manifested themselves?"

"Well," said Anakin, grasping at straws. "You never know. They could have. That barve Durd miraculously manifested himself. Besides, I'm complaining for a reason. We need to fuel ourselves, Obi-Wan. Being able to scrape by on three mouthfuls every second day is a survival trait. We're looking at a bit more activity than just surviving. Although that's pretty much at the top of the list."

Annoyingly, his former apprentice had a point. The next day or so would see great demands placed upon them. Doubtless they would be using the Force not only to gain access to Durd's compound for a second time, but afterward to escape it and then escape Separatist-controlled Lanteeb altogether. And using the Force extensively required deep physical reserves—which required adequate nourishment.

"I know," he said, and shifted around a bit himself, stuck under his wretched desk. "But we'll be fine."

Beyond the confines of the boarded-up electronics shop, another new day was stirring. They could hear ground traffic now, and ships thundering out of the spaceport. Soon there'd be foot traffic, too, and more battle droid patrols. They'd have to remain completely silent. One wrong sound might lead to discovery, and death.

Restless, Anakin crawled out from beneath the counter and bounced to his feet. "Toss me the comlink. I want to contact Bant'ena."

"There's nothing new to tell her, Anakin."

Anakin frowned. "We can tell her she hasn't been forgotten."

"I'll tell her," he said, and activated the link. "Doctor Fhernan. Doctor Fhernan, are you there?"

"Yes, Master Kenobi. I'm here. What's happening?"

Instead of answering immediately he took a moment to read her, as well as he could. He sensed tension. Fear. A heightened level of anxiety. Of course, she'd lived with intolerable stress for some time now.

"Best I not elaborate, Doctor," he said, habitually cautious. Unlike Anakin, he was still not ready to fully trust the woman. "Events are in motion. All you need to do is hold tight—and stall working on the Project, if you can. Tell Durd—"

"*I don't need to. He's gone to see Dooku. But he'll be back tomorrow. Can you get me out of here tonight? There'll only be me and the droids here. We might not get another chance. And—and I'm afraid, Master Kenobi. I think Durd's regretting his decision to keep me alive.*"

And that would explain her increased fear and anxiety. He glanced at Anakin, who nodded, his expression fierce. "Yes, Doctor. We can do that. Though it's only fair to warn you that we might not have a full report on the status of your loved ones."

"*You've said you'll see them safe, Master Kenobi. You're a Jedi. I trust your word.*"

"Do you think there's a chance Durd has changed his mind and taken the bioweapon formula with him to Dooku?"

"*No,*" said Dr. Fhernan. "*I told him I'd found an instability in the primary chained molecule sequence. He was very angry. He—he—*" Her voice broke. "*He beat me again. Please, Master Kenobi. Please get me out of here.*"

With a muffled curse, Anakin used the Force to pluck the comlink from his grasp. "We will, Bant'ena. We'll be there after dark. Be ready. Hold on. Can you hold on? It's nearly over."

"*Yes,*" she whispered. She sounded on the verge of tears. "*But not for long.*"

"It won't be for long, I promise. We end this tonight."

As Anakin disconnected the comlink, Obi-Wan raised an eyebrow at him. "Snatching is discourteous."

Ignoring that, Anakin tossed the comlink back to him. "I was still hoping there'd be a way to take that barve Durd home with us."

"So was I," he admitted. "We'll just have to make him our next mission."

Anakin grinned fiercely. "That sounds like a plan."

"Now I suggest we sleep for a few hours. Conserve our energy. We can contact the Temple again later, before we go to retrieve Doctor Fhernan."

"Sleep?" Anakin groaned. "How do you expect me to sleep when I'm starving to death? Are you *sure* there aren't any bis—hey! Don't do that."

The last words came out muffled, because he'd used the Force to plaster a sheet of old flimsi invoice across Anakin's face.

"Hush," he whispered severely. "Before somebody hears us."

And having managed the last word, for once, he rolled onto his side—and summoned sleep.

THE LONG LANTEEBAN DAY dragged on, unbearably slow. Though they tried to sleep, true rest proved difficult to find. Acutely aware of their precarious position, they kept startling to wakefulness, alerted by passing battle droid patrols or the boom of a departing starship's thrusters. Being hungry didn't help, either. A groundcar collision right outside their hiding place had them sweating. The drivers started fighting, raised voices attracting unwanted attention. Then the spaceport's Magna-Guards weighed in to the altercation. Soon after that they heard weapons fire and screaming—and then silence, shot through with a woman's wild weeping. A final round of blasterfire silenced that.

"The same thing's happening everywhere, you know," said Anakin in a low voice, once the droids had moved on and it was safe to speak. "Everywhere the Separatists have taken over, people are dying."

"Yes, they are," said Obi-Wan, just as quietly. He had himself in hand. He did. Yes, there was grief for that unknown woman and for the three men who'd also died—who had been murdered. A Jedi could feel grief . . . but a Jedi did not lose himself in grief. That was the difference. "But you must remember, Anakin, that there has to be consolation in the knowledge that we're saving as many people as we can. It's just—you know as well as I do, we cannot save everyone. For your own peace of mind I wish you'd find a way to accept that."

Feeling a death through the Force was never pleasant. Distressed and resentful, Anakin closed his eyes. "How can you ask me to accept it? Our mandate is justice, Obi-Wan. What's happening now is our fault. We're to blame for things falling apart."

"That's not true, Anakin," he protested, shocked. "The Jedi are not responsible for Dooku's turn to the dark side. He chose—"

Anakin's eyes snapped open. "I'm not talking about Dooku! I'm talking about how the Jedi claim to defend those who can't defend themselves yet leave so many defenseless people at the mercy of gangsters and slave traders and starvation and poverty."

"That's not us, Anakin," he said wearily. "That's the Republic. It's politics. The Jedi do not involve themselves with politics. You know that, too."

"Then maybe we should," Anakin retorted. "Maybe if the politicians won't do what needs to be done, *we* need to do it. Because somebody needs to. You wonder why people believe the lies Dooku and his cabal tell them? It's because they're desperate. The Republic's abandoned them—or it never cared in the first place. In the end it's the same thing. The rich stay rich and they make sure the poor stay broken and ignorant in the gutter."

Obi-Wan stifled a sigh. *Oh Anakin.* This was about his childhood. Again. About the indelible fingerprints slavery had left on his soul and his psyche. *Qui-Gon, did you never once stop to think of that? Did it never occur to you the damage might run too deep?* "Anakin—"

Anakin flicked him a frustrated look. "I know you think you understand. I know you *want* to understand. But if you haven't lived it, Obi-Wan, you can't. And you never will."

They really shouldn't be talking. Even keeping their voices low almost to whispering, it was dangerous. But if he shut down the conversation now, if he refused to hear what Anakin had to say, he'd pile damage upon damage. And this wasn't the time to be at odds. Not with so much depending upon them.

Another transport blasted out of the spaceport. The shop's boarded-up windows rattled. The desktop above his head vibrated, and the counter Anakin curled beneath. A pile of flimsies thudded to the floor, raising dust. Obi-Wan smothered a sneeze in the crook of his elbow.

"Anakin," he said, when he could trust himself to speak again, "I've never said the Republic's perfect. It's not. But the Senate—"

"The Senate's corrupt," Anakin declared. "It's been corrupt for years, long before the Trade Federation's blockade of Naboo. You know that, Obi-Wan. You've been lecturing me about the perils of politicians ever since we met."

"That's true," he acknowledged. "But hope isn't quite lost. Bail's not corrupt. Neither is Padmé."

For once, the mere mention of her name didn't provoke a reaction. "And neither is Palpatine!" Anakin replied hotly. "But that's three politicians out of more than a thousand. And instead of the Jedi standing up to them, we go along. We do their bidding. We prop them up while their governments exploit the weak and the helpless. How can you tell me that's right?"

With an effort Obi-Wan held on to his temper. "I never said

it was right, Anakin. I deplore it. But at this moment, flawed as it may be, the Galactic Republic is the best system we have. It's the only system we have. And it's better than a dictatorship—which is what Dooku is after and what we're here trying to prevent. If you're so concerned about galactic injustice, my friend, I suggest you talk to *your* friend Palpatine. He is the Supreme Chancellor, after all. Presumably he has an interest in preserving the Republic."

Anakin stared at him, incredulous. "You don't think he *knows* the Senate's rotten? Obi-Wan, *he knows*. He knows better than anyone. He sees it day in and day out. And if he could fix it he would, but he can't, because there are too many Senators who like things the way they are. If he had more control over them he could fix what's wrong. He *would* fix it. But then people like you would say he was just being a typical politician, grabbing power for its own sake. So you tell me, Obi-Wan. What's the answer?"

"I don't know, Anakin," he said, abruptly so tired, and so dispirited. "All I can tell you is we're not going to fix the problem while holed up in this abandoned electronics shop, hiding from battle droids and MagnaGuards and Separatist forces. So let's focus on what we *can* do, shall we? Which is stop Lok Durd and Dooku from murdering countless innocents with their filthy new weapon."

"I'm sorry," Anakin murmured, contrite. "I know it sounds like I think you don't care. I don't think that. I don't."

And if he says it enough times, will he come to believe it?

But that wasn't fair. Anakin wasn't entirely wrong about him. He'd never been a slave. He'd never been beaten for making a mistake. Never crawled beneath threadbare blankets, starving, and fallen asleep with his mother's tears on his cheeks. He didn't remember his mother. He'd been raised in the Temple, safe and loved.

I have compassion. I have empathy. What I don't have are scars.

"See if you can sleep again, Anakin," he said softly. "I estimate four hours, a little less, until sunset. We can try contacting the Temple again then."

Anakin nodded. "How late do you want to leave it before we head back to Durd's compound?"

"As late as we can. The Seps believe their curfew is working. We should take advantage of their complacency."

"Okay," said Anakin, and rolled his eyes. "More sleep it is. And with any luck, I'll dream about biscuits."

TWENTY

"Ahsoka."

Startled out of her doze, Ahsoka slid off the soft chair and onto her feet. "Taria—I mean, Master Damsin. You—you look better."

Master Damsin flicked a quick look around the softly lit Healing Halls antechamber. "We're alone. Taria's fine."

"All right. Taria," she said, feeling a warm wash of pleasure despite her various worries. "Are you feeling better?"

Taria wrinkled her nose. "As better as I'm likely to. Look— Ahsoka—"

"No. You don't have to explain. It's none of my business."

"True, it's not," said Taria. "But I know you're curious. Are you hungry, too?"

Hungry? She was starving. "I could eat."

"And so could I." Taria stepped back. "Come on."

"You mean Master Vokara Che's not keeping you here?"

"Trust me, Ahsoka, a stampeding herd of wild banthas couldn't keep me here," said Taria, backing up another step. "Don't worry. I've been given the all-clear, I promise."

Not disbelieving, just a little bit doubtful, she bit her lip. On the way home to Coruscant, their mission accomplished, Taria had bled some more and been in obvious pain. "Are you sure?"

Taria rolled her eyes. "I'm sure. Stop fussing, you old woman. One Vokara Che in my life is enough."

It occurred to Ahsoka then that the Jedi Master was teasing her, bantering with her the way Skyguy and Master Kenobi bantered with each other because they were friends.

Does that mean Taria and I are friends? Is that how easily it happens?

From the way Taria was smiling at her, it seemed the answer was yes.

Wow.

They made their way to the nearest dining hall in companionable silence. It looked like word of their exploits on Corellia was yet to circulate—there was nothing more than simple friendliness in any of the nods and smiles they received from the other Jedi they encountered on the way.

"So," said Taria, once they were seated in a private booth with bowls of steaming bean soup and fresh, crusty bread. The dining hall's air was warm and scented with good food. Scattered, cheerful conversations provided a backdrop of sound. "To make a long story short, Ahsoka, it's called Borotavi syndrome. It's not contagious but it is terminal. Eventually."

Ahsoka felt her mouth suck dry. Terminal? But—but—*She's so young and strong and amazing. So alive.* "How did you get it?"

"I ate the wrong kind of shellfish on Pamina Prime." With a wry smile Taria stirred a pinch of salt into her soup. "Turns out it's the blue-shelled mollusk with the *green* stripe you need to watch out for. Blue mollusks with black stripes you can eat till you burst." She sat back. "Just a little tip to stand you in good stead, if ever you find yourself on Pamina Prime."

She'd never even heard of the place. "I'll—I'll try to remember that," she said. All of a sudden she wasn't hungry anymore. "Taria, I'm—"

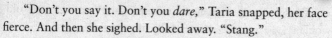

"Don't you say it. Don't you *dare*," Taria snapped, her face fierce. And then she sighed. Looked away. "Stang."

"No," she said quickly. "It's all right. You don't want pity. I get that. Skyguy—I mean, Master Skywalker—he's the same about his arm. You know. The one Dooku cut off."

Taria pushed her spoon around her soup, then finally swallowed a mouthful. "Anakin's lucky to have you, Ahsoka. You handled yourself brilliantly against that kriffing Anzati."

"Oh." Embarrassed now, she pulled her bread to crumbs. "I just followed my training. I mean, *I'm* lucky to have *him*, Taria. If you could see him in battle—or even when he's just sparring with Master Kenobi—he's—he's—"

"Something special," said Taria, nodding. "I've heard. I guess that's the reason they call him the Chosen One."

"He hates being called that, you know," she said, dropping her voice just in case. "He never says so but—well, I've felt it."

Taria spooned up more soup. "Can you blame him? Talk about a weight of expectations . . ."

It was her new friend's instinctive understanding that loosened her tongue. There wasn't *anyone* she could talk to about this. "I get so scared," she murmured. "When it comes to fighting the Seps, Skyguy's fearless. He just—he throws himself at them like he's indestructible. And he's not." She felt a cold shiver run through her. "He nearly died on Maridun, you know."

Taria nodded. "I heard that, too. I hear a lot of things, Ahsoka, even though these days I'm stuck here in the Temple. Things like Anakin's not the only one who thinks the Seps can't kill him. And after seeing you in action—well. I'd have to say that rumor is true."

Suddenly she was interested in her soup after all. "I don't know what you mean."

"I *mean*," said Taria, "that it looks to me like you're learning more from your Master than a few fancy lightsaber moves."

She shrugged. "Fortune favors the bold."

"Maybe so," Taria retorted, "but the Force isn't an all-purpose cheating-death security pass, Ashoka. Be careful you're not so caught up with worrying about Anakin that you forget to worry about yourself. The Order needs young Jedi like you. This war's taking a heavy toll. We've already lost too many good people."

She didn't know what to say, hearing that. She wasn't used to lavish praise—it wasn't Anakin's way. It wasn't the Jedi way. So why—

"Dying gives me a unique perspective," said Taria, easily reading her troubled thoughts. "Life's too short not to tell the truth."

Ahsoka was ambushed by a sharp and selfish grief. *We've just become friends and now I have to lose her? I hate this. It's not fair.* And then the grief was swamped by hot shame. *At least you're not dying. Wait till you're dying then moan about not fair.*

Taria dunked bread in her bean soup, chewed, then swallowed. "So, while I was being fussed over by Vokara Che—I don't suppose you heard how Obi-Wan and Anakin are getting on, wherever they are?"

Ahsoka shook her head. "Not a word. Not even a whisper. I wish I was brave enough to ask Master Yoda."

"Ha!" said Taria, amused. "I doubt even your Skyguy is brave enough for that."

"I tried to see for myself," she confessed. "In the Force. But all I got was a headache. I guess I've still got a lot of learning to do."

Pushing her bowl aside, Taria frowned. "Don't blame yourself, Ahsoka. The Force on Coruscant is . . . cloudy. I've tried as well and I can't see anything, either."

Ahsoka tried to smile. "I wish that made me feel better, but it doesn't. Even without seeing through the Force, Taria, I—" She pressed a fist to her chest, where her heart was bumping hard. "I've got a bad feeling, here. Something's not right. I think Skyguy's in danger. Well, more danger than he's usually in, if that makes any sense."

"Oh, it makes sense," said Taria grimly. "I've got the same bad feeling about Obi-Wan. And since they're together—"

"Then what should we do? What *can* we do?"

Taria shrugged. "We can wait."

"Wait? For what?"

"For the clouds to clear."

"That's *it*?"

"Pretty much," said Taria, her smile darkly amused. "Unless you want to make a run at Master Yoda, after all."

No, no, no. She didn't want to do that. She tucked her chin and folded her arms. "I *hate* waiting," she muttered.

"You and me both," said Taria. "So I suggest we keep ourselves busy. I'm not quite up to sparring yet, but if you like I can watch you go a few rounds with a training remote, give you some pointers. How does that sound?"

Ahsoka had to smile. "That sounds great."

"Then let's do it," said Taria, and slid out of the booth. "Last one to the dojo has to buy the drinks. Go!"

SENSING BAN-YARO'S EAGER APPROACH, Yoda looked up from the datapad he was reading. A moment later the transparisteel doors to the Temple's high-security comm center hummed open and the communications chief joined him.

"Master Yoda. It's Obi-Wan."

"Excellent," Yoda said, dropping the datapad into his hoverchair's side pocket. Hoping to hear from Obi-Wan again, knowing that time was in short supply, he'd elected to spend the night in the comm center so that if his two Jedi on Lanteeb did contact the Temple, he wouldn't have to make them wait while he was sent for. "Speak with him now, can I?"

"The signal's come through on a different relay this time," said Ban-yaro. "I'll have it patched through to you in a moment."

"Thank you," Yoda said, and guided his chair to the nearest comm console. When at last Ban-yaro gave him the signal, he toggled the switch. "Yoda this is, Obi-Wan."

"Master, we have the chance to get Doctor Fhernan off-world within the next few hours," said Obi-Wan. *"This might be our only chance. Have you had any success securing those hostages?"*

The signal from Lanteeb was faint, Obi-Wan's voice slushy with interference. Yoda looked at Ban-yaro, but the comm chief shook his head. This was the best he could do.

Resigned to that, Yoda leaned close to the comm console vocoder. "Yes, Obi-Wan. Rescued is your scientist's family, and all of her friends save one. The last friend now are we trying to find. Enough that should be to secure her cooperation."

"It should be, but—Master, I'm afraid she might balk at coming with us if there's a chance that even one person could be hurt because of her."

"Then lie to her you must, Obi-Wan. Tell her everyone is safe."

"Lie to her?" Even through the interference Obi-Wan's shocked dismay was palpable. *"But Master—"*

"Happy with the notion I am not, Master Kenobi," Yoda said. "Even less happy am I with the thought of thousands falling to Lok Durd's evil weapon. Remind you must I that we are at war?"

"*No, Master,*" said Obi-Wan, chastened. "*Of course not. I'll secure her cooperation and we'll contact you again as soon as we can. Kenobi out.*"

The lights on the comm console died as the signal was disconnected.

Discreet as always, Ban-yaro stopped a few paces distant and cleared his throat. "Master Yoda? Do you require anything else?"

With a weary sigh Yoda shook his head. "No. To my private chamber I will go now, Ban-yaro. But alert me you must if word we receive from the last retrieval team, no matter how late the hour. Or if from Obi-Wan we hear again."

Ban-yaro bowed. "Of course, Master. I'll contact you the moment there's any word."

"Thank you," he said, and left the comm center to meditate in private and wait for news.

It was all he could do. It wasn't enough, but he'd long ago learned to take what he could get . . . and trust in the Force to provide the rest.

ANAKIN STARED AT Obi-Wan as he quickly dismantled the jerry-rigged comm hub. He wished they didn't have to, but it was too dangerous a clue to their presence to leave behind.

"What?" said Obi-Wan, not looking up. "Anakin, so help me, if you say one more word about biscuits I'll—"

"Biscuits? I don't care about biscuits. Obi-Wan, am I hearing things or did you just agree to lie to Bant'ena?"

The merest hint of a hesitation, then Obi-Wan kept on ripping out circuits and datachips. They'd only turned one lamp on this time, just to be safe. In the dim illumination his expression was opaque. Utterly unreadable.

"I've been thinking about how we're going to get from

Durd's compound back here to the spaceport," he said. "And then through spaceport security without our local ID chips *and* with Doctor Fhernan in tow. It's going to be tricky, but—"

"Yeah, I've been thinking about it, too," Anakin said, impatient. "Never mind that for now. Obi-Wan, what's going on? We are Jedi, and Jedi don't lie."

No answer. Obi-Wan Force-pulled the torsion pliers to him and wrestled with a recalcitrant circuit.

With an effort, Anakin tamped down his rising anger. "Obi-Wan, *talk* to me."

Still Obi-Wan wouldn't look at him. "There's nothing to say, Anakin. You heard Master Yoda. We're at war, and war compels us to perform distasteful acts. Besides, it's more than likely that by the time we reach Doctor Fhernan the last of the hostages will be in safe hands."

"You don't know that! *Yoda* doesn't know that! I can't tell Bant'ena we've saved all her family and friends if we haven't."

"You won't have to. I'll tell her. And it's *Master* Yoda."

Yeah, yeah, whatever. "Obi-Wan—"

"*What,* Anakin?" Obi-Wan demanded. "What would you have me do? Defy Yoda? Abandon Lanteeb without completing our mission? Sacrifice thousands, perhaps millions of lives so I might keep my conscience unsullied?"

"This isn't about you!" he said, tempted to let his temper loose entirely. "It's about right and wrong and not breaking our word. We promised Bant'ena—"

"No, Anakin, *you* promised!" said Obi-Wan, close to losing his own temper. "Yet again you allowed your emotions to rule you. Well, this time, Master Skywalker, you'll *control* yourself, is that clear? What we are facing is bigger than Bant'ena, bigger than your muddled, misplaced emotions—bigger even than our Jedi honor. This might be the moment in which the war is lost or won—and I will *not* allow you to lose it for fear of hurting that woman's feelings!"

Stunned, he stared at Obi-Wan. "So you're saying you're all right with lying to her? That it doesn't bother you if—"

"Oh, Anakin, of *course* it bothers me!" said Obi-Wan, hands fisted on his knees. "How can you claim to know me, be my friend, and ask if it *bothers* me?"

"So it bothers you," he said, feeling suddenly calm. "But you'll still do it."

Obi-Wan nodded. "If I have to." His lips twisted. "Just as you defied the Council by going to Geonosis with Padmé. So what is this, Anakin—do as I say, not as I do?"

Oh, well, that was just playing dirty. "I defied the Council to save *you*!"

"One man," Obi-Wan retorted. "*I'm* trying to save thousands. *We're* trying to save thousands. Aren't we? Or is this where we part company, Anakin?"

Part company? "I'm not going anywhere," he said tightly. "I promised Bant'ena I'd get her off this rock, and that's exactly what I'm going to do."

"And to do that it looks like you'll have to lie," said Obi-Wan, challenging. "Are you telling me you can't lie in a good cause?"

Padmé. Anakin felt his guts twist. *Who am I kidding? My whole life is a lie. I lie to this man every time I draw breath—and next to him, Bant'ena Fhernan means nothing.*

"You're right," he said, and raised his hands. "I'm sorry."

Now it was Obi-Wan's turn to stare. "Just like that?"

"You'd rather I kept arguing?"

"No, of course not, but—"

"Then let's move on," he said flatly. "Our exit strategy. What are you thinking?"

Instead of answering, Obi-Wan finished dismantling the old

comm hub unit. His face was utterly unreadable, his feelings tamped down tight. When the hub was at last scattered around him in bits and pieces, he fished out the betraying Republic-issue scrambler chip, tucked it into his shirt's shielded pocket then turned off the lamp. Instantly they were plunged into darkness.

"All right," he said, as though they'd never once exchanged heated words. "Here's how I propose we extricate ourselves from Lanteeb. We return to the spaceport in the official ground-car we first followed to the compound—"

"With Bant'ena driving and us as collateral," Anakin interrupted. "She can tell anyone who challenges us at the spaceport that we're human test subjects. The Seps probably won't bat an eyelid. But if they do we can mind-trick them. Although I doubt they will. They know who she is, who she works for. Not even droids will be stupid enough to question her authority. Then we load into the ship and get out of here."

Obi-Wan's silence was eloquent.

"Hey," Anakin said, shrugging. "I told you I'd been thinking."

"Apparently," said Obi-Wan. He almost sounded amused. "Then we're set? We can go? No—last-minute qualms?"

"None. I'm good." And of course that was a lie—but who cared? He was practicing for Bant'ena. Getting in the mood.

In the darkness, there was a soft sigh. "Anakin, how are you feeling? Truthfully?"

If he said *hungry*, Obi-Wan would throw something at him. But he was. He was ravenous. And he hated, *hated*, feeling hungry. The sensation stirred too many memories. Distracted him with the past when he needed his mind on the present.

"I feel sad," he said at last. "If it turns out we weren't able to save that last hostage, I hope Bant'ena can forgive us. I hope she'll help us anyway."

"If she's the woman you believe her to be," said Obi-Wan, "she will. She'll not punish thousands of innocents because we failed—or lied."

"Do you believe that?"

"I'd like to," said Obi-Wan. "This time I'd very much like to be wrong."

Despite the cloaking darkness, he smiled. "Well, you know what they say. There's a first time for everything."

"And I'm sure this will be it."

But Obi-Wan didn't sound sure. He sounded doubtful and pressured and yes—a little bit sad. Not the right frame of mind to be taking into a mission that promised to be as precarious as this one.

And that's partly my fault. I started the fight.

"Hey," he said. "You know what else I feel? Hungry. Go on. Hit me. You know you want to."

To his great relief, Obi-Wan managed a faint chuckle. "No. It's all right. Truth be told, I'm hungry, too. It's unfortunate but it can't be helped. We'll manage."

Of course they would. They'd manage by drawing on the Force to fuel them. Which it would, but at a steep cost to their overstretched bodies. And when the inevitable crash came afterward it was going to be messy.

"I can cope with the burnout," Anakin said. "But what about you?"

"You let me worry about me."

He really wished he could see Obi-Wan's face. It was much harder to read him in the dark. But there was no point pushing. First rule of managing Master Kenobi: *Pick your battles.*

"Now I suggest we meditate until it's time to go," Obi-Wan added. "We'll need all our wits about us for this one."

"I couldn't agree more," Anakin said. "Meditation it is."

· · ·

FOUR HOURS LATER they stirred and unfolded themselves from beneath cramped counter and desk. They took a few minutes to limber up, warm their muscles, encourage the Force to burn more brightly in their blood and fill them with borrowed strength for the challenges facing them.

Anakin eased himself upright. "You don't think we should warn Bant'ena that we're on our way?"

"I'd rather not risk it," said Obi-Wan. "She'll be ready. She knows this is her only chance."

"Okay. Then can we go? I'm not getting any younger."

Obi-Wan snorted. "Who is?"

Wrapped in the Force, they abandoned their hiding place and reached out with their senses to taste the night. Beyond the harshly lit spaceport the city was again eerily dark. A miserly scattering of stars and a pinched cheese-rind of moon shed little light. Nothing stirred. It was a dead place reeking of fear. They could feel the arrogance of the human Separatists over the road, in the port. Could see MagnaGuards and battle droids unmoving at their posts.

"All right," said Obi-Wan. "Let's do this, shall we?"

Lok Durd's compound was a long way away, and this time there wasn't a droid-powered trundle cart to make life that little bit easier. With their destination too far for Force-sprinting, they opted for the less draining technique of enhanced, short-burst running. Speed and slow. Speed and slow. Hearts pounding, breathing deep.

Gradually the city fell behind them. They swam through the night like fish in the deep. Twice they encountered Separatist patrols, twenty battle droids on droning STAPs, hunting for humans to chase and kill. Twice they avoided detection, flung facedown on the cracked, crumbling edges of the ferrocrete road, plunged as far as they dared inside the shrouding Force.

Then a swift tap on the shoulder. An answering nod. And it was up and away again, speed and slow, speed and slow. Reached the right-hand turn leading off the main highway, they padded, quiet and cautious, through the echoingly empty streets of the industrial district. The area felt like a graveyard. Buried hopes, buried dreams—everything decent crushed by the dark side. It was draining. Oppressive. Misery like soaking rain.

Anakin ran through it, teeth gritted. *Get me out of this place.* Obi-Wan ran beside him, every emotion locked-down tight.

At last they reached the top of the street that led to Durd's compound, and Bant'ena. They stopped running and stepped into the deeper shadows of a squat, low-roofed building.

"What do you think?" Anakin asked, catching his breath. His heart was pounding harder than normal, his hungry body's resentful response to the demands he was placing on it. "Do we wait here and hope for a truck, or risk going in the way we got out last night?"

Obi-Wan's breathing was the smallest touch ragged. He was feeling it, too. "A truck would be nice—but we can't wait for one indefinitely. For all we know they only turn up once a week."

That was unfortunately true. "We should've asked Bant'ena about the compound's delivery schedule when we had the chance."

"No doubt, but let's keep our minds focused on the present, shall we?"

Obi-Wan hated making mistakes. "How long do you want to wait, then?"

"I suggest we play it by ear."

"Suits me."

There was silence. And then, after a little while, Obi-Wan stirred. "I don't sense Durd's presence. Not even that odd, slippery deflection."

"Why are you even checking for it?" he said, surprise shading to annoyance. "Unless—what, you think Bant'ena's lying?"

"You know the drill, Anakin," said Obi-Wan, deliberately patient. "Trust but verify. I'm not in the mood to walk into a trap. Are you?"

"No," he muttered, and reached out with his feelings. *I'm not doubting her, I'm just being careful.* "I don't sense Durd, either. But I can feel Bant'ena. She's scared. No . . . terrified." Her fear made him feel sick.

Obi-Wan shrugged. "Who can blame her? You think I don't know what I'm asking of her, Anakin, but I do. And I'm not unsympathetic."

That was true. He wasn't. But he was coldly capable of denying sympathy and compassion if the task at hand required him to be hard. Obi-Wan Kenobi was a far more complicated man than a first glance would suggest.

"I'm not sensing any hint of trouble. Are you?"

"No," said Obi-Wan, after a pause. "But don't get complacent, Anakin. Fueling ourselves with the Force as we've been doing can muddy perception. Take nothing for granted."

"Trust me, I wasn't planning to."

"Good, because—"

"Yeah," he said, as Obi-Wan's fingers brushed his arm. "I can hear it. Looks like we're in luck."

Or they would be, if the approaching vehicle was heading for the compound. But it had to be, didn't it? Where else was there to go around here?

"Steady," murmured Obi-Wan, as the first sweep of headlights dazzled the night. "Steady. This might be our only chance."

There wasn't a handily deep-set doorway to hide in this time, so they ducked around the edge of the building and flattened themselves against its rough wall. The truck came closer . . . closer . . . turned into the street . . .

"Now," said Obi-Wan, and they made their move.

Lying prone on the truck's roof, anchored in place by the Force, Anakin tried to ignore his body's fresh protests, and their echoes in Obi-Wan prone beside him.

We'll be paying for this for weeks, I bet.

Squinting ahead, he saw the brightly lit compound gates. Felt the buzzing tingle of the laser grids. The truck slowed. Slowed again. Negotiated the first security checkpoint. Crawled forward. Negotiated the second, then entered the compound proper. So now it was just a simple case of repeating their previous fun and games—slip off the truck as soon as it reached the loading dock, wait for the droids to stack the delivered crates on antigrav pallets and float them away, get up to the main building undetected, crawl through its extensive ducting—*oh, my aching back*—grab Bant'ena . . . and run.

He felt another tap on his shoulder and nodded to let Obi-Wan know he was ready. Then he took a deep breath and tensed himself, ready to leap.

Not quite halfway to the loading dock, the delivery truck stopped. Anakin turned his head and looked at Obi-Wan. For the first time he felt an inkling of something wrong.

"What were you saying about taking nothing for gr—"

The night lit up with the power of a thousand suns.

Training-honed instinct took over. Anakin had his lightsaber out and ignited before his booted feet hit the stalled truck's roof. So did Obi-Wan. They were targets up here, but at least with height they could see what they were up against.

Starkly lifted out of shadow, marching clear of the concealment—battle droids. The Sep compound was suddenly full of them. Skinny clankers. Super battle droids. Vultures. Droidekas.

"Oh no," Anakin breathed, staring. "Where the stang did they come from?"

"Where do you think?" said Obi-Wan. He sounded sick with disgust. "They're a gift from Doctor Fhernan—and General Lok Durd."

"No," Anakin said, abruptly light-headed. "No, she wouldn't betray us, Obi-Wan. I felt her. I *read* her. She wouldn't throw us to—"

"We can argue about it later," said Obi-Wan, his voice tight, his presence in the Force alight with a rare fury. "Right now we—" There was a high-pitched humming, and an ominous rattle in the dark. "*Jump!*" he shouted . . . and the massed ranks of battle droids opened fire.

Lightsabers whirling, they leapt to the ground. Leapt back-to-back and began fighting for their lives. It was Geonosis all over again, only this time there was no Padmé to provide blaster cover, no Mace Windu, no Yoda. No clones in their gunships swooping in to save the day.

Don't look now, Obi-Wan, but I think we're in trouble.

Blasterfire was coming from every direction. They were managing to deflect each volley, they hadn't been singed or struck yet, but it was only a matter of time before the enemy scored a hit. Even though they'd inflicted some damage they were still brutally outnumbered. Anakin felt the world shift and blur around him as he sank deeper into the Force than he'd ever gone before. It was almost painful. Nearly too much to bear. As hard to endure as Bant'ena's betrayal.

Why? Why? How could I not see it?

"Forget about it, Anakin!" yelled Obi-Wan over the whine and sizzle and crump of the enemy's attack. "Focus on this! What will the *why* matter if we're dead?"

Good point. Slowly but surely the battle droids were closing in. They had to get out of here. They had to—had to—

"Obi-Wan, the groundcar! If it's here—if any kind of groundcar is here—if we can get to it—" Oh, he was crazy. *I'm crazy. If I try this I'm going to get both of us killed.* But if they stayed they were dead, too, so—*Anakin, pick your poison.* "If you can hold off these blasted clankers long enough for me to rig the groundcar's systems, I can fly us out of here!"

"You can *do* that?" Obi-Wan shouted, incredulous, almost drowned by the high-pitched buzzing whine of their lightsabers and the booming and shrieking of the droids' concerted attack. The air stank of heated plasma and burned grass and desperation.

"Yes!" he shouted back. "Maybe. I don't know."

"Anakin, *make up your mind*!"

"Yes! Yes, I can do that!" he said, and risked a look at Obi-Wan. His friend's face was streaked with sweat, eyes almost blank with a fierce concentration. Beneath the concentration was a dangerously escalating exhaustion. "If we make it to the parking area in one piece can you hold off these barves?"

"By myself?"

"Yes!"

"While you play with a groundcar?"

"*Yes!* Obi-Wan, will you try?"

The droids were meters away now, closing fast. They were moments from death. If they were going to do this—if they were going to try—

"Oh, why not?" said Obi-Wan, and actually laughed. "I've nothing better to do. So what are you waiting for, Master Skywalker? *Run!*"

Raggedly Anakin reached for the power to Force-sprint. Heard himself shout in pain, because he'd used too much of himself already. Even the Chosen One had his limits, it seemed. He shouted again then, and heard Obi-Wan's equally pained cry as they Force-pushed their way through the droids firing at them almost point-blank. He felt another pain, sharper and hotter, sear its way along his ribs and knew he'd been clipped by a blaster bolt. But he could worry about that later.

First rule of business: Keep us alive.

Reaching the compound's roofed parking area they staggered out of their Force-sprint, and he nearly sobbed aloud. The fancy groundcar was still there. But there was no time to give thanks because rolling right behind them were five shielded droidekas, and, marching behind *them* countless undamaged droids.

He saw blood, but looking at Obi-Wan he couldn't tell where it came from. *Focus. Focus. He's not dead yet, and neither are you.* "We can do this. Do you want my lightsaber?"

"No," said Obi-Wan tightly. "You might need it. Get to work, Anakin. I'll hold them off for as long as I can."

As Obi-Wan turned to face their attackers, lightsaber in one hand, the other extended ready to Force-repel the approaching droids, he took a deep, painful breath—and extinguished all emotion, narrowing his focus to this thing, this one thing, that he knew how to do better than any other thing he had learned in his life.

Machines, and how to make them. How to mold them. How to rule them.

Dimly aware of Obi-Wan's furious defense of him, with no time for care or finesse, he used the tip of his lightsaber to slice off the groundcar's rear engine housing, then rested the weapon on the vehicle's roof. It was a beautiful machine, sleek and powerful. It pained him to mutilate it, but he didn't have a choice.

Come on, Anakin. Think. Locate the antigrav platform. Isolate the repulsor circuits and cross-wire them. Rip out the height limiter. That's all you have to do.

The groundcar's engine was an elegant model of simplicity. He'd never seen its design before, and yet with one look he knew it, he *knew* it, as intimately as he knew the curves and planes of Padmé's beautiful face. It had been this way his whole life. Machines spoke to him. He understood instinctively every last one of their sweetly whispered secrets.

And there was the antigrav platform. There were the repulsor circuits. Hello, circuits, meet your new best friends. Goodbye, height limiter. Knuckles skinned and bleeding, horribly aware of the blasterfire behind him, around him, screaming past him close enough to crisp his hair and his clothes, he worked the machine harder and faster than he'd ever worked one before. And then he saw the state-of-the-art security tracker and fried it with his lightsaber, for good measure.

"Anakin!" called Obi-Wan. "Anakin, hurry up! I don't— I can't—"

Looking over his shoulder he saw that Obi-Wan was swaying, the thrust and slash of his lightsaber weakening. Hardly any of the attacking droids were falling now. A blaster bolt ripped by him and blew a hole in the ferrocrete less than a meter away. Any moment now they'd be surrounded—and dead.

He dropped his weapon and hotwired the groundcar's ignition. The machine roared into life, a promise of speed and power and life.

"Obi-Wan!" he said, yanking the front passenger door open, then summoning his lightsaber to his filthy, bloodstained hand. "I've got this. I'll cover you. Get in, we've got to go."

Obi-Wan turned, almost overbalancing, and stumbled for the groundcar. Half falling, half crawling, he got inside and pulled the door shut after him. Anakin, the blood roaring in his head, the Force howling in his blood, threw himself forward and flung every last bit of himself at their swiftly closing enemy. The first two rows of clankers tumbled like leaves in a storm. He screamed with the effort, screamed with the pain.

And as the droids clattered and shot one another and fell to pieces on the ground, he turned and ran back to the groundcar. Obi-Wan opened the driver's-side door for him. Deactivating his lightsaber he clambered in, slammed the door closed again, and grabbed hold of the controls.

"Get the shield up. Find the shield," he snapped at Obi-Wan as he fired the engine harder. Oh, it was sweet, this thing, it was sweet like a bird, sweet like honey on the tongue. Eager and responsive almost to a thought.

Obi-Wan found the shield switch on the console and flipped it, just in time. A barrage of blaster bolts smacked them from every side.

"Hold on!" Anakin said, his breathing ragged, his vision bleary with sweat and sudden fear. "This might not be pretty."

And he rammed them out of the roofed parking area, scattering droids like skittles.

With the height limiter ripped out and the repulsor circuits enhanced, the groundcar soared upward like an airspeeder—sort of. The droids fired after them, to no avail. The ground fell away. The droid army swiftly dwindled. Shuddering, awkward now but still with glorious power, they flew over the compound fencing and into the night-dark sky.

Exhausted, hurting, Anakin smiled and smiled and smiled.

Beside him, Obi-Wan nodded. "You did it. Well done."

He sounded shattered. He looked worse, pushed almost to passing out, his face chalky white in the console's pale running lights. There was more blood, too, on both arms and legs. His pathetic Lanteeban clothing had been no protection at all.

Anakin felt a thump of fear. "Hey—are you okay? You're not going to faint on me, are you?"

"Faint?" said Obi-Wan, somehow managing to sound offended. "Don't be ridiculous. I'm fine. In fact that was so entertaining I say we go back and do it all over again."

"You're a riot, you know that?" he retorted. "No. We are not going back."

"Oh, well," said Obi-Wan, with a small, pained shrug. "It was just an idea."

Beyond the shielded front viewscreen the night stretched on, seemingly limitless. Anakin could see no ground lights, nothing that might indicate their location. The groundcar's controls felt heavy in his hands, but they were doing all right. They were airborne—and alive.

Stang. I am good.

"So, Obi-Wan," he said, sideways glancing again. "What's the plan? I don't think we can risk the spaceport, do you?"

Obi-Wan snorted. "Hardly. They'll be on full alert by now. We wouldn't make it five steps. What's our altitude?"

Anakin looked at the console. There was no altimeter. "Your guess is as good as mine. You seem to be forgetting that this thing's not meant to fly."

"And yet here we are, flying," Obi-Wan murmured. "How long before we stop flying and start falling, do you suppose?"

"Ha," he retorted. "You need to have more faith, Master Kenobi."

Obi-Wan gave him another pointed look. "Really? Well, I'll certainly try to take your advice, Anakin. Though I feel bound to point out to you that since we've no idea where we are, or where we're going, or what we'll do when we get there, my supply of faith is sorely overstretched as it is." He peered out the passenger window. "It's as dark as the inside of a bantha out there. Can't see a blasted thing below us."

"And I can't see a blasted thing in front us," Anakin said.

But I'm not worried. I'm not. I'm not. "No way we can risk putting the headlights on. Cross your fingers that we don't fly into a tree."

"Or a house," said Obi-Wan. "Or a hill. Or a droid ship. Really, the possibilities for disaster are endless."

He was sounding almost *cheerful*. Maybe a piece of flying droid had clipped him on the head . . . "So maybe I should turn around and go back after all?"

Obi-Wan looked at him. "Please don't."

The groundcar was shuddering a little now. Fighting him. *Great. The blasted machine's scared of heights.*

"Okay," he said, wrestling the vehicle back under control. "The Lanteeb briefing notes Agent Varrak gave us. What did they say? They said one city, with the space port, then nothing but scattered villages. So we head for the country. Fly this thing until it's ready to drop then ditch it somewhere it won't be found and lay low in a village until we can work out how to get off this rock."

Obi-Wan spared him another eloquent look. "Yes, that sounds terribly plausible, Anakin, except for the part about this groundcar not being found. In fact I expect the Seps are already tracking it, which means—"

"No, they're not," he said smugly. "I burned out the transponder."

"Oh," said Obi-Wan, after a moment. "Good job."

That first wild burst of elation and adrenaline had faded, leaving an uncertain dread in its wake. But somehow he managed to dredge up a smile. "No big deal. Just doing what my Master taught me."

"Of course you were," said Obi-Wan. Then he sighed, and all his escaping pain was in the sound. "So. Here we are in dire straits. Again. Really, I should be used to this by now."

The groundcar's blunt nose dipped, threatening a dive. With a head-throbbing effort, Anakin wrenched it up again.

"It's okay, it's okay, we're okay," he said, risking another sideways look at Obi-Wan. "We're okay."

"Oh, Anakin," said Obi-Wan. There was no color at all left in his face. "Let's not kid ourselves, shall we? You and I are *any-thing* but okay."

Anakin wanted to argue. He wanted to say, *Obi-Wan, you're wrong.* But he couldn't. How could he?

Stang. Stang. We really are in trouble.

And at that moment, for the life of him, he couldn't see a way out.

Read on for an excerpt from *Star Wars:
Fate of the Jedi: Outcast* by Aaron Allston

Published by Arrow

○

ONE BY ONE, THE STARS OVERHEAD BEGAN TO DISAPPEAR, SWAL-
lowed by some enormous darkness interposing itself from above
and behind the shuttle. Sharply pointed at its most forward position, broadening behind, the flood of blackness advanced,
blotting out more and more of the unblinking starfield, until
darkness was all there was to see.

Then, all across the length and breadth of the ominous
shape, lights came on—blue and white running lights, tiny red
hatch and security lights, sudden glows from within transparisteel viewports, one large rectangular whiteness limned by atmosphere shields. The lights showed the vast triangle to be the
underside of an Imperial Star Destroyer, painted black, forbidding a moment ago, now comparatively cheerful in its proper
running configuration. It was the *Gilad Pellaeon,* newly arrived
from the Imperial Remnant, and its officers clearly knew how to
put on a show.

Jaina Solo, sitting with the others in the dimly lit passenger
compartment of the government VIP shuttle, watched the entire
display through the overhead transparisteel canopy and laughed
out loud.

The Bothan in the sumptuously padded chair next to hers gave her a curious look. His mottled red and tan fur twitched, either from suppressed irritation or embarrassment at Jaina's outburst. "What do you find so amusing?"

"Oh, both the obviousness of it and the skill with which it was performed. It's so very, *You used to think of us as dark and scary, but now we're just your stylish allies.*" Jaina lowered her voice so that her next comment would not carry to the passengers in the seats behind. "The press will love it. That image will play on the holonews broadcasts constantly. Mark my words."

"Was that little show a Jagged Fel detail?"

Jaina tilted her head, considering. "I don't know. He could have come up with it, but he usually doesn't spend his time planning displays or events. When he does, though, they're usually pretty . . . effective."

The shuttle rose toward the *Gilad Pellaeon*'s main landing bay. In moments, it was through the square atmosphere barrier shield and drifting sideways to land on the deck nearby. The landing place was clearly marked—hundreds of beings, most wearing gray Imperial uniforms or the distinctive white armor of the Imperial stormtrooper, waited in the bay, and the one circular spot where none stood was just the right size for the Galactic Alliance shuttle.

The passengers rose as the shuttle settled into place. The Bothan smoothed his tunic, a cheerful blue decorated with a golden sliver pattern suggesting claws. "Time to go to work. You won't let me get killed, will you?"

Jaina let her eyes widen. "Is that what I was supposed to be doing here?" she asked in droll tones. "I should have brought my lightsaber."

The Bothan offered a long-suffering sigh and turned toward the exit.

They descended the shuttle's boarding ramp. With no duties required of her other than to keep alert and be the Jedi face at this preliminary meeting, Jaina was able to stand back and observe. She was struck with the unreality of it all. The niece and daughter of three of the most famous enemies of the Empire during the First Galactic Civil War of a few decades earlier, she was now witness to events that might bring the Galactic Empire—or Imperial Remnant, as it was called everywhere outside its own borders—into the Galactic Alliance on a lasting basis.

And at the center of the plan was the man, flanked by Imperial officers, who now approached the Bothan. Slightly under average size, though towering well above Jaina's diminutive height, he was dark-haired, with a trim beard and mustache that gave him a rakish look, and was handsome in a way that became more pronounced when he glowered. A scar on his forehead ran up into his hairline and seemed to continue as a lock of white hair from that point. He wore expensive but subdued black civilian garments, neck-to-toe, that would be inconspicuous anywhere on Coruscant but stood out in sharp relief to the gray and white uniforms, white armor, and colorful Alliance clothes surrounding him.

He had one moment to glance at Jaina. The look probably appeared neutral to onlookers, but for her it carried just a twinkle of humor, a touch of exasperation that the two of them had to put up with all these delays. Then an Alliance functionary, notable for his blandness, made introductions: "Imperial Head of State the most honorable Jagged Fel, may I present Senator Tiurrg Drey'lye of Bothawui, head of the Senate Unification Preparations Committee."

Jagged Fel took the Senator's hand. "I'm pleased to be working with you."

"And delighted to meet *you*. Chief of State Daala sends her compliments and looks forward to meeting you when you make planetfall."

Jag nodded. "And now, I believe, protocol insists that we open a bottle or a dozen of wine and make some preliminary discussion of security, introduction protocols, and so on."

"Fortunately about the wine, and regrettably about everything else, you are correct."

AT THE END OF two full standard hours—Jaina knew from regular, surreptitious consultations of her chrono—Jag was able to convince the Senator and his retinue to accept a tour of the *Gilad Pellaeon*. He was also able to request a private consultation with the sole representative of the Jedi Order present. Moments later, the gray-walled conference room was empty of everyone but Jag and Jaina.

Jag glanced toward the door. "Security seal, access limited to Jagged Fel and Jedi Jaina Solo, voice identification, activate." The door hissed in response as it sealed. Then Jag returned his attention to Jaina.

She let an expression of anger and accusation cross her face. "You're not fooling anyone, Fel. You're planning for an Imperial invasion of Alliance space."

Jag nodded. "I've been planning it for quite a while. Come here."

She moved to him, settled into his lap, and was suddenly but not unexpectedly caught in his embrace. They kissed urgently, hungrily.

Finally Jaina drew back and smiled at him. "This isn't going to be a routine part of your consultations with every Jedi."

"Uh, no. That would cause some trouble here and at home. But I actually *do* have business with the Jedi that does not involve the Galactic Alliance, at least not initially."

"What sort of business?"

"Whether or not the Galactic Empire joins with the Galactic Alliance, I think there ought to be an official Jedi presence in the Empire. A second Temple, a branch, an offshoot, whatever. Providing advice and insight to the Head of State."

"And protection?"

He shrugged. "Less of an issue. I'm doing all right. Two years in this position and not dead yet."

"Emperor Palpatine went nearly twenty-five years."

"I guess that makes him my hero."

Jaina snorted. "Don't even say that in jest . . . Jag, if the Remnant doesn't join the Alliance, I'm not sure the Jedi *can* have a presence without Alliance approval."

"The Order still keeps its training facility for youngsters in Hapan space. And the Hapans haven't rejoined."

"You sound annoyed. The Hapans still giving you trouble?"

"Let's not talk about *that*."

"Besides, moving the school back to Alliance space is just a matter of time, logistics, and finances; there's no question that it will happen. On the other hand, it's very likely that the government would withhold approval for a Jedi branch in the Remnant, just out of spite, if the Remnant doesn't join."

"Well, there's such a thing as an *unofficial* presence. And there's such a thing as rival schools, schismatic branches, and places for former Jedi to go when they can't be at the Temple."

Jaina smiled again, but now there was suspicion in her expression. "You just want to have this so *I'll* be assigned to come to the Remnant and set it up."

"That's a motive, but not the only one. Remember, to the Moffs and to a lot of the Imperial population, the Jedi have been bogeymen since Palpatine died. At the very least, I don't want them to be inappropriately afraid of the woman I'm in love with."

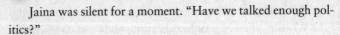

Jaina was silent for a moment. "Have we talked enough politics?"

"I think so."

"Good."

HORN FAMILY QUARTERS, KALLAD'S DREAM VACATION HOSTEL, CORUSCANT

Yawning, hair tousled, clad in a blue dressing robe, Valin Horn knew that he did not look anything like an experienced Jedi Knight. He looked like an unshaven, unkempt bachelor, which he also was. But here, in these rented quarters, there would be only family to see him—at least until he had breakfast, shaved, and dressed.

The Horns did not live here, of course. His mother, Mirax, was the anchor for the immediate family. Manager of a variety of interlinked businesses—trading, interplanetary finances, gambling and recreation, and, if rumors were true, still a little smuggling here and there—she maintained her home and business address on Corellia. Corran, her husband and Valin's father, was a Jedi Master, much of his life spent on missions away from the family, but his true home was where his heart resided, wherever Mirax lived. Valin and his sister, Jysella, also Jedi, lived wherever their missions sent them, and also counted Mirax as the center of the family.

Now Mirax had rented temporary quarters on Coruscant so the family could collect on one of its rare occasions, this time for the Unification Summit, where she and Corran would separately give depositions on the relationships among the Confederation states, the Imperial Remnant, and the Galactic Alliance as they related to trade and Jedi activities. Mirax had insisted that Valin and Jysella leave their Temple quarters and stay with their parents while these events were taking place, and few forces in the galaxy could stand before her decision—Luke Skywalker certainly knew better than to try.

Moving from the refresher toward the kitchen and dining nook, Valin brushed a lock of brown hair out of his eyes and grinned. Much as he might put up a public show of protest—the independent young man who did not need parents to direct his actions or tell him where to sleep—he hardly minded. It was good to see family. And both Corran and Mirax were better cooks than the ones at the Jedi Temple.

There was no sound of conversation from the kitchen, but there was some clattering of pans, so at least one of his parents must still be on hand. As he stepped from the hallway into the dining nook, Valin saw that it was his mother, her back to him as she worked at the stove. He pulled a chair from the table and sat. "Good morning."

"A joke, so early?" Mirax did not turn to face him, but her tone was cheerful. "No morning is good. I come light-years from Corellia to be with my family, and what happens? I have to keep Jedi hours to see them. Don't you know that I'm an executive? And a lazy one?"

"I forgot." Valin took a deep breath, sampling the smells of breakfast. His mother was making hotcakes Corellian-style, nerf sausage links on the side, and caf was brewing. For a moment, Valin was transported back to his childhood, to the family breakfasts that had been somewhat more common before the Yuuzhan Vong came, before Valin and Jysella had started down the Jedi path. "Where are Dad and Sella?"

"Your father is out getting some back-door information from other Jedi Masters for his deposition." Mirax pulled a plate from a cabinet and began sliding hotcakes and links onto it. "Your sister left early and wouldn't say what she was doing, which I assume either means it's Jedi business I can't know about or that she's seeing some man she doesn't *want* me to know about."

"Or both."

"Or both." Mirax turned and moved over to put the plate down before him. She set utensils beside it.

The plate was heaped high with food, and Valin recoiled from it in mock horror. "Stang, Mom, you're feeding your son, not a squadron of Gamorreans." Then he caught sight of his mother's face and he was suddenly no longer in a joking mood.

This wasn't his mother.

Oh, the woman had Mirax's features. She had the round face that admirers had called "cute" far more often than "beautiful," much to Mirax's chagrin. She had Mirax's generous, curving lips that smiled so readily and expressively, and Mirax's bright, lively brown eyes. She had Mirax's hair, a glossy black with flecks of gray, worn shoulder-length to fit readily under a pilot's helmet, even though she piloted far less often these days. She was Mirax to every freckle and dimple.

But she was not Mirax.

The woman, whoever she was, caught sight of Valin's confusion. "Something wrong?"

"Uh, no." Stunned, Valin looked down at his plate.

He had to think—logically, correctly, and *fast*. He might be in grave danger right now, though the Force currently gave him no indication of imminent attack. The true Mirax, wherever she was, might be in serious trouble or worse. Valin tried in vain to slow his heart rate and speed up his thinking processes.

Fact: Mirax had been here but had been replaced by an imposter. Presumably the real Mirax was gone; Valin could not sense anyone but himself and the imposter in the immediate vicinity. The imposter had remained behind for some reason that had to relate to Valin, Jysella, or Corran. It couldn't have been to capture Valin, as she could have done that with drugs

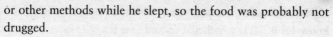

or other methods while he slept, so the food was probably not drugged.

Under Not-Mirax's concerned gaze, he took a tentative bite of sausage and turned a reassuring smile he didn't feel toward her.

Fact: Creating an imposter this perfect must have taken a fortune in money, an incredible amount of research, and a volunteer willing to let her features be permanently carved into the likeness of another's. Or perhaps this was a clone, raised and trained for the purpose of simulating Mirax. Or maybe she was a droid, one of the very expensive, very rare human replica droids. Or maybe a shape-shifter. Whichever, the simulation was nearly perfect. Valin hadn't recognized the deception until . . .

Until *what*? What had tipped him off? He took another bite, not registering the sausage's taste or temperature, and maintained the face-hurting smile as he tried to recall the detail that had alerted him that this wasn't his mother.

He couldn't figure it out. It was just an instant realization, too fleeting to remember, too overwhelming to reject.

Would Corran be able to see through the deception? Would Jysella? Surely, they had to be able to. But what if they couldn't? Valin would accuse this woman and be thought insane.

Were Corran and Jysella even still at liberty? Still *alive*? At this moment, the Not-Mirax's colleagues could be spiriting the two of them away with the true Mirax. Or Corran and Jysella could be lying, bleeding, at the bottom of an access shaft, their lives draining away.

Valin couldn't think straight. The situation was too overwhelming, the mystery too deep, and the only person here who knew the answers was the one who wore the face of his mother.

He stood, sending his chair clattering backward, and fixed the false Mirax with a hard look. "Just a moment." He dashed to his room.

His lightsaber was still where he'd left it, on the nightstand beside his bed. He snatched it up and gave it a near-instantaneous examination. Battery power was still optimal; there was no sign that it had been tampered with.

He returned to the dining room with the weapon in his hand. Not-Mirax, clearly confused and beginning to look a little alarmed, stood by the stove, staring at him.

Valin ignited the lightsaber, its *snap-hiss* of activation startlingly loud, and held the point of the gleaming energy blade against the food on his plate. Hotcakes shriveled and blackened from contact with the weapon's plasma. Valin gave Not-Mirax an approving nod. "Flesh does the same thing under the same conditions, you know."

"Valin, what's *wrong*?"

"You may address me as Jedi Horn. You don't have the right to use my personal name." Valin swung the lightsaber around in a practice form, allowing the blade to come within a few centimeters of the glow rod fixture overhead, the wall, the dining table, and the woman with his mother's face. "You probably know from your research that the Jedi don't worry much about amputations."

Not-Mirax shrank back away from him, both hands on the stove edge behind her. "What?"

"We know that a severed limb can readily be replaced by a prosthetic that looks identical to the real thing. Prosthetics offer sensation and do everything flesh can. They're ideal substitutes in every way, except for requiring maintenance. So we don't feel too badly when we have to cut the arm or leg off a very bad person. But I assure you, that very bad person remembers the pain forever."

"Valin, I'm going to call your father now." Mirax sidled toward the blue bantha-hide carrybag she had left on a side table.

Valin positioned the tip of his lightsaber directly beneath her chin. At the distance of half a centimeter, its containing force field kept her from feeling any heat from the blade, but a slight twitch on Valin's part could maim or kill her instantly. She froze.

"No, you're not. You know what you're going to do instead?"

Mirax's voice wavered. "What?"

"You're going to *tell me what you've done with my mother*!" The last several words emerged as a bellow, driven by fear and anger. Valin knew that he looked as angry as he sounded; he could feel blood reddening his face, could even see redness begin to suffuse everything in his vision.

"Boy, put the blade down." Those were not the woman's words. They came from behind. Valin spun, bringing his blade up into a defensive position.

In the doorway stood a man, middle-aged, clean-shaven, his hair graying from brown. He was of below-average height, his eyes a startling green. He wore the brown robes of a Jedi. His hands were on his belt, his own lightsaber still dangling from it.

He was Valin's father, Jedi Master Corran Horn. But he wasn't, any more than the woman behind Valin was Mirax Horn.

Valin felt a wave of despair wash over him. *Both* parents replaced. Odds were growing that the real Corran and Mirax were already dead.

Yet Valin's voice was soft when he spoke. "They may have made you a virtual double for my father. But they can't have given you his expertise with the lightsaber."

"You don't want to do what you're thinking about, son."

"When I cut you in half, that's all the proof anyone will ever need that you're not the real Corran Horn."

Valin lunged.

KAREN MILLER is a speculative fiction novelist who lives in Sydney, Australia, and writes full time. When she's not having too much fun adventuring in that galaxy far, far away, she's writing fantasy novels under her own name and her pen name, K. E. Mills.

THE POWER OF READING

Visit the Random House website and get connected with information on all our books and authors

EXTRACTS from our recently published books and selected backlist titles

COMPETITIONS AND PRIZE DRAWS Win signed books, audiobooks and more

AUTHOR EVENTS Find out which of our authors are on tour and where you can meet them

LATEST NEWS on bestsellers, awards and new publications

MINISITES with exclusive special features dedicated to our authors and their titles

READING GROUPS Reading guides, special features and all the information you need for your reading group

LISTEN to extracts from the latest audiobook publications

WATCH video clips of interviews and readings with our authors

RANDOM HOUSE INFORMATION including advice for writers, job vacancies and all your general queries answered

Come home to Random House

www.rbooks.co.uk

Fate of the Jedi: Outcast

Aaron Allston

**THE EXTRAORDINARY NEXT EPISODE IN THE STAR WARS
GALAXY BEGINS HERE . . .**

The Galactic Alliance is in crisis. Worse still, the very survival of
the Jedi Order is under threat.

In a shocking move, Chief of State, Natasi Daala, orders the
arrest of Luke Skywalker for failing to prevent Jacen Solo's turn
to the dark side. But it's only the first blow in an anti-Jedi
backlash fueled by a hostile government and a media-driven
witch hunt. Facing conviction, Luke must strike a bargain with
the calculating Daala – his freedom in exchange for his exile
from Coruscant and from the Jedi Order.

Though forbidden to intervene in Jedi affairs, Luke is determined
to keep history from being repeated. With his son, Ben, at his
side, Luke sets out to unravel the shocking truth behind Jacen
Solo's corruption and downfall. But the secrets he uncovers
among the enigmatic Force mystics of the distant world Dorin
may bring his quest — and life as he knows it — to a sudden
end. And all the while, another Jedi Knight, consumed by a
mysterious madness, is headed for Coruscant on a fearsome
mission that could doom the Jedi Order . . . and devastate the
entire galaxy.

arrow books

Fate of the Jedi: Omen

Christie Golden

**The second novel in a bold, new Star Wars story arc –
Fate of the Jedi!**

The Jedi Order is in crisis. The late Jacen Solo's shocking transformation into murderous Sith Lord Darth Caedus has cast a damning pall over those who wield the Force for good. Two Jedi Knights have succumbed to an inexplicable and dangerous psychosis. Criminal charges have driven Luke Skywalker into self-imposed exile. And power-hungry Chief of State Natasi Daala is exploiting anti-Jedi sentiment to undermine the Order's influence within the Galactic Alliance.

But an even greater threat is looming. Millennia in the past, a Sith starship crashed on an unknown, low-tech planet, leaving the survivors stranded. Over the generations, their numbers have grown anew, the ways of the dark side have been nurtured, and the time is fast approaching when this lost tribe of Sith will once more take to the stars to reclaim their legendary destiny as rulers of the galaxy. Only one thing stands in their way to dominance, a name whispered to them through the Force: Skywalker.

arrow books

Fate of the Jedi: Abyss
Troy Denning

The third novel in a bold, new Star Wars story arc – Fate of the Jedi!

Luke and Ben Skywalker arrive in the mysterious part of space called The Maw in search of more clues as to what caused Jacen Solo's fall to the dark side. But they are not the only ones exploring The Maw: a Sith Master and her apprentice arrive – determined to kill Luke. And they're not the only ones with plans for Luke Skywalker. There's a powerful being hiding in The Maw, enormously strong and purely evil . . .

arrow books

Fate of the Jedi: Backlash

Aaron Allston

Repercussions from the dark side's fatal seduction of Jacen Solo and the mysterious plague of madness afflicting young Jedi continue to wreak havoc galaxy-wide. Having narrowly escaped the deranged Force worshippers known as the Mind Walkers and a deadly Sith hit squad, Luke and Ben Skywalker are in pursuit of the now Masterless Sith apprentice. It is a chase that leads to the forbidding planet Dathomir, where an enclave of powerful dark-side Force-wielders will give Vestara the edge she needs to escape – and where the Skywalkers will be forced into combat for their quarry and their lives.

Meanwhile, Han and Leia Solo have completed their own desperate mission, shuttling madness-stricken Jedi from Coruscant to safe haven in the Transitory Mists and beyond the grasp of Galactic Alliance Chief Natasi Daala. But the bold manoeuvre has intensified Daala's fury, and she is determined to shatter Jedi Order resistance once and for all.

Yet no greater threat exists than that which still waits in the depths of the distant Maw Cluster: a being or pure, ravenous dark-side energy named Abeloth calls out across the stars to Jedi and Sith alike. For some it may be the ultimate source of answers crucial to their survival. For others it could be the ultimate weapon of conquest. But for all, it is a game-changing – and life-altering – encounter of untold magnitude and a tactical gambit with unimaginable consequences.

arrow books

Fate of the Jedi: Allies
Christie Golden

What began as a quest for truth has become a struggle for survival for Luke Skywalker and his son, Ben. They have used the secrets of the Mindwalkers to transcend their own bodies and speak with the spirits of the fallen, risking their very lives in the process. They have faced a team of Sith assassins and beaten the odds to destroy them. And now the death squad's sole survivor, Sith apprentice Vestara Khai, has summoned an entire fleet of Sith frigates to engage the embattled father and son. But the dark warriors come bearing a surprise proposition that will bring Jedi and Sith together in an unprecedented alliance against an evil more ancient and alien than they can imagine.

Wil the Skywalkers and their Sith allies set off on their joint mission into the treacherous web of black holes that is the Maw, Han and Leia Solo risk arrest and worse to aid the Jedi imprisoned back on Coruscant. Tyrannical Chief of State Natasi Daala has issued orders that will open a permanent schism between her government and the Jedi Order - a schism that could turn all Jedi into renegades and wanted criminals.

But it is in the depths of the Maw that the future of the galaxy will be decided. For there the Skywalkers and their Sith allies will engage a true monster in battle, and Luke will come face-to-face with a staggering truth.

Century · London